W0008054

GRIMOIRE OF STONE

★ ★ ★ ★ ★

A Romance of Water

By
Keith Harvey

Copyright 2014 © Keith Harvey

All rights reserved. No part of this book may be reproduced in any form or by any electronic or mechanical means, including information storage and retrieval systems, without written permission from the author, except in the case of a reviewer, who may quote brief passages embodied in critical articles or in a review.

Trademarked names appear throughout this book. Rather than use a trademark symbol with every occurrence of a trademarked name, names are used in an editorial fashion, with no intention of infringement of the respective owner's trademark.

The information in this book is distributed on an "as is" basis, without warranty. Although every precaution has been taken in the preparation of this work, neither the author nor the publisher shall have any liability to any person or entity with respect to any loss or damage caused or alleged to be caused directly or indirectly by the information contained in this book.

This is a work of fiction. Names, characters, places, and incidents either are the product of the author's imagination or are used fictitiously, and any resemblance to actual persons, living or dead, events, or locales is entirely coincidental.

Interior formatting by ePubConversions.com
Cover by Michael Atman - www.MichaelAtman.com
Editing by Roberta Binder - www.RobertaEdits.com

Table of Contents

Time present and time past
Are both perhaps present in time future
And time future contained in time past.

T. S. Eliot from *Burnt Norton*

Along with terror, there sweeps over the warrior in a seething tide of blood-red waves, ecstasy.

Ernst Jünger

You could not step twice into the same river; for other waters are ever flowing on to you.

Heraclitus, quoted in Plato's *Cratylus*

About the Author

Keith Harvey is the author of four novels, *Vogel Flies South*, *Vogel and the White Bull*, *Cave Gossip*, and *Grimoire of Stone*; and two books of poetry, *Petroglyphs*, and *Sea-Snails on a Black Chow's Tongue or, a Castaway's Poems in a Bottle*.

In addition to writing, he practices international law and divides his time between his offices in Frankfurt am Main, Germany and Dallas, Texas.

In 2009, his fantasy novel, *Okeanus*, was a semi-finalist in the Amazon/Penguin Breakthrough novel contest.

He is currently writing the sequel to *Grimoire of Stone* and short stories set in an alternate history, code-named: *La Ciudad*.

You can read about Keith's books at
www.amazon.com/author/keithharvey

★ Grimoire of Stone ★

From **LEMEGETON CLAVICULA SALOMONIS**

The 41st spirit in order is called Focalor he is a great duke & strong, & appeareth in ye forme of a Man with griffins wings; his office is, to kill men, and to drown them in ye waters, and to over throw ships of warre, for he hath power over both winds and seas, but he will not hurt any man or Thing, if he be commanded to ye contrary by ye Exorcist; he hath hopes to returne to ye 7th Throne after 1000 yeares; he governeth 3 Legions of spirits, his seal is this wch must be worne as a Lamin.

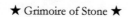

Chapter One: Out of the Frying Pan

THREE WEEKS OUT OF MONTAGNE, the northernmost city of Mexico, Stern, a blacksmith, rode his black gelding toward a copse of pines that grew thickly on a small rise above a dry ravine south of the Azul Mountains. Tugging on a thick, hempen rope, tied to the horn of a silver pommel, he urged his two white mules, loaded heavily with supplies, to follow him further up the steep hill. In the distance a fire serpent glided languidly on currents swirling above the ravines and passes of the mountains and higher still a pair of blue-back dragons circled.

He had purchased the mules in Montagne with silver furnished to him by the priests in La Ciudad. The cover story they spread throughout the ancient city was that he was moving his smithy from the capital of Mexico to the Santa Rey Pueblo north of the Azul Mountains and the crumbling Anglo wall. His real mission, however, was to deliver three *bullae*, priestly edicts – one to the Cardinal in Santa Rey, one to the head of the Brotherhood in the Martinelle Pueblo and one to the bishop of the Nord Pueblo – and enlist their help in tracking down the home of the blue-black dragons.

Before he left Montagne, Father Gonzales introduced him to an Argyle prospector, Mime, who drew a series of maps, showing him the way to the Santa Rey Pueblo, identifying the last known location of *indio* camps, the highest infestation of the blue-back dragons, the scourge of Mittilagart, their world, and any burning cities along the route.

After the officious Argyll left, smelling of cinnamon and tobacco, Father Gonzales said, "Your ultimate mission must be secret. Do not lose the *bullae* and do not open them. It is better you destroy them rather than let them fall into a stranger's hands. North of the Rio Concho you will find many people who hate us. Be careful of strangers and especially the ones that call themselves Freedmen."

"Are they making trouble again?" asked Stern.

The priest caught Stern's eyes and grasped his hands, "They refuse to serve the Holy Father; these godless ones; the ones who walk alone. They continually vex us." Still gripping his hands, he asked, "Shall I hear your confession son?" Stern shook his head and pulled his hand away from the priest. Unperturbed, Father Gonzales handed him a silver talisman. "Take this. It was made before the war, before the burning cities and the great dragon plague. It was forged by one of our greatest smiths." Pulling the chain of the talisman over his head, somewhat ashamed he continued to believe in the Black Robes' magic, he said softly, through pursed lips, his anger barely in check, "Father, promise on the sacred book to take care of my son."

The old man grimaced, embarrassed by the ex-priest who had brought up the fact he had illegitimately fathered a son with an Argyll woman, while on campaign in the jungles of the south, and said, "He is in God's and our hands now." The blacksmith, his anger rising, frowned and shook his head. He didn't believe anymore in their professed infinite mercy, although he went to great pains to hide it from the Black Robes. When the old man turned and raised his hands in prayer, Moses Stern, known now simply as a blacksmith among the Pope's Swiss Guards and warrior priests, shrugged and strode away from Gonzales; his silver spurs singing on the seared marble of the cathedral's floor.

Days later, stopping at the crest of yet another hill, Stern stood in the stirrups and leaned forward over the gelding's neck and surveyed the north, his eyes scanning the area up above a range of middling mountains, where dark, threatening clouds, surged toward the south. He watched several blue-back dragons, the size of a dray horse, running from the storm and then a sliver of silver lightning split the bruise-black clouds. His mules in a panic jerked the line. In response, he tugged harder on the rope forcing the skittish animals to move closer to him as he whispered to them in *lingua*, the language of the Central Kingdom. From the bottom of the hill in a dry ravine his two dogs, Phobus and Deimos, barked, turned and ran toward him and he smiled grimly, as he turned his horse toward a forest that spread across the valley.

Hours later underneath tall resinous pines, Stern swung out of the saddle and untied the mules. The gelding with its reins hanging free pulled at a clump of grass that protruded from the thick bed of dried needles that covered the ground, as Stern led the mules into the trees where he stretched a rough hempen rope between two firs that towered above him and swayed gently in the rising wind. With the mules tied off, he extracted two leather feed bags from a wooden pallet on the nearest mule, partially filled the bags with dry oats and wrestled them over the mules' ears. He then unloaded both pallets and carried the supplies deeper into the woods where he stacked them and covered them with a waterproof tarp, which he secured to the ground with six steel pegs he had forged in his smithy in La Ciudad. Finished unpacking, he retrieved the grazing gelding and removed its saddle and rubbed it down with dried grass before filling its feedbag with grain.

He lifted the saddle and carried it on his shoulder into the woods, away from the mules and the horse and placed it beneath a rock that extended from the curve of the hill and formed a rough and ragged roof. He slid the single shot carbine, which he had also manufactured in his shop, from the saddle's leather boot and examined it proudly. He had fashioned the carbine from an ancient, discarded plan that one of the blue-skinned Argyll prospectors had retrieved from the wreckage of an ancient city on the banks of the Rio Concho and sold to him for the outrageous sum of one gold angel. Leaning the gun against the rock, he untied a waterproof slicker and a blanket from the *cantle* of the saddle, removed the *mochilas,* and slung them, the slicker and the blanket under the rock roof. Lying on his back and using the saddle as a pillow, he stared up through the pine needles and observed black clouds passing quickly over him.

A storm had caught him. He expected the rain to fall at any moment; and with the clouds and the wind picking up from the north, he knew the temperature would drop. Standing, he tugged the black slicker over his head and set about gathering twigs and broken branches to make a fire beneath the rock, where the two dogs now lay, stretched out near his saddle, watching him, their pink tongues lolling from their square jaws, saliva curling thickly across their wide paws. Clicking his tongue, he attracted the attention of the female, who moved toward him, but he ordered her back. She was pregnant and he hoped the puppies held off until he reached the Santa Rey Pueblo and the compound of the Black Robes.

He had bought the dogs at a *baratillo* near the *zocalo* of the capital city from an old *mestiza,* who had reached out and grabbed his robe as he passed. "Father," she said, "buy one of my puppies." He remembered bending down and uncovering a paper box where four black puppies, asleep, lay in a warm huddle like worms, unearthed. "Four coppers for each. They are weaned and ready to go. They will make good breeding stock. Or if you are a gourmand, then a delicious meal or two." They were perfect as best he could tell. Their line seemed pure so he bought two and put one in each of the pockets of his black robe. As he walked away from the *zocalo* he felt their reassuring warmth in his pockets, balanced like the two revolvers he now wore on his hips. Back in his shop, he built a wooden box, filled it with fresh hay, placed an old horse blanket on top of it, and moved it near the fire. He laid them on the blanket and placed a bowl of milk near them.

Brushing away his memories, he tended his small fire beneath the overhang, sat back and filled his pipe from a leather pouch, containing tobacco, slices of dried apples, and currants. The single-shot carbine leaned against the back of his makeshift dugout within reach and one of his revolvers rested in his lap, with the hammer half-cocked. He smelled the coming rain, as he pushed his worn sombrero off his head and his black hair fell forward into his eyes. Rubbing his left hand over his thick blue-black beard, he yawned and leaned against his saddle and closed his eyes, thinking about Mara, the Argyll girl, he took as his woman during the campaign against the Mayans and the mother of his son.

The first cold drops of rain splattered onto the red sand in front of the overhang and a raven, seeking shelter and maybe food, landed in a fir tree near his rugged rock roof, shook its wings free of water, and turned its head from side to side. The two dogs, startled by the bird, snarled, while the skittish mules strained against their rope. The gelding, too, seemed restless. The blacksmith, who was on the edge of sleep, opened his eyes and peered into the rain as he pulled the silver talisman from beneath his slicker and his black linen shirt with his right hand and unholstered the second revolver and pulled the hammer back with his left. He pushed himself further back under the rock into the shadows of the overhang and rubbed the talisman, not because he thought it provided him with any help, but because it had been made by a man like himself, another smith, who worked with metals, blessed by the priests.

Minutes passed as he stared into the rain. Seeing nothing but the sheets of water and the silhouette of the drenched bird, he relaxed and, overcome by a sudden inexplicable fatigue, he fell back asleep and dreamed he was working in his shop. Later, he awoke to the sound of a twig snapping; the dogs heard it, too, growled and moved forward, ready to attack. He whispered to them to sit.

Suddenly, a rattler twisted out of the rain and landed near his feet. He jerked back surprised and aimed at the snake but Deimos moved in front of him, ready to pounce, blocking his shot. Before the dog could reach the snake, a black arrow flew from darkness and penetrated the snake's head, pinning it to the ground, its tail thrashing wildly in the rain, flicking dark drops of water toward the man's boots and the dog's eyes. Then, from the shadows, a voice calling in *lingua* said, "I'm a friend. Don't shoot."

The blacksmith, pulling the hammers all the way back on the twin revolvers, readying them to fire, called out to the voice, "come forward!" A short, slight man appeared, holding a bow and arrows in his left hand and a steel knife in his right. With a wide grin that showed his mouth of white teeth, he moved forward toward the snake and cut its head from its body in one fluid stroke and then grabbed the rattlers and shook them. The dogs snarled and backed away, as the blacksmith aimed his guns at the man, who stood before him, naked in the driving rain, shaking the snake's tail and grinning widely.

"Friend, please," the man said with a laugh.

"Who are you?" asked Stern.

With his arms raised, holding a knife in one hand and the remains of the rattler in the other, the man said in his strange accent, "You have some tobacco for me and maybe a little dried meat?"

The blacksmith asked again, "Who are you?"

"I'm nobody, Black Robe. Just a hunter in these mountains." He pointed back over his left shoulder.

"I am not a Black Robe."

The man squatted in the rain, his long black hair clinging to his back. "You come from the Black Robes. My nose is cold and wet and yet I can still smell incense and cinnamon on your skin. You are not one of those crazy *indio* prospectors nor one of the blue-skin Argyll; maybe you're one of the first ones, who came with the dragons?"

"What do you know about incense or dragons for that matter?" he asked, as the mention of the 'first ones' tickled his conscious mind and memory.

"Don't worry Black Robe. I'm not your enemy. Your enemy lies there." He pointed toward the Azul Mountains in the north and said, "Where the burning cities light the night and the undead track the living. Where the thorns of the other worlds pierced our world's skin and allowed the dragons to enter. And where the lunar *bruja* search for warriors to transcend the spheres and return the dragons to their homes."

"What the hell are you on about? There are no undead or witches, only perverted men. And as far as the dragons are concerned, they came from the north."

"If you say so Black Robe then I'm sure it must be true. But maybe you have never seen a lunar *bruja*, a moon witch, in her white robes, flying through the night on one of those infernal machines?" He squatted down near the fire and rubbed his hands. "I'm very hungry. Doesn't your book tell you to feed the hungry?"

"You are no *indio*. What are you?"

"I'm a drowned man, who is hungry, cast from the sea into the desert," he said. "Feed me now. This rain is cold and I'm tired. Let me stretch out beneath your rock roof and sleep next to the warm dogs. Let me sleep like your shadow."

The blacksmith noted the dogs had calmed, their heads rested on their paws and they were almost asleep. He released the hammers on the pistols, easing them down, as he motioned the man to come closer. As he approached, the blacksmith detected a bitter, rank odor; the feral smell of a predator. He had smelled it before, when a mountain lion sprain upon one of his pack animals in the Coral Mountains down south near the waist of the world, where he first met Mara, before they coupled in the rain under a *coaba* tree in the dark jungle. That time he had escaped but the pony he rode died before he could kill the cat.

He had also smelled it when he stumbled upon a female coyote and her pups in a den in the desert, south of the Rio Concho. It was a mixture of musk and rot, piss and sweat. Holstering the guns, he reached into his saddlebags, pulled out some beef jerky, and carved off a piece for each of the dogs. He then cut a smaller piece for the man and one for himself. Crouched on his haunches near to the fire, the man smiled and chewed the beef strip. Stern observed him through half-closed lids. He wore only a loincloth and carried a leather bag on a wide strap hung nonchalantly over his left shoulder. He was lean, his hairless skin darkened by the sun and his black hair wet, braided into one long strand that was tied off at the tip with rawhide.

The blacksmith broke the silence between them by asking once again, "Who are you?"

The man held the blacksmith's eyes and said, "I'm a hunter from North of the Rio Concho."

The smith fingered the hammer of one of the revolvers. "You don't look like one of the Freedmen."

"I'm not a cannibal, if that is what has frightened you, Black Robe. That is only the Easterners anyway, the ones that live near the great gulf at the mouth of the wide river. I was cast onto the Big Waste and adopted by a tribe of *indio* near the Sun Mountains, the home of the father of the dragons to the west of Santa Rey. That's how I know you are a Black Robe, sent by the Sacred Father to study dragons."

Stern cut off another chew from the jerky and stuck it in his mouth. "Castaway, are you?" he asked, with a note of derision in his voice. The man ignored the tone and the question. "I'm curious, Black Robe. Usually your ilk travel with a column of dragoons up from the south and they certainly do not try to cross the Azul Mountains alone."

"I told you I am no Black Robe. I was once but no more."

The blacksmith passed a large canteen over to the *indio*, who took several short swallows, and then handed it back. A clap of thunder shook the rock above their heads and rain ran off of the rock and down the hill into the ravine.

"How do you know where I go?"

"I crossed your trail three days ago and I have followed you. If you continue on this route you will cross into the Azul Mountains and then come to the Rio Concho. If you do this, I think you will surely die."

"Assuming you are correct, what do you care if I die or cross the Rio Concho?"

The *indio* waved his hand vaguely. "I do not care. I'm just curious. The coyote is a very curious animal. Usually, the Black Robes and their Argyll allies search the ancient cities for something. What do they seek, these Black Robes?"

"They are looking for history, for the past."

"Why?"

"Power is there. Knowledge and technology is hidden in the burning cities."

"What?" asked the man.

Stern pointed at the man's belt and said, "The knowledge to make a knife like the one on your hip."

"A corpse gifted me this knife, Black Robe."

"And where did the dead man get it? Someone made it from steel. Do you know what steel is?"

"The knife comes from the original ones."

"Exactly," answered Stern.

"Are the Black Robes looking for their ancestors?"

"That's as good an answer as any."

The man swallowed the last of the jerky and the blacksmith cut off another piece and tossed it to him across the fire. Sparks flew up as the meat passed through the flame.

They chewed in silence until the blacksmith asked, "If you were going home to Santa Rey, how would you go?"

The man scratched his inner thigh before answering. "I would not cross the Rio Concho. Too many dangers, too many dead lands. Travel with the sun to the west toward the Sun Mountains."

"That's dragon territory. Even the dragoons are afraid to go there."

"Go west until you can see the night glow of the burned cities on the edge of the Sun Mountains and then turn north. You will find a town there, a free town, called Camaron. There are about two hundred souls there, civilized *indios,* and people who fled the cannibals, the sickness, the witches, and the undead. From Camaron you can go northeast and cross the Rio Concho south of the Santa Rey Pueblo. One of the ancient roads runs from Camaron to Santa Rey. It is crumbling now but it is still there and you can make good time on it."

"Doesn't the road run through the burning cities?"

"Of course, but get off and go around. Everyone knows that."

"Where did you learn the common *lingua*?"

"From the people in the Santa Rey Pueblo," said the man, who looked away, as if he were lying.

"Not the Black Robes?" asked Stern, noticing the deflection.

"If I learned from the Black Robes, I would be a Black Robe, just as you are."

"How did you keep up with me for three days?"

"The coyote runs faster than you."

"I have heard that some *indios* shift shape."

"What are fairy tales to the coyote?"

The man shrugged, ignoring the statement. The rain fell steadily and they talked about mundane things, as they ate. When they finished, Stern handed his tobacco pouch to the *indio*, who fished a short corncob pipe from his leather bag and filled it with the sweet tobacco. He returned the pouch to the blacksmith, who refilled his pipe and lit it with a twig from the fire.

"The bitch will soon birth," said the *indio*.

"How do you know?"

"I can feel them. There are three."

"Three!"

"They will come soon." The man chuckled. "Go to Camaron, sell the puppies there."

"That's a hell of reason to go days out of my way, just for a litter of pups."

"It could save your head and your liver." The man shivered.

"You cold?" asked Stern, pulling his slicker close to his body. "Temperature is dropping."

The blacksmith pulled the gelding's blanket from behind his back and threw it to the man, who quickly wrapped himself in it and fell asleep.

After he finished his pipe, the blacksmith fished the three *bullae* from his saddlebag. Each roll was wrapped in soft leather, sealed with red wax by the seal of the Holy Father. 'The *bullae* are too important to be lost. I will go west to Camaron,' he thought.

Pulling the arrow buried in the head of the snake from the ground, he examined the primitive flint stone with its hundreds of tiny cuts and thought. 'The man probably made it himself. Here is what the old Black

Robe was talking about. This man has the knowledge of steel but not the capacity to make it. Only civilization has the ability and the means to make steel.'

The fire died and the blacksmith crossed himself and silently recited his prayers in the ancient language of the church before he lay back and fell asleep. 'Old habits die hard,' he thought.

During the night, the rain stopped and sometime before morning the man left.

The blacksmith awoke about an hour before sunrise, coaxed the fire into life, and boiled some coffee. Phobus and Deimos were nowhere to be found and the mules were restless, waiting for their food.

After the blacksmith fed the animals, he inventoried his supplies. Everything was there except for a long hempen rope he suspected the man had taken.

As the sun rose, the day became hot and humid. Water rushed through the ravine below and Stern could not leave his camp until the waters receded. Late in the afternoon, he crossed the ravine and rode west away from the Azul Mountains, heading due west toward the Sun Mountains and the pueblo of Camaron. He camped that night on the banks of a turgid stream, filled with the runoff from the hills to the east, and slept fitfully, waking before the sun rose. While relieving himself on the edge of his camp, he gazed up at the stars in the now clear sky and focused on the moon.

The Argylls that lived in the crumbling adobe cities around Ciudad believed that before the coming of the dragons, before the fires and the sickness, the gods opened up a crack in the sky and shot the Northerners into their world. According to the legend, the gods chose the fittest and smartest and tied them onto a silver arrow and shot them into the sky. On Mittilagart they built great pyramids and floated on barges on canals in fertile lands to the south. But the gods left the fissure open, letting the dragons through that brought desolation, drought, and dread to all the people of Mittilagart.

The *indios*, though, believed something else. They tell tales of the spines of other worlds piercing the skin of this world causing wounds and breaks that allow demons and dragons to enter the world. To them, the world is body and witches, demons and monsters are an infection that must be fought and overcome. It was this legend that the old man referred to last night. There was also another legend, he remembered, one about a trickster god, called Coyote, who could shift shape. Coyote wandered in the desert. Sometimes he would help men in distress, other times he would steal them blind or seduce their women. Coyote was a great lover and a monstrous liar.

A real coyote yelping in the desert interrupted his thoughts and out of religious habit, he turned back to his chores and said a prayer, as he boiled coffee and ate iron rations, which consisted of dried nuts, berries, oats and wheat squeezed into a square bar.

Two days after the night in the rain with the *indio*, the blacksmith noticed a cloud of dust in the south, moving parallel to him. He led the mules up onto a small rise and stared at the dust until he could discern riders, maybe five or six of them. He cursed the man, who sent him west, away from the north, where it was easy to hide in the folds of the land. He waited throughout the morning for the riders to disappear over a hill and then he cut back south to cross their trail and fall in behind them.

Later in the day, as he approached an arroyo, a giant *kakapo* crossed his path, startling his horse and mules. He pulled firmly on the reins and after a few seconds the horse calmed. But suddenly hundreds of the flightless birds appeared on the horizon, running north, cutting him off from the arroyo and forcing him to turn north and run ahead of the stampeding birds; otherwise, the flock would have taken him and his animals down. In the thundering rush of the birds, he heard his errant dogs barking and he saw Deimos biting at the birds' legs as they tore up the earth in their fright. "Damn their eyes," he cursed the wayward dogs and whistled for their return. Finally, he found some rugged rock to protect him from the flood of bird flesh. He reined his horse and the mules to a stop behind the strength of crumbling stones to allow the flock to pass.

When safe, he turned back toward the west and entered the desert, where the sand was thick and red and large cacti dominated the ground. Because of the broken terrain and the cacti, he could no longer see further than a couple of hundred meters. The dust in the south had disappeared and in the afternoon he spied a herd of dromedary moving languidly to the west. He had considered buying camels rather than the mules in Montagne but in the end he preferred the mules to the foul-smelling dromedaries.

The next day, he ran upon a caravan of Argyll prospectors. There were twelve of them, each riding a donkey and each leading ten pack animals, a motley collection of camels, mules, donkeys, and llamas. He kicked the gelding to catch up with the train. The Argyll wore colorful shirts and pants and tall straw hats. When they saw him, they pulled up and raised the shortened flintlocks preferred by the Ciudad dragoons in a salute. He waved at them and announced he was a friend in their language. They waved him in calling out in their sing-song voices for the Black Robe to join them.

He camped with them that night on a hill covered with tall cacti. As he listened to them telling their stories about winged serpents, blue-back dragons and silver arrows, he felt good for the first time in weeks. They served him *frijoles* in a red clay bowl and *tortillas*. When he finished he cleaned the bowl with a corn tortilla and washed it down with fresh water from a leather bag. The Argyll slept and he sat by the fire and smoked his pipe. A raven landed on the thick arm of a cactus near the fire and he suspected he would soon see the man, he now identified as Coyote. And, as if on a cue, he heard the yelps of a coyote and the roar of a mountain lion. Deimos moaned in her sleep and Phobus lifted his head, as one of the Argyll turned in his blanket and called out for his wife or lover.

As he rode out the next morning, waving to the Argyll that were turning to the northwest, while he continued due west, he saw a coyote on a rise, watching him. The animal lacked fear and as he drew nearer it ran across his path and Phobus and Deimos, disobeying his command to heel, chased after it. The coyote turned north and the Blacksmith imagined he heard the voice of the man saying, 'turn north now.'

He ignored the voice in his head but when the dogs did not return, he turned north to find them. As he rode, he blew a silver whistle but he heard no response. Toward sundown, he camped in a formation of red rocks, great boulders spread around the mesa like children's blocks. A kilometer from the rocks, he caught the outline of five men, riding hard toward him from the southeast. Kicking the gelding, he forced it into a full gallop, as the mules brayed in panic behind him.

Up among the rocks ahead, he saw Phobus and then Deimos, barking and baying at him, to ride to safety.

He rode into the rocks, slid from the saddle, pulled his carbine from its boot, climbed a giant red sand stone, and lay flat on its top.

As the five riders drew near, he recognized them as *indios* and took aim. A peregrine falcon circled above his head and he heard its screech on the wind, as he squeezed the trigger of the carbine. The round struck one of the attackers square in the chest, pitching him backwards off his painted pony's bare back. He ejected the empty casing, placed it into his vest pocket, and inserted another round. In that short moment, the other horsemen drew even closer. He fired a second time but missed. He then drew one of the revolvers and fired almost point blank into a second *indio*, who had ridden to the base of his rock and swung at him with a wooden mallet.

A black arrow thumped into the rock and then a second slammed into his left shoulder, protruding like a black flag. Squealing with pain, he dropped his revolver, his vision blurred and he felt faint. Crouching down, he steeled himself against the pain and picked up the revolver and shot two rounds at his antagonists. The three survivors withdrew and pulled their horses up outside the range of his pistols. Reloading his carbine, he aimed and fired. A pony buckled but its rider rose unharmed, as the three men withdrew behind a rise.

The blacksmith cursed the pain in his shoulder. As he watched blood drip onto the red sand stone, he pulled his sombrero onto his head to protect himself from the sun and wondered if he should try to reach the canteen still fastened to his saddle by a strip of black leather. He knew if he moved off the rock, the *indio* would surround him, so he pivoted to see the position of the sun and calculated he had another two hours of light. Once it was dark they would take him and his mission would fail. He might kill one but not all three. He pulled the silver talisman from beneath his shirt and began to say the last rites. Mumbling the ancient *lingua* words, a tear rolled down his cheek.

He both hated and loved the Church and all of its rituals.

The rituals were probably the things he missed the most. But after Mara's death and their taking his son to live in an orphanage to be trained as a Black Robe, he found he could no longer tolerate their prejudice and hypocrisy. He wiped his eyes at the sound of Deimos whimpering and he turned on the rock to see her. She was anxious for him but he could not help her now. He wasn't afraid of death but he mourned the failure of his quest. He had been entrusted with the holy patents, the three *bullae*, and now he feared he might fail and if he failed the Black Robes then his son, who they controlled, would suffer.

He needed water so he crawled backwards off the rock to the ground where his animals waited patiently. As soon as his feet touched the ground, he heard the *indio* shifting to new positions. Hearing them, too, Phobus growled and moved toward the south, while he untied the canteen and swallowed several mouthfuls of the water. His thirst quenched, he slipped the carbine back into the saddle boot; for the coming fight he would only need his knife and pistols. He took the gelding's reins and led it and the mules deeper into the rocks. As he passed, a rattler coiled under a rock rattled its tail, warning him off, and he steered the horse and mules away from it.

Within the mound of red rocks he found a small space that resembled an antique arena with only two paths leading into it. To reach him, the *indio* would have to use one or the other or climb over the rocks. He led the animals to the northern wall and then he moved to the opposite side, where he could watch both entrances. Finding shade in a recess in the rocks, he sat. Drawing his pistols, he rested them in his lap and stuck his knife into the ground next to him. Phobus was lying in the shade across from him and Deimos was near the mules. Cicadas clicked the only sound and he suffered the pain of his wound, as three sparrows played in a mesquite bush and a spider spun a web in a nearby crevice.

He closed his eyes and thought about the story the *indio* had told him. Lunar *bruja* flew from the moon and searched the battlefields of man, looking for men that they could use to find a way to remove the dragons from this world. The catch was that the men they chose were dead warriors, men killed bravely in battle. He licked his lips and imagined the witches coming for him. He would like to be one of those men: a dead warrior at the service of beautiful women.

He awoke with a start; the arena dark and the cicadas silent. The mules were moving about but he could not see the dogs. Suddenly, he heard the snake's rattles and then a scream. One more man down, he thought. The moon rose and cast an eerie glow over the red rock, the stars were brighter than the night before and the blacksmith saw the outline of a man on the rocks up above the mules.

He took aim and fired both guns and the figure fell and rolled across the rocks and then dropped to the floor of the arena, where Deimos and Phobus tore into his body. Moments later, silence returned and the cicadas started their mechanical song. Listening, he watched the moon cross the sky above the arena's floor. He dozed off several times but he quickly caught himself. Once he awakened in the middle of a snore. The moon directly overhead filled the arena with light.

He fell asleep and then awoke with a start. Three figures, barefooted, wearing white robes with hoods, stood arrayed in the middle of the arena. The middle one, the tallest, disengaged from the display and walked slowly toward him, pushing the hood off her head. Her feet shone a luminous white in the moonlight. For a moment, he imagined they were Northerners, come to take him home to their paradise in another universe, parallel to his, but he shook his head and said, "Clap trap."

He pulled the hammers back on both the guns but he heard a voice in his head that said softly, gently, sweetly, "Don't shoot." Bound by some magic, he could not stop the guns from falling into his lap. She stood at his feet, bent down on one knee, and leaned toward him. Her long black hair fell forward, covering her green eyes. She pulled the hair from her face and pressed her lips against his, then withdrew slowly. "All is well, my friend," she whispered so low he had to lean toward her to hear. "You are not dead yet but soon. Then you shall be my warrior and I will send you through the spheres to the home of the dragons."

She smelt of cinnamon and smoke and her presence comforted him but he suspected he was delirious from the fever in his wound. She touched the arrow and a savage pain pierced him and he cried out. It was as if his bowels had been opened by a great sword. How could a woman so beautiful cause him so much pain? He cursed her and tried to lift his guns. She whispered into his ear. "Be calm; the pain will pass. The arrow was dipped in poison. That is why you sleep." She held him down as she licked the blood from around the arrow's shaft and sucking the blood and poison from the wound.

He was dreaming, he was sure of it, as he faded slowly away into a deep sleep. In his dream he heard a howl and he saw a great black wolf pad into the arena. At its side were his dogs, Phobus and Deimos. The wolf jumped into the air and landed at his feet and the woman turned and then calmly backed away, while Phobus and Deimos growled at her two companions.

Before he awoke, he dreamed another dream. He was standing on a hill overlooking the mouth of a wide river that emptied into the Middle Sea with the same woman, now wearing red robes, standing beside him and whispering into his ear. "I love you." And he answered, "And I you." She then raised her arms and began to float into the air above the rushing river and he heard a great horn and saw a white boat with a paddle wheel, like the ships that arrive at ports from the eastern continents. She extended her hands away from her body and spoke in a strange language, guttural and harsh, which he somehow translated: "Do not fret I will find you in the end, but first I will send a woman warrior to you on an island in the North and she will birth the sisters of your son and the four of you shall one day find a book made of thorns. But before then you must leave this land and find your people."

Chapter Two: The Hanged Man

STERN AWOKE to the smell of coffee boiling and smoke from a small fire made from oryx dung. Next to the fire, the man he called Coyote bent forward, stirring the pot and chewing a strip of jerky. "Morning," he said cheerily, as if nothing had happened over the last few days.

"How long have you been here?" asked Stern.

"Since last night," he answered, pouring some coffee into a tin cup.

"What about the *indio*?"

"Dead,"

"All of them?"

"Yes."

The blacksmith groaned from the dull ache in his shoulder.

"Can you pull this thing out?"

"No. But help is at Camaron. It is only two days away."

"I'm not sure I can ride."

"You will ride, Black Robe."

The man extracted two small leather pouches from his bag and approached the blacksmith. Squatting next to him, he opened the first pouch, which contained a yellow powder. Taking a pinch with his thumb and index finger, he blew it into his face. "Pollen from the corn," he said. The powder smelled acrid and irritated Stern's eyes but the pain in his shoulder lessened. The man opened the second pouch, which contained a red powder. "Chilies," he said, repeating the pinch but this time he pulled the blacksmith forward and sprinkled the powder in the wound.

"That *bruja* cleaned your wound last night."

"What are you talking about?" he asked; the memory of the woman coming to him in a rush of both panic and erotic tension.

"That witch last night sucked out the poison and cleaned the wound."

"She was real?" he asked, knowing now that she was real and the story the old man had told him about the lunar *bruja* was true.

"What did you think?"

"I thought I was dreaming."

The man grunted and then pulled the mouth of the pouches shut and stowed them in his bag.

"They took the *indio* bodies and probably would have taken yours if I hadn't shown up."

"Why didn't they?"

"You tell me."

"I don't know. I saw a wolf, a great black wolf."

"Coyote has been watching you, following you."

The Blacksmith grabbed the man's arm and said, "This is madness. It was you, wasn't it? You are Coyote."

"Maybe in your world but here, in the desert, near the dragons' lair, it's madness not to believe."

The man retrieved another cup from the blacksmith's saddle bags and filled it with coffee and then handed it to him. As Stern sipped the bitter brew, he asked, "Who is she?"

"She's a lunar *bruja*, a moon witch, who lives in the stone fortress in the Southern Bayou, the marsh land next to the Middle Sea. I have never seen them come this far into the desert."

"You saw her?"

Coyote shrugged.

"Why did she taste my blood?"

"You would have to ask her, but I know one thing. You and she are tied together now. She knows you. Your blood will lead her to you anytime she desires to see you. As long as your heart pumps you and she are connected." He paused and said with a crooked grin. "You Black Robes are forbidden by law to have women, aren't you?"

"I am not a Black Robe." Not anymore, he thought, not after Mara and the birth of his son. He pushed the thoughts away.

"So you said."

Later that day, Coyote helped the blacksmith into the saddle and they moved out, away from the rocks, heading north now toward Camaron.

That night they camped on a hill. In the distance, a herd of a thousand oryx passed in the night and the blacksmith fell into a deep sleep. He dreamed he was a great black wolf and that he led a pack of wolves against the oryx and they separated a female from the herd and he and his pack mates brought the oryx down. He woke from the dream and he heard a coyote yelping on a mesa to the east.

The next day Coyote said the red glow in the west was a dead city. They camped along a dry creek bed, and Stern, now feverish, shook from chills. In a dream, he saw the *bruja* standing on the ramparts of a walled city on the shore of a great sea, calling for him.

Several days later, they reached the outskirts of the adobe walls of Camaron and two men on donkeys, wearing homespun clothing and carrying flintlocks across their saddle horns, rode out to meet them. A tall black man, on a white donkey, called out for them to stop and Coyote, who had been leading the gelding, turned and handed the reins to the blacksmith, who was slumped forward in the saddle, shivering and mumbling in an antique language. "Talk to these Freedmen, Black Robe," he said. The blacksmith tried to focus his eyes and his mind. "I was attacked by *indio*," he mumbled. "I'm a blacksmith on my way to the Santa Rey Pueblo," he said, as he fell from the saddle.

He heard the tall black man order the other to ride to the town and fetch help, as he dismounted his donkey and brought his canteen to the blacksmith. Stern looked up to address Coyote but he was gone. The black man, the bailiff of the town or the Dorf, as they called it, held his head, as they waited for help. Soon a ragged group of people, wearing motley clothes, emerged from the adobe walls of the Dorf. Friend Alyse, her long black skirt dragging in the red dust, led the way, while Hermann Braith and his brother Detlef hurried behind her, carrying a stretcher.

A few minutes after Alyse's group exited the Dorf, another group on horseback exploded from the gate, quickly passing Alyse. It was a man named Dom Angelo and three of his sons. The Bailiff groaned. "Damn Freedmen," he cursed under his breath, "do they have to control everything, stick their noses in everything."

"Johnston, what is it?" asked Dom Angelo.

"He's a Black Robe from La Ciudad."

"Look, father, "said one of Dom Angelo's sons. He pointed at the dogs and the horse and the mules. "The man is rich."

"I will be claiming his kit," said Dom Angelo quickly.

"Why you?" asked the Bailiff.

"It is recompense for the raid on my cattle by those dragoons last winter."

"We will take his stuff legal-like if he dies. If he lives, he will have some explaining to do before we split up the booty," said Johnston.

Dom Angelo stood in his stirrups and called out to Friend Alyse, "Now you don't be saving this man. I want his kit."

"He is a child of the gods. I will be saving him, if you don't mind."

She had now reached the blacksmith. "Turn him over onto his stomach. I want to look at that arrow wound."

Johnston slowly turned Stern onto his stomach, as the two dogs approached him and lay down in the red sand near him. The woman examined the wound and said, "It's fairly clean; just a minor infection, yet. You, boys, get him to my surgery. We will have that arrow out."

One of Dom Angelo's boys was already leading the horse and mules away.

Johnston said, "Dom Angelo, that's his property until the town takes it through a lawful action."

The large Freedman leaned over his saddle horn and pushed his wide brim hat back off of his forehead and said, "Certainly, Bailiff, certainly. But I aim to have that saddle and carbine."

The Braith twins placed Stern on the stretcher and then headed toward the white bleached walls of the Dorf, while many of the Dorf's citizens lined the path, watching them carry Stern into the compound.

Alyse led the way, taking long strides. Suddenly she broke into song in her deep resonant voice, "What friends we have in gods. . . ."

Johnston shook his head, as he swung his right leg over his donkey, and Dom Angelo and his three boys galloped ahead of him into the Dorf, leading the Blacksmith's gelding and mules behind them. The two dogs followed the Braith brothers. Johnston was the last one to enter the Dorf. The half-conscious Stern caught a glint in his left eye and turned to see a coyote run beneath a sage bush into a gully that ran near the Dorf, where the latrine emptied.

The Braith brothers carried the man to the Hospice, where two young girls, members of the Friends, helped them stretch him out on a gray slab. The girls undressed him, cutting away his leather vest and shirt underneath, then washed him and prepared him for surgery.

Friend Alyse arrived dressed in a white dress, washed her hands in a clay bowl and examined the wound. She then asked for a scalpel. Before she cut, she said in a loud voice, "Dear gods above, thank you for this day and this job. Guide my hand for the glory of the deities and save us from those dragons and corrupt witches!" She then cut the wound open and widened it to remove the arrow.

The Blacksmith passed out under the pain and dreamed his bowels were being ripped open by the talons of a great black bird. The pain was excruciating and he too called out for his God to help him. But in his dream no help came; instead, the bird tore at his entrails and pulled them out of his body, leaving his corpse ripped and distended. He awoke later in darkness, lying face down on a cot snuffed with hay. He was completely naked and the room was cold. His shoulder felt stiff and he smelled a medicinal odor. A coyote yelped outside and he shivered. The bastard had led him into a trap and then deserted him. He felt his forehead and it was hot. He stood up after some struggle and surveyed the tiny chamber. There was the bed, a great iron door and a window with three bars. He climbed up onto the bed and looked out into the night. A huge yellow moon rose in the east. He tried to remember how he had come to this place. He remembered the arrow and the black man on the donkey but he could not remember anything after that. Suddenly, he realized he had failed. He had been stripped of everything and the three *bullae* were gone. He lay back down on the hay and for a long time he thought about his plight and he prayed for help, for deliverance from this cell.

Sometime later, he fell asleep and dreamed the *bruja* was standing next to his cot. She wore a white diaphanous gown and her hair was loose, falling onto her shoulders. She sat on the edge of the bed and touched him and he felt the fever lessen. Rather than shivering he felt warm. She turned him over onto his back and she kissed him and then she straddled him. He shuddered because this dream was not right. It was a venal sin. He said, "Don't, it is a sin."

She laughed and continued to move. She whispered, "You failed your God and your order a long time ago in the jungles of the south. You are no longer a Black Robe. Join me and I will save you. You will go through the tear in the sky to Okeanus and land in a villa on the red cliffs. You will shepherd blue-back dragons and balance the worlds and they shall move like the innards of a great clock." She cried out in pleasure and dug her nails deeply into his chest.

Later, lying side by side, he said, "I must deliver the *bullae.*"

"Why? "she asked. "They mean nothing, they do nothing. The Black Robes are blind, all men are blind."

"Because I gave my word," he mumbled.

"Can you be trapped so easily in a false quest? The demons will use your words to destroy the balance of the worlds. Be true to yourself and fear the help of demons but promise me that if I help you, you will join me," she said.

"But you lead the dead," he interjected. She smiled and leaned forward and kissed him and he felt great warmth fill his whole body and for a moment he was happy. For a moment he did not care he had failed the Black Robes.

"Do not argue like a barrister. Just agree and you will survive these monsters' ministrations." He nodded in agreement.

The next morning he woke to the sound of the iron door opening. He was hungry and thirsty and his fever was gone.

Johnston stood in the doorway.

"So you are alive?"

"Who are you?"

"The Bailiff of this Dorf," he answered before asking. "The more important question is who are you?"

"Moses Stern, a blacksmith from La Ciudad. I was on my way to Santa Rey Pueblo, when I was attacked."

"Why were you traveling alone? The people here think you are a scout."

"A scout?" he asked, although he knew exactly what the man was saying.

"A scout for the dragoons," said Johnston, knowing the man was acting ingenuous.

"I am no scout, just a blacksmith."

"Did you make those guns you were carrying? And the ammo, did you make the ammo?"

Stern nodded and the man grinned: "You are a talented man. The kind of man we could use in this pueblo."

"Thank you," said Stern.

"You hungry?" the Bailiff asked. "We will feed you and then we will have the trial."

"The trial?" asked Stern, somewhat confused by the way the conversation swerved off in the opposite direction from which he thought they were heading.

"Yep," said the man. "Oh, by the way, your bitch whelped last night and we have parceled the puppies out to some of the town's members."

Stern put his head into his hands and then asked, "What happens at this trial?"

"If you are found guilty you will die. The Friends don't let us hang people no more, so we exile you to a place where you will either starve to death or die of thirst."

"What does that mean?" he asked, somewhat confused by the bailiff's tone. It seemed to Stern the man was joking.

"You read the good book?"

"Of course I've read it."

"Then you know the ending."

"What story are you talking about; there are a thousand stories."

"If you are found guilty, we take your things and then throw you into a well out in the desert. It is all legal and book-like. It is just like Joseph and his brothers. You had the beautiful clothes and the guns and mules and we, your brothers and sisters, were jealous. Now we have your things and you are either going to die or end up in some foreign land." He laughed and continued, "The Friends and Freedmen like it that way, all legal and tidy. On this matter they are in agreement. Most times they can't agree on the time of day. I think it's a lot of foolishness. If you are going to steal from a man, just steal his things, take it while he is looking down the barrel of your guns. It is more honest and realistic. But they like it metaphorical."

"Why are you doing this to me?"

The man laughed and said, "Because you're a stranger and because you have some valuable things. This desert is hard scrabble. That is what it is and to live here you have to take. Besides, your Pope has sent dragoons here to steal our stock. They have killed our people and burned our homes. It seems he wants as much land as he can grab. We fight back but he is stronger. We can't let strangers in, especially someone like you. I mean you have the papist smell all over you. Even the way you talk gives you away."

"Have you thought that maybe I look the way I do and speak the way I do because I have nothing to hide."

"Who knows who or what you really are? I'm just telling you what I see."

"I'm a blacksmith."

"There is the rub, for me, at least. We could use a blacksmith. A man that can make guns like you do could be valuable to us."

Stern rubbed his forehead and tried to think. "Maybe I could work here for a while, make guns, shoe some horses. "

Johnston looked at him and shook his head. "Tell them but I wouldn't put much hope in it. Dom Angelo wants your things and the Friends love to chastise sinners. I mean exile sinners."

Later that day, he stood naked in front of a tribunal of three: Alyse Guterschein, Dom Angelo and Ralph Johnston, the bailiff's brother. Ralph Johnston suggested they hold him as an indentured servant but Dom Angelo demanded they hang him as a spy or scout; while Friend Alyse pointed out he was a heretic and must die by exile. After a few preliminaries, he was quickly adjudicated a stranger, a heretic, a Black Robe and a spy for the Emperor's dragoons. Alyse pronounced the sentence of exile and then asked if he had any last wishes.

"I had three letters with me. Could I be exiled with them?"

"Papers?" she asked, puzzled. "Are you asking for some papers?" Alyse looked at the other members for some guidance and then asked him, "Why do you want them?"

"They are sacred to me."

"They a part of your religion?" asked the woman.

"Yes," he lied.

"If we can find these letters we'll throw them into the well with your body."

After the trial, the bailiff, riding Stern's mule, led him by his tied hands from the Dorf, toward the east, while Dom Angelo rode the gelding and his three sons followed at a distance. At sunset, they arrived at the well, which was only a dry hole in the ground. Stern looked over the edge and it was dark and he could not tell how far the bottom was. The bailiff dismounted and untied his hands.

"You want to jump or should I push you."

"I'll jump."

He looked up at the sky and saw the moon rising, which seemed closer than ever and then he jumped into the darkness, grabbing at the side of the wall to slow his descent and minimize the damages to his legs and feet. He fell twelve feet onto a pile of bones and debris at the bottom of the dry well; his nails and hands bloody from scraping the rough walls of the well. Spiders and rats and maybe snakes rustled and stirred in the detritus. He sat down on a pile of bones and heard Dom Angelo laughing. He sat for a long while before he slept.

He awoke to the yelp of a coyote and looked up to see the moon hanging full and yellow over the well's mouth. He began to hum Friend Alyse's song and a tear rolled down his cheek. Rats' red eyes shone out at him. Time passed and he thought about his life in La Ciudad, about the Priests and about his mission. The sun shone into the well and then it grew dark and the moon rose again.

That night he killed his first rat with a rock and tore its foul fur from its body with his teeth. "Just like chicken," he said and then laughed. After his meal he slept again. When he awoke, he crawled through a short narrow passage and entered a larger chamber. Bones evidenced other men and he supposed he was not the first man to crawl into this stomach-like hole.

As afternoon approached the light faded in the larger chamber so he crawled back to the floor of the well to take advantage of what little light was left to him. Even though they expelled him several years before, the Black Robes continued to call upon his talent as a smith and an explorer. They would bring him documents or artifacts and then ask him to rebuild or explain their function to them. Sometimes he would ask them where they found the object.

Many times they only brought him a piece, so he would travel to the location and search about, trying to find the whole relic. He had become an expert on things of the past, as the Argylls and the Priests continued to deliver things at his door. His service kept his child alive in the miserable Black Robe orphanage in La Ciudad. He had suspected from the first that the *bullae* concerned some artifact; otherwise, why send him, a defrocked priest? They wanted him in Santa Rey Pueblo for a reason and the reason must involve an artifact.

As the hours passed, he killed another rat and then another, until he no longer saw their red eyes peering at him from the darkness. He found a yellow and black snake coiled in the corner and he killed that too and ate it; then he was sick. Nearly every time he fell asleep he dreamed of the *bruja*. She came to him at night and they did things he never imagined men and women could do together. When he broke his vows and made love to Mara, they never did anything like the *bruja* showed him. He wondered at his sanity and believed demons were visiting him.

Because of the dreams, he preferred being awake and he feared that soon he would die. As he fought sleep, he thought about food. In particular, he day-dreamed of a restaurant near the *zocalo* called *Villa*'s, which served fat pork tamales and saffron rice, with cold *cerveza*. On Saturday nights, a forty-piece band would play and people would dance and drink tequila from clay jugs. He liked to sit in the corner and sip tequila and smoke his pipe and watch the blue-skinned Argyll girls whirl around the dance floor to the sound of guitars and horns. He would never have known about *Villa*'s if the Black Robes had not thrown him out of the Order for breaking his vows. For this he was thankful. They could have kept him and simply punished him. By expelling him, they had freed him. He laughed. He was a Freedman after all.

Three days after being cast into the well he awoke from yet another dream of the *bruja*. This time they were standing together in a great building where hundreds of smiths were forging metals. Huge kettles with melted copper, tin, gold, and iron glowed as Stern and the woman walked among them, their faces lit by the bright fires. 'Was this hell,' he asked himself? When he woke, he crawled to the shaft of the well. It was night again and he looked up to see the moon but he also saw the snout of a coyote at the lip of the well. Then, he heard, "Black Robe, what are you doing in this dry hole? It's as dry as old badger's woman's womb."

"Coyote, thank God."

"You want out?"

"Please."

A hemp rope, his rope, fell into the well and he reached for it. The man pulled him out because he was too weak to help. All he could do was to hang onto the rope. He lay on the ground panting and Coyote ordered him to lie still and said he would soon be back with food. Stern said a prayer of thanks.

Soon Coyote returned with a gourd filled with water and two doves.

"Can you pluck those birds, while I look for firewood?"

He sat up and held the bloody birds, one in each hand, as tears rolled down his cheeks.

Later, as they ate, the Coyote asked, "you still going to Santa Rey Pueblo?"

The Blacksmith looked up, the juice from the birds dripping onto his thick black beard.

"What else is there to do?" He asked the question because at that moment he was empty. There was no desire to move on. He was simply hungry and thirsty.

"Where are you going?" he asked Coyote.

"Going?" he asked and then said, "Nowhere. I'm here."

Stern smiled.

At sunrise they set off toward the north. As his bare feet flopped firmly onto the hot red sand, he hummed Friend Alyse's song under his breath. He wore nothing, carried nothing, thought nothing, except that he must keep moving.

That night, as they slept in a stand of stubby mesquite trees, the *bruja* overcame them in their sleep and cast a spell on both of them. Then, with the help of a dozen of her sisters, she carried their bodies to a clearing where they had landed their ornithopters. Preparing to take off, she tied them supine to the struts of her craft; and in the air, she whispered into his ear: "We fly to the walled city at the mouth of a great river, where I will open a portal to Okeanus and send you through into the watery world. There you must find Bedwyr and learn the magus' craft and the secret of the blue-back dragons. Only when you learn these things will you be able to return. Remember this though, mark your entrance to the world and return from the same spot. To return from somewhere else will have fatal consequences. And never trust a demon. Every word a demon speaks is a lie."

He felt cool air against his face and the will of the *bruja* permeate his soul. "Promise me you will do as I say," she whispered into his ear, releasing the binding of his mouth.

"I will do as you say."

"Promise me on the souls of your son and your children to come."

"I promise."

She then spoke the words that bound him and he felt his physical body strain as a great force pounded against it. The spell prevented him from speaking but he repeated over and over the question in his mind until he lost consciousness, 'Why are you doing this to me?' Then, he thought, 'Who are you?' And finally, 'is this magic?'

Chapter Three: Home Sweet Home

STERN OPENED HIS EYES to find himself lying on the patio of an antique villa, situated on the edge of a sheer red, rocky cliff, on the coast of a mountainous island, surrounded by a violent and purple sea. Above his head, on a redwood lattice, flowering vines grew thickly and giant yellow and blue butterflies, honeybees and bumblebees fluttered. The air, redolent with the cloying smell of the flowers, vibrated with the buzzing of bees. Above him, in a stubby olive tree, growing on the lip of the patio, nine parrots with yellow, green and blue plumage sat, squawked and spread their multicolored wings, beating them angrily.

He realized he was alone, cast into an alien world by the lunar *bruja*; his fellow captive, Coyote, was nowhere to be seen. As he stood the parrots paced back and forth, following him, shaking their heads up and down in disapproval, like pompous and pious Black Robes. Dizzy and nauseous from being transported from his world to this place Stern fell onto the tessellated floor of the patio; however, the fact he lay prostrate on his back, helpless and disoriented, although frightening to him, seemed to calm the parrots. Up above, through the spaces between the vines and the lattice, he saw a rosy sky filled with pink clouds. But to his right, far in the distance, a yellow bolt of lightning split the bruise-black heavens, and the odor of ozone permeated the air. He waited for the sound of thunder. When it arrived, it was so loud he covered his ears. An icy breeze accompanied the thunder, a harbinger of winter.

He stood as his nausea passed and the parrots immediately responded by parading nervously about the gnarled limbs of their olive tree. To pacify them he moved slowly to a wall that he thought faced north, it was shorter than the other three walls. With a minimum amount of disturbance from the parrots, he crept up and peered over its side and surveyed his surroundings. His villa was one of thousands built or carved into the side of a sheer mountain wall. He was located, he reasoned from the facts he had, in the center of a salmon-colored city, built or carved from the side a massive red cliff on a balcony perched high above a rock-strewn beach on the edge of a restless, raging sea. And then a thought occurred to him that maybe he was dreaming or maybe he was dead.

High above him, a falcon screeched and dropped from a pink cloud onto a flock of pigeons that circled below his ledge, grabbed one in its talons and then spread its wings, turned and climbed toward Stern, who backed away from the edge. Reaching the wall, the bird dropped the bloody pigeon onto the red tiles, hopped down onto the floor, and quickly ripped its chest open with its hooked beak. In response the parrots squawked and beat their wings. Undisturbed by the parrots, the falcon continued to devour its prey, while Stern's mouth watered. He felt an urge to rush the falcon and steal the remaining bits of the pigeon but he feared its blood-soaked beak.

The crimson sun set and Stern shivered at the anticipation of his first night in the strange world. His stomach rumbled and he knew that tomorrow he would have to explore the city to find food. He stretched out on the tiles underneath the arbor and remembered the myths he read as a child, where the hero landed in a new world and immediately began to explore, usually discovering a naked woman in the alien landscape. Unlike the brave, adventuresome protagonists of those stories, he had remained in the same spot throughout the day. It was important for him, he reasoned, to become accustomed to his new surroundings before he set out and to somehow come to grips with his unusual predicament, cast by a witch through a portal into an alien world, with instructions to find Magus Bedwyr.

Later, staring up at the now dark sky, he generalized that so far this world consisted of red mountains, blue sea, an aggressive falcon, pigeons, parrots, bees and butterflies. Consequently he deduced this world was a world of red things with wings. He laughed and the parrots squawked an agitated and angry answer, as he fell asleep, shivering as the last light of the day disappeared.

Stern awoke to the raucous shriek of the parrots, running along the lattice roof of the patio, bouncing and bobbing their heads in anxiety and anger. Shivering from the early morning chill, he rubbed his eyes, stretched broadly and walked to the shortest wall to urinate over the side. He was stiff, hungry and his back ached. The falcon, perched on a brick column above the patio, with its head buried beneath a mottled wing, awakened and flew toward the beach, as Stern rubbed his beard and scratched his arm where something had bitten him in the night. His stomach rumbled and he knew his time of inaction was up, he had to find food and water. In an alcove of the patio, he discovered a locked door with large iron hinges and handle. He attempted to force it open but he failed, so he climbed the northern wall and jumped to an adjacent patio which was similar but smaller than his and without a lattice.

This patio also had a door and it too was locked, so he traversed its northern wall and discovered yet another patio, a patio, however, that possessed a gurgling fountain. Dropping to its floor, he ran to the fountain and drank the brackish water from cupped hands. Later, the falcon, returning from its hunt, dropped a dead rabbit onto the flat clay tiles of the patio. Stern somehow understanding it was for him approached the carcass while watching the falcon. When the falcon did not react, he frantically tore raw flesh from the bone of the rabbit but as he began to eat, thirty or more parrots descended upon him. The falcon, in his defense, spread its wings and beat back the birds, as Stern wiped blood from his mouth with the back of his hand and cursed the parrots.

In the late afternoon, purple clouds gathered in the north above a now turgid sea and a colder wind stirred dead leaves on the patio, causing the parrots to huddle together. The naked Stern shivered too while his guardian, the falcon, rose into the air and flew toward the storm, freeing the parrots to creep once again closer to him.

Later, an orange bolt of lightning ripped the sky and through the menacing clouds a dark shape emerged, flying faster than the wind. Circling the patio, the falcon screeched a warning and the parrots scrambled to their original perch as the unknown creature turned slightly adjusting its trajectory. 'It was either a great bird or a small dragon,' Stern thought as he scuttled away from the wall and crouched in a corner. Soon, he heard leathery wings flapping dully and he rose to see the creature clearly hovering above him. It was no bird, it was a humanoid with wings. The parrots flew up and away, as the winged creature, now almost on top of Stern, turned slowly. Its bare cloven hooves touched down gently, almost elegantly, onto the tiles of the patio. Folding its leather wings tightly against its back, it opened its mouth in a gesture, resembling a yawn, exposing sharp white teeth and filling the air with the taint of brimstone, as it spoke to Stern in a guttural language.

"I don't understand you," Stern said.

The creature smiled, its black eyes blinking rapidly under its thick brow: "I know your language. Do not fret." It drew a deep breath, expanding its broad chest covered by a black leather vest and croaked: "Welcome to Okeanus, man of Mittilagart." It paused and attempted a parody of a smile before asking: "How are you called?"

"My name is Stern."

"Stern," the creature repeated. "Do you fly, Stern?"

He shivered, maybe from the cold or maybe from fear, and said, "No, I don't fly." And then he felt the need to explain; "No man can fly. That is no man can fly with his own wings like you."

"Oh no, then how do you explain him?" The creature pointed to the falcon.

"What do you mean?"

"This bird, this falcon, is a man like you."

"A man?" questioned Stern, as the falcon screeched, as if in agreement.

"He is a man in his basic form, one of the animal people, one of the hidden ones. Surely, you know the nature of the man you travel with? To not know is irresponsible."

Stern whispered, "Coyote?" The falcon hopped in answer.

Stern turned to the creature and asked, "Why is he in this form?"

"You have reached the watery plane, the first level of the lower worlds."

"Is this hell?"

"Do you ask if this is the world of the dead?" asked the creature, spreading his wings and Stern nodded in the affirmative.

"This is the watery plane, a material realm, a realm between the worlds of air and fire."

"Then who are you?"

"I'm Focalor and I have come to guide you."

"Guide me where?" asked Stern.

"I will help you as much as possible but as I said I am simply a guide." He paused and looked toward the parrots. "We must get you away from the silent city because you are in danger."

"Danger?" said Stern, suspicious of the creature that looked and smelled like brimstone.

"Those petty daemons of Elysium desire your soul."

"The parrots?" he asked looking around the patio.

"They are pitiful petty daemons that have a great hunger for your soul. Only the presence of the falcon prevented them from devouring you."

Stern swallowed and then asked, "How do I get off this ledge?"

"We fly. You must shift into animal form."

"I cannot fly."

"My dear Stern, you can fly. I assure you. I will help you."

"If I can fly, it is news to me?"

"Close your eyes."

Stern leaned against the stone of the patio's wall and, as instructed, closed his eyes and, in the process, disregarded the lunar witch's warning to avoid all demons.

"I want you to clear your mind and then tell me what images float into your mind."

"I see a landscape. The sand is dark red, much darker than the stones of this building."

"What else?"

He concentrated and out of the dark he saw two eyes and a hooked yellow beak.

"I see the head of a bird. He has a white cap and dark eyes."

As he imagined the bird, it stretched its large white wings and began to fly. He described the bird to Focalor, recognized it and named it. "It's an osprey."

"An osprey?" asked Focalor, smiling, mouthing the new word. "Like your friend, you can shift. Keep your eyes closed and imagine you are the osprey and I will help you change."

Stern felt the being's hands on his bowed head radiating heat. As he waited, meditating on the osprey, he became painfully aware that Focalor's hands were becoming hotter and hotter until his touch seemed to blister his skin.

Focalor whispered into his ear, "What is the osprey doing now?"

"It's gliding over an ice-covered mountain and a frozen lake."

Suddenly, there was a crack of lightning and Focalor's voice boomed out, "Dive, Stern, for the fish!"

Stern was no longer aware he was meditating; instead, he was soaring over snow-covered mountains, where, in a valley, lay a frozen lake, with a tiny break in the ice. In the open water, he spied a great salmon near the surface. He dived and soon he felt himself flying away from the lake with a great fish in his talons. He landed on a jagged peak above the lake, where he dropped the salmon and held it still with his right talon before ripping into its flesh with his great curved beak. He tasted the salmon's flesh. The scene faded and he saw Focalor and the falcon.

"Where am I?" he asked.

However, his words echoed in his mind, as Focalor stretched his great leather wings and ordered, "Follow me."

Chapter Four: Learning to Fly

STERN FOLLOWED COYOTE, the falcon, and Focalor, the guide, as they lifted off the patio, flew up above the city and turned south away from the storm. As he rose higher, Stern realized the plateau dominated a small island. When he flew even higher, he recognized the island was one of many in a great purplish-blue sea. He remembered a word–archipelago–and he knew he was now flying over an archipelago that stretched for hundreds of miles. Stern could no longer speak, he screeched and squawked but he could discern something in his mind, a faint echo of words and he concentrated to understand. Finally, he heard, "Fly faster, Stern." He was sure this was the message. 'Who speaks?' He thought.

"*It's Coyote. You're falling behind.*"

Communicating without speech, he thought, 'Where are we going?'

The answer came almost instantly. "*Focalor says we fly to find Typhon.*"

"*Who is he?*"

"*You think I know. I cannot speak nor can I shift from this shape. We're trapped in the creature's magic, just like that witch trapped us in the desert.*"

"*What do you mean?*" Stern asked, beginning to panic.

"*I mean he has sealed us in these forms.*"

"*Why? What does he want from us?*"

"*He wants us to accompany him to Typhon. That's all I know.*"

40

"You're falling behind," yelled Focalor. "Stay close to me."

Stern flapped harder and he began to catch up. He concentrated on Focalor, calling his name repeatedly in his mind. Finally, Focalor shouted, "Would you shut up?"

"*You can hear me, too?*" He asked telepathically.

"Of course, you fool."

"*Where are we going?*" asked Stern, ignoring the creature's anger.

"Coyote told you. We fly to Typhon's island in the far east."

"*Who is Typhon?*"

"He is a powerful being in this world. He will tell you what you need to do."

"*Is he the same as you?*"

"No. He is something else. He lives on a small volcanic island near the equator in the eastern ocean."

"*What does this Typhon do?*"

"He makes things through the use of fire from the minerals of this earth. Now be quiet and fly."

They passed over another island and Stern asked, "*Was that place, where we arrived, part of an archipelago?*"

"It is a known land and it lies within the known sea of the North. We are now flying toward the unknown sea in the East, away from the magicians, witches, and kings," responded Focalor.

'I'm hungry,' thought Coyote, and they all heard his thoughts.

"You creatures are pathetic," said Focalor. "The sea is full of beings. Fly down and see what you can catch. But be careful that one of them does not catch you."

Coyote fell like a stone toward the sea and Stern squawked nervously, watching him plummet downwards. Far below them, the falcon leveled out above the water and glided several inches above the frothy waves. Finally, Stern saw a splash of blue and then Coyote began to ascend toward them, a great yellow fish, thrashing back and forth, in his talons.

"Now that you have your fish how are you going to eat it?" asked Focalor with a laugh.

Coyote did not answer. The weight of the fish caused him to lag and as the sun began to set, Stern feared the night and asked, "*Would Coyote lose them in the dark?*"

Just before the sun sank beneath the horizon, Focalor dipped his right wing and turned toward the south. Stern followed and soon spied a green speck in the distance, a small island, shimmering from the fading light. Focalor landed, folded his wings, and squatted with his head against his knees on the small, flat island, composed of volcanic red rock, pitted and scarred from erosion. Stern came to rest near him and asked: "Would you help me shift back to my human form?"

"Why would you do that?" asked Focalor. "You will be naked, exposed to the wet and the cold. It is safer to stay as you are."

"*But I am hungry.*" Stern, who had never cried in his life, now whined in sheer frustration.

"Then find something to eat. It's time you learned to feed yourself in this world of making."

Stern was struck by the expressions and linguistic constructions Focalor used when talking with him. It was as if the creature were trying to communicate some hidden message about the nature of the world in which the witch had cast him. Focalor called this plane the world of making and the material world. 'What does that mean?' He thought, consciously projecting the question to the dozing humanoid: "*Why do you call it the world of making?*"

Focalor lifted his head and grimaced in a way that communicated Stern's ignorance was annoying. "The base elements are here. The materials necessary to build a world are here: iron and gold, silver and tin. They are all here in this world. The Great Goddess takes them and mixes them and forms things. It is a world in constant movement. The earth shifts and the volcanoes spurt lava into the sky. There is ash and embers in the wind and we change with every explosion." He closed his eyes and for a moment Stern thought he had fallen asleep but then he opened his eyes and said, "Now fly off and find us something to eat. I must sleep."

Stern spread his wings and rose into the dark sky. As he flew above the water's surface, he smelled sulfur and brimstone spewing into the atmosphere from the active volcanoes and wondered at what he now was: a bird flying above the waters of an alien world. For the first time that day he remembered why he was sent to this place: to find a magus, another blacksmith, named Bedwyr and to learn the secret of the blue-back dragons and their coming to Mittilagart.

As he said the name of his world and repeated the command of the witch, he realized it was becoming more and more difficult for him to remember the other world–the middle world–his world of origin. The bird's brain was taking over and he struggled against it, forcing his memories to remain and not fade. He suddenly remembered the witch's warning to mark his entrance into the watery plane and he realized he hadn't marked the spot nor did he have the faintest idea on how to find the island of the rose-colored city. And then he remembered her other warning to never trust a demon.

A burst of light, emanating from a creature, sporting the head and body of a lion, the leathery black wings of a bat, and a long hairless tail with a spike at the end, interrupted his worried train of thought. This creature, this dragon lion, spit another bolt of flame across the water and illuminated the surface of the sea, revealing a school of flying fish just a foot or so beyond the reach of its large golden paws.

Suddenly hundreds of flying fish sprang from the sea foam and sailed for thirty or forty feet before they splashed against the water and disappeared. Stern realized quickly that if he flew up above the dragon lion he could dive onto the flying fish, grab one in his talon, and be gone before the heavier dragon lion could respond to the theft of his prey. His birdbrain was taking control of his rational human mind, which seemed to be receding into some dark unconscious realm. The thought of the taste of the fish outweighed the danger of revealing himself to the dragon lion. So, when the dragon lion illuminated the surface again with a yellow burst of fire, Stern climbed above it. Then, when the fish sprang from the water, he folded his wings and fell upon them, caught a large one in his talon and climbed higher into the sky.

He believed he had succeeded in his tiny theft but suddenly he felt an excruciating pain in his right wing and smelled the sickening odor of burnt feathers. The dragon lion had abandoned its fish hunt and was now closing on him. Stern painfully flapped his wings to gain altitude and speed but the large flying fish hampered his efforts and unbalanced him. Fear filled his mind. He could not fly directly back to the island where Focalor and Coyote waited with the dragon lion following him so closely, so he dipped his left wing and turned abruptly to the west. The turn surprised the dragon lion, which was not as fast as Stern and by the time it had corrected its pursuit, Stern was several yards ahead.

As the minutes passed the dragon lion fell further and further behind until Stern could barely make out its image. When he could no longer see the lion, he dipped his right wing and circled back toward the south. If the dragon lion still pursued him, he thought, it might continue west, unaware the bird had fled south. But to be safe he shifted his direction again, now flying east, hopefully, heading toward the island where the others waited.

As he flapped his wings, he sent his thoughts frantically out to Focalor, begging him to answer but minutes passed without an answer and his wings ached and smarted from the burns. Fear that he was lost on this strange world filled his mind, embarrassing him because he was a Black Robe, at least he once was, and he was trained to bury his fear. Now though in this strange world, his feelings seemed to bubble to the surface and he felt child-like in his terror and apprehension.

Later, he spied a large island different from the small one where he left Focalor and Coyote. This island, covered with lush vegetation, possessed several tall mountains, some of them smoking. As he approached, he could make out dense forests and fields, deep valleys and many fjords. Even though he knew this wasn't where he left his companions, he decided to land, eat his fish and rest. He glided toward a forest near the northern end of the island and as he drew closer, he leveled off and made a pass over a red sand beach, a dense savannah that spread out in all directions for several miles and the forest itself. Three passes over the savannah to make sure it was safe and then he landed.

There were no other birds in the sky, a fact, which if he had taken a moment to think, might have disturbed him. He set down on an elevated knoll in the center of the savannah, dropped his flying fish onto the yellow grass and waited a few moments before ripping into its pink flesh. He did not want to start eating and then have to flee the dragon lion. When he was satisfied he had escaped he ate. With half the fish eaten, he heard the dull thump of leather wings of a giant dragon hovering high above him. He froze and waited, praying the dragon would not see him. Minutes passed and finally the beast turned and flew toward the south, toward the mountains. As the dragon's image faded and disappeared, hundreds of sea birds flew up out of the forest, circling the savannah and heading toward the sea.

Stern squawked and finished his fish, then flew toward the edge of the forest, landed on the limb of a gnarled and weather-beaten hard wood of some unknown variety, and hid himself amongst its dark foliage. Thousands of birds of all types flew through the forest, their calls filling the sky. Many of the birds were parrots: green, yellow and red. He feared they might be spirits seeking his soul. Frightened he called out to Focalor and Coyote but he heard nothing.

Finally, he placed his head beneath his right wing and slept. He dreamed of the *bruja*. He was in a large rambling stone house, full of women and children. As he walked through the house, he talked with children who stopped their play and hugged him. He felt love for all of them although he knew they were not his. He came to a door where he stood and looked out onto a gravel drive, where the *bruja* waited with two baby girls in her arms and a young boy standing at her side. The Argyll, his woman, the mother of his son, now dead, stood next to her. Another woman, someone he had never seen, took the babies from the *bruja*'s arms and placed them in his arms. He felt their warmth and loved suffused his body and he knew they were his.

As suddenly as he realized the children were his, he feared the babies would change into birds or perhaps worse a baby with a bird's head. He felt panic and embarrassment. The babies did not change in the dream and he awoke with a numinous feeling still vibrant in his mind. This feeling quickly passed over to fear when he awoke. He quickly realized he was once again in his human form and the limb of the tree where he perched was bending under his weight. He fell several feet to the ground, where he lay naked, cold, bruised and afraid.

Stunned from the fall, he gathered the strength to crawl under a thick bush growing next to the tree and tried to calm down. He had wanted his human form back but now he was trapped, alone and naked, on an island that housed a great dragon, a dragon much larger than those he saw flying over the Azul Mountains. He could no longer sleep and he waited for sunrise. At dawn, a pair of wild boars emerged from the undergrowth of the forest and he climbed a tree to avoid being gored by their curved tusks. After spending most of the day in the tree, he decided to take his chances in the savannah or better yet on the beach, where he could at least see the creatures before they were on top of him. Late in the day after a quick march through the thick grass, he found something that resembled clams half-buried in the red sand along a creek that ran to the sea and pried them open with a sharp stone and swallowed the contents raw. When night came he climbed a tree and settled between its gnarled, rough limbs.

The next day it rained in the morning and he shivered under the trees' thick foliage. In the afternoon, he reached the ocean and discovered a small turtle emerging from its white foam. Grabbing it, he cracked its shell with a stone and ate it along with some clams. He did not relish another night in a tree, where he barely slept out of discomfort and fear. Searching, he found a grassy knoll between the savannah and the beach and lay there looking at sea birds floating on the air until he fell asleep.

During his third day on the island, while searching the sand for more clams, a humanoid emerged from the high green grass of the savannah, riding a pony or something that resembled a pony. Stern glanced here and there for a hiding place but it was useless. The humanoid was heading his way. He had obviously been discovered. Frankly, he was tired and ready to be found. When the creature drew near, he realized her pony was a zebra and the humanoid was a woman, naked like him, riding bare back. Tall and lean, with dark red hair that fell in thick curls around her shoulders, she carried a wooden stave in her right hand and held the reins of a hempen bridle loosely in her left. Halting the zebra a few feet from Stern, who now stood on the edge of the beach, she dismounted the zebra and let the rope fall. Stern raised his right hand and waved. Smiling, revealing strong white teeth, he pointed to his chest and said, "Stern."

She watched with a bemused grin on her young face and said, "Gotha."

He repeated her name and she smiled again.

"Come," she said, in a deeply accented version of his language.

"You speak my language."

She frowned, not understanding what he was talking about. Instead, she answered: "We must leave. This is a dragon island. No humans live here."

"What are you doing here, then?" he said.

"My queen sent me to check the North." She paused and then pointed her spear over his shoulder, where the dragon was once again languidly flying over the savannah, seeking its prey.

She jumped onto the zebra's back and reached for him, urging him to climb on behind her. As soon he slid against her he became painfully aware of their nakedness. She turned and said, "Forget that. We must cross the island before nightfall. Do you want a dragon to eat us?" She kicked the zebra and they galloped through the tall grass of the savannah toward the darkness of the shadowed forest, as he realized she was the woman in the dream.

Chapter Five: To Build a Fire

HE HAD NOT YET VENTURED so far into the forest of the island. Together they rode along a narrow path that wound through and under massive trees. The further they rode, the denser the forest became. The sun disappeared and the shadows of the trees merged. 'It is like the darkest night,' he thought, 'under these trees.' Gotha forced the zebra to jump some gnarled roots that had overgrown and blocked the trail and he unconsciously put his arms around her waist to prevent himself from falling. She relaxed and moved toward him so he remained as he was; his arm around her, his chest pressed against her back. She was warm and firm and he felt happy. It was an odd emotion to feel at that moment but having her with him changed his mood.

Before she arrived he was afraid and now he wasn't; she appeared confident and strong and he took solace in that. They rode for an hour and then stopped at a stream that eroded the trail; she dismounted and walked up stream, squatted and drank. He followed her, imitating her actions. The water was brackish and tasted of iron. He walked back toward the zebra that was grazing on a patch of gray-green grass, climbed a shallow bank, and sprawled on a thick, mossy tuft. A ray of sunlight penetrated the foliage and a giant bat circled above him. He sprain up and ran to Gotha, who was swimming in the brackish stream. "I saw a giant bat, there." He pointed.

She squinted in the feeble light and said, while treading water, "A fox bat. They are usually harmless, if you leave them alone."

As if on cue, the red-furred fox bat glided toward them and he shuttered. "Do all creatures in this world fly?" he asked.

She laughed, as she emerged from the water. "I do not fly. In fact, no human flies, nor do the other races, neither the Silenoi, Reavers, Dra'ghan, Tarn, or Bouc." She paused and scratched her naked thigh. "The Keltoi and Skaellanders are called shape-shifters and there are tales that some of them fly, when they are in their totem form."

"The Silenoi?" he repeated softly. "That name is familiar. We have legends about them. They are half-men and half-goat. We call them the children of Silenus."

"The Silenoi are not goats but they are wild and some have thick hair on their chests and backs. They form *thiasos* traveling throughout our world on masted ships, trading and conveying messages between the islands. They are great craftsmen and a friend of Bedwyr, the Magus. They worship Pannus, a god of Chaos and are distantly related to the Bouc of Grun."

Hearing the name, Bedwyr, caused him to pause. Perhaps these Silenoi could take him to the Magus. "Are there any Silenoi on this island?"

"This is a dragon island. The only semi-sentient creatures here are the dragons."

He looked at her directly, as a thought struck him. "Gotha, what are you?"

"What do you mean?" she asked, pushing her wet thick hair back with her left hand.

"You are not a fox bat or a Silenoi. What are you?"

She laughed. "I'm a woman, just as you are a man."

She lay down in the moss and crossed her legs. She held her head up with her hands and stared off into the distance. Suddenly, he felt the need to tell her about his journey to Okeanus, his capture by Focalor, his flight to the island in the guise of an osprey, and his transformation back into human form. She listened patiently and did not act surprised by his weird story. After a while, she rubbed her chin and said, "I don't think your totem is a bird."

"My totem," he asked. "I don't have a totem; I was transformed by Focalor's magic."

"Maybe," she said, "maybe not. Focalor is powerful but he cannot create what does not exist. My guess is you have the power to shape shift. Do you have Skaellander blood? Are you one of the dragon people?"

"As I told you, I'm from Mittilagart. I do not have the power to shift shape. That is something that Focalor did with his magic."

She sat up and scratched a bite on her leg. "You have a totem. I can sense it but I don't think it is a bird."

"If I am not a bird then what am I? How could I have shifted into the osprey?"

"Tell me about the transformation?" He repeated the story of his encounter with Focalor and the transformation. When he finished, she said: "You were tricked. Focalor wanted you to be a bird so he turned you into one so you could fly with him."

"Coyote was a bird from the start," he said.

"He is obviously a shape-shifter, like the Keltoi. But you are not a bird. I don't think the bird is your spirit animal. It is something. I can feel it but not identify it. Not yet but it will come to me. However, the osprey is now a part on you, it is a result of Focalor's magic."

Stern examined her face to determine if there was any guile there. All he saw was a sincere young woman; a sincere naked woman, puzzling over his spirit animal.

Suddenly, a strong swoosh of air across their heads startled them and she sprang to her feet, holding her stave across her chest, her knees bent ready to spring. The fox bat turned and glided back toward them and Stern searched the ground for a rock or a stick. When the bat was a few inches from Gotha, she rose up on her toes and whacked it squarely between its eyes. It smashed into her and knocked her off feet. Stern grabbed its thick reddish fur, yanking the creature off her chest, and threw it against one of the trunks of one of the great, gnarled trees with a sickening thud. Recovering from the collision, Gotha delivered a deadly strike to its head with her stave.

"Dead," she said. "We must leave now. They fly in pairs and the female is far fiercer than the male."

They retrieved the zebra grazing on the gray grass along the creek, mounted, and rode across the stream and up a slippery red clay embankment. After an hour of riding Stern noticed the trees were smaller and spread further apart. Light filtered through their leaves illuminating small clearings, where he spied several large piles of sawdust, shaped like haystacks.

"Those mounds, what are they?" he asked softly in her left ear.

"Nests of wood ants," she answered.

"Are they dangerous?"

She laughed. "Of course, they are. But only if we disturb them."

Finally they emerged from the forest and rode into a broad field of red grass that stretched miles before them. In their flight, they had turned east, moving away from the red iron mountains, the home of the dragons.

The grass rippled in the wind and great insects, dragonflies and butterflies hovered above the undulating waves of grass. The day waned and he wondered if they would spend the night in this sea of grass. He remembered the wood ants and the fox bats and he shuttered.

"Will we sleep here tonight?"

"There is a shelf of rock ahead. We will reach it before dark?" She said nervously.

"Are you afraid?" he asked, sensing her mood had changed.

"What do you mean?" she said, deflecting his question.

"What creatures should we fear here in this prairie?"

"Dragon lions, hyenas, winged snakes, badger dogs, sand scorpions."

"Enough, I get it."

She laughed nervously and leaned into him. Without talk they had grown intimate. They reached the rocks at the very moment the sun disappeared behind the giant forest and left the zebra in a draw and climbed the red iron stones of a wide outcropping. When they reached the top, which was six or seven meters above the draw, they found a small shallow recess that could provide shelter.

Stern rubbed his flat rumbling stomach and Gotha smiled. "I will find food. You build a fire."

She took her stave and descended the rocks, as Stern searched about the top of the outcropping, finding nothing he could use to ignite a fire. He decided to climb down from the rocks to search for dry brush to burn. Faint red haze rose off the ground. Gotha had disappeared into this reddish gloom and he feared he might lose his way. Before setting off, he faced north toward the trees to situate himself and then turned east because he was right handed and that seemed to be a logical direction to go. As he walked slowly examining the ground for twigs or brush, the rough red and yellow grass scratched his legs, hips, and thighs.

After thirty or forty minutes he had found enough sticks and twigs to make a middling fire. Turning back to the west, he squinted against the haze. The rocks were indecipherable in the crimson gloom, although he was confident he knew the way back. But it drew darker and the night filled with metallic clicks of what he guessed were insects. He moved slower through the grass, afraid he might disturb some deadly creature. The wind rustled through the thick grasses, then he heard a roar in the distance, a lion's roar, he was sure of that. He moved faster than before. After a short time, he stopped and rubbed his face with his right hand. Listening intently, he heard the sound of an animal grazing to his left; he was certain it was the zebra. He altered his course and found the rocks.

As he climbed the rock, a lion roared nearby and he hurried to the top, where he found Gotha, sitting on her haunches, plucking feathers from two multicolored birds, resembling the speckled grouse of Mittilagart. He dropped the twigs and sticks in front of her and she commanded, "Make a fire."

He found a small hole in the stone, filled it with moss, bark and dead leaves, which he crumbled into small bits, then thrust the end of the stick in the hole and rolled it between the palms of his hands, pressing hard against the wood. Soon his hands and arms ached, as wisps of smoke rose from the moss. He added bits and pieces of wood and feathers to the timorous flame until he had a dancing fire. Gotha brought the plucked birds to the fire and skewered them on sticks and then fashioned a makeshift frame to dangle the birds over the fire. She took over from him and nurtured and built the fire up until bright yellow and blue flames bounced and pranced on the rocks. She said with a toothy grin, "Stop grinning like a piebald monkey. Anyone can make a fire."

"Sorry but I am happy. I'm hungry, cold, naked, sun-burned and raw but I'm happy."

She smiled. "This is a good land. But you have to be tough."

"Is this island like your home?"

"No." She leaned toward the fire on her haunches. "There are people there. Children of Bedwyr, the Brotherhood, Reavers, some Silenoi, Dra'ghan and Brasilikans."

"Are there a lot of creatures there, like here?"

"Not like here because we have hunted out the most dangerous."

"Did you hear the lion before?"

"How could I not?"

She turned the grouse on the spit.

"Do you think the zebra is safe?"

"She will run if the lion comes. We are the ones that will not be safe."

"Is it a lion like on my world or a dragon lion?"

"I know nothing of your world but this creature isn't a dragon lion. It's a green lion. There are two types on this island—the red and the green. The green is the most dangerous, although the red is smaller and smarter. Sometimes you can escape the green only to run into a pride of the red."

"Lions are blond in my world."

"Blond?"

"Yellow."

She turned the birds on the spit and he asked: "Where are we going?"

"I'm surprised you waited so long to ask. We are going to the east coast. I hid my boat in cave there."

"Will we reach it tomorrow?"

She shook her head and turned toward the birds.

"Maybe day after tomorrow," she said, "if we are lucky." She stared at him for a long time and then asked, "What did you feel when you heard the lion roar?"

"Fear," he answered.

"Nothing else?" she asked, watching his face for a lie.

Suddenly, a red and gold snake crawled into the light and she smashed its head with a red stone. "Fire attracts all creatures."

They sat, quietly, for a long time, listening to the sound of the fire and he found himself stealing glances at her lithe form and thick hair. 'She's a beautiful woman,' he thought. She caught him looking at her and smiled a crooked smile, her white straight teeth glistening in the firelight. She rose up off her haunches and moved toward him quickly, pushing him onto his back, straddling him and grinding back and forth. Although startled, he lay back and let her work. As soon as he was ready, she slide onto him and rocked back and forth until she came. She paused and then continued until he too spent himself. With a grunt she fell onto him and rested until she smelled burning meat. She leaped up and turned the grouse.

Stern sensed creatures in the night watching them just outside the circle of light. As he was tearing flesh from a leg, he heard the lion roar nearby. She pulled her stave closer to her feet and continued to eat. When they finished, she extinguished the fire and moved toward him. They lay on the rocks and slept like spoons until dawn.

Chapter Six: Hot Springs

THE ZEBRA WAS GONE. Gotha leaned on her stave and stared at the horizon, while Stern wondered how many days had passed on his world since the witches expelled him. Gotha scratched her thigh vacantly, as she straightened. "Time to move," she said and then set off through the tall red and yellow grass. Watching her disappear into the grass, Stern sighed before following her. They walked east for several hours and not once did they emerge from the tall grass. Along the way, Gotha killed several creatures, resembling rabbits with stubby leather wings. The creatures could not fly but the wings helped extend their long leaps in the grass. Her method to bring them down was ingenious. Once she spied them hopping about, she dropped to the ground and crawled toward them. She, then, crouched in the center of their playground and waited until one leaped over her and in its mid-flight she sprang and hit the creature with such force that it folded into a limp ball and dropped to the ground. Before it could recover, she grabbed it and wrenched its neck, breaking its spine. Then she threw the dead creature to Stern to carry. Soon they had gathered four, more than enough for a meal.

At mid-day they stopped and lay in the grass. After thirty minutes of sleep she awoke and straddled him again and satiated, they set off. Late in the afternoon, when they noticed a dragon flying languidly toward the mountains in the southwest, they squatted in the grass and did not move until the dragon passed. During those tense moments, Stern thought once again of Mittilagart, his failed mission for the Black Robes and his encounter and expulsion into this world by the witches. Looking down at his hands and legs, he saw he was burned a deep red from the sun and filthy. Gotha, too, he observed, was covered with blood and dirt and grease and they both smelled sour from sweat and sex. When the passing dragon was a speck on the horizon, she signaled him to follow her.

They walked until well past dusk and then threw themselves on a small rock outcropping, where they made a fire and tore the skin from the flying rabbits and cooked them over a small fire until the meat turned clay-red. Later, as they ripped the seared flesh from the bone with their teeth, they laughed, expressing contentment. Extinguishing the fire, they cuddled together before falling asleep.

No lions roared that night. Stern woke at one point and gazed up into the night sky, filled with millions of stars, a star system exactly like his, and he wondered at this similarity until he drifted back into sleep. They awoke with the sun and finished the rabbit. At mid-morning they came to a small stream where they fell on their hands and knees and drank. Animal tracks covered both banks and Stern, after drinking his fill, was anxious to move on. Gotha, however, studied the tracks and said, "Zebra."

She tracked the animal for hours with Stern following. When they found the zebra grazing on succulent green plants growing on the banks of a creek bed, Gotha approached the animal, whispering in a guttural language Stern did not recognize. The zebra did not bolt; it allowed her to take the reins and mount. Stern ran to her and grabbed her right arm and swung himself up behind her.

They set off to the east again and Stern realized they would spend yet another night on the veldt. At dusk they stopped at a pool of water in a draw and tied the zebra to a fallen tree next to the pool. As Stern gathered wood for a fire, Gotha hunted. An hour passed and she returned with three long green snakes with the same circumference as her wrist. With a sharp rock she skinned them and hung them above the fire. Wrinkling his nose in disgust, Stern almost gagged at the thought of eating the snake but being hungry, he forced himself.

Afterward, they climbed a tiny rock ledge that emerged from the stone wall of the narrow draw, had sex and slept. Before he fell asleep, Stern spent a few moments praying. It was the first time he had thought about God since arriving in this world. As he prayed, Gotha snuggled next to him and he put his arm around her and pulled her close to him. During the night he dreamed he was a jaguar sleeping on the limb of a tree in a dark green jungle. Colorful parrots filled the trees and he roared at them. Rain fell and dripped heavily from the leafy roof of the vast forest. The next morning as they finished the snake, Stern recounted his dream and she said, "This jaguar seems closer to your soul than the bird. Maybe it's your totem."

Stern laughed. "I don't feel like a jaguar."

She asked seriously, with a slight frown on her face, "What do you feel like?"

"I feel like your child."

She blushed and turned her head. "I have no children but you can be my man."

Stern was touched by her pronouncement. He knew he could not stay in this world but he didn't want to hurt her so he said, "If you want me to be your man, it would be my pleasure?"

She smiled and said, "We will see when we return to my home." They mounted the zebra and rode out of the draw into the sea of red and yellow grass. Several hours later they spied a pride of dragon lions flying parallel to their course. Gotha tensed, pulled back on the reins and turned away from the lions and rode north at a gallop.

An hour after that they turned back toward the east. It was past noon and they had not eaten but she did not want to stop so close to the sighting of the dragon lions. They barely talked during the day and only whispered together in the evening over the fire. She asked him questions about his world and he answered the best he could. She told him her world consisted of islands, some large, some tiny. Her world was large and she had only seen a small portion of it. Her tribe numbered less than a thousand members but there were other tribes on her home island. She was eighteen-years-old and her father's youngest child, although he had just signed a contract with a new woman, a twenty-year-old warrior, and she expected to have more brothers and sisters soon. Her father had signed many contracts in his long life and fathered many children with the female warriors of his clan.

Stern asked her, "Why have you come alone to this island naked and armed with only a stave? Where are your clothes and armor?"

"It is our custom to fight naked when on a dream quest and I am forbidden by my leaders to bring a panoply of weapons. The ancient daughters of my clan fought this way."

"Why did your ancestors fight naked?"

"They believed it is not honorable to clothe yourself in armor. Some do it but I am a Tandraxx warrior. Do you understand this designation?" When he shook his head, she continued. "The female clan warrior arose from the cult of Tandraxx."

"Tandraxx?" he asked, trying to capture the same guttural pronunciation she used.

"She is a female warrior, mistress of the bow, daughter of the first mother."

"A god?" he asked.

"Yes, but she lived as one of us, a member of our race. Tandraxx warriors never marry; instead, they live together without men."

"But you referred to your father? If your mother did not marry, how did you come about? I'm confused."

"My father contracted with my mother. It required her daughters to join her on the island of Tandraxx and the sons to reside with him. My mother had no sons, so my father has no sons but many daughters."

"When you say I can be your man, what does that mean?"

"It means I will contract with you to have a child. If it is a girl, she will join me. If it is a boy, you will take him."

"What if I am not here? What if I am killed by a dragon lion?"

"Then my father will raise him."

At mid-afternoon, she forced the zebra up a steep dune. At the top, a wide red beach spread out before them and Gotha pointed to a pile of red rocks protruding into the sea. Great waves beat against the rocks, as rain clouds gathered out over the ocean.

"There is a cave there where I hid my boat. I brought clothing and supplies for both of us."

"A storm is coming." Stern said.

"We will make it to the cave before the storm hits."

She kicked the zebra and rode at a gallop toward the cave. Stern felt a pang of sadness at the thought that they were leaving the island. He had been afraid and cold for days but he had been happy with her. He imagined their lives over the last few days had been like those of the sacred couple."

As they neared the rocks Stern saw a giant black dragon flying just above the surface far out at sea. He pointed to the creature and Gotha acknowledged it. "He is hunting for a leviathan. He will take no notice of us."

The rocks hid them from the dragon and Stern held the zebra's reins as Gotha entered the cave. In a few moments she returned with a leather bag, which she handed to Stern. He uncorked it, sniffed the contents, and took a swig of a sweet wine, quickly feeling its warmth permeating his body. He handed the bag to her and she pressed a dried shriveled apple into his. The wine and the apple were like ambrosia. He sat on the sand and slowly chewed the apple, as Gotha removed the zebra's bridle and shooed it away. At first it stood a little ways away, looking at them, then it turned, kicked out its hind legs and ran south across the beach, up the red sand dune and then over it.

Stern followed Gotha into the cave, where she showed him the small boat that had been stored in the dry cave, away from the water and any prying eyes. She opened a large canvas bag lying on the bottom of the boat and extracted a pair of scissors, large straight razor, bar of rough soap, wooden comb, and a towel. "Come," she said with a smile. They left the cave and then walked away from the rocks. They soon crossed a stream running from the mountains to the south into the sea. She followed the stream across the beach and the dunes and then into an evergreen copse several hundred yards from the beach. Hidden away in the copse was a pool of hot mineral water. Stern smelled the rotten-egg odor of the hot springs; and, when he saw the pool bubbling and gurgling water, he ran to the pool, bent down, cupped his hands and splashed water onto his face.

Gotha walked to the edge of the pool and gently lowered herself into the hot water, moaned softly and then slowly swam across the natural bath. Steam rose from the surface, as she disappeared in the mist. Stern lowered himself into the water, swam to the center and floated on his back, where it was deep and wide and the water hot. He closed his eyes and thought about Mittilagart and the Argyll woman, mother of his son. It all seemed so far away now.

Gotha took his hand and led him back to the edge of the pond. She climbed out of the water and retrieved the bar of soap and returned to him and beckoned him to stand on the flat stone facing her. She lathered his whole body, rubbing hard, removing the grime and filth from the past days. When finished, she told him to wash her.

She laughed when he became aroused while scrubbing her. She took his member in her hands and held it. She dived into the pool and washed off the soap then instructed him to sit on the rock as she trimmed the wild fringe that had grown around his ears with the scissors. When his hair was cut close to his scalp, she lathered his head and face and shaved both his beard and head.

Afterward, she trimmed and cleaned their nails on their hands and feet and walked to a shrub with red berries and cut two small twigs and fashioned a toothbrush for the both of them. When they were finished she lowered herself back into the water and called him to her. In the middle of the pond they made love and he almost fainted from the heat of the water and the force of his desire for her.

Later they lay upon the rock and slept.

In the late afternoon they returned to the beach. She had combed her long red hair and braided it. Once inside the cave, she stored away her tools and presented Stern with a pair of loose fitting woolen pants, a rope belt and vest, leather sandals and a gray cloak with a hood. She dressed in an identical fashion, however, she wore a wide leather belt and attached a sheath, which held a long curved dagger. He placed the cloak in the boat and then searched for wood to build a fire. That night they sat on the beach and ate a bowl of hot cereal and dried fruits and drank sweet wine. They slept in the cave and the next morning, before dawn, they launched the small boat into a rough sea and raised the single sail.

Chapter Seven: The Storm

THROUGHOUT THE NEXT DAY they sailed due east. Flying fish and dragon lions, sea birds and massive creatures, which she called leviathans, gamboled near the boat. Near dusk she turned the small craft and soon, just as the light was fading, Stern glimpsed a green dragon flying parallel to them. They took turns steering the boat's tiller throughout the night. During the next day they talked about their history. She told him about her life among the Tandraxx and he told her about Mittilagart and the Black Robes. Both stories seemed to be fantasies to the other but Stern liked the woman's simplicity and her physical presence. He imagined a life with her on this plane. Mittilagart, the *bruja* and the Black Robes seemed further away every day, although the promise he made burned in his mind. He wondered at times if he had dreamed it.

Midway through the second day, Stern noticed a black cloud, the size of a man's hand in the north. "A rain cloud," he said pointing the cloud out to Gotha, who was half asleep at the prow. She awoke and then turned toward him in panic.

It was really the first time he had ever seen her afraid. She took control of the tiller, turning the boat toward the south. "Bad storm," she said in a whisper.

As the day wore on the cloud grew until it almost covered the whole northern sky. They traveled further to the south, trying to outrun the coming storm. Near dusk the black cloud overtook them and Stern felt the wind kick up and the temperature drop. Gotha let the heavy winds push them before the storm. The sea now roiled and heaved with the wind and Stern felt sick. Heavy rain beat down on them and Gotha gripped the tiller with both hands, straining to keep their boat on course. A flash of lightening illuminated the sea and Stern saw a great leviathan swimming parallel to them. It, too, was trying to outrun the storm.

Another bolt of lightning brightened the water around them. They could see that it was alive with leviathans, maybe ten or fifteen, all swimming away from the squall.

An hour into the run the waves deepened and widened until they found themselves falling into a trough and then suddenly being cast upward. Gotha began to chant in a language Stern had not yet heard her speak, her face locked into a grimace. Pitch black, the waves grew even larger in size. At one point the boat rose up out of the water and flew. In mid-air, the sail whipped about and smacked against Stern's back, throwing him from the boat. He felt the sickening fear of falling and then he hit the bottom of the trough. The collision knocked the air out of him and he sank.

He sank for several seconds, unconscious, before he awoke in a panic and began to thrash. The sea whirled in all directions and he had no idea which way was up. His heart pounded and he was frightened. A thought flitted through his mind, 'I am going to die now. I am going to drown in an ocean in a strange world alone. No one is going to rescue me. This is it. This is the end.'

With this thought, he stopped thrashing and relaxed. He waited for his death and when he did, when he stopped fighting, his body began to move upward toward the surface. Bobbing on the surface, he coughed and breathed deeply, now treading water in the chaos around him. He could not see the boat or Gotha. He floated on the waves for hours. Finally, the storm passed. He was exhausted but if he fell asleep he would drown.

The sun appeared on the horizon and he turned to face its warmth. The ocean was flat and calm now. When the sun rose above the horizon, one of the leviathans swam past him, heading south. He watched the long sleek body of the beast vanish into the haze. Later, in the day a school of flying fish swarmed around him and agitated the water with leaps and bounds.

He was hungry and thirsty and his arms ached. Soon he would give up and sink to the bottom of the blue-green waters. By mid-afternoon he knew he was finished. He remembered the Argyll woman, his son, the *bruja* and Gotha. He prayed for help but he suspected his prayer was too feeble and his faith too weak to elicit God's attention.

He was still floating at dusk, as he watched the sun dip beneath the horizon. He closed his eyes and felt sleep taking him. As his eyes closed, he saw a blue dragon flying over La Ciudad. The capital was burning and his son screamed his name. "I cannot help you," he mumbled. "I cannot help myself." He felt great sorrow. He was dreaming. He was drowning.

Chapter Eight: the King's Assassin

HE WASHED UP on a black beach. Rough volcanic sand scratched his face, as he crawled away from the water into the dunes, where he fell asleep. He slept on the warm sand like a sea turtle and dreamed he laid a thousand eggs before crawling back into the sea. He cried out, "I am not a bird or a turtle. I am a man."

He awakened to the sound of a horse, opened his eyes and saw a black gelding a few yards up the beach coming toward him with a man, dressed in black boiled leather, sitting astride its back. When the horse reached Stern, the man leaned forward, resting his right forearm on the pommel of the saddle, and gazed down on him. The man was young with long black hair and clear pale blue eyes. A claymore was strapped to his back and two long curved daggers were attached to a wide black belt, wrapped twice around his narrow waist. When he realized Stern was alive he nudged the horse's flanks with his spurred heels and moved the horse closer to the drowned man.

To his chagrin, Stern realized he was nude again. He lost his clothes in the ocean.

The man spoke in a guttural language, which Stern did not understand. He shrugged his shoulders and said, "I don't understand."

The man grinned, "I speak the language of the Northern clans, castaway."

Stern stood, covering his groin with his hands and said, "Thank you." The man spoke *lingua*, just as Gotha had.

"For what?" the man with a grim smile on his wolfish face asked.

"I guess for understanding me," said Stern, moving away from the horse that seemed skittish and dangerous.

"Were you cast overboard in the storm?" asked the man, pulling back on the reins to settle the horse.

"Yes," said Stern.

"What was your destination?"

Stern did not know whether to lie or not but he wanted to find Gotha and he couldn't do it without help. So he decided to tell the truth. "I was on the way with my companion to find the blacksmith, Bedwyr."

The man's expression changed. No longer did he look amused. "You mean the magus, Bedwyr."

Stern decided not to address the comment. He dissembled instead. "I was traveling with a woman warrior, a follower of Tandraxx, to find the blacksmith, Bedwyr."

The man changed his tack and asked, "Was she beautiful, this Tandraxx?"

"Yes, very beautiful. She saved my life."

"You are very far from Bedwyr's island. And there are no Tandraxx here to protect you."

"Am I in danger?" asked Stern, backing away from the man and the horse.

"You tell me castaway. You are naked on the beach of an island that you do not know, lost and hungry, talking to the King's assassin."

Stern studied the man's lean face and could not discern his intentions. He decided to play along as best he could. "How shall I address you?"

"I'm called Flymtt, castaway."

"Do you have a title other than assassin?"

With a sudden laugh, that startled the horse, he said: "To name a few, I am a thief, murderer, factotum, rogue, and King's dogsbody. And you castaway, do you have a name?"

"Stern."

"Any titles?" asked the man, growing more serious.

Stern was about to say—blacksmith or Black Robe—but he changed his mind. "Just Stern," he said.

The man unfastened a canteen tied to the saddle by a leather strap and threw it to Stern, who drank deeply.

"Better?" asked the man, as he leaned from the saddle and accepted the canteen from Stern.

"Much," Stern said, wiping his mouth with the back of his hand.

The man tied the canteen to his saddle and then slowly turned his horse around and ordered, "Time to go." He looked over his shoulder and said to Stern, who had not yet moved. "Are you coming?"

Stern walked slowly; his whole body sore and swollen from his hours in the sea. He staggered a bit and then followed the horseman off the beach and into a field that stretched out in front of them, where workers, both men and women, harvested grain, stacking bundles of yellow stalks into piles and loading them onto great wagons pulled by four oxen each. As they passed, the workers stopped to gawk at the naked man following Flymtt, who rode ahead silently, refusing to glance at them. Soon they had cleared the boundaries of the field and turned onto a black two-rutted road that meandered toward a stand of tall hardwoods.

Flymtt rode quietly, while Stern struggled to keep up. He stumbled once, stubbing his toe on a rock protruding from the black volcanic soil. After an hour or so on the ragged road, they met four riders, cavalrymen, wearing black and white uniforms. One called out to Flymtt in the same guttural language in which Flymtt had greeted Stern and laughed. Stern suspected jokes were being made at his expense. The men soon tired of their jesting, especially after Fymtt growled something in his language, and they rode past them toward the grain fields and the beach.

"Who were those men?" asked Stern, running to catch up with Flymtt.

"Some of the King's musketeers," answered Fymtt and then spat on the ground.

"They obviously found me quite funny."

"Can you blame them? You're pretty ridiculous."

"I spent two days floating in the sea," said Stern, growing angry. "How do you think you would look?"

Flymtt swiveled in the saddle to observe Stern's face. "I apologize. It is no mean feat to survive the anger of the storm. You are a lucky man. They say that Bedwyr brings luck to those he helps. Maybe he was looking out for you in the water."

"I have never met him. I'm simply trying to find him."

"Why?" asked Fymtt.

"I was sent to him, to ask his help in dealing with a dragon."

"You mean to kill a dragon?" said the man with a raised eyebrow.

"Maybe, I'm not sure what the solution is."

"Kill it. We need no more dragons. They are as thick as fleas. You can keep your dragon."

Stern asked, "Where are we going?"

"Ultimately, to see the King, he likes oddities, freaks, and anomalies."

"Will it take long to get there?"

"Three or four weeks, if we are lucky," he said with a grin. "Tonight, however, we stay at an inn I know and I will find you some clothes. Winter is coming. I can feel it. Maybe it is acceptable in your country to travel naked but here it is frowned upon." He laughed loudly and urged his horse into a trot.

Chapter Nine: The Drowned Man

STERN FOLLOWED FLYMTT for hours, falling further and further behind the man on horseback. Terrain changed and they entered a land of rolling hills and orchards and the grainy lava trail they strode morphed into black sticky clay that stuck to Stern's bare feet. Near dusk, Flymtt rode over a hill and disappeared from Stern's line of vision and he panicked, fearing that this most tenuous of lifelines in this unknown world had slipped through his fingers. He took a deep breath and pushed himself harder, trying to keep up with the rogue. Over the hill, a small community nestled in a shallow valley, consisting of a two-story wooden building and four or five small houses, a corral and a log blockhouse. He limped slowly toward the village, where Flymtt waited in front of the two-story building. A painted sign above the door of a man drowning, his arms flailing, with dragon lions circling above him, named the place for the illiterate. As Stern stumbled up the steps of the porch, Flymtt laughed and said, "Yes, this tavern is called *The Drowned Man.*"

Several children of the village gathered around the naked Stern; laughed and pointed and commented on his appearance in their guttural tongue.

"Let's get you some clothes before the women of this village either stone you or mount you," said Flymtt.

One of the children called out, "Forest Father!"

Flymtt shooed the children away and pushed Stern into the tavern. "What did he call me?"

Flymtt explained: "A Forest Father. Men who see visions leave the villages and wander into the forest, where they live like animals, naked and alone. The people believe them sacred because they say they contact the spiritual plane."

"Have they?" asked Stern.

"Of course not," barked Flymtt. "They have simply gone insane."

It was dark inside the empty inn and Stern waited while his eyes adjusted. Flymtt called out, "Siggi!" There was no response. Stern began to make out the outline of tables and chairs, barrels and boxes and he imagined at dusk the place came alive with patrons. Flymtt called again, "Siggi!"

A tall full-bodied woman emerged from the rear of the great room, wiping her hands on her apron. "Flymtt, you demon!" she called out in the strange language with a laugh. Then she saw Stern and her laugh died. "A Forest Father," she whispered and crossed her chest in some emblematic ritual.

"No," said Flymtt, "a drowned man."

"Truly?" she asked with a gasp.

"Can you find him some clothes?"

Siggi approached Stern cautiously, sniffing the air as she moved. "He must bathe and shave before I find him clothes."

Flymtt laughed. "A steam would be good for both of us. Come, little star, let's walk to the bath house."

Stern blushed and bowed his head before turning and following Flymtt outside and set off down a path worn into the black clay leading into a dense evergreen copse.

"Be careful of snakes and don't touch the wolf's bane," warned Fymtt, unbuttoning his leather vest and removing it.

"What is wolf's bane?"

"It is green lichen that grows on the trees. It is highly poisonous."

"This world of yours is full of danger," sighed Stern.

"Isn't yours?" laughed Flymtt. "You have a dragon don't you. Surely there is danger in your land," argued Flymtt. Stern thought for a moment and shook his head in agreement and asked: "Are there dragons on this island?"

"Not here, as I said earlier. We have spent generations battling them. Every once in a while, a green dragon tries to land but someone raises the alarm and we destroy or drive the lizard off."

They walked through a stand of what seemed to be immature aspens and Stern glimpsed a large lake through the trees and heard a sound that resembled the call of the loon.

"You said you were a rogue and a murderer, when we met."

"I did."

"Is that true?"

"Of course, it is true," the man said proudly.

"Who have you killed?"

"The King has enemies and I eliminate them."

"What enemies?"

"Other nobles who wish to take his throne. Ours is the only true free kingdom in the North. Our ships sail far and wide and we make enemies. There are people who resent the King. They question his authority to land on their islands and force his will on them. We just finished a war with Brasilika because the Witch Queen refused the King's God-given right to rule this world."

"They have a point don't you think?" said Stern without thinking. Flymtt turned angrily toward him. "Keep your heresy to yourself. If someone else heard you talk, I would have to kill you to preserve the King's honor."

His eyes narrowed and his mouth became rigid and Stern feared he had gone too far. Flymtt shrugged and Stern followed him to a wooden building on the south side of the lake, where a short man, with a thick red beard, wearing a black linen shirt and black hemp pants, sat in a natural pine rocker on the deck of the building. "Fredegar, two for a steam and bath," said Flymtt.

"Two copper, Flymtt," responded the man, rising slowly from the rocker. Flymtt dug into his pocket and counted out two battered coopers from a fat leather pouch then walked to a roofed patio and undressed, hanging his clothes and weapons on a wooden peg. As he waited, Stern noticed a loon-like creature floating about thirty yards off shore and beyond that a black cloud forming in the north.

Undressed, Flymtt signaled Stern to follow him into a pine building a couple of yards away from the building. Inside, he sat on a wooden bench as Flymtt poured water over lava rocks, stretched out on a wooden plank directly across from him, and closed his eyes. "Now," he said, "tell me about your dragons and your dangerous journey."

Stern cleared his throat and began at the beginning. During his story Flymtt stopped him when he mentioned Gotha, demanding Stern describe her in detail. Rather than being annoyed, Stern enjoyed telling his story, even embellishing certain points. At the mention of Focalor, Flymtt sat up and growled his disapproval of the daemon's behavior and abandonment of

Stern. "Anyone from the spirit plane is trouble," he spat out in a grunt. "They are daemons, demons, or angels and none of them bring good news. They don't mix in our business unless one of them is running a scam or planning a coup."

"I don't understand."

But before Stern could respond, a woman opened the door and said, "It's time for your bath and shave."

Flymtt hopped up and Stern followed him to the main building, where two tall blonde women with birch limbs in their hands waited. Stern began to ask, "What are they...." But he did not finish; the two young women began to beat them vigorously.

Flymtt laughed and advised, "Relax, little star, and enjoy."

After a thorough thrashing they entered the bathhouse, where, one of the women, Pella, told him to stand in a wooden tub. She then lathered his body from head to toe with herbal-scented soap, poured several buckets of scalding water over him and then dumped two buckets of ice water over his head. As he stood shivering, she laughed and pointed to a large tub where Flymtt was already sitting in fragrant hot water.

After soaking for several minutes, a young woman with dark black hair and pellucid blue eyes called for Stern. She handed him a cotton robe he wrapped around himself, as she pointed to a barber's chair. Seated, she lathered his face and shaved the thick black stumble on his face, then combed the hair that was just growing back. Finished, she ordered him to take off his robe and return to the tub where he lay quietly for another half hour. He fell asleep in the water and slept until Siggi shook him and announced she had some clothes for him. He followed her to a dressing area, where Flymtt was pulling on his boots.

Siggi had found him a pair of worn leather boots, some brown hempen pants, a red linen shirt, and black leather vest. Dressed, they walked back to the tavern, his mouth watering at the thought of food. After a meal of what Stern thought was venison and wild berries, he and Flymtt sat next to a large open fireplace and drank ale, watching the inn fill with people, many of whom had ventured out to see the Forest Father.

"Do you know how to use any weapon?" asked Flymtt, puffing on a pipe.

"You mean weapons like you use?" asked Stern suddenly desperate for a smoke.

"Of course," said Flymtt around the stem of the pipe.

"I have been trained in hand-to-hand combat, staves, and knives. I can handle a bow but I'm no good at it. I prefer a carbine or a brace of pistols."

"What is that?" asked the assassin.

"You would probably call it a musket," answered Stern.

"Ah. Good. Tomorrow we will buy you a weapon and a horse."

"How will I repay you?" asked Stern nervous about obligating himself to the man.

"Not me, the King. The question is how you will repay the King."

Suddenly, it thundered loudly and the people jumped, as rain mixed with hail pummeled the roof. Someone began to play a lute and the dark-haired girl from the bath began to sing a song in the guttural language. Stern felt safe for the first time since the witches sent him to the watery plane. As his mind calmed, he felt settled and at home in the inn of *The Drowned Man*. He began to doze but stirred with a start at the sound of a wolf's howl amidst the sound of thunder and falling rain. He imagined a black wolf with green eyes. Now, fully awake, he looked around the room to see if the others had heard the wolf but no one seemed disturbed. Flymtt had moved to a nearby table, where he leaned against a busty blonde, his hand exploring inside her blouse. The young woman with the black hair and blue eyes was singing another tune soulfully but he could not understand the words, although the language no longer seemed so alien. He closed his eyes and concentrated, attempting the exercise Focalor suggested before he had shifted into the osprey. He let the images work their way from his unconscious mind into his conscious mind. First, he saw a raven and then a wolf's head and finally a dragon's maul more like the snout of a wolf than a head of a reptile. He relaxed into the image and then he felt himself flying. He was no longer a hawk or an osprey. He was the dragon; he was a flying wolf.

"Stern, wake up."

Flymtt shook him violently. "Wake up man. You were moaning."

With everyone in the inn watching him, Stern shook himself and ran his hand over his short hair, slick with sweat. His body was warm and feverish.

"Let's get you to bed. You are exhausted."

Flymtt extended his hand and pulled him forcefully to his feet. They climbed some stairs near the back of the tavern to a small room on the second story, overlooking the woods. The sole window was open and a cool wind blew into the room. Stern shivered as he climbed fully clothed beneath a feather comforter into one of the single beds. Flymtt blew out the candle and Stern drifted into sleep.

Chapter Ten: Lights in the Forest

STERN AWOKE SUDDENLY into a dark and frigid room with Flymtt standing over him and whispering. "Get up. We're leaving. The horses are saddled downstairs."

"What time is it?"

"Four."

"Why so early?" he asked pulling on his britches.

"It is better we leave in the dark. There were several strangers in the tavern last night and I didn't like the look of them."

Stern rubbed his eyes, as he pulled on the boots and shivered from the cold. "It is colder than yesterday," he said.

Flymtt nodded: "There is a coat next to your saddle bags. I also found an oaken stave."

As Stern pulled on the woolen coat, Flymtt swung his saddlebags over his shoulder and pointed at some bags on the floor with his left, indicating Stern was to pick them up.

Flymtt's horse was tied to a tree in the back and next to it was a gray mare of fourteen hands, which appeared, when compared to the assassin's warhorse, like a pony.

"The mare is a good horse," observed Flymtt. "She is small but fast; a pony from the Aegean archipelago."

"Where is that?" asked Stern.

"Far to the southeast; near the equator, where it is hot," answered Flymtt, tightening the straps and cinches of his saddle.

Siggi walked out of the shadows of the tavern and handed them each a hot biscuit and an apple. Once they had tied their bags onto the saddles they quickly wolfed the food down. Shivering from the cold, she pulled her shawl tight around her shoulders, hugged Flymtt, and then disappeared back into the dark building.

"Let's go." Flymtt said, inserting his left foot into a stirrup and swinging his right leg over the back of the gelding. Stern rubbed his hands together and patted the rear flank cf the pony, mounted and followed Flymtt around the building.

"You do ride, don't you?" asked Flymtt over his shoulder

"Of course," grunted Stern.

By mid-morning Stern was hungry again. They rode through a wide valley with a number of what Stern took to be farms. It had warmed up considerably and he had removed his coat. Flymtt had not said anything for several hours and Stern chose not to talk either; instead, he studied the land and concentrated on his horse. He was beginning to get the hang of the pony's gait and personality. The little horse had a mind of its own and several times it wanted to stop but Stern forced it on. He felt they were beginning to understand one another, as Flymtt pushed them forward at a steady pace. Finally, halting near a stream bed to let the horses drink, Stern stretched his arms out wide and walked in circles, as Flymtt watched with a bemused look on his face. When he finished stretching, Stern asked, "Did you really think we were in danger?"

Flymtt's smile disappeared. "Yes, especially after your howling in your sleep."

"Why then?"

"Because the common folk of the island are afraid of shape-shifters, they kill them."

"I am not a shape-shifter," Stern paused, remembering his transformation into an osprey.

Flymtt looked at him dubiously before saying, "Maybe not. But your howls were quite realistic."

Stern looked away and then said, "Are there many here, many shape-shifters?"

"On this island, you mean?" He shook his head. "No. When discovered they are killed or exiled."

"Are they so dangerous?"

"Some are, some aren't."

"Which ones are dangerous?" he asked, thinking about the osprey or his friend, now a falcon.

"The most dangerous were the dragonkin, the Skaellanders. But they are all gone now, wiped out by years of warfare. Only their abandoned red cities in the far north near the ice sheet remain."

Stern appeared startled. "You mean they were able to shift into dragons?"

"Dragons, wolves, bears," said Flymtt, "don't you know anything about Okeanus."

Stern pondered this new fact as he chewed some hardtack and jerky that Flymtt tossed him.

"When you finish that, we must be on our way. See that black cloud in the distance?"

Stern nodded.

"It is another cold front. It could bring snow and sleet."

"Winter arrives fast here," he said naively.

"Very fast and very hard," answered Flymtt.

An hour later a hard cold rain fell but Flymtt refused to stop until a yellow blast of lightning rent the blue-black sky asunder. He turned his horse off the road and forced the gelding into a gallop toward a thick stand of hardwoods to the east. The dark forest was so thick and dense that as soon as they entered Stern had the impression that all light had been extinguished. They worked their way through the trees slowly until they reached a point where the leafy roof was so thick the rain could not work its way through the upper mat of leaves. Flymtt dismounted and stripped his body of any metal, laying his weapons in a pile of leaves under a great oak.

"Afraid of attracting the lightning," he said, as Stern dismounted and tied the mare near the gelding.

"We will stay here until the storm clears. But I warn you. Do not wander away from this camp. This is an eldritch wood and once lost, very few have ever found their way back."

Stern moved to a tree opposite the great oak and sat upon the ground, pulling his coat tightly against his body, as Flymtt retrieved a gray blanket tied to his saddle and wrapped it around his shoulders before sitting. "Why don't you tell me more about your country while we wait out the storm?" asked Flymtt. Stern thought a moment, editing his tale, sanitizing it to fit what he perceived were Flymtt's prejudices and realized he knew nothing of the man or of his land.

"Flymtt, how do you know my language?" asked Stern, ignoring the assassin's request for a story.

"I learned it from a bar maid in Tarnyvyk, a tiny fishing village on the northeastern side of the island."

"And your language, what is it called?"

"It is *íslenska*," answered the man.

"And the name of your country?" continued Stern.

"We call it *íslensk* or the Island. Now shut up and stop asking me stupid questions that you know the answers to."

Thunder rumbled in the distance followed by a strident sizzle before the strike of lightning. Flymtt covered his head with the blanket and soon he began to snore.

While Flymtt slept, Stern surmised that this elemental plane had a number of parallels to his own and that, geographically, the island, Flymtt's island, was in the western hemisphere in the far north. As he imagined this world's geography, he saw a flicker of light to his right, in the direction of the heart of the forest, away from the road. He concentrated on the light until it seemed to bounce. Soon the bouncing light joined another and then another, until there were twenty or thirty flickers of light dancing in the interstices of the trees. Unlike a character in a fairy tale, which he was very aware of, he did not intend to stand up and investigate the light; instead, he sat still, barely breathing, watching the display and when he realized they were growing larger, these spots of light, and approaching them, he shook Flymtt, but to no avail. The rogue seemed to have fallen into a heavy sleep.

Chapter Eleven: Black Wolf, Yellow Eyes

THE ELDRITCH LIGHTS stopped two or three yards from the horses, illuminated the surrounding forest and caused the intervening trees to cast long gray shadows. From the gray shadows forming from the lights like tendrils on a *koaba* tree, a tall, thin, blonde woman, with green eyes, wearing a scarlet robe and carrying a long wooden staff, approached Stern. She stepped over the sleeping Flymtt to reach him and took his right hand in her left. "Come with me, shifter and I will teach you the spell of the wolf heart."

"Shifter?" whispered Stern.

She smiled at him and said, while extending her other hand to help him stand, "Do you think a simple human from Mittilagart could shift into an osprey or a wolf?"

"What am I then, a shape-shifter?"

"You are a bare-sark. You must know this."

"I'm a blacksmith from La Ciudad and a Black Robe," he answered.

She frowned and said, refusing to acknowledge his speech, "You are a bare-sark from the north and I am Keltoi."

"A Keltoi," he sputtered. "I came to your world with Coyote. We were sent here to find Bedwyr but a daemon captured us." He felt tears welling in his eyes and he was embarrassed.

"And so you shall find Bedwyr but first you must come with me. If you stay, he will take you to the King and the King, once he knows your mission, will relieve you of your head."

"What about Flymtt?"

"Unfortunately," she whispered and then spat on the ground near the assassin's head, "you are fated to meet him again."

Stern felt an extreme pull toward the woman but he feared she was another daemon, like Focalor, and he asked ingenuously, "Are you a daemon?"

She laughed and said, "No, as I said, I am a Keltoi, one of the hidden ones."

The pull on him to follow her now was illogical but irresistible and he suspected he was once again caught within a sorceress' spell. He felt himself standing and changing under her will and her magic. His body, now under her mind's control, morphed into a great black wolf with luminous yellow eyes. Transformed, the woman patted his head and rubbed his fur. "See," she said, "you are a changeling." Then she, too, shifted into a great white wolf and they bounded off into the woods, as the two horses pulled against their reins and reared in fear at the smell of the wolves.

The wolves ran through the woods at a great speed and Stern became aware that other wolves were joining them, forming a pack and slinking silently through the deepening forest. After many hours they reached a stream where they stopped and drank. As he lapped up the water, his nostrils flared and he detected the scent of a deer, a doe, in heat and nearby. The others picked up the scent as well and they were off. The deer's ears pricked up at the sound of the wolves bounding through the thick underbrush. It paused, analyzing its sense data, a fatal error, because the wolves were on it before it could move. Stern was one of the first to reach the doe. His great fangs tore into its rear rump and it began to fall. Then the others arrived and their teeth sealed the doe's fate.

Stern awoke from the wolf form ten days later, naked once again, on the side of a mountain, far to the south of the black forest where he left Flymtt. Covered with dried blood, he swallowed and coughed up a fur ball. He smelled wolf, as he slowly rose and surveyed his surroundings. Behind him was a structure: a platform with tall white columns, where the Keltoi woman stood on massive marble steps beckoning him to approach.

"Damn," he said, as he walked toward her, and vomited onto the ground. Once again, he thought, as he was heaving, he was naked and once again he had fallen into the hands of some sinister force. When he finished, he rubbed away the sputum with the back of hand and climbed the steps. Reaching the top, he followed the Keltoi up the side of the mountain, as flakes of snow flew in soft circles against an azure sky, while down below a turbulent sea roiled in the distance and above a falcon circled on the frigid currents of air above him. He thought: 'Coyote.'

The woman stopped and said, "Stop day dreaming and follow me. He is waiting for us and he does not like to be kept waiting."

"Who is waiting?" he growled, almost unable to form his words.

"You will find out, bare-sark."

"You called me that before. What does it mean?"

"You are a *beserker*. Did you not know this?"

"I thought because I changed into a wolf I was a Keltoi like you."

"You are no Keltoi. I caused you to change. That was my magic, my spell." She said with a laugh.

As Stern continued to climb, he wondered what being a bare-sark meant and what significance it had. He remembered the warnings of the witches and he feared what new daemon or *eudaemon* awaited him at the top of this mountain. When they reached the summit and a marble building perched on the edge of the cliff, the woman pointed to a marble fountain and said, "Clean yourself." The water was freezing but the wolf scent was overpowering on his skin, so he splashed the freezing water over his face and chest, wishing Siggi and her girls were here. Finished, he stood naked, shivering, waiting for the next step, when another woman appeared. She, too, was tall and blonde but younger, carrying towels in one hand and a robe in the other. She rubbed him down with the towels and then massaged warm aromatic oil into his shoulders, chest, back and thighs. His skin tingled and he felt his body relax, as she handed him a ruby red robe and issued an order in the guttural language of the Island.

The other woman translated, "Put on the robe, bare-sark."

The robe was soft and warm and he smiled, thinking that if he only had some socks and mittens, he might not be so cold.

A man, wearing black boiled leather armor underneath a red robe appeared on the doorstep. He too was blond, almost a twin to the woman.

"Bargi is ready for the bare-sark," he said sharply.

"Go. Follow him. And bare-sark, it was an honor to hunt with you." She bowed and moved towards the steps.

Stern followed the warrior into the building. Oil lamps lit a long corridor that led toward the sea side of the mountain. At the end of the corridor, they entered a room open on three sides and from there, Stern saw the sea and the sky. A man with long thick white hair sat in a chair made of oak and leather. He, like the warrior, wore a leather harness and leggings and a dark blood-red robe covered his shoulders. As the man stood, Stern realized, although he was tall and thin and youthful in appearance—no wrinkles or scars marked his smooth white skin—he was much older than the others. Self-conscious, Stern rubbed the thick black stumble on his face and coughed, catching a whiff of his still wolfish breath.

"Stern, welcome," said the man, his voice deep and soft, like the voice of an actor. "Tangr, bring another chair and build a fire. Our friend is cold."

The man sat and crossed his long legs at the ankles, put his two hands together as if in prayer and touched his nose with his two index fingers. "You were an osprey, when you flew over the red waters. Have you tried to fly over land?"

"No," said Stern, running his tongue over his gritty unwashed teeth, wondering how the man knew of his change into the osprey.

"Close your eyes and imagine yourself flying over a corn field," ordered the man.

Stern dutifully closed his eyes. He thought of thieving crows. Suddenly, he saw the head of a raven, with its black beak and black eyes and imagined himself sitting on a wooden fence, a cornfield spread out before him, the sky dark blue and menacing. He heard the caw of the crows and he tasted the crisp sweetness of the corn. He opened his eyes and he was flying over the sea. He circled the mountain and he saw a woman descending the marble stairs and the great black forest to the North and he felt the presence of a falcon above him.

"Return bare-sark!" The Bargi's command thundered in his head and he knew he had to obey. He landed on the arm of an empty chair across from Bargi, then changed and fell backwards onto the marble floor. A fire was now burning in a circular fireplace in the center of the room. Once again he was naked, his robe lying on the floor of the room. He stood up, walked to it and hastily pulled it over his shoulders.

The Bargi laughed and said, "Nakedness is the life of the Keltoi."

Stern laughed too, at the absurdity of his position. "At least you are all beautiful."

The Bargi smiled and nodded his head in acceptance of the compliment.

"Listen, Stern, I have interrupted your journey and our time is limited. The Norns are busy weaving and they do not smile when we interfere." The man sounded like one of the Black Robes.

"Go on," said Stern, pulling the robe tightly against his skin.

"Focalor is following you. He was one day behind you when we snatched you from the rogue. The rogue does not want you to reach Bedwyr, any more than Focalor does, so beware his advice. We say this because it is your fate to meet him several times on your journey."

"You can see my future?" asked Stern, startled by the pronouncements of the Bargi.

"I see several possible strands for your future and I know your past. The Keltoi serve the Norns and the Norns tell us their secrets."

"Do you have any stake in my journey?"

"You were sent here to do something that cannot be done. I don't know if it was a ruse or just stupidity on your part. I suspect it was a bit of both."

"What do you mean when you say a ruse?"

"Whoever sent you here doesn't know all. Their vision is limited. The dragons are a symptom of the sickness that reigns in your world; removing them is not the cure. But returning the blue-back dragon to our world will be a start in curing the sickness. All the planes are currently out of balance. Whether it began here or in your world, I don't know. Your world began as a world of lizards and dragons and then the imbalance came. They died out and your world changed. Then the they returned and your world changed again. Someone in your world wants imbalance: a world without dragons. The King of this island wants the same. Both parties are wrong."

Stern's left hand began to shake, an involuntary response to severe anxiety. "I never suspected this absurd quest might be based on a lie," he said.

The Bargi softened his tone. "Your quest is real. I am sure of that. But the narrative framework contains nothing but nonsense. Bedwyr is the key so continue your journey to him."

"Should I see the King? Flymtt wanted to take me to the King."

"Focalor knows you were on your way there. To resume that journey would be dangerous. You and the King share a time line, a future and a past. To see him now would be folly and dangerous."

Stern did not understand the man's comments but he decided to ignore them as nonsense. "Then how do I get to Bedwyr?"

The man rubbed his chin and said: "We could smuggle you onto a ship."

"Is there another way?"

"With your susceptibility to shape shifting you could fly or swim there but it would take weeks, maybe even months."

"What are you saying?" he was startled by the Bargi's characterization of his ability to shift his shape, his entrapment in a wolf form had not been pleasant, more a punishment than a pleasure.

The man turned to the warrior and commanded, "Tangr, summon Kylla."

Tangr disappeared through a passageway that led into the mountain.

"While we wait for her, let me show you a map of the world." He led Stern to the southern edge of the marbled floor, where a map was imprinted in the floor. Runic writing in golden script marked it and the

Keltoi used his staff to point out and name the major islands. As he pointed, he explained the world to Stern. "This is a map of Okeanus, the watery plain. Here is the north. We are in the northern most quadrant of the Northern Sea. Bedwyr's island, this tiny speck, is in the southwest quadrant of the northern sea but it abuts and extends along the edge of the western sea. It is warmer there and more populated; and as a rule there are more pirates and dragons in the western sea than anywhere else, except the southern Xippon Sea. By ship from the King's port, it will take you approximately twelve weeks to reach Bedwyr's island."

Stern studied the map intently. There were thousands of islands and archipelagos in the northern quadrant of the Western Hemisphere and he realized he could study this map for ages and not know all of them.

"What lives on these islands?" he asked.

"Thousand are uninhabited. On others there are creatures and races known and unknown. No one has ever explored every rock or sand barge."

Stern turned at the sound of Tangr returning with a woman following him. She too was tall, thin and wearing robes similar to the Bargi. Her hair was a dark burgundy, plaited and hanging to her waist. Her green eyes sparkled and a band of freckles crossed her aquiline nose.

Tangr pulled a chair to the right side of the Bargi and the three sat.

Without introduction, the Bargi asked: "Kylla, can you help us? Can you see our little brother's fate?"

She leaned forward and reached for his hands. Her hands were dry and warm and Stern felt self-conscious: his hands were cold and his nails dirty.

After a long time, in which Stern barely breathed, nervous to be so close to her, she said in a steady voice that was deep and resonant, "He must go to Bedwyr, as is his purpose."

"How should he go?" asked the Bargi quickly.

Stern interrupted, "is the rogue trustworthy?"

Squeezing his hands, she frowned; irritated he interrupted the Bargi. After a moment, she said, "the rogue is not trustworthy but it doesn't matter, your fates are intertwined, you will meet again. But for the voyage you must go alone, although others will find you and guide you."

"How will I get there?" asked Stern, echoing the Bargi's inquiry.

She pressed his hands firmly between hers and said, "Close your eyes." He did as she instructed. "What do you see?"

"Just blackness," he answered softly but then raised his hand, warning her to be quiet. "Wait, something is coming." The darkness cleared and lightened, as a black trireme with a red mainsail sailing on a violent green sea emerged into his conscious mind so vividly he tried to pull away from her and avoid the inevitable collision.

"Tell me quickly, what did you see?"

He opened his eyes and described the vision that still glittered in his mind's eye. Once he completely described his vision and then answered her questions, she released his hands and closed her eyes and recited something in the guttural language of the island. After several moments, she opened her eyes and gazed directly at him. "You shall go to Bedwyr in the company of reavers, witches and dragons. At times you will be in the shape of a bear, at others a bird and ultimately, you will disappoint and betray the witches and lose those who you hold most dear."

He ignored the ultimate sentence of the prophecy and concentrated on the first part instead, forgetting for the moment the young woman who saved him and pledged to contract with him. "Are you saying that I can transform or shift into these animal forms?"

The Bargi answered, "You are a bare-sark. With training you could be a shaman. We have not seen a bare-sark shaman in three hundred cycles, not since the passing of the Skaellanders of the northern most islands, the islands within the ice. If you are indeed a bare-sark, you can spell yourself into a transformation into any creature you possess an affinity."

"How can I train myself?" Stern asked vaguely. "Although, I am not sure I believe it is really possible. This trip seems to be a dream of madness or death itself."

"We will train you if you tarry with us," said the Bargi.

"How long must I stay?" he asked, thinking about the dragons burning the cities of Mittilagart and the threats of the witches.

"As long as it takes," answered Kylla.

"But my son," he uttered. "I must get back."

"How can you save him if you are unprepared?" asked the Bargi.

Stern asked himself how many would die before he returned. However, he also asked himself how many would die if he failed because of a lack of training. "I will do it," he said. "I will train with you but who will teach me and guide me on this journey?"

Kylla looked at the Bargi and then said in a low voice, "Besides me," said Kylla, drawing on her powers of precognition, "I see several others: witches and mages."

"What?" he asked startled by her clearly enunciated prophesy.

"It will all be revealed through your training."

"Then let's begin as soon as possible."

"Not tonight. We will start at first light. Tankr will lead you to your chamber and provide a bath and anything else you need."

Chapter Twelve: The White Wolf

STERN FOLLOWED TANKR into the mouth of a tunnel descending into the mountain. They soon reached a great chamber that resembled a giant hub of an ancient wheel, with passageways, like spokes, radiating from its center. They turned left and entered another passageway much narrower than the original, and stopped at a stout wooden door and pushed it open. "Have a good sleep," he said abruptly and left Stern alone.

The room was essentially a cell with a wooden half bed, a table with a candle, and a porcelain bowl on the floor. Stern sniffed the room and bed linens that seemed clean and smelt of resin and pine pollen. He sat on the cot, while a small candle flickered and illuminated carvings in the smooth white stone of the wall. The carvings told a tale of a round, naked woman who traveled the world and met several outlandish creatures. Strangely, the small cell reminded him of his room in La Ciudad. He blew out the candle and lay down.

Stern awoke in the dark with Tankr shaking his shoulder. "Kylla is waiting for you in the great room," he said.

Staggering off the narrow bed, Stern relieved himself in a porcelain bowl on the floor and then adjusted his robe. "All right, I am ready."

Tankr set off down the tunnel and he followed. When they arrived at the hub, they turned left and entered yet another spoke of the great wheel.

Stern heard laughter, utensils hitting plates, and the murmur of many people talking, as Tankr led him into a large hall with long wooden tables running down its middle. A hundred or more Keltoi sat at the long tables, as other Keltoi ran up and down the aisles serving food. Kylla, at the far end against the wall, wore black leather leggings, a red tunic, leather vest and boots, and a loden-green cape over her shoulders.

Stern still filthy and disheveled, smelling of wolf, sat next to her. "May I wash my hands?" he asked. She pointed at an alcove in the corner of the room, where he found fresh water, soap and several large cotton towels. When he returned, someone placed a bowl of hot porridge in front of him and she said, as he took his first bite: "Eat up. We leave at first light." He nodded, his mouth watering, and took fresh black bread from the table and spread thick honey over it, as a server filled a tankard with aromatic mead. As he wolfed the hunk of bread down, he almost howled, and she said with a laugh, "You can slow down. We are not in that much hurry." When he finished he looked about for more. She, however, noting he had finished, signaled him with a turn of her lithe body that it was time to leave. He reluctantly stood up and followed her to a large oak table near the exit, where she took a blackthorn stave from the table and a long, curved dagger, which she attached to her wide leather belt. Adjusting her weapons on her narrow hips, she said: "Let's find you some shoes and pants."

They followed the main tunnel back to the great hall, crossed the hub, and took yet another spoke that led to a work area, where a man, with gray hair and a long beard cobbled shoes. "Aegr, have you some shoes for this man?" The man studied Stern's filthy feet and coughed: "I have a pair of doe-skin moccasins that might fit him." He rummaged through a pile of shoes near his workbench and threw a pair at Stern, who jumped back.

"Now for some pants and maybe a vest," she said.

They forged deeper into the mountain and stopped at a door painted a bright red with a painting of a woman who resembled the one on his cell wall. Kylla used her staff to knock twice and a teenage girl with bright green eyes and dark black hair opened it and Kylla said in her language: "Myr, is your mother here?" The girl smiled shyly and bowed, as Pyr, her mother, entered, wiping her hands on a leather apron and grinning at Kylla, who bowed and said, "Pyr, I need clothes for this man." Pyr examined him closely. "I have clothes I bargained for at the summer fest that might fit him." She left the room and returned with a brown linen shirt and some woolen pants, which she handed Stern, with a sniff. He blushed, knowing he stank of wolf. They fit and he bowed to the woman, trying to convey his gratitude.

"How do I pay for these things?" he asked Kylla.

"You don't. Our society is one of barter. They will come to me later and ask to be paid in a certain way. Pyr may want a love potion to help find her a man or Aegr might ask me to rid his chamber of mice. You never know what they will want or need."

She scratched her nose and said suddenly, "Come, I feel the sun rising, we have a long walk ahead of us."

"Where are we going?"

"To the forest, of course," she answered.

They left the mountain refuge, waded through a wide swath of dry, dead grass, and entered the forest. The darkness of the forest descended upon him like a wet woolen blanket. His nostrils flared with the smell of rotting leaves, pollen, mold, and an unidentifiable sharpness, like aging cheese and mushrooms, which caused him to sneeze. She turned with a smile and said something in her language. "I know the forest is rich with odors but from this point you must be quiet. Although the King and his soldiers have tried to tame this island there are still things here, in this forest, that are dangerous. Also, Focalor is searching for you and we must avoid him at all costs. Trust me. Follow me and be quiet."

Stern bowed his head. The woman made embarrassed him. Ever since he had arrived in Okeanus, he had felt childlike and helpless. He reminded himself he was a highly-trained and even though he was in an alien world, he could take care of himself. He followed Kylla, as she wound her way through the forest, stopping once at mid-morning to eat some cheese, which she pulled from a pocket of her cloak, and to drink from a stream. As he bent down, Stern noticed a myriad of tracks in the mud around the banks, where other creatures had stopped to drink.

Hours later they halted on the edge of a small lake, where a loon-like bird slowly floated. Kylla sat on a fallen log and fished out another hunk of cheese and a black roll from her leather bag and divided it with her dagger. Stern had not spoken since his sneeze.

"We are about two hours from the clearing."

"What clearing?" he asked, chewing his food.

"It is a sacred place the Hidden Folk have carved from the great forest. We will stay there until your training is complete."

"How long will that take?"

"I don't know. It will be up to you and your powers of concentration."

He took another bite of cheese and bread and asked with a grin, "How much cheese do you have in your pockets?"

She laughed and the beauty of her face struck Stern with a strident pang of loneliness. She noticed the look on his face and lowered her voice: "From this moment on I will begin to speak to you in my language. I will teach you the ancient tongue of the Keltoi and the runes you must know if you are to develop into that which you are."

"What do you mean—develop into what I am?"

"We are like an acorn, predisposed to be what we are born to be. The acorn, however, falls where it falls. Maybe it falls on stone, where it rots and dwindles into its basic elements. Or perhaps it falls in dark black loam and grows into a mighty tree.

"Your kin dropped into the middle world, away from ours, and became lost, forgetting who or what they were. There was no soil for you to grow and so you withered. Now, you have been transplanted into a soil full of nutrients. You can grow to be what you are."

"What am I to be?" He asked, not believing anything she just said. He was no bare-sark and this world was not his home. Mittilagart was his home.

"Only the goddess knows."

With the mention of the goddess, Stern immediately thought of the carvings in the mountain citadel and intuited those carvings were representations of the goddess. He was about to ask another question, when she stood and said something in her language.

"What?" he asked with his mouth full.

She repeated the statement and lifted her staff and pointed it across the lake. He assumed the words meant, "Let's go." From that moment on, as she walked, she pointed to things and said a word in her language. Slowly, he learned the words for walk, trees, feet, hands, eyes, leaves, lake, path, sky, rain, sit, loon, squirrel, and stop. As twilight approached, she began to walk in a small circle, then a larger one until she found four great oaks growing close together on a slight rise. Dead leaves lay thick on the ground and their rich acidic aroma of decay filled the air and tickled his nose, as she gathered them to make two beds. After her preparations she sat with her back against one of the great trees and pulled out more cheese and bread.

As night fell he heard the somber hoot of an owl and in the far distance, in the direction of the lake, a loon-like creature called out into the night for its mate. Next to him, Kylla pulled the hood of her cape over her head and snuggled into the folds of the garment. The temperature was falling and Stern saw his breath. "Could we make a fire?" he asked and Kylla stirred as if awakened. "No. Not in the forest."

"Are you cold?" she asked softly. "Come close to me."

He moved next to her and she wrapped her cape around his shoulders. It was warmer beneath the cape but sitting so close to her was disconcerting. He felt nervous, bashful even, to be so near her. And he knew he stank of wolf, a feral smell that bothered even him.

"Do not be nervous. Think of me as your sister."

He tried to settle down and just enjoy her warmth. He consciously tried to slow his pulse and he used tricks he had learned over the years. He talked to each part of his body, starting with his feet and told them to calm down and just enjoy the sensation of the moment. Once he completed his bodily inventory, his breathing had slowed and he felt more relaxed. He began to feel himself drifting into sleep, but suddenly he remembered the Black Robes, his son, and the witches and his mind began to race once again.

Sensing his new agitation, she said softly, "Leave the thoughts of your world behind and concentrate on the now. Sense the wonder of the forest. Listen to its sounds. Smell its odor. To battle the witch or the demon you must prepare yourself. You cannot prepare yourself if you are constantly worrying about the battle to come. There is nothing that you could do now, even if you were there. You are too ignorant and unprepared."

"How long will it take me to learn what I need to know?"

"If you are to become what you are, it will take the rest of your life. To fight a dragon will only take a short time. Fighting dragons is one of the first levels of knowledge. Now I am going to repeat everything that I just told you in my language. Listen carefully."

After several minutes, she said, "Let's sleep. We must continue at first light. We will turn toward the north soon, where the woods are thicker, darker and colder."

He awoke stiff and cold, very cold. She had already awakened and was sitting on her haunches regarding him. "You sleep like a rock." She laughed.

"Is that bad?" he asked, stretching his arms.

"No, it is very good. Tonight, we will sleep the sleep of the wolves."

"What is that?"

"You will see my little star, you will see."

They broke fast with the last of the bread and cheese.

"What will we eat tonight?" he asked.

"The goddess will provide."

Suddenly, she slapped her hands together and pointed her staff to the north and repeated the phrase that he now understood to mean 'let's go.' Throughout the morning they worked their way through the thick forest. At mid-morning they stopped to drink rainwater trapped in the boll of a great oak but ate no food. Stern had not been fat or weak but he realized that over the past few days, he had grown leaner and stronger. He imagined the land trimming the fat from his body.

At noon they rested in a stand of ash trees. He saw a large bird fly under their limbs and he heard a cuckoo in the distance. He noted that a tree had fallen in the stand and that termites busily worked on its decaying bark. He closed his eyes and he heard a squirrel chattering in a nearby tree. He pulled his robe close to his chest for warmth and wondered if she would mind his snuggling against her for warmth. He smiled because he suddenly remembered snuggling against his mother on a fall day in the *Gardens of the Forking Paths* in La Ciudad. He recalled the vibrancy of the colors as the leaves turned. His mother was sitting on a wooden bench reading and he had been playing, sailing his sailboat on one of the pools of one of the great fountains. A cold breeze had blown across the waters, chilling him. He remembered the coldness of his hands and his nose, as he ran to his mother, who enveloped him in her arms, closed his jacket and wiped his nose with a perfumed cloth. Her body was warm and soft and he felt her love.

His growling stomach interrupted his memory of his mother, as Kylla struck off once again to the north. They walked in almost complete silence. Stern realized she made no sound and that the pounding, thrusting, grating noises on the trail were his. He tried to imitate her and soon he too was walking silently. From time to time she stopped and sniffed the air like a sleek greyhound moving through the forest, following a trail of odors. In mid-afternoon they reached a large oak; someone had carved the image of the goddess into its bark. She knelt in front of it, bowed her head, and said what he interpreted as a prayer to the image, so he too knelt and said a prayer. However, he prayed not to the representation in the tree but to the Holy Mother of God. When Kylla finished, she said, "We are near the sacred grove. We must find a place to camp."

"Isn't it still early?" he asked dumbly.

"We must start your training, if we are to eat tonight. You have eaten all of our food."

As she did the preceding night, she began to walk in ever widening circles until she found what she was looking for, an evergreen copse on a slight hillock. She found a depression in the earth at the top of the hill, which formed an indenture protected on three sides by clay walls, with the fourth open to the east, and began gathering leaves to make a bed as she did the night before; but this time she made only one. She then took off her great cape and laid it onto the bed of leaves. She then undressed completely and folded her clothes on the edge of the cape and then placed her dagger and staff on top of the folded clothes.

"Undress and set your clothes next to mine."

As Stern undressed, he began to shiver.

Kylla sat upon the cape; her back straight and her legs crossed, as if preparing for meditation or prayer. When he was completely undressed, she commanded him to sit directly in front of her and take the same position. He tried not to stare at her body or to concentrate on his body's reaction to her nudity. She noted his discomfort and said, "Simply sit and close your eyes." He arranged himself directly in front of her. "Now, place your right hand on top of my left palm." He did as she instructed. His hand was cold whereas her hand was as warm as a baked muffin. "Hold your left out, palm up." She placed her right hand on his. "Open your eyes and look directly into mine. Look deeply and try to see my soul. Do not think of anything else."

They stared deeply into each others' eyes and he slowly felt her warmth embracing him.

"Close your eyes and describe the first image that materializes."

From the darkness of his unconscious mind came a pair of yellow eyes and then he saw the dark black fur of a wolf. He shuddered as he vaguely remembered the hunt in the forest.

"I see a black wolf with yellow eyes."

"Before you ran rampant with a pack, now I want you to be conscious of the wolf. Do not allow the wolf to eat you. I want you to eat the wolf. Imagine swallowing the wolf."

Stern imagined swallowing the wolf and he laughed as the bushy tail of the wolf disappeared into his mouth. After he visualized the eating of the wolf, Kylla asked, "Where is the wolf?" The rational answer would be, he thought, "in my stomach." But he felt her pushing him to concentrate, to visualize the wolf's presence. He relaxed and slowed his breathing, he searched for the wolf and then it dawned on him. The wolf's yellow eyes gazed through the lens of his green eyes. He had swallowed the wolf and he had become the wolf. He was still Stern but he was also the wolf. Before Stern lost consciousness and the wolf controlled him but now he was both wolf and Stern and he was awake and aware.

"Imagine now you're consciously taking on the form of the wolf."

He relaxed and imagined it and felt the transformation. Suddenly, he was aware of odors and smells he had not been aware of before. He also heard sounds he knew were miles away. He opened his eyes to see a great white wolf sitting on its haunches before him. He felt a sense of vertigo as he rose up on all fours. He could no longer hear her voice because he was now a wolf and the conscious human being, Stern, was receding.

The wind shifted and Kylla's ears perked up. She issued a slight woof as she turned with her bushy white tail extended straight out and bounded off into the darkness of the woods. Stern followed her and the two sped through the woods, tracking the scent wafting on a slight breeze from the north. As he ran, he saw the vision of a creature, a deer-like creature, a third the size of a Mexican deer from the Azul Mountains. He now discerned two different scents, male and female, and he hurried in his hunger behind Kylla.

As they drew near, Kylla slowed and approached the clearing where the two beasts grazed. Stern followed her lead, when she stopped a few hundred feet away and waited. The male lifted its head, its nostrils flaring and Stern knew it had detected their presence. Kylla must have sensed it as well because she sprain forward, heading for the female, catching the deer on her rear haunch just as it was about to spring. Stern took the other side and together the wolves pulled the doe to the ground. Once down Kylla held the doe with her paws, as Stern ripped its throat open.

They devoured the steaming entrails of the doe in the clearing, as flakes of snow drifted lazily down out of a gray sky. Satiated, they returned to their camp and formed two warm balls, their snouts buried in their thick winter's coats. Stern dreamed of deer, bison and rabbits.

He awoke shivering. A light patina of snow had filtered through the thick needles of the trees in the evergreen copse and covered his naked body. Kylla, already awake, was scrubbing her face with a handful of fresh snow. He quickly cleaned himself with snow and leaves, then dressed. The memory of the hunt returned and he shyly looked at Kylla, who seemed unmoved or troubled by the night's grisly events.

"I awoke when you shifted in the night. We will concentrate tonight on your controlling your shape."

"Is there a way not to lose my consciousness?"

"You were conscious."

"Yes, I was aware of what was happening but I wasn't me."

"You were you as a wolf. You can learn to have more control over that state but you will never be truly you in the skin of a wolf."

"When I was a bird, Focalor talked to me."

"That was more a function of Focalor' power and control over you than of you."

He paused and scratched his chin. "What is Focalor?" he asked.

"He is a messenger and a daemon. You know this."

"But what is his goal? Why has he involved himself in my business?"

She laughed. "This is not your business. You have involved yourself in their business. The dragons belong to this world." She wrapped her cloak tightly around her shoulders. "The blue-back dragons and their riders were exiled to your realm through the machinations of magic and you have somehow been interjected into that event. You are not the main player in this drama, nor is Focalor for that matter."

She entered the woods, heading due north. "Who is?" he asked hurrying behind her.

"Typhon commands Focalor." She stopped and he almost collided into her. "We will talk of Typhon when we reach the sacred grove and not before." She smiled and touched his face and rubbed his coarse black beard. "You should let it grow."

She turned, strode ahead and he remembered her as a white wolf.

Chapter Thirteen: Focalor's Dogs

THEY CONTINUED NORTH throughout the morning, stopping only to drink at creeks and springs they stumbled onto along the way. As they walked, Stern thought of the previous night and he tried to recall as much of the events as possible. He found it troubling to lose consciousness of his self. All his life he had tried to maintain control; however, the more he struggled to maintain order, the more chaotic things became. He had pushed and pulled, studied and strategized to reach his position in the Black Robes, only to be undone by his love for a Argyll woman. Now what was he? Some freak of nature caught in a nightmare? In this nightmare, Gotha and Kylla seemed to serve him in the same way. Was God sending emissaries to help him or undo him? Such a thought seemed to emanate from Kylla's teaching or from a remnant of the magical thinking instilled in him by the Black Robes. And yet he could not shake off his fears, especially when he added to the list of "helpers," the Argyll woman and the lunar *bruja*. A total of four very different women had entered his life so far and prepared the ground for his quest.

The pines gave way to a forest of aspens and snow fell through the wide-spread boughs. Kylla broke trail for them now and her strength and endurance impressed him, as he struggled against the snow. In the afternoon, when the snow stopped and the sound of the forest was muted by the snow, he heard a woodpecker tapping against a tree; and, as he searched for the bird, he saw a falcon circling high above them. He touched Kylla's shoulder and pointed.

"Focalor hunts us," she whispered.

"You mean the falcon?" He pointed up at the bird of prey circling in the frigid air.

"It is your companion, Coyote. Focalor controls him."

"How do you know?" he asked, watching the bird circling against the clear, bright sky.

"A Keltoi can always discern a shape-shifter from a real animal. That bird is a shape-shifter. I believe it to be the being you described to us as your traveling companion."

"Has he seen us?"

"I do not know but we should move. The snow has slowed us and I fear we will not make the sacred grove by nightfall."

"Will we hunt again?"

"If you plan to eat we will."

In response his stomach rumbled.

As they pressed on and entered a clearing, Stern wished for the dark dense shadows of the pine forest. At dusk, Kylla found a shallow dry cave in the bank of a hill. Tufts of fur caught on the rock fluttered around its mouth and she said it had once housed a bear. The thought of bears terrified Stern. He had seen people mauled by them and he felt an inordinate fear of their size and strength.

"It denned here long ago." She said, sensing his trepidation. "You have nothing to fear but it does give me an idea. Tonight we will meditate on the bear to see how strong your powers really are. Collect leaves to make a bed."

Gray clouds rolled in from the north and Stern smelled fresh snow. "Do you think we could make a fire tonight?"

"No fires." She said before moving off into the forest. Fat wet flakes began to fall and Stern wondered if he would ever be warm again. He thought of his room in La Ciudad and imagined eating a steak and drinking a bottle of red in front of a blazing fire in his favorite tavern on the *Zocalo*.

The sound of baying dogs, emanating from the south, from the way they had come, shattered his daydream and he hurried back to the cave to find Kylla, standing on its lip, her staff held defensively in front of her chest; she too had heard the dogs.

"What do you think?" he asked.

"Hunters and several hounds," she whispered. "We are not safe here. We must lose them but first I want to know who and what they are."

She quickly undressed, handing Stern her clothes. It was an intimate gesture and for the first time he felt something akin to love for his teacher.

"Take my things and head north as fast as you can. When possible, run on rock or through streams. Do anything you can to throw off the hounds. I will find you soon."

She sat on the leaves and closed her eyes. The change was sudden and mesmerizing. A large white owl now perched on the bed of leaves where Kylla had sat and in a flurry of wings and feathers she was airborne, rising quickly above the aspen forest. She flew in a widening gyre, climbing higher and higher, as Stern watched her, praying to God to protect her. He remembered her goddess and he addressed her, too, petitioning her for her grace to protect Kylla.

He heard the hounds baying this time from the west and he wondered if there could be more than one pack. Were they surrounding him? He ran north at a comfortable pace. He had always been a good runner and the last few days had strengthened and hardened him. Thirty minutes later he crossed a creek, doubled back and waded, thigh deep, into the water and moved downstream, heading toward the southeast, following the stream for almost an hour before he emerged, his legs and feet numb from the icy water and ran toward the north again. He had not heard the hounds for almost an hour and he hoped he had lost them. A half-hour later he stopped and wrapped himself in Kylla's cloak. He would rest for a few minutes and then set out again.

Night fell and it became more difficult for him to maintain his pace because of the dense root system of the trees. He slowed to a walk and used her staff. It was snowing heavily now, which was good, because it would cover his tracks. By morning he was wading in thick snow. He had reached the edge of a great clearing and he dared not cross it and leave the security of the woods. He climbed an oak on the edge of the clearing and found a place high up, where three limbs emerged, forming a saddle, and settled down to sleep. Wearing Kylla's cloak over his robe for warmth, he braced her staff between two limbs to secure his position. Eventually he fell asleep and dreamed of Gotha. She wore black leather and a black helmet with a black face guard and above them he heard the sound of leather wings flapping and the screech of the dragon's roar.

He awoke to a white world. Snow fell heavily onto the clearing and the forest, stripping the trees of the last autumn leaves. Above the forest, flying slowly toward the north, was Focalor. The sound of the leather wings in the dream must have been his. He watched from his hiding place as the daemonic messenger disappeared into gray clouds and falling snow. Although the snow muffled all sounds of the forest, he dared not move lest Focalor hear or see him and decide to turn back. He remained in the tree until nightfall. Slipping twice on the icy bark, he climbed down, his hands and feet frozen and stiff. North was across the clearing but he would not chance crossing it; instead, he worked his way around its edge.

He walked all night and found a fir tree on the bank of a frozen pond. He climbed it and settled among its aromatic needles. In the afternoon, he awoke to a black boar sniffing among the roots of the trees; its acrid porcine stench overcoming even the rich scent of the tree's resinous sap. Fearing the wild strength of the boar, he watched and waited from his safe perch. He was not foolish enough to climb down now. After a while he closed his eyes and dozed off into another dream. This time, he dreamed he hunted a wild boar from the back of a roan mare. Dressed in silver mail and carrying a long spear, he stabbed the boar. It turned and tore at the spear in fury; as it struggled, it transmogrified into a woman with auburn hair and green eyes. Startled, he pulled the spear from her and dismounted. She however once again transformed into the boar and gored him, ripping him from crotch to throat before he knew what had happened. As he was dying, he heard the woman's voice say, "do not fear me, embrace me."

He awoke to find a white winter owl perched on the limb next to him with a snow rat dead in its beak. He rubbed his eyes. It was even colder than the day before and he wondered if this intense, extreme weather was usual for the island. The owl blinked and then glided to the floor of the forest. Once there it tore the rat apart with its beak. The owl was Kylla. He climbed down carefully and laid her clothes and staff on the snow. He was hungry, too, but he had no interest in snow rat, at least not in his current form.

When the owl finished with the rat, leaving only bones, Stern noted a change in its form. First it grew in size and then transformed into Kylla, who stood before him naked and shivering. He quickly handed her the clothes. Once she was dressed he hugged her, trying to provide warmth. As soon as she stopped shivering, she said, "They are hunting us. There are twenty men with eight dogs. They have split up in four groups and they now surround us. The nearest group is about a day's run to the east. Focalor leads them and your friend Coyote reluctantly spies for them."

Stern's heart shuddered. His initial reaction was to run but he did not know this world well enough to know where. He replayed Kylla's message in his mind and then he asked, "Why reluctant? How do you know the way he feels?"

"I was able to get close enough to him to feel his anger at being controlled by Focalor, who has somehow locked him into the bird form."

"Do you think we could free him?"

"If I were able to touch him, I think I could break the bond. However, they will be upon us before we can reach the sacred grove. You have wandered away from our trail and I had a difficult time finding you."

"Sorry."

"No, this is good. We cannot reveal the location of the sacred grove to Focalor."

From the beginning of his journey, Stern had been led, chased and abused. He was not accustomed to his current impotence. He had to think, devise a plan to escape the hunters. A vision of La Ciudad burning flashed in his mind and he shivered. Where had this apocalyptic vision come from? He said, "We have to break out of the circle, but because of the dogs, it will be difficult. We could use Coyote's help so we should try to free him from Focalor's spell."

She sat, with her back pressed against the fir tree, watching him as he nervously paced back and forth.

"We have to destroy one of the groups to clear a path." Stern said, remembering his training from the wars on Mittilagart.

"Destroy? You mean kill five men and two dogs?"

"Exactly," he said grimly, trying to take control of his destiny for the first time since he had set foot on the watery plane.

"How do we do that?"

"Slowly," he said. "Here's my plan."

Later, they ran toward the east in their wolf forms, Kylla leading the way, sniffing the air, adjusting their course in order to approach downwind of the group. At dusk Stern sniffed the strong odor of the hunters: sour sweat, urine and musk, plus man-made odors of tobacco, alcohol, cooked meat and wood smoke. He also detected the smell of the dogs, one was a female coming into heat.

They made a large semi-circle run around the group and continued east for another hour until they found a secluded spot to transform into their human forms. Earlier that day Kylla had transformed first and Stern had tied their clothes and her staff and dagger to her back. He dressed quickly and took her dagger. She kissed him on each cheek and they headed out toward the hunters. They soon found their trail in the snow and followed it. As night approached, new snow fell. They walked for an hour or two and then Kylla stopped suddenly and pointed her staff to the northeast. She whispered in his ear, "They have camped. I smell wood smoke."

She began to undress, handing him her clothes, which he folded and placed between the gnarled roots of a great oak. Once undressed, she sat upon the snow, closed her eyes, and transformed into a great black boar. Stern instinctively jumped back, as the boar sniffed and turned toward the smell of smoke. Stern followed her until he could hear talking. He then found a suitable tree and climbed up a few feet, while Kylla waited below. She sniffed the tree, rooted around its gnarled roots and shook her curled tail.

As soon as he was situated on a large limb above her, she moved through the woods toward the camp. The first thing he heard was the baying of the hounds, then the excited shout of the men. They were trying to control the dogs that were now agitated and full of rage. He could hear it in their barking, as he tried to calm his breathing. His body was awash in adrenalin as he hoped he had the strength and courage to do what he had planned.

The sounds of the dogs grew louder and he knew she was leading them to him. Soon she passed directly underneath the tree with two dogs following closely. Several minutes elapsed and the baying hounds' barking faded, as they disappeared into the east. Finally, two men approached, running at full speed, at least three minutes behind the hounds, carrying cudgels, axes and polearms. A larger man wielding a sledgehammer of some sort jogged beneath the tree and a few minutes after him a short squat man approached, hoisting a crossbow over his shoulder and wearing ragged leather armor.

As the last man passed under Stern, he jumped from the limb, knocking the man to the ground, quickly forcing his right knee into the small of the man's back, grabbing his chin with his left hand, and then cutting the man's throat from left to right. As the man struggled to live, his blood pumping wildly onto the snow, Stern turned him over and relieved him of his belt, which held a short sword and quiver of short iron bolts. He picked up the crossbow and then hurried after the group. He could no longer hear the dogs.

He ran as hard as he could and in minutes he heard the labored breath of the large man carrying the sledgehammer. As soon as he was close enough to the man, who had not yet heard him, he stopped, knelt on one knee and aimed the crossbow, releasing the safety and letting the bolt fly. It struck the man between the shoulder blades, and he fell into the snow. Stern also slit his throat fearing there might still be life in him.

He reloaded the bow before setting off behind the men, who were tiring; it was not long before he caught sight of the third man, who, although lean and fairly fast, carried a heavy ax and wore a metal helm and a leather vest over his wet, woolen clothes.

Stern closed on him and, as before, as soon as he drew close enough, he knelt and fired the bow. This time, because of the man's speed, he missed his back, striking him instead in the thigh of his right leg. The man screamed with pain and fell, trying to dislodge the dart. Stern dropped the bow and pulled the short sword and closed on the man, who now struggled

95

to his feet. As Stern drew near, the man swung the ax wildly at him. Stern jumped back, fearing he might throw the weapon. The man swung again and Stern blocked it with the sword and then pushed in with his dagger, thrusting it under the man's ribs. The cut was slight because of the resistance and thickness of the armor the man wore, but the pain shocked him and he impulsively released the ax and grabbed the hand thrusting the dagger. Stern pushed harder on the dagger and simultaneously swung the sword, as the man fell back, trying to avoid the dagger. With room to work, he brought the sword down on the man's shoulder cutting deeply, catching the sword. The man staggered, fell to his knees and died.

Stern, exhausted and covered in blood, felt bile rush into his mouth and threw up upon the snow. Wiping his mouth, he slowly rose, found the bow and reloaded it, extricated the sword and pushed it into its scabbard, retrieved Kylla's dagger, hoisted the ax onto his shoulder and followed the trail of the last two men.

He was exhausted but only two men were left. These two men were the fastest and probably the best hunters. His plan was for Kylla to lead the dogs as far away from the men as she could and then transform into the owl and leave them wandering in the woods. He no longer heard the dogs so he feared she may have already escaped, which meant the men and dogs would turn back toward their camp. With this in mind, he devised a new plan. He left the trail and circled back to his last kill, where he climbed a nearby tree and waited.

He dozed in the tree and awoke to the curses of the men, who had found the body of the ax man. One knelt at the corpse while the other paced in the snow, cursing loudly, thrusting his polearm into the air. As he turned with the weapon raised high, Stern let loose a black bolt that struck the man in the forehead. He fell dead into the snow. The other man turned, looking about frantically, to find the direction and source of the attack. Stern cocked the weapon, which the man heard, and hurriedly loaded another dart. The man turned to run but a black boar blocked his path and ripped him open from groin to chest.

As Stern descended the tree and approached the bodies, Kylla stood in front of him naked and shivering. He unfastened the bundle he had strapped tightly to his back and handed her the clothes, bow, belt with the quiver and her dagger. He searched the bodies of the two men and found a long curved dagger, which he thrust in his belt and a short dagger in the boot of another, which he slipped in his own boot. One of the men wore a sheepskin hat; he checked it for lice and found it malodorous but vermin free and pulled it firmly onto his head.

Kylla said, "We should head north as fast as possible. We may find help at a spiritual retreat in the hills northwest of the sacred grove."

"What about Coyote?"

"We will deal with him later. It won't take long for those dogs to pick up our trail. We must get as far away as possible."

Now armed and dressed warmly, they struck out through the trees toward the north again. They jogged for an hour without talking and then stopped at a half-frozen creek to drink.

"I was astonished at your fighting abilities," she said.

Stern wiped his mouth on his sleeve and smiled at her.

"We should make the mountain retreat by night fall."

"What do you expect to find there?" he asked.

"There should be two or three pilgrims in the retreat. I will ask them to watch the ways to the sacred grove as we train. We will require all of our energies if we are to train you properly and we cannot be concerned about an attack."

Chapter Fourteen: Lessons

ONCE THEY CROSSED the stream, they marched toward the northwest and left the dense forest behind them and entered a beech wood. Light filtered through its leaves and Stern soon felt a slight elevation. The snow had stopped and the sun shone sharp and straight off the white powder before him. They emerged from the trees and trudged through the thick snow directly toward a band of hills and mountains in the distance. Startling him, a snowshoe rabbit bolted from a slight indenture in the snow and Kylla raised the crossbow and let fly a black bolt that struck its hip. Blood splattered on the snow as the rabbit writhed against the bolt. She hurried to it, broke its neck and stuffed it under her belt.

"The retreat is located in the rocks of a hillock beyond these low hills," she said.

"What are these pilgrims doing at the retreat?"

"Meditating and making vision quests."

He shrugged and she continued, "One meditates and enters into a trance, freeing the subtle body from the physical body. The others guard the physical body, protecting it from daemons that might seek to take control of the body."

Stepping over a fallen log, he asked. "Where do they go on these quests?"

"It depends on the experience and the training of the dreamer. I have heard tales that some have even traveled to the deepest darkest depths of Niflheim, the land of death. Others have taken control of lesser creatures in order to experience their lives. There is a story of Dymr, an ancient and revered Keltoi, who entered the body of an elk when he was a young man and who did not return to his body until he was middle-aged. My grandmother told me the tale of Dymr and the ice dragon every winter solstice. In that one, Dymr took control of a lazy ice dragon to fight off a horde of black dragons that invaded the island."

He wiped his hands and leaned back. "Flymtt said the King has killed all the dragons on the island?"

"The King's men attack any dragon they find. That is true. Every year in the spring, dragons attempt to nest in our mountains but the King's men are constantly vigilant. Some say it was not the King but the Keltoi that rid the island of the fiery beasts. But if that is true it was a long time ago and we no longer remember it."

"You said that Focalor was a daemon?"

"He is a servant of Typhon."

"How can he exist here and dragons don't?"

"If the King's men found him they would cut off his head and burn his body."

"So he is as much a fugitive as I?"

"More so. He has made you a fugitive but he hunts here against the King's desire and design."

"Typhon, Focalor also mentioned him. Who is he?"

"We have never seen him but the legend is he is the son of the great mother and the ouroborus worm."

'The great mother?" he asked, as he trudged behind her.

"She is the first mother, the mother of all the gods."

"So Typhon does not exist. He is simply a myth?"

"No, he is very much alive. He has followers here and he has messengers such as Focalor to do his bidding." She paused and then continued, "Before visiting this realm, if someone told you that there was a race of people on another realm that could shift shape and project their subtle bodies into other worlds, you would think they were crazy. Now you know we exist and you have experienced our abilities. We are real to you and you would never deny our existence. You also have experienced other realms and now your idea of reality has changed."

He asked, "Do the carvings in the trees have something to do with the Great Mother?"

She did not answer immediately; instead, she marched on, her breath billowing from her nostrils, as she labored against the snow.

"The carvings are a representation of a goddess not the great mother."

"Do you worship Typhon's mother, as well?"

"Typhon's mother was the great mother, the mother of the worlds, the mother of all being. Some legends picture her as a spider that gave birth to thousands of offspring that sprung fully-grown from her. The great goddess, the goddess of this realm, was one of those gods born of her."

"The great goddess is sister to Typhon?"

"A stepsister," she said. "Typhon was the progeny of the mating of the ouroboros and the great mother. All the gods sprung from the one and it is our belief that they will all return to her in the end."

"The end of what?" he asked.

"The end of the gods...the end of everything...it is the return of all into the one."

"So what role does Typhon play in this story?"

"Typhon believes all dragons came from him and belong to him. He is half man/half dragon, part man and part worm."

"What does that have to do with me? Why is Focalor trying to stop me?"

"My guess is he desires dragons to live in your realm so that he can extend his power to your world, he wishes dragons to exist on all the spheres. You are here to free your world of dragons. Consequently, your goal is antithetical to his."

A few moments later, he asked, "What would happen to me if the King captured me?"

"I don't know. He might hold on to you as an oddity or he might send you away as a madman. The King does not believe in the elemental worlds. He no more believes in your realm than you believed in his before coming to this world."

Stern heard the expression—elemental worlds—and stopped. He suddenly envisioned his world contiguous to Okeanus but that could not be right. He asked: "Is my world contiguous to yours?" She paused and placed her right palm down on her left hand and said: "Two planes touching at every point." He thought about the image and said, "Like two pieces of papers, stacked one on top of the other?"

She nodded but then added: "Think of it as an onion with layers."

"So there is more than one sphere or layer?"

She shook her head affirmatively.

"If people want to hurt me for being here on this sphere, do you believe my quest is fated to fail?"

"I cannot judge whether you are fated to fail or not? That you have arrived here in my keeping, I believe, means the great mother is guiding your steps. If she intends you to succeed, you will succeed."

"Why would she want me to succeed?"

"Legend tells us she plans to rehabilitate Typhon and his ilk and adjust the balance of the planes. Your desire to return the dragons and foist Typhon's plan seems to fit within her grand design."

Once they reached the top of the first small hill, she pointed her staff to a taller hill in the distance. "The retreat lies in the valley beyond that hill."

"Will we make it before dark?"

"Maybe, if we hurry."

"I don't wish to spend another night in the open."

"Nor do I."

They moved as quickly as possible through the deep powder. Soon he was sweating, his muscles aching and his breath labored. Although the few days in this realm had strengthened him and stripped pounds from his body, even Kylla was having trouble with the fresh snow.

After two hours they stopped on the crest of the larger hill and peered down into a shallow valley that flattened out in the north, where he spied a copse of fir trees.

"The retreat is there in that copse."

He took a deep breath and said, "Let's go."

She smiled and shook her head in agreement.

Chapter Fifteen: Dryrrt the Drac

AS THE SUN SET in a red and yellow explosion against the darkening sky, they entered a dense copse of fir trees. A gray owl perched on a rowan limb hooted as they entered the quiet calm of the trees and a tall man with long blond hair, braided down his back, emerged from the shadows. He wore green boiled leather armor, carried a long bow in his right hand, with a heavy woolen cape draped over his shoulders, and sported two short curved swords on his hips. He raised his hand in greeting and Kylla said, "Well met, Brydr."

"Welcome Kylla to the quiet repose of our retreat."

"Before we enter I must warn you that Focalor trails us."

He frowned and blinked, demonstrating a facial tic that reminded Stern of the gray owl perched at the entrance of the stand of trees. He whistled and another man with long red hair, carrying a long bow, appeared.

"Brae Syrl, they say they are followed by Focalor, would you see if he is near?"

"Per Brydr, I will."

Syrl stripped, sat and closed his eyes. In a matter of seconds he transformed himself into a white snow owl. As he flew up and away, Brydr gathered up his clothes and weapons and said, "Follow me. There is a stone hut nearby. We have lit a fire and Myrr is preparing soup."

Inside the hut, Myrr squatted in front of a small fire burning in a stone fireplace, stirring a pot of soup that hung from an iron hook protruding from the wall of the chimney. Stern's mouth watered. He shrugged his wet cloak from his shoulders and pulled off his boots. His whole body was cold and he luxuriated in the heat of the hut.

Myrr was older than the others. He had long gray hair that fell naturally onto his shoulders and a full salt and pepper beard. He wore a gray hooded robe over black leather armor, a silver dagger hung from his belt and a long oaken staff leaned against the wall near his hand.

"Kylla, we welcome you and your companion to our retreat."

"You don't look like you're in retreat," observed Stern.

He smiled and answered, "We were but our solitude was disturbed several nights ago by a band of bandits."

"We are being pursued by such a band, led by the daemon Focalor. Maybe there is a connection," said Kylla.

He turned from his cooking to examine Stern. "Perhaps they chase your companion."

"You are quite correct." She paused and then said, "I came here for protection. He is in training and I need uninterrupted time in the sacred grove to finish his initiation."

"What is he?"

"I suspect he is a descendant of the lost tribe of the North."

"He has fallen out knowledge?"

"Yes, but he has incredible powers, warrior powers. He may be a bare-sark."

"Truly?" he asked, with one eye half-closed, an expression of his disbelief.

She nodded.

"Then how can you initiate him in a matter of days? It takes years for a bare-sark to develop into that which he truly is."

"I can only show him his potential."

Myrr rubbed his beard and stood. He was taller than the rest. "We can watch for you but I don't know how long we can hold them off if they arrive in force."

Syrl opened the door. Naked, he moved quickly to the fire to warm himself. Brydr handed him his clothes and rubbed his shoulders as he pulled on his leather pants.

Kylla asked, "Did you see them?"

"I saw nothing. I flew in a series of expanding circles and I spied nothing except your tracks marking the snow. A blind man could follow them."

Myrr scratched his head and said, "After we eat, we will move to the retreat for the night and erase our tracks as we go."

After Syrl passed out clay bowls and wooden spoons, they dug into the soup. The food and the heat of the hut made Stern drowsy and he did not relish a further march in the cold to the retreat. Myrr, however, was adamant that they leave so he began to clean up the hut as soon as they finished eating. Stern reluctantly pulled on his wet boots and shrugged into his damp cloak.

The night was clear and Stern glimpsed thousands of stars through the evergreens. They left the trees and climbed the eastern side of the valley, heading up another hill. Several hours later they entered a narrow ravine. The snow here was particularly deep and the way was difficult and time consuming. Finally, they reached a stone ledge that overlooked the valley, behind a lone cedar tree, an entrance. They squeezed past the cedar one by one and entered a small dry room with a flat stone floor. Another, smaller entrance lay before them. Myrr bent down and slithered through the narrow opening, followed by the others, until only Kylla and Stern remained outside. Stern swallowed and crawled through the narrow opening. The tunnel ran for almost four meters before it opened into a huge dry chamber, its flat stone floor covered with aromatic fir boughs. Myrr lit several oil lamps, which illuminated the rounded stonewalls that were covered with thousands of ideographs, pictographs, and runes.

"We will be safe here tonight and then we will send Syrl out in the morning," said Myrr.

They settled into the cavern and Byrdr showed Stern a recessed space in the north wall where he could place his weapons and cloak. Once he had settled in he joined the others in the center of the cave. Myrr handed him black bread and passed him a leather flask that contained an alcoholic drink. After finishing eating, Myrr turned to Kylla and asked, "Where are you in his training?"

"He has mastered a few transformations and he can control his animal nature to some extent. As you can see he has absorbed a great deal of our language. He knows nothing of our beliefs and religion nor has he been touched by the Goddess."

"You know, Kylla, that it takes a lifetime to understand our ways and our power. It is dangerous to show him a little and then drop him into the world."

"But he is not of our world and he is a grown man, nay he is almost an elder."

"Thanks," said Stern hurt by the reference to his age.

"I have heard of cases like his, people of our world that have fallen into ignorance."

"So what happened to them?" asked Stern.

"Some learned quickly, others did not learn at all. It depends on their natural abilities."

"I think he has the ability," said Kylla.

"What totems has he?" asked Syrl.

"The wolf so far but I do not believe that these beings are representatives of his authentic self. The Bargi says he is bare-sark and that he has seen the vision of the turtle."

"The turtle?" whispered Syrl. "Our people never see the turtle."

"The Skaellanders, the northern people, saw them and worshiped them."

Myrr said, "But did the northern sea people even exist? Have we ever seen them or heard them?"

"I believe the stories of the ancient sea peoples and so does the Bargi. There are the red ruins in the north."

"Could he truly be one of the lost northern sea people?" asked Brydr.

Stern felt odd, trying to follow the twists and turns of their guttural language. There were moments when he felt he understood every word and then he lost track of what they were saying.

"He is not a northern sea person," said Myrr. "I don't intuit any sea element in him. He is something else and I agree with Kylla; he is not a wolf, although he has the ability to morph into one. The Bargi may be right in naming him a bare-sark."

"Most bare-sarks have three totems—the wolf, the bear and the dragon," whispered Syrl, frightened by his own statement.

"How many bare-sarks have there been?" asked Brydr. "I will tell you, maybe two in my lifetime and they are all dead now. Have you ever heard of a dragon bare-sark?"

"Dryrrt," said Kylla.

"Dryrrt, the Drac, is a fairy tale, a myth, made up to scare Keltoi children by the shamans," said Myrr.

"Suppose he is a mix, part sea people and part Skaellander," postulated Kylla.

"Don't be silly. The sea people and the Skaellanders are figments of the shamans' imaginations. We are the only shape-shifters, only us and those that were carried away by the thorns."

"Who is Dryrrt?" asked Stern. "What thorns?"

They looked startled. They had almost forgotten he was there and his asking them about Dryrrt in a sentence in their own language amazed them. Myrr cleared his throat and said, "He was a shaman king of the Keltoi many years ago. How long ago we are not really sure. At that time the Keltoi dominated the world, our world. They ruled from an island in the north near the ice wall. At that time, the Keltoi were craftsmen and artisans, dealing in gold and silver goods. We sent our miners out in long boats to explore the world looking for metals. On one of those voyages, the miners landed on an island far to the west inhabited by fire drakes, who not only destroyed the miners and their ship but who through their sense of smell tracked the ship back through every stop made until they reached our Keltoi home. When they reached our shores, the age of the dragon began and the Keltoi began to disappear. It was then we became the hidden people."

"But who was Dryrrt?"

"When the dragons appeared, Dryrrt was but a teen, indentured to Skadlr, the silver smith. He lived in a small village on the northern coast of the northernmost islands. Because the island was so far north, its harbor was iced over for at least half of every year. During those cold cruel months, the inhabitants stayed underground in elaborate caves, warmed by hot springs, and worked at their crafts.

"Because of the ice and cold, the dragons had been on the island for almost eight months before Dryrrt's village learned of the invasion. It was almost a year, however, before the dragons molested one of the villages, burning its houses and driving the survivors into the surrounding mountains, into their winter homes, the caves. Dryrrt and a few others survived underground until the next winter but then the really hard times began.

"One of the survivors was Lyzarr, the shaman of Dryrrt's village. He was old then and no one expected him to survive the winter. Sensing his death he began to train Dryrrt in the ways of the shaman. At first, Dryrrt seemed to be just an intelligent young man but soon Lyzarr realized he had a prodigy on his hands. He learned the medical skills rapidly and casting his subtle body seemed child's play. All the while Lyzarr worked with Dryrrt, he was trying to discern the source of his power and his authentic totem. It was not until Dryrrt was caught alone on the ice by a young female dragon that the truth was revealed. During their battle, Dryrrt unconsciously transformed himself into a polar bear. When the dragon wounded him in the bear form, he became so angered or frightened, we are not sure which, he fell into the emotional state of the bare-sark and began to rage uncontrollably against his dragon opponent.

"He struck out with such tremendous speed and fury that he shifted into the shape of his enemy; in an instance, he became a white dragon male, larger and fiercer than the female he fought. In this new form, he quickly dispatched her with such ferocity and anger that there was little left of her but scales and burned flesh.

"He remained in the form of the white dragon for two days, circling the Keltoi's mountain hideaway. Finally, Lyzarr after several hours reached Dryrrt's conscious mind through mind speak and guided him back to his Keltoi form.

"Once he shifted he fell into a deep sleep that lasted for almost a week. When he finally awoke, he was no longer Dryrrt the boy; instead, he was Dryrrt, the Drac, a shaman and shape-shifter. Throughout the winter he and Lyzarr meditated together exploring the boundaries of his authentic self but even working together they were unable to penetrate his limit of power. In fact, the more they learned about his powers, the greater his unknown potential seemed to loom over them.

"After several weeks, Dryrrt announced he was going to lead the Keltoi away from their island home in the north. They would travel south and find a place to hide until they could rebuild their strength and power. He led the Keltoi here and we took up a life in the mountains of this island, many years before it became the King's Island."

Stern yawned and so did Kylla.

"You should rest" said Myrr. "We will watch this night and tomorrow we can determine what we should do."

Stern walked to his nest in the stone recess and lay down, pulled the dead man's cloak over his body, and fell into a deep sleep.

Chapter Sixteen: Rogue's Return

STERN DREAMED several giant red dragons circled above the cathedrals of La Ciudad. Smoke rose from buildings and he heard the thump, thump, thumping sounds of the witches' ornithopters approaching from the south. Trumpets wailed and women screamed as the dragons broke from their circle and burned their way up and down the streets. He saw his son running away from the mayhem. In the next instance, he was with him, watching in horror as a dragon descended toward them. He embraced his son and felt his warmth and in that moment he was filled with anger and hate against these dragons that threatened them. He shifted into a seething monster with leathery wings and a huge gaping maul. He was now a dragon, too, and he intended to burn all those who stood against his will. He rose up and spat a fiery blast.

Stern awoke with a start. Kylla was gently shaking him, saying, "You must get up. It the hour before dawn and Syrl has found someone camped near the retreat." He rubbed the sleep from his eyes and followed her to the tunnel. Myrr stood just outside the entrance to the cave, his long bow in his right hand. All the clouds had disappeared and it was a clear frigid night.

Kylla whispered, "What news?"

"There is a man camped in a small clump of trees near the valley's mouth."

"Have there been any sightings of Focalor or his men?"

"Brydr saw campfires far to the southeast, near the place where you said you confronted Focalor's men."

"Is this man a scout, then?"

Myrr shrugged and gazed into the night. "Listen, Syrl returns."

Syrl landed in the form of a white snow owl and then shifted. Myrr handed him his clothes and weapons; and as soon as he was dressed, he said, "A man camps at the valley's entrance. He is wrapped in a blanket and shivers next to a small fire."

"Describe him," ordered Kylla.

"He is young, tall and slim with thick black hair and blue eyes. He has not shaved for several days and he has the beginnings of a thick beard. He wears boiled leather and he carries two curved daggers."

"Is he riding a black horse?" asked Stern.

"No horse, pack or supplies. He seems in bad shape."

"It is the rogue," said Stern.

"I agree," added Kylla. "He is the King's man and he is looking for Stern. He must be some tracker to find us here."

"I sensed he is starving. If we don't help him, he will die."

"We cannot bring him here to the cave. We can escort him to the stone hut."

"You should not expose yourselves. Let me take him to the hut," said Stern.

"When he recovers he will try to deliver you to the King."

"I cannot stay here forever," he said, remembering his mission.

"You have not been trained. If you leave now, you will not have the power to protect yourself."

"I cannot let him die. He helped me on the beach."

"Then I will travel with you," said Kylla.

"You needlessly place yourself in jeopardy," warned Myrr.

"The Bargi made me pledge to train him and I will not violate my oath to him, our tribal leader."

"Neither one of you should go. Let this man die. The King has been no friend of ours and we do not know if he works with Focalor," said Myrr.

"I have been battered about since I came to this world," Stern said. "I must help Flymtt and trust that he is what I think he is, a good man."

"You are very naïve," whispered Myrr, turning his back and entering the cave.

"Gather your things, while I find some food for this rogue," ordered Kylla.

Thirty minutes later Kylla led the way through the valley toward the stone hut. Syrl circled high above them, surveying the sky for any sign of

Focalor or Coyote. When they reached the hut, Kylla left the provisions and they set off toward the trees where they last saw the rogue. It took them almost an hour to trudge a mile through the deep snow. As they neared the copse, Stern smelled the faint smell of wood smoke. Kylla nodded, indicating that she, too, smelled the fire. They soon found the man, wrapped in a horse blanket, lying next to a dying fire.

Stern bent over him and Kylla warned: "Take his knives. If he wakes up he might lash out."

Stern relieved Flymtt of his daggers and stuck them in his belt. He continued to shake him and call his name. Finally, the man opened one eye and grunted. Stern shook him harder and the man weakly lashed out and murmured: "Let me die in peace."

"Flymtt, it is Stern. We have a warm cabin nearby and food. Wake up."

The man stirred and tried to sit up. It took both Kylla and Stern to get him to his feet. He was groggy and his step hesitant. However, after a few steps he began to respond and awaken. He looked into Stern's face and said, "I knew I would find you." He looked over and saw Kylla, standing straight, holding a long bow. He turned back to Stern and said, "Your Tandraxx is beautiful."

"She is not my Tandraxx. She is my teacher, Kylla."

"Teacher,' he asked with a wink. "What does she teach?"

"Save your energy and just walk. We will talk once we are at the hut."

Stern was sweating by the time they had wrestled Flymtt to the hut, stripped him down, and hung his clothes to dry. Kylla built a fire, as Stern wrapped him in the cloak he had taken from the dead man in the snow. Flymtt fell asleep immediately and Kylla set about making a stew. Once it was bubbling over the fire, she said, "You watch him while I go back and cover our tracks."

Stern sat next to the fire watching the man, who was now moaning lowly and shivering. He added a few pieces of dried wood to the fire.

Stern closed his eyes and after a few moments, he dozed. Just at the edge of sleep, he caught, out of the corner of his eye, a vision of white light. He blinked, not knowing if he were awake or asleep, dreaming or seeing. The *bruja* bent down and placed her right hand on the rogue's head and he stopped his moaning and shivering. In fact, the whole room felt warmer and dryer than before he had entered. She no longer wore the white robes, instead, she wore crimson.

"Witch?" he whispered."

"Stern," she answered.

"I saw you in my dream."

"You felt my presence and incorporated it into your sleeping thoughts."

"I'm failing my mission, every step is blocked."

She smiled and said, "You are going where you must go. You must remain until it is finished."

"Can I trust this man?"

"It is not clear. He is not here for you. He has his own duty to perform."

"What about Kylla?"

"Learn everything you can from her."

She turned and began to fade. "What about Coyote?"

Turning toward Stern, she said, "He may be saved yet."

She disappeared as Kylla opened the door, followed by Syrl, who knelt next to the rogue and touched his head. "His fever is gone. He may live after all."

"Any sign of Focalor or his men?" asked Stern.

"None," said Syrl.

Kylla checked the stew and then spooned several spoonfuls into a clay bowl.

"We must wake him and feed him, otherwise he will never recover."

When Stern shook him this time, he quickly responded. His eyes were clear and he seemed rested. "I dreamed I saw a bright light."

"Death is not far away this day," said Kylla.

"I thank each of you for my life."

Kylla and Syrl bowed their heads, acknowledging they received his thanks.

His hand shook as he quickly ate the stew and asked for more. At that point each took a bowl and filled it and they joined him in the meal.

"Is it still snowing?" asked the rogue. "This storm appeared freakishly early for this time of year."

"It has stopped and the temperature has warmed," said Kylla.

"I lost my horse in the snow. It broke its leg in a narrow ravine covered with snow. I had to leave it and continue on."

"You did not put it out of its misery?" asked Syrl.

"I didn't have time; the hounds were almost on me."

"What hounds?" asked Stern, knowing the answer but asking it anyway.

"There was a group of bandits chasing me. They had a couple of those long legged wolfhounds, barking their heads off like the hell hounds they resemble."

"How many were in the group?" asked Kylla.

"Five or six men and two dogs," he responded.

"How did you escape?"

He smiled and then said, "I found a creek, not much of anything, half frozen really, and ran through it until I couldn't feel my feet any longer. I'm lucky I didn't lose any toes. I followed it until I reached a frozen pond, which I basically crawled over, fearing I would fall through the ice." He paused and then said in a whisper: "That's how I lost them—by crossing ice and water."

He yawned and Kylla urged him to go back to sleep. "We will take the watch. Rest easy and tomorrow we will decide what to do."

Flymtt wrapped himself in the horse blanket and the dead man's cloak and was soon asleep.

Chapter Seventeen: Gyylr, the Spider God

ONCE THE ROGUE was asleep, Kylla said, "We must use our time wisely. I have yet to find your totem animal and we are losing precious time. You must have this totem available as a representation of your essential self. It will ground you and strengthen you in the coming fight with Focalor."

"Is this all you need to teach me?" asked Stern.

"No, of course, not," she answered quickly. "I have to teach you the way of the bare-sark and the Keltoi. To be one of us involves more than shape shifting. There is an entire system of living based upon the wholeness of nature that must be absorbed. In addition, there is our language, our religion, our system of justice, and our spiritual values that must be absorbed. To those with talent, I teach the nature of herbs and the preparation of potions and medicine, the art of the bow and arrow, the skill of tracking, basket weaving, and thought talking."

"What is thought talking?"

"Communicating without speaking," she said with a grimace at his sheer ignorance.

"Like Focalor?"

"What do you mean?"

"When he helped me shift into the form of the osprey, he talked to me telepathically."

"What?"

"He spoke in my mind, openly and clearly, just as we are speaking now."

"You must have a high aptitude for thought talking. Are you sure you have never had these experiences before coming here."

"No, in fact, to the chagrin of the Black Robes, I was one of the more pious of the unbelievers."

She thought for a moment, digesting what he had told her of his experience with Focalor. Then, she straightened up, closed her eyes and folded her hands into her lap and thought, "*Speak these words in my language if you hear me.*" She then thought the question, "*Where does the truth lie?*" Moments of silence passed and then he said the words just as she had spoken them.

"When did you hear my words?"

"Earlier, but I was not sure if you sent them or I imagined them."

"You spoke them perfectly. Did you intuit their meaning?"

"Oddly, I understood not only the words but I pictured the grammar."

"Grammar?" she asked.

"Never mind," he said with a smile.

"Let's try something. Who in this world other than Flymtt and me would you like to speak to?" She said.

"Bedwyr or Gotha," he quickly answered.

"You have never met Bedwyr so let's try Gotha. Call to her and ask if she is well."

"You mean silently call to her?"

She nodded in the affirmative.

He closed his eyes and imagined Gotha as he had first seen her many days ago. At first, there was only his memory of her, her hair cascading onto her shoulders, her freckled skin, her long legs, firm back and stomach, her small breasts, and ruddy nipples. Then, there was a small whisper in his mind, an intimation of her calling him, asking where he was and what had happened to them in the great storm. He answered on faith that it was her voice that spoke and not his imagination. "*I washed ashore in a land called the Island. Where are you?*" He faintly heard her reply, "*I am sailing into the harbor of Tylynna, an island of the Tandraxx. I can see the towers of the Keep, rising from the verdant hills.*"

"*Isn't it cold there?*"

"*Not yet. Winter is behind me. I outran it but it follows quickly.*"

"*I am glad you are safe.*"

"*Thank you, my man, for I now travel for two. I carry your child and she sits as a woman in my womb. I sailed here to find counsel with the Matron Warrior.*"

Stern felt the room turn and he became nauseous, as he woke from his trance.

"What is it?" asked Kylla.

"I felt sick suddenly."

"Did you contact her?"

"I think so. I cannot be sure. I don't trust this magic."

"It is not magic. It is a natural skill."

"She said she was sailing into the harbor of Tylynna, the home of the Tandraxx."

"Tylynna is an island southwest of here. It is a small island but it is the home of a Tandraxx Keep. Haven't you heard of this place before?"

"No. She told me she was a Tandraxx but she never mentioned a place. She said she had sailed to Tylynna because she was pregnant and had to consult with the Matron Warrior."

"This child is yours, I suppose?" Kylla said with a strange look on her face, which Stern could not interpret.

"That is what she said. She said we have a contract and if the child is a girl then she will be raised as a Tandraxx"

"That is the custom." She paused and then asked, "Why did you swoon?"

"Out of fear and anxiety at the thought that I have produced a child in an alien world with a woman I do not know. I have lost one child to the Black Robes and now it seems I have lost another in an unknown realm. I am running from a daemon and I have sired a child. The absurdity of it all made me ill."

Kylla shrugged her shoulders. All of the madness of the last few days came crashing down on Stern and he collapsed into a depressed heap. Everything seemed black and he questioned his own sanity. He was caught in a nightmare that he could not awaken from, descending, he feared, into even darker madness. Suddenly, he thought of the night he met the Keltoi, of their rampage through the woods, the hunt of the pack and the killing of the deer. He tasted its bestial blood and smelled the musk of its hide as his teeth tore into its flesh. He felt another spasm of vertigo but before he fell onto the stone floor he glimpsed the maul of a great black bear that rose up on its hind legs and pawed viciously at the air.

He saw, as if outside his body, Kylla catch him as he fell and lower him to the floor. She silently spoke to him and he saw in her mind's eye a black bear running into the shadows of his own mind. In her subtle body, she followed him to the last visible boundary of his conscious mind before she reached the total blackness of Stern's unconscious. At first, the expanding darkness, which washed against his conscious mind, like the surf on a sandy beach, was black and opaque, but then a faint light appeared, allowing him to decipher the outline of a giant black bear, backing into a darker hollow of his un-thought thoughts. She called to the bear and it growled and pawed the ground, its anger frightening her. He felt her think: *Stern appears to be gentle, almost childlike, but here in this recess is a shadow creature filled with anger and hate.* He felt her fear as she quickly retreated from his mind. She whispered, "I cannot leave you as long as the bear lurks, wounded and hidden in the dark recesses of your unconscious mind. I must help you lure this creature out into the light of day and tame it."

She sat next to him on the floor and wrapped her left arm around him. He closed his eyes and re-envisioned the bear. Later, he whispered, "Is this bear, my authentic self?"

She spread her cloak over them and whispered into his ear, "No, but he is the messenger. He will lead us to your authentic self. The next time we shift, you must concentrate on the bear, no matter how much he scares you. He is a representative of the *prima matera.*"

"What?"

"It is the original matter, that from which we spring and come into being. The Bargi calls it the god seed, god in us, the Keltoi. In order to find the authentic self, you must find in yourself the prime material of being or the god seed."

"How does one find the god seed?"

"If we had time, we would seek it through quests and meditation but we do not have that time. Sometimes it reveals itself suddenly in visions, such as you have just experienced."

"You spoke of the great mother?"

"I have told you before of Gyylr, the great spider, the mother of all. She, like your bear, is blackness incarnate."

"A spider?" he shivered.

"She is a great black spider that births thousands of beings at a time."

"Do you pray to this god?"

"Pray? You mean do we petition her for help?"

"Yes."

"No, that would be useless. She does not answer petitions and we are not beggars. She has given us being, why should we ask for anything more? Besides, once we find the god seed our need is over and our journey is then clear."

"What is that journey?"

"Every being must follow the dictates of the god seed and grow into that which Gyylr intends us to become."

"The bear will lead me to the god seed?"

"One way or the other it will."

He felt himself falling asleep in the warmth of her arms. This, he thought, must have been what it was like to be a child, resting on his mother's breast. As he slipped into sleep, he saw Gyylr scampering over rugged mountainous terrain, a thousand tiny spiders following her trail and he heard a priest of the Black Robes say, "Being is God."

Chapter Eighteen: To Stormcrow Keep

WHEN STERN AWOKE, Kylla boiled oats, while Flymtt washed from a large clay bowl filled with melted snow.

"Finally awake I see?" said Flymtt.

Stern stretched and rubbed the sleep from his eyes as the assassin continued. "The weather has changed again. This is the strangest weather I have ever encountered. Fall has returned and the snow is melting. It will be almost impossible for them to pick up my trail now."

"What do you intend doing?" asked Stern.

"Deliver you to the King at Stormcrow Keep."

"What if I choose not to go?"

He frowned and wiped his face on his undershirt.

"I thought you wanted to see Bedwyr. The only way you will be able to catch a ship is through the King's harbor and no ship will grant you passage without leave of the King. As I see it you have only one of two choices: stay here and hide from those thieves that are chasing you or come with me to the Keep."

"They are not thieves," said Kylla. "They are Focalor's minions."

He whistled and then continued, "It is even more important we reach the Keep. Only the King's priests can battle Focalor."

Stern bowed his head, trying to decide what the best thing to do was. Could the King help him get to Bedwyr? Suddenly, he envisioned a black bear running from its hiding place and rearing before a man draped in silver plate mail astride a giant black horse.

As the vision passed, he asked: "What type of a horse does the King ride?"

"A great black charger, big enough to carry the King in his plate armor," answered Flymtt.

"And the color of the armor?" asked Stern.

"Silver with gold flourishes," said Flymtt, throwing the towel to the side.

Stern closed his eyes again and watched the horse rear in panic before the bear and throw the King from his silver saddle.

"I will go with you," he said, as the image faded.

Kylla frowned and then said sadly, "I will accompany you to the Keep."

Stern was touched by her loyalty but he feared for her safety. "It is not necessary. I owe you my life but my journey is not yours."

"You are right. Your fate is not mine. The great goddess has given me my own. I saw in a dream that I am to accompany you."

Flymtt slapped his hands together and asked, "When do we leave?"

After eating, they packed up their few possessions, mostly weapons and a sack of oats. Kylla filled her quiver with arrows, and Stern traded his sword for a polearm and borrowed a pair of leather gloves from Syrl. Myrr handed them a goatskin water bag, which Fymmt carried, dangling from his right shoulder. Kylla hugged and kissed her three kinsmen, who stood in front of the hut, watching the three set out toward the west.

They would journey due west until they reached the King's Road, which ran from the Northern Keep, a fortress on the coast near the spot where Stern washed ashore, to Stormcrow, the King's massive keep on the southern heights above a fjord that extended one mile from the sea and opened up into a natural harbor called Wyvernne. Once they made the road, Flymtt said, they would head south to Milieu, a town in the middle of the great forest, to obtain horses and supplies.

Later, as they walked, Stern asked, "How long will it take us to reach the King's Keep?"

"We will plan to reach the King's Road in three or four days and then it will take another three weeks to get to Milieu. The journey from Milieu to Wyvernne is a fortnight on horseback and another two days from Wyvernne to the Keep."

"I thought you said Wyvernne was only a mile from Stormcrow."

"By boat in the fjord but you cannot reach the Keep from the water. To get to Stormcrow from Wyvernne, we will have to travel a very circuitous route through the surrounding mountains."

"Will I be able to find a ship to take us to Bedwyr's island?"

"It is possible, if the King grants you leave?"

"Does every person seeking to depart the island have to pray for the King's leave?"

"Of course not," answered Flymtt.

"Then why should I seek his leave or even travel to Stormcrow?"

"You must go because you are not one of the King's subjects." Flymtt stepped toward Stern, his eyes flashing, his hand reaching for one of his curved daggers. "That's the second time you implied disobedience to my liege."

Stern sighed and said, "If I must see your king to book passage on a ship then I will see your king." Stern noticed that Kylla had moved to his right and he suspected she was prepared to strike Flymtt if he attacked Stern.

Flymtt relaxed, "You are different from when I pulled you off the beach, Stern, and more confident than when I found you naked. You also speak my language well. How has this happened?" He paused and rubbed his chin. "Were you lying before?"

Stern had been unaware he was speaking the guttural language of the island.

"I have had a good teacher these last few days."

Flymtt smiled grimly and turned his back on Stern. "Let's waste no more time talking about kings."

Stern felt better today for some reason. He had somehow overcome some of the fear and anxiety that had haunted him since he had fallen into this world from Mittilagart."

They spoke little as they walked. The snow was melting and it was much warmer. The remaining leaves on the trees, however, frozen in the unnatural storm, were falling and the earth was wet and muddy. Near dusk, Kylla left their party to scout out a suitable spot to spend the night, as Stern and Flymtt continued their westward trek.

"I thought your woman was about to attack me earlier."

Stern said nothing. After a while Flymtt continued, "Who is she?"

"She protected me from Focalor."

"Is she one of the hidden people?"

"Hidden people? I don't know what you are talking about?" He dissembled.

"If she is, you should take care. They are werewolves."

"You think she is a *lykan*."

"What does that mean?"

"It means wolf-man. There is an ancient myth of a man, Lycaon, a king by the way, who fed a god human flesh and the god punished him by turning him into a wolf."

"Exactly," he said. "I think she is a wolf-man or I guess a wolf-woman."

Stern laughed, not because he thought Flymtt would be deceived by his laughter, but because Flymtt had no idea of Kylla's abilities or his and this thought provided him a little solace.

Kylla waited for them beneath a birch tree.

"I have found an outcropping of stones ahead that will provide shelter for the night."

Flymtt cleared his throat of phlegm and spat onto the ground in arrogance. "Lead on," he said gruffly, looking over his shoulder at Stern, who smiled and winked at Kylla.

She sent him a question silently, *"What does that mean, that signal with the eye?"*

"It means take care around Flymtt. He suspects you are a werewolf."

"A werewolf!" she exclaimed. *"I should strike him down right now."*

"Calm down. I need him to obtain passage on a ship."

"I fear you're walking into a trap. His King is not noted for his good deeds."

They bedded down in a recess in the stone outcropping. Flymtt offered to take the first watch. Stern and Kylla wrapped themselves in their cloaks and fell into a deep sleep. Several hours later, Flymtt shook Stern awake, whispering: "I can't keep my eyes open. You take the watch."

Stern stood still at the opening of the stone's recess. A full moon illuminated the forest, causing dramatic gray shadows to stretch silently beneath the trees. An owl hooted in the night, as another type of bird glided beneath the branches of the trees and landed on a twisted limb of an ancient oak nearby. Stern pushed a thought at the bird then jumped, startled by Coyote's clear response. *"Help me, Stern. He has trapped me in this bird's body."*

Stern answered, *"I do not possess the power to free you but Kylla may. I will talk with her."* He felt Coyote's suffering but he needed to know about Focalor. *"Where is the daemon?"*

"He is a day behind you. One of his dogs picked up your trail early this morning and he is pushing hard to catch you."

"Are they still moving?"

"They stopped for the night."

"Will you tell them you have found me?"

"I must. I cannot keep him from my mind."

"Have you told him already?"

121

"He is sleeping."

Stern moved to Kylla's side and gently shook her. She immediately awoke and he whispered into her ear, "Coyote is in the big oak, there." He pointed toward the tree. She squinted and eventually made out his silhouette framed by moonlight. Stern watched as she strung her bow, pulled a long black arrow from her quiver, and, carefully, nocked it. He sighed heavily as she pulled the bow back and let fly the deadly dart. Coyote's shock and pain filled his mind, as he heard the bird fall from the tree onto the earth. Tears coursed down his cheeks. "He was a friend."

"I know but he was trapped. He would not be able to keep our location from Focalor and neither you nor I had the power to free him in time. If he lived, he would have disclosed our location."

Stern felt a physical ache as sharp and hard as the pain he suffered at the death of the Argyll woman, who gave birth to his son. He had not even winced when he killed the men in the forest but Coyote's death shook him. He now resolved he must not let anyone or anything prevent him from reaching Bedwyr; he owed Coyote the success of the mission and Focalor a death. He resolved he would destroy the daemon, if possible.

Kylla left the camp and did not return until dawn. When she appeared she carried two rabbits, skinned and gutted. Flymtt awoke and stretched, unaware of the fall of Coyote. When Flymtt saw Kylla, he frowned and asked, "Where have you been?" She raised the rabbits and said, "Hunting, but unfortunately, we do not have time to cook these now. Focalor is only a day's march behind us."

Flymtt scrambled to his feet and pulled his few possessions together. "We had better move, then."

Within moments of his rising they were running through the forest at a steady but comfortable stride. Flymtt led the way, followed by Kylla and Stern, who tightened his belt, steadied his breathing, and jogged behind the two islanders. Slowly, he fell behind, unable to keep up their pace. He had spent his life on the back of a horse. In the Black Robes, he was a *jinete*, a mounted soldier. He determined to call for a stop, only if they disappeared from view.

After two hours, Flymtt stopped by a rivulet of running water and drank. Stern collapsed on the ground as soon as he reached them. Flymtt sternly commanded, "We will rest for a quarter of an hour and then move on." Later, somewhat recovered, Stern tightened the laces on his boots and secured his weapons, then bent down and drank from the stream with his right hand, as Kylla watched the way they had come.

"What is it?" asked Flymtt.

"I hear hounds."

"Where are we?" muttered Flymtt to himself. He scraped the ground clear of snow and dead leaves and drew a quick map with a dried twig. "I think we are half way to the road. If I am right, there is an outcropping of rocks here. If we turn south and head to the rocks, we might lose the hounds."

Kylla interjected: "A good plan but I have one suggestion. When we reach the rocks I will stay behind and fight the dogs."

The rogue smiled. "Brave suggestion but we will have better luck if we all stay and fight. We will kill the dogs and bury their bodies. Our attack will cut off Focalor's nose and buy us some time."

"I hope you're good with that bow," said Flymtt. "We should also make some spears." Turning to Stern, he said: "If you see any limbs that might make a spear, pick it up. Also, you can no longer linger behind us in this run. From now on, you will run in the middle and keep close to me. And watch the end of that polearm, I don't relish being skewered."

A few moments later Flymtt said, "Ready. It is time to fly." He turned toward the southwest and bolted across the stream and set a steady pace. Stern fell in behind him and ran as hard as he could, while Kylla took up the rear, carrying the long bow in her right hand.

Several hours later, as the sun descended and the shadows of the trees lengthened, Stern heard the first baying moan of the hounds. Flymtt picked up the pace and breathlessly called out: "The rocks are near. Run hard and good luck."

At the sound of the hounds, Kylla passed them, lengthening her stride in a brave attempt to reach the rocks first and prepare their defense. By the time Stern reached her, Kylla stood behind a makeshift wall of gray stones. She had pushed eight black arrows into the earth around her feet and nocked an arrow in her bow. The rogue took up a position next to her and began to sharpen the end of one of the limbs he had picked up on the trail, while Stern pulled off his cloak, hid it in a recess in the rocks, and discarded any other excess items he carried. Flymtt handed him the water bag and his cloak to place with the other items.

They stood ready, listening to the dogs rushing through the woods. Stern knew some would be faster than others and he hoped they would come at them piecemeal. A vision of the black bear sprang into his mind and he felt dizzy, as if the bear were pushing him aside to take his place in battle. He swallowed and shook his head, trying to focus on the coming attackers. He saw a large, short-haired dog emerge from the woods, its tongue lolling from its great head. Kylla released her first arrow, which took the hound squarely in the chest. The dog sprang up, its paws scratching at the shaft of the arrow that was buried deep into its flesh. Blood spurted freely as the dog tried to escape the pain of the wooden shaft, twisting and turning in agony. Before the arrow struck the first dog, Kylla had nocked another arrow.

Flymtt, in an adrenaline rush, sang out to the sky, "What a woman!"

Stern turned the polearm in his sweaty palms, waiting for the next hound to appear. Three dogs rushed from the woods together but slowed and stopped to sniff at the now still body of the red dog, lying in a pool of blood. In that moment, Kylla let one and then another arrow fly, both of which found their targets. The last dog standing turned in a circle, confused and frightened. Kylla strung a third arrow and downed the hound, as Flymtt jumped up and down in excitement at their luck and Kylla's skill.

Stern said, "Calm down. That's only four. We know that there are at least eight."

As Kylla extracted five more arrows and stuck them into the earth, Stern heard a thrashing from the forest and then the next brute emerged from the trees. He gasped at the size of the creature. "That couldn't be a dog," Stern whispered. The rogue groaned and said, "that's no dog; it is a kroaxx."

"A kroaxx?" asked Stern, his mouth open in shock.

"I thought the King rid this island of those benighted creatures years ago," observed Kylla.

"He did. It's a crime to breed them or to house them," answered Flymtt.

The kroaxx lumbered onto the first stones of the escarpment and stopped. A white glob of saliva fell from its wide snout onto the earth, as Stern gasped at its saber tooth-like canines protruding from its black maul, its massive chest moving in and out like a blacksmith's billows and the thick massive bone that formed its square head and flat skull.

"We can outrun them," said Flymtt nervously.

"He is too close to run. He will spring if he sees you run," responded Kylla calmly.

"Can't you down him with an arrow?" asked Stern.

She shook her head and then to prove her point, she nocked an arrow and let it fly. It struck the kroaxx in the head and bounced off, leaving a bright red tear in the monster's blue-black hide.

As they watched the beast, two more emerged from the shadows of the forest.

Letting out a sigh, Kylla said, "You must back away slowly. I will hold them here as long as I can." As she picked up another arrow, she said: "Leave the polearm here for me. I will need it."

"I can't leave you," said Stern, moving to her side. "We will fight together."

"Don't be stupid. You must reach Bedwyr and I must do what I can to help you on your way."

The rogue was already backing away from them. Once he was several yards away he turned and ran across the escarpment, picking up his cloak and their water on the way, jumped off the rocks and sprinted toward the west, heading for the King's road.

Stern pulled on Kylla's arm, like a worried child. "We will go together."

"No, these creatures are bred to fight dragons. We cannot defeat them but I can keep them busy. As soon as you are away I will change into the boar and lead them away but I can't do it if you are standing here. Go, follow the rogue, but don't trust him or the King." She turned and noted the figure of the rogue disappearing over the horizon. "Never mind, he's gone. Don't follow him; run south. As soon as you reach the woods, transform into the wolf and stay a wolf until you are far away from here."

She kissed him on the cheek and then pushed him away from her side, as the kroaxx bristled and growled at the sudden move. "Run now. They are about to attack."

Stern turned, saddened and disgusted with himself. He could not run; he would not run. He took his polearm from her hand and said, "I will stand with you."

"But who will deal with the dragons in your world? If you remain with me you will die."

The largest kroaxx began its march up the gradual incline of the escarpment. Seeing that he meant to stay, Kylla smiled and turned from Stern with a shrug and pulled the string of her bow back and let go another arrow that pierced the nearest creature between its black beady eyes. The beast simply shook its head and continued forward, while the other two followed in its wake. Stern was initially terrified; however, as the kroaxx drew closer, he became angry. He imagined killing Focalor because he now blamed Focalor for the dragons flying over Mittilagart, the death of Coyote, and the challenge to Kylla. As an addendum, he vowed to kill Flymtt for his cowardice.

The kroaxx's movement was slow and deliberate and Stern was losing what little patience he had. Kylla had released two more arrows into the beast. Except for some black blood, Stern could see no effect. Kylla dropped her bow and pulled her two short swords and prepared to attack. When she plunged forward, Stern ran next to her, screaming at the top of his lungs. She struck at the creature's front legs, as Stern rammed his polearm deep into the kroaxx's massive throat.

The kroaxx cracked the polearm in two with one mighty swing and then pounced on Kylla. The blow broke her right arm and threw her back onto the rocks of the escarpment. Stern jumped on the animal's back and stabbed his dagger into its thick muscles at the base of its skull. The kroaxx reared, throwing him back, as one of the smaller beasts ripped through his pants, cutting deeply into his thighs.

Stern lay stunned on the rocks; however, before the kroaxx could strike again, the hidden black bear appeared in his conscious mind as real as if he saw the creature on the side of a mountain in mid-day. His whole body shuddered and shook with the might of the creature, darkening his mind with a vicious, raging madness, and he swiped at the smaller kroaxx with a gigantic black paw that ripped open its dry hardened skin, exposing guts and spraying blood. The other kroaxx, smelling blood and exposed bowel, turned away from Kylla, who now lay unconscious on the rocks, and moved toward the black bear that stood on its hind legs, bellowing threats.

The bear attacked the largest kroaxx first, fending off its attack with several quick blows to its left side. Soon the creature was blind and bleeding and the bear finished the animal by tearing the sinews of its great neck with its massive jaws. The smaller kroaxx attacked the bear's left hind leg and tore flesh. With the pain of the wound searing his mind, Stern's rage became so great he lost all consciousness of himself and what was happening. He became the bear completely and as the bear he ripped and tore relentlessly into the kroaxx, until his fur was drenched in their blood. Even when they were dead he continued to rampage across the rocks, tearing their bodies into pieces and feeding on their entrails until he collapsed. When he awoke he was lying in a puddle of blood, naked and cold. The bodies of the kroaxx were ripped and scattered over the escarpment.

Stern staunched the wounds on his legs with remnants of his clothes. He then crawled to Kylla, whose crushed, lifeless body lay between two large rocks several meters to the north. Tears welled into his eyes and he moaned at the fading light, as night fell. Sometime near dawn, he awoke from a feverish sleep. Kylla's body lay inert next to him. He heard voices in the distance and he smelled wood smoke. Focalor was near.

Stern remembered Kylla's last words to him. As she instructed, he sat, as they had sat many nights and meditated on the wolf. He saw its great yellow eyes and black fur first and then he consciously shifted his shape into a large black wolf with yellow eyes and great white fangs. He sniffed the air and counted the men in the woods; he paused over Kylla's broken body on the rocks then he marked the rocks of the escarpment with his scent before bouncing off toward the south, away from Focalor, away from the King, and away from Flymtt, who, he had now decided, must die like the kroaxx and Focalor.

Chapter Nineteen: The Brotherhood of Mithlass

THE WOLF WITH THE YELLOW EYES slunk south through the shadowed woods. Its intent was to reach the Wyvernne harbor and take passage on a ship to find Bedwyr. In his wolf's brain, Stern had not worked out all of the details, he simply padded south, covering twenty to thirty miles a day, bypassing any communities, and feeding off rabbits, mice and squirrels. Finally, he paused on a hill overlooking a primitive community at the crossroads of two wide roads. One road he knew was called the King's Road and it ran from a keep in the north to the king's fortress in the south. The other extended from east to west and he had no idea of its name. He left the hill and slept in a shallow cave until sunset. In the dark, he crossed the new road and entered the woods about a mile south of the city, which he guessed was Milieu.

He wandered in the woods southwest of Milieu for almost a week, always moving in a southerly direction. After a time, his human mind fell into a stupor and he was more wolf than a man. Sometimes, he dreamed of the bear and the bloody battle with the kroaxx. At other times he dreamed of the Argyll woman, the *lunar bruja*, Kylla, and Gotha. In those dreams the four women seemed one. In his reveries, they were mothers, ministering to him, sacred women.

The weather changed yet again. At first, it was unseasonably warm and then the rains began. He huddled in a hollow, rotten tree for several days as the rain poured down on the island. Then, the cold returned and the ground froze and the sky turned a steel gray, impenetrable in its sharpness, as he resumed his journey.

At dusk, several days later, he reached a wide clearing. Rolling green hills lay before him and he smelled sheep, pigs and rabbits. In the distance he saw a villa with several outbuildings and barns. When the wind changed he picked up the scent of two men. He sought them out and watched as they cut several dead trees up for firewood. They worked steadily, each wielding double-headed axes. They wore brown linen pants and gray cotton shirts and their heavy woolen coats were draped over a stump. They laughed and sang as they worked and something about their jocularity touched his mind. He was lonely and his innate humanness demanded a return to the world of men; however, he was suspicious of the islanders now, so he decided to watch these humans for a few days before he revealed himself. Other than the axes, he saw no other weapons and he suspected they were workers indentured to the villa.

The next day, a group of men exited the villa early in the morning, carrying large scythes on their shoulders, marching in a single line to a field in the eastern corner of the clearing to cut wheat. So far, he had seen no children or women.

That night it snowed. He decided he would reveal himself tomorrow, so when the sun began to rise, he lay in a hollow beneath a great tree and meditated on his humanness as Kylla taught him. It was difficult to concentrate because his wolfishness now willed to dominate and control him. But finally he shifted.

He was filthy and smelled of wolf. The wounds on his legs had healed but vicious ugly scars remained. He searched for an evergreen tree, broke-off several boughs from the trunk and made a makeshift skirt. He scratched his long beard and hair that crawled with lice and fleas, as he marched from the woods and moved slowly toward the villa. He hoped he could attract someone's attention before he came too close to the buildings and the dogs of the house. He had become very leery of dogs; they sniffed the wolf within him and reminded him of the kroaxx.

Several meters from a smokehouse, Stern came upon two men watching him. One pointed at him and called out a warning. In response, four men emerged from a stone barn, one of whom brandished a large pitchfork, then all six men moved toward him. Stern remained still and waited.

They stopped about two meters from him.

"I have been attacked and robbed. Can you help me?" croaked Stern.

The men did not answer and he wondered if they understood him. Maybe, he thought, people in the south speak a different language. A man riding a large white horse and wearing a wide slouch hat, a brown leather coat and brown woolen pants and black work boots, galloped from the villa. He drew back hardily on the reins, halting the horse, and calling out to Stern, without dismounting, "Who are you and where do you come from?"

"My name is Stern and I am from an island in the north," dissembled Stern. "I shipwrecked on your northern coast and I'm traveling south to book passage on a ship."

"Stern, you tell me nothing. What island in the north? Where in the south? What is your destination?"

Stern cleared his throat and rubbed his tongue over his teeth before answering. "I am from a small, nameless island in the north, and I travel to Wyvernne to catch a ship to Bedwyr's island."

"That is better. I have never heard of an unnamed island. If there are people, there is always a name. However, there are as many islands as there are stars, some are inhabited, others are not. However, Noirrith, Bedwyr's home, I know. It's a small rugged rock that houses monks and magickers. Why do you seek the shadow master?"

"I seek Bedwyr, the blacksmith, only. I have heard he can provide me with a weapon to rid my island of dragons. As to this term—shadow master—that you use, it is the first time I have heard it."

The man relaxed in the saddle and leaned forward to address Stern. "Why do men fear dragons? Dragons are the prime beings of this world. They are as natural as the water that flows around the earth, as light as the air, and as hot as the hottest fires," he spoke haughtily. Stern suspected the man was ridiculing the king and making fun of him at the same time.

"This dragon kills the people of my island. They huddle in fear in their homes, afraid to walk the earth. We are trapped and intimidated by these flying snakes. Besides, I understand your King hates the dragons and battles them wherever he finds them."

"See, there is the rub. The King is afraid and your people are afraid. They see the dragon as something unlike them, as another. How do you imagine the dragon views you?"

"Obviously as food," said Stern, growing tired of the man's pompous tone.

The man laughed and shifted in the saddle. "Exactly," he said with a laugh. "You are but a part of the food chain."

Stern shivered. The wind kicked up and snowflakes fell gently. He cursed his luck. It seemed he was destined to walk through the elemental world naked.

"I see you are cold. Tell me about these rogues that robbed you."

"I was traveling with two companions—a servant of the King that I met at the inn of *The Drowned Man* and a woman we encountered in the woods. Men and dogs set upon us. The rogue fled and the woman was killed in the fight. I survived, although I suffered many wounds as you can see. They stripped us of our armor, weapons and coins."

"Where did this attack occur?" the man asked; his eyes half-closed, as if he were bored or sleepy.

"South of *The Drowned Man* and north of Milieu," answered Stern quickly because now he was telling the truth. "We left the road to escape them but the dogs caught us on a stone escarpment."

The man stared at Stern for a long time and he felt a vague tickle as the man tried to discern the truth of his tale. From his experience with Kylla, Stern knew this man had a rudimentary talent for thought talk, yet the extent of his power manifested itself in intuition only. Stern, sensing the man's limitation, sent the thought, *"trust me."*

Finally, the man straightened in the saddle and said in a loud voice, as if addressing the group, "I trust this man and I believe his journey, though wrongheaded, is righteous.

"Stern, follow young Jarllx to the bathhouse. He will administer to your needs. Steam and bathe and when you are finished we will have clothing and a meal for you. Then I will ask you to meet me in the Round Room to discuss your journey in detail.

"Jarllx, send word to the surgeon to have him examine Stern and ask Maskkus, to provide clothing for him."

Jarllx bowed and then signaled Stern to follow him to the bathhouse on the eastern side of the villa. Once there, Jarllx suggested they start with steam and then hot water.

Stern lay on a wooden bench, as the heat penetrated his sore body and opened his pours. Jarllx dripped water over the heated rocks; their bodies were slick with sweat. He, then, showed Stern how to scrap his body with a sharpened bone to remove the dirt and grime.

After the steam, Jarllx pointed the way to a small door that opened upon a stone room with a large heated pool. As they entered, he took a large bar of soap and a pumice stone from a table made of pine and handed it to Stern.

Finished with the bath, Jarllx asked Stern, "Shall I shave you?"

"Do you have a mirror?" asked Stern, rubbing his fingers through his beard.

"A mirror?" asked the young man.

"Yes, to see myself. Also, I would like to clean my teeth and trim my nails."

Jarllx left and returned in a few minutes with a crude mirror, a straight razor, scissors, and a small brush for his teeth. Stern grunted his thanks and then cleaned his teeth and cut his nails. Examining his beard in the mirror, he decided to keep it. He trimmed the prodigious mustache and rounded the beard, then asked Jralxx to shave the top of his head.

Two hours after arriving at the villa, Stern was clean and groomed and wearing a pair of brown linen pants, a woolen shirt, and leather vest. Instead of boots, the inhabitants of the villa, when not working, wore thick woolen socks and leather sandals. To top off his outfit, Jarllx handed Stern a red, knit cap that covered his bald pate.

Snow was falling as they left the bathhouse and the temperature had dropped. Jarllx led Stern through the powdery snow to a long rectangular stone building that possessed two stone chimneys, one at each end of the rectangle edifice. As they entered, Jarllx pointed out that the building served as a kitchen, smokehouse, storage, and dining room.

A man, wearing a white woolen smock, placed a bowl of porridge on a long wooden table and pointed at it with one hand, as he took his seat and reached for a wooden spoon with the other. As Stern took his first bite, the man with the white smock placed a pewter stein of beer next to his bowl. He slurped the simple fare down in a most wolfish way and washed it down with the brew. Finishing quickly, he asked for a second bowl but the man in the white tunic shook his head and called for Jarllx, who was sitting next to the fire, smoking a pipe. Jarllx tapped his pipe against the stones of the hearth and signaled for Stern to follow him to a stone building in the center of the compound. Passing through its double-door entrance, they climbed wide, oaken stairs to a cubicle on a crowded second floor, where, in the cubicle, they found the pompous man on the horse sitting behind a large desk. He motioned for Stern to take the only other chair. The gesture, so bureaucratic, reminded Stern of the Black Robes; and he asked himself, "*How many days have passed?*" And realized he had no idea.

"Stern, I am the Magister here. My name is Blut, so I am called Magister Blut. Do you understand?"

"Yes, I am to call you Magister Blut," said Stern solemnly.

"Correct. By using my title you're honoring Him, who we serve."

"May I ask, to whom you are referring?"

"You really are a barbarian, aren't you?"

Stern shrugged his shoulders.

"We worship the god of war, Mithlass, first begotten of the mother."

"The great goddess?" he asked, trying to remember Kylla's instruction.

"No, the great mother, the mother of us all," the man snapped.

"You mean the spider god?" It was beginning to come back to him.

"Yes, the begetter of the world."

Stern sat quietly for a few moments, thinking about Kylla, before Blut interrupted his thoughts. "Mithlass is the lion god and we are his servants. We are monks and soldiers, mercenaries really, who hire ourselves out to the kings and queens of this world. We use our earnings to buy land and build our sanctuaries. This compound is one of the oldest."

"I did not see many men."

"That is because the King sent five thousand of our best men to their deaths in the south in a stupid trade war against Brasilika and the followers of Tandraxx. We are now starting over, seeking out young devotees to take the pledge."

"You fought the Amazon warriors of Tandraxx?"

"Does that surprise you?"

"But why would you fight them?" He worried about Gotha's safety.

"I understand your point. They follow Tandraxx, Mithlass' sister, the warrior witch, their sacred goddess. They should be our allies. I agree but they aligned themselves with Brasilika against the King. It is true that he is a pragmatist, power hungry and willful. He tolerates us only because we provide warriors stronger and more determined than his musketeers. For this he pays us and we fight for him. We fight even against our natural allies."

Stern winced.

"Have I said something that disturbs you?" asked the Magister, noticing the look on Stern's face.

"I am a foreigner here and I do not want to contradict your laws and beliefs but I am contracted with a Tandraxx to father a child and one of my most trusted mentors was a Keltoi."

"Stern, you are very trusting man. These facts alone could cause your death on this island."

"Perhaps, I misunderstood you. I felt you were being candid with me, so I am being honest with you."

The man leaned forward and extended his hand across the table. "Take my hand in friendship and trust, Stern. However, do not share this information with my men. Do you hear me?"

Stern gripped his hand and, suddenly, unbidden, a tear welded up in his eye and ran down his cheek. Stern attributed his sudden emotion to his loneliness and the stress he had been under for the last few weeks. Additionally, he was relieved although he had not trusted the man at first and thought him a self-righteous prig.

Blut cleared his throat and said, "It is good that we speak frankly. When you told me of your plans I was somewhat startled because it was as if fate had presented you to me at the most opportune time."

"How so?" asked Stern, wiping his eyes.

"We have a brother monastery and contingent of warriors seconded to Noirrith and I need to send a message to the Magister there. I was prepared to use one of the younger men but I cannot afford to lose anyone at this time. I only have forty men and twenty-seven of them are novices. The King's hubris has nearly destroyed us. Magister Blatt has ten thousand men situated in four large camps on Noirrith and I am petitioning him to send my three thousand brothers back to us.

"I will be even franker with you," he continued. "The King has decided to revoke our charter. Because of our losses in Brasilika, the land lies fallow and its resources must be worked. This is a valid reason to reject the charter I suppose but I fear there is another reason. He wants to rid the Island of us because we refuse to bend entirely to his will."

"Why do you find it difficult to serve him?"

"We are loyal only to Mithlass and the one who hires us can only rely on us as long as the contract lasts. Besides, we control vast estates rich in minerals, woods, horses, cattle, sheep, and cleared fields, which the King wants."

Stern stroked his beard and said: "I will gladly take your message to Magister Blatt."

The man smiled widely and rubbed his hands together. "In return, I will arm you, provide money for your passage, and send you to Wyvernne with an escort of eight warrior monks."

Blut stood and they shook hands again with genuine feeling.

"When should I leave?"

"Winter is coming and when it arrives the harbor will be frozen for at least six months. If you are to leave this year you must go immediately."

"The sooner, the better for me," said Stern, imagining the ocean freezing solid.

"What is your weapon?" asked Blut, warming to the subject. He was a man of action and now something was happening.

"Polearm and daggers," said Stern, remembering the fight with Kylla.

"Excellent choice," he said and then yelled: "Jarllx!"

The young man stuck his head around the corner. "Take Stern to the armory and help him select the weapons of his choice. Also provide him with leather armor and saddlebags. He will need some extra clothes and personal items such as straight razor, toothbrush and under clothes.

Turning back to Stern, he said: "You will leave at dawn. Tonight dine with me and by tomorrow I will have the message ready. I will ask you to memorize it in case you are captured and I will require you to take an oath of loyalty to Mithlass."

Stern rubbed his bald head and felt a moment of resistance and a pang of guilt at the thought he was not only being asked to swear an allegiance to a pagan god but out of necessity he was in all likelihood going to do it. He weighed his loyalty to his mission against the greater good and found his fear of the witches and the protection of his son greater than any oath. But he did not have to choose at this moment; instead, he pushed the nagging ache of guilt out of his mind and followed Jarllx to the armory, where he selected two long curved daggers and a six-foot long polearm. He also took two short dirks that he fit snugly into his boots and a leather baldric in which he inserted four throwing knives. In another room, he gathered up in his arms a black leather jerkin, a pair of matching leather pants, a steel helmet, painted black, and an all-weather cloak made of wool.

As Jarllx helped him squeeze into the armor, he asked, "What about a bow?"

"I have had no experience with it," said Stern

Jarllx handed him a crossbow. "You think you could handle this? It is easier to use than the long bow."

Stern smiled and said, "This I can handle."

Jarllx removed a quiver with thirty black bolts from a hook on the wall and handed it to Stern, who looked around the room and asked, "Gloves?"

Later in the day, after Stern had stored away his new clothes and equipment, he met Blut and Jarllx in the common room of the dormitory for dinner.

"It is very quiet here," noted Stern looking up from his food.

"You should have seen it when we had our full complement of monks," growled Jarllx, his mouth full of roasted duck.

Blut drank some of the golden mead brewed by the monks and said, "We made a tactical mistake, believing in the King. I now think he knew he was sending our men to their death and that was his intention all along. He desires our land." He shook his head and wiped froth from his mouth.

"This King controls only this island?" asked Stern.

"He also rules a few worm-eaten colonies in the south."

"It is a very small kingdom," said Stern absently.

"What is your point?"

"My point is that the world is large and this kingdom is quite small. If the King is as greedy as you say, then he will not just stop with your lands. Does he have aspirations for a larger kingdom?"

"Our world is covered almost entirely by water. There are thousands of islands and only two larger lands. The King has sent ships all around the world looking for habitable islands to establish colonies, he has such a small army and navy that he has been frustrated in his ambition. That is why he hired us to battle Brasilika."

"What is Brasilika?"

"It is a large island to the south. Its Witch Queen, Sycorax and her son have conquered and colonized over fifty islands. Her latest conquest is an island just six weeks voyage from Wyvernne. It is the nearest inhabited island without a nest of dragons and that is where we engaged her army."

"Have you thought of taking one of these islands as your own?"

"What do you mean?"

"I am asking you why you sell your sword. Why not take one of these islands for your own or for Mithlass? That would make the most sense."

Blut looked as if he had seen a ghost. "You mean act autonomously against the King and establish our own country?"

Stern answered quickly: "Or against a queen, a daemon, or a magus. You have the power and the expertise obviously to conquer an island and inhabit it. What do they have, except some pretended right to sovereignty? Through your own choice, you would gain land for your order and you would no longer wager your lives on the whim of a monarch."

"You are a revolutionary!" gasped Jarllx.

"No, I'm a simple man, a blacksmith by trade."

After dinner, a short, stout man with a thick black beard entered the room, carrying a valise.

Blut said, "This is Karlxx. He will mark you for the ceremony tomorrow."

"What type of mark?" asked Stern.

"He will use inks and needles to tattoo your skin with the mark of Mithlass."

"Show me this mark."

Blut rolled up the sleeve of the silk shirt he wore and showed Stern a tattoo on the forearm of his left arm of a figure with the head of a golden-maned lion, a man's torso, and the lower body of a fish. The inked avatar held a trident in its right hand and wand in the other.

Stern gulped and Blut slapped him on the back and asked: "Are you ready? You should drink some more mead to dull the pain of the needles."

Stern rolled up the rough linen sleeve of his shirt and took a seat beneath a gold candelabrum. He heard the wind kick up outside the dormitory and he shivered.

Blut drinking yet another tankard of mead said, "Winter is approaching. It is good you are leaving tomorrow." Jarllx handed him another tankard, which he noisily drank down in one long gulp.

Later, he awoke in a narrow cell on the third floor of the dormitory. Dreaming, he stood on a vast field on a great island, where two armies faced each other on a rolling plain, and in the center a beautiful woman with long black hair, wearing red armor, stood in a silver chariot drawn by three black stallions. She chanted loudly and the clouds gathered at her back and the armies cringed at her power, as she reached out her hand and called for the blue-back dragon warriors to join her.

Awake now Stern realized he had to relieve himself and he found a clay pot under the bed. His arm ached and his head throbbed. Finished, he crawled back under the rough blankets, pulling them over his head. For a moment he thought of Gotha and then Kylla. Kylla seemed more real to him at that moment. He heard her voice say, "Remember the Keltoi." Later, Jarllx nudged his shoulder, awakening him from yet another dream. His throat was dry but his headache was gone and his arm no longer hurt. He looked at the tattoo and he admitted he liked it. He washed, shaved his head, and combed his voluptuous black beard. With a smile, he pulled on the leather armor and adjusted his weapons. His green eyes sparkled with energy he had not felt in weeks.

He joined twenty of the monks in the dining hall and ate a hearty breakfast of porridge, bacon, and flagons of mead. As he finished eating, Blut stood, recited a prayer and then called Stern to the front. He ordered him to kneel and repeat the oath of Mithlass. Afterwards, the men stood and raised a cheer.

Blut accompanied him outside, where he handed him a small leather pouch he pinned to his linen shirt underneath his leather jerkin. Jarllx, mounted on a tall roan gelding, held the reins of a black mare, only fifteen hands high. Stern's poleaxe was in a scabbard astride the horse's flanks and his saddlebags and bedroll attached to the saddle. Eight mounted monks waited, each equipped with black armor, silver helms molded to mimic the head of Mithlass and dark red cloaks. Stern shook Blut's hand and Blut asked him to repeat the message into his ear, which he did.

Mounting his horse, Stern followed Jarllx toward the compound's gate, as the escort of monks fell in behind, two abreast. Stern turned in the saddle and waved to Blut. He squeezed his thighs and the mare cantered to the front of the line next to Jarllx. T-hey exited the compound, heading east on a wide stone road, the horses' shoes clacking against the slate gray cobblestones. As the men cleared the gate, they shouted in unison, "May we soon lie between Bestar's thighs."

It was cold and Stern smelled snow. Somewhere ahead he imagined Focalor waiting for him.

Chapter Twenty: Wounded Daemon

THEY FOLLOWED THE ROAD throughout the day. Jarllx said he was happy the weather held and the men piped up that they were happy to be on the road and not working in the fields. They camped in a clump of trees a few hundred yards off the road at dusk and Jarllx said to Stern, as they stripped the saddles from their horses, "Tomorrow, we will reach the end of this trail then we'll take the King's road all the way to Wyvernne. It is not as good as our roads and there will be others on it. Be aware the inhabitants of this island do not love us. They think we are rich and that our god is a demon; consequently, do not engage anyone in conversation and if they taunt us ignore them.

Later, they ate hardtack and drank tea beside a fire. The night was cold and the monks predicted snow. Stern rubbed his hands together and asked Jarllx about Mithlass.

"What do you want to know?"

"I don't know, really. Is there a book of holy writings?"

"There are writings but not by Mithlass. Just stories really. Mithlass is a warrior god and warriors are not great writers or readers for that matter. We don't believe in magicking or incantations. It is simply prayers and offerings."

"Offerings?" asked Stern, trying to keep the discussion going.

"We sacrifice a bull before battle. The priest, if there is one about, will read the entrails."

"Are there stories about his birth?"

Jarllx turned on his side and rested his head on his right hand. "Of course there are. There are many; some of them contradictory. What is agreed is that Mithlass was the first born son of Okeanus, the father of this world. Okeanus was born of Gyrrl."

'The Spider god?" asked Oiseau.

"That's what some call her. In our language, it is *Großmutter* or *Mutti*. In the common tongue of the Island, it is Great Mother or Mother Goddess."

"The Great Mother," repeated Stern.

"From her darkness, the Mother birthed a legion of gods into the universe. Okeanus, one of the nine first born, created this world from his body and from the world, which he called Erde, he sired Mithlass. And, as his firstborn, he was told to guard the world from nothingness and from any brothers and sisters that emerged from nothingness."

"Was there any danger in the void? I mean there was nothingness, yes?"

"Being, in form of the first gods, emerged from the void and was susceptible to falling back. The void or Chaos constantly called out for the baby gods to return. When Mithlass heard the call, he answered it with a threat."

"What type of threat?"

"Mithlass threatened to end nothingness's darkness by filling the void with light. That is why Mithlass is also called the god of light because it was he who brought the sun to drive back the nothingness of the void from which the Mother Goddess gave birth to the first gods."

"So, nothingness did not back down when Mithlass threatened to bring the sun."

"No, nothingness renewed its call for all beings to return to it and so Mithlass brought forth light, as he threatened."

"How did he do that?"

"He struck two stones together so hard that sparks flew into the void and became the stars. The closest star is our sun."

"Ah," said Stern, recognizing the usual tropes of pagan creation tales emerging from Jarllx's disquisition. "Then what happened?"

"Mithlass prayed to Okeanus for help in protecting the newborn gods. Okeanus heard his plea and created the sea and the islands. He then gave refuge to all the gods and spread them over the face of the watery world. Some landed on islands, while others splashed into the sea."

When he finished his story, Jarllx lay back and fell asleep. Stern rested on his back, gazing into the night sky, darkened by a mass of gray snow clouds, extinguishing a multitude of bright stars. In the distance he heard an owl and thought of Kylla; his world seemed a distant gaudy memory. He imagined Mithlass, the sun god, and he felt it all seemed so familiar. Eventually, he fell into a restless sleep and dreamed of a great black spider writhing in birth, spewing thousands of tiny black spiders from her womb out of the void. In his sleep he called out for the Mother Goddess to guide him.

He awoke in the dark. Sometime in the night he had pulled his woolen blanket over his head; nevertheless, he still awoke cold and stiff. He heard the men moving about the camp and he smelled porridge boiling. He crawled from beneath the blanket, which was covered in a fine patina of dry snow and ice, staggered to the edge of the camp and relieved himself against a dark green bush, drooping with red berries. Returning to the campsite, Jarllx handed him a cup of green tea, a tin of hot porridge and a biscuit. "When we reach the end of our road, we will cut across country until we reach the King's road. There is a large farm to the south where we will camp tonight."

Three hours later they reached the end of the Monk's road and Jarllx scanned the south. "See those two large oaks?"

"Yes," answered Stern, standing in the stirrups to garner a better view.

"We will head for them and then turn to the southwest. There is a trail in the woods that we will follow to the farm." Jarllx raised his right hand, signaling to the troop to move forward and the riders in column of twos stretched out over the clearing.

Stern enjoyed traveling with these monks, they were disciplined, professional and they effortlessly projected a sense of camaraderie. He felt some primal connection to them, a feeling of belonging, which he had not felt in years. Even though he wore a savage, primitive costume, he felt authentic and real in the saddle of his warhorse. Once they reached their goal, the two great oaks, Jarllx swung the column to the southwest and the forest.

They drew closer to the trees and Stern saw a wide worn path winding through a dense forest of hardwoods. They were riding in the rough now, away from the monk's well-maintained road. As predicted by Jarllx, the trail was more difficult. Stern found himself paying close attention to the trees and low-lying limbs. He was no longer aware of time; instead, he focused all of his attention on the trees and his horse. Jarllx, who had pulled ahead of him, riding authoritatively through the woods, pulled his horse brutally to a halt. Responding to his raised right arm, the column spread out in the woods behind him and halted. He dismounted and dropped the reins to the ground and his horse slowly edged to a clump of dried grass pushing up through the snow and began to graze. Stern, too, dismounted and approached Jarllx, who was examining the bark of a beech tree.

"The bark has been rubbed off and there is fresh blood," he whispered.

Walking around the tree, he muttered: "More blood here." He snapped his fingers and then held up two. The first two monks in the column, Martz and Cleave, dismounted and rushed to his side. "Track this spore. We will wait here. Don't do anything. Just find out what is going on." They shook their heads affirmatively and then unsheathed their swords.

Jarllx turned to Stern and said, "The farm is near. Finding blood is not a good sign." As he waited, Stern concentrated on sounds from the woods. He heard Martz and Cleave moving through the thick underbrush. One of them stepped on a rotten limb and he heard a dull crack. A flake of snow landed on Stern's nose, startling him, and a raven, disturbed by the sound, cawed and bolted from a naked black limb. Stern examined the clouds. Smelling snow, he remembered his plan to set sail before the waters froze and shivered, fearing he would not make it off the island before winter arrived.

They were coming back. Martz, the tall blue-eyed northerner with thick blond hair, led the way through the trees, while Cleave, the short, swarthy southerner, with almond-shaped eyes followed. When he reached Jarllx, Martz removed his helm and shook his head slowly. "There are five dead in a gully. One is a woman, who has been stripped and violated."

"Did you recognize anyone?" asked Jarllx.

Cleave pushed forward, "They were hands from the farm. One of them was Mattix, the goatherd."

Jarllx placed his hand on his sword and asked: "Did you see any tracks?"

"It was a large group," said Martz.

Cleave added, "They're headed toward the farm."

This fact seemed to galvanize Jarllx. "Martz, you and Cleave, follow the tracks through the woods. We will continue down the trail." Jarllx called out to Hemple, a young monk from an island in the west. He had red hair and a thick red mustache. "Scout ahead and keep your eyes open." He walked to his horse and, as he mounted, he called out: "Forward in a column of twos. Trantor and Millz take the point. Be on guard for a possible ambush."

The men mounted up quickly and formed up behind Trantor and Millz. When they were ready, Jarllx gave the command and Trantor and Millz moved forward in a gallop.

The column rode through the forest. All the while Stern concentrated on the woods. He felt his body shake with adrenalin and an image of the bear appeared in his mind. He fought the image away. He could not let these warrior monks know he was a bare-sark. If they knew, they would probably kill him.

They rode for almost an hour before they found any more signs of the marauders. At a bend on the forest trail, Cleave sat on a fallen tree, eating some hardtack. Even though it was very cold, he was sweating.

Trantor and Millz dismounted to talk to the southerner, but Jarllx called out for them to keep going, to scout the trail ahead. He then halted the column and dismounted to receive the scout's report, as Stern and the rest of the group remained mounted.

"What is it?" asked Jarllx.

"We tracked them to the edge of the great field that lies in north of the farm's compound and found another six bodies, lying in a heap near a hayrick. They are all farmers. We were about to sneak up on the compound when were heard musket fire."

"Muskets?" asked Jarllx in a gasp.

"A squad of musketeers was firing on the compound. We think the marauders have taken control of the farm and the musketeers are trying to root them out."

"Where's Martz?"

"He went down to talk to the musketeers and I came back to tell you."

"Damn it, Cleave, don't you men have any sense?"

"What's wrong, sir?"

"What makes you think the musketeers didn't kill those people?"

A look of horror spread across Cleave's face. "But Martz went to talk to them."

"Exactly my point, brother, mount up and let's go."

The column rushed at full gallop through the remnants of the forest and emerged on the edge of a broad wheat field. On a rise in the middle of the field was a walled compound that consisted of a large stone house, several barns and sheds and a small blockhouse. A contingent of musketeers—about thirty—was spread out around the west side, firing sporadically at the walls. Jarllx observed the scene for a few minutes and then commanded the column forward at a walk. Minutes later, he ordered them to stand ready and the brothers responded in unison by pulling their long swords from their sleeves and resting them on their shoulders. Stern pulled his polearm from his makeshift scabbard and held it forward like a spear. He felt the spirit of the bear rise and he caught a vision of it rearing and pawing the air, as three men disengaged from the musketeers and marched toward them. Jarllx called the column to a halt, when he realized that Martz, the blond Northman, was one of the three men marching up the hill toward them.

Martz approached Jarllx and saluted. "Brother," he said, turning toward a short swarthy man, dressed in the black and white uniform of a King's musketeer, "this is Captain Gonzalzz."

141

Gonzalzz bent at the waist and said, "My pleasure, sir." He paused, straightened up and added, "I am glad you have arrived. We have ten to fifteen marauders trapped in the farm's compound and we can use your help."

"I would think thirty King's musketeers could subdue fifteen marauders,"

"I have fifty men, actually. They are spread around the compound to keep the marauders entrapped. The problem is that they are led by a daemon, a big one with leather wings."

Stern felt his world twist, he was losing his balance in the saddle, and he knew the feeling arose from both guilt and fear because the daemon was obviously Focalor and it was his fault the farmers had lost their lives.

"A daemon?" sputtered Jarllx.

"Yes, sir," said the musketeer. "So you can see why I am happy to see Mithlass' own warriors enter the field."

Stern cleared his throat and studied the walls of the compound, trying to envision Focalor strutting about the compound with his leathery wings spread wide. He thought about Kylla and Coyote and their deaths and he felt the bear stirring inside him. He feared the feckless Focalor but he also hated him and he did not want anyone else to be harmed because the daemon hunted him.

"What is your plan, captain?" he asked, trying to control his emotions.

"Unfortunately, we don't have much daylight left. If we are going to take them, we need to do it before the sun sets."

"The daemon could leave at any time," said Stern.

Jarllx turned in the saddle, surprised at the tone of Stern's voice.

"What do you suggest brother?"

Stern straightened in the saddle and cleared his voice, "Jarllx, I have had some experience with daemons. I suggest you allow me to go in first and kill the daemon before you charge in with your men."

"How are you going to kill the daemon? You barely know how to use that polearm."

"I don't intend to use the polearm. I am going to borrow two of the captain's pistols."

"Have you had training in pistols?" asked the captain.

"In my land, to the north, we use mostly guns and I'm a bit of an expert."

Jarllx stared at Stern for a few moments and then said, "If you think you can kill this daemon, it will save a lot of lives."

"I can kill him."

"What about his men? What will you do about them?"

"I have no idea. I would suggest when you hear the discharge of the pistols you rush the compound."

"When do you want to make your attack?"

"At dusk," he answered. "I would appreciate the captain pointing out the best way in."

The captain walked towards the compound and then pointed. "There is a wooden wall about five feet high on the north east corner. I think it is a pig sty. That is where I would attack."

"Perfect. I will need some time to camouflage myself."

"What?" asked Jarllx.

"I will make myself look like the terrain. Relax, it is not magic. It is a tactic that I learned from our warrior chiefs."

The brothers moved back behind a slight hill that hid their presence from the marauders viewing the field from the wall of the compound. The captain sent a runner to retrieve two flintlock pistols, as Stern stripped his clothes off and asked a few of the men to start cutting grass.

Within an hour of intense work, Stern resembled a straw man. The only article of clothing he wore was a pair of laced sandals retrieved from one of the brother's saddlebags. He tied a dagger to his thigh and carried the pistols underneath a particularly thick clump of wild grass tied to his back.

One hour before sundown he began to crawl slowly toward the wooden fence. As agreed five minutes before he set out, the Captain and his men made a feigned attack on the western gate.

It took Stern almost an hour to reach the wooden wall and scale it. Once inside the compound he stripped off the camouflage and checked the pistols. Now completely naked he moved from one shadow to another. Dead bodies lay broken and bent along the pathways and dried blood soured in the soil of the compound's floor. To clear his mind, he began to think of Kylla. He felt his rage rising and this time he did not dismiss the bear, he prayed for it to be ready because he intended killing, not only the daemon, Focalor, but each and every one of the men, who had perpetrated their violence on so many innocent people.

One of those men stepped out from the corner of a shed near the blockhouse and Stern laid the pistols on the ground and removed the dagger from its sheath. When the man cleared the protection of the building, Stern grabbed him over his mouth with his left hand and struck him quickly and repeatedly in his kidneys with his right. As the man fell he cut his throat. When he was sure he was dead, he removed his hand from the man's mouth and let him crumple to the earth.

Covered with the sickeningly sweet smell of the man's blood, Stern pulled the body into the shadows. Picking up the pistols, he moved to a shadowed niche of the blockhouse, where he listened, trying to discern the presence of the daemon. The daemon, however, sensed him first and called him.

"Ah," he said, "you are back. I knew you would pass this way. You have changed. You are different, my friend."

Once the daemon touched him mentally, his position, as well as Stern's, was no longer a secret. Focalor was on the far corner of the small square in front of the stone blockhouse. He hid in a shadow of one of the stone paths, leading to the farmer's house.

"How have I changed, daemon?" asked Stern, as he moved toward him.

"You are no longer innocent of your nature. You have made the first steps toward being the being that you are."

"Watching your friends die does that."

"If you had come with me, they would all still be alive."

"Perhaps, but what about the people of Mittilagart; what will become of them?"

"Alas, that does not concern me. Only you concern me. Are you ready to fly away from this place?"

"What about your men?"

"They must fend for themselves."

Stern felt Focalor directing his men to surround his position. As he concentrated, he intuited not only Focalor's position but also his plans. He could even hear faint echoes of a conversation that Focalor was conducting telepathically with another daemon far away from the field of battle.

Stern realized if he did not move, he would soon be taken. He leapt up and ran across the small square, lifting and cocking both pistols as he sprinted across the clearing. Three quarters across, he saw the daemon clearly. He fired one pistol at the space between the creature's eyes. He fired the second at the heart. Both balls hit their mark and the creature reeled back, his great wings spreading, as if to lift him away from earth toward a place of safety.

Stern dropped the pistols and pulled his dagger. He plowed into the daemon with his left shoulder and then rammed the dagger beneath Focalor's ribcage and pushed upward into the heart. The creature struck him away with a mighty swing and he slammed against one of the dormitories' stone walls.

Stern expected this onslaught. That is the reason he entered the compound naked. He did not believe he could kill the daemon with a dagger or with a pistol. He knew he would have to summon the bear. With the shattering pain of the daemon's blow rushing throughout his body, the bear surged against his mind. Rather than fight the bare-sark's transforming, he let go and berserker rage filled his body.

From where Stern fell, now rose a large black bear that, in one mighty thrust, crossed the empty space and slammed into the body of the daemon, who was as surprised as his men to see the mighty creature lumbering at him in a bestial rage. In one blow, the bare-sark tore one of the daemon's wings half way from his body. Focalor cried out in wounded rage and fled toward the southern rampart, as black blood flowed from his chest, head, and shoulder. He could not fly over the wall, but he scaled it and jumped from the wall and ran toward the darkening wood, as snow began to fall heavily upon the farm.

Several musketeers, seeing the daemon running across the field, fired into the creature, eliciting new groans of rage and pain. Inside the compound, the bare-sark began to hunt the marauders, killing one after another in his rage, until they were all dead. His body covered with cuts and his fur matted in thick drying blood, the great beast crawled underneath a wooden stairway that led to the northern rampant and collapsed into an exhausted heap. Within a few minutes of his collapse, the bear form disappeared, leaving Stern bloody, crumpled, unconscious and shivering in the quickening snow.

An hour later, a musketeer scaled the eastern wall and opened the gate. Soon, almost sixty men filtered into the compound, their eyes wide, startled by the extent of the carnage. Thirty members of the farmer's family lay dead, along with thirteen marauders. Jarllx and his brothers searched among the bodies for Stern. The southerner, Cleave, found him, shivering underneath the stairs, his body covered in dried blood, and called out for Martz.

Martz and Cleave picked him up and carried him into the nearest dormitory and began to clean and dress his wounds. The rest of the men searched the compound and dealt with the dead. They could find not one survivor.

Jarllx and the captain decided not to follow the daemon into the woods. Night was descending and it was snowing. Neither man wanted to lose any more men in the woods, battling a daemon. They decided to wait and talk to Stern as soon as he recovered to discover what had happened within the walls.

The men, however, were already talking. Stern, in a matter of minutes, had achieved a reputation as a formidable warrior that would resound throughout the island kingdom until even the King eventually would hear of his reputation. However, now it was not clear if he would even live through the night.

Chapter Twenty-One: Mithlass and Bestar

STERN DREAMED GOTHA handed him a baby girl, wrapped in wolf skins, and asked: "What shall we call her?" He held her and gazed down upon her flaming red hair and dark green eyes and said, "We shall call her Ourssa, daughter of the bear." He then saw her running through the forests, brandishing a great sword, her long red hair flying behind her. He awoke with tears in his eyes, grieving for his unborn daughter who would live on another plane.

Jarllx sat next to the bed. "Bad dream?" he asked.

"Yes," he grumbled, pulling a blanket up to his chin.

"I can imagine you do have bad dreams, brother. You committed wholesale slaughter here last night."

Stern looked at Jarllx, trying to discern if the man was judging him or worse aware he was a bare-sark.

"It is not the first time I have killed."

"From what I have seen of your handiwork, you must be one mighty warrior. In fact, I would like you to consider joining us."

Stern breathed a heavy sigh of relief. Obviously, Jarllx did not suspect the truth. "Brother, I am on a journey, as I am sure you know, I have never felt more comfortable in my life as I do riding with the brotherhood."

Jarllx smiled, truly touched by Stern's statement.

"Do you feel well enough to ride today? I hate to rush you but the weather is changing."

"Is it still snowing?"

"Light snowfall and it is still too warm but I can tell that winter is finally coming. Gonzalzz and his men will remain here until the King sends out a new group of farmers."

"How far away are we now from the harbor?"

"We have two full days of riding ahead of us."

"I am anxious to continue so I will do my best not to slow you."

"Brother, we know your quest. You do us a great service, so we will make sure you make it on time, even if I have to persuade that big ox Martz to carry you on his shoulders."

Stern laughed. "Is there a place I can bathe?"

"The farmers have a bathhouse." Jarllx called out for Cleave, who quickly appeared at the foot of Stern's bed. "Help our brother get bathed and dressed and then we leave."

Stern needed Cleave's help to stand. He was sore and bruised and covered with shallow cuts. They staggered to the bathhouse where he bathed in the hot water for almost an hour. Martz arrived carrying his clothes and weapons. While he dressed, Cleave fetched a bowl of porridge and a tankard of ale, which he ate in front of a big-bellied stove in the bathhouse's dressing room.

With Cleave's help he staggered out of the bathhouse where the brothers' waited, each mounted. As he pulled himself onto the saddle, Martz raised a cheer, which all the brothers, plus Gonzalzz's men, joined. Tears formed in his eyes. He realized how lonely he had been in La Ciudad after the Argyll's woman's death. Odd, he thought, he should find friendship in the watery realm.

They rode out of the farm compound in a column of twos, Stern next to Cleave, who was prepared to reach out and grab him, if he were to slip from the saddle. Light snow fell. Two hours later they found the King's road. Now it was simply a matter of hard riding, he thought.

They stopped midday and ate. Cleave once more helped him off his horse. Slowly he felt his strength returning and he knew that by evening he would not need Cleave's help. He suspected the spirit of the bare-sark was helping him to recover. It was a strength he had never felt on his plane.

At mid-afternoon they left the forest and entered a country of rolling hills and farms. A considerable amount of traffic on the now muddy road slowed them, and they had to work their way around wagons and carts. At one point they came to a complete stop, as a goatherd led two hundred goats from the road.

"I thought Stormcrow was in the mountains," asked Stern, stirring his horse past a ragged cart.

Cleave answered, "Tomorrow the land will change. You will see mountains in the distance. Stormcrow stands on a rocky cliff overlooking a narrow valley. The valley leads to the sea and Wyvernne lies at the end of the valley. Beyond the port is a great fjord that stretches several leagues to the ocean.

They camped for the night on the edge of a small village. Cleave and Martz entered the settlement and returned with fresh bread, dried fruit, and roasted fowl. Later the brothers sat around a roaring fire, eating and telling tales. "Tell me a story of Mithlass," asked Stern. The brothers stopped their talking and turned to Jarllx, who wiped duck grease from his mouth and cleared his throat. "Would you like to hear the one about Mithlass and the sea lass?" The brothers smiled and punched themselves. This was obviously one of their favorite stories. "As you know Mithlass loved his beautiful younger sister Bestar but he was prohibited from lying with her. In fact, Okeanus sent him on a phony quest to the Xippon Sea to separate the two. He left in a dragon ship with a crew of forty men and sailed for half a year until he found an emerald island in the wine-dark sea of the tropical south. It was so hot the men wore no clothes during the day and fainted from the heat as they pulled the oars.

"Bestar missed her brother more than she was afraid of her Father. She knew that Mithlass liked athletic women so she decided to surprise him. On the day he left, she set sail in a fast dragon ship, manned by twenty of her strongest female retainers. The women pulled at the oars day and night and arrived at the Xippon Sea weeks ahead of her brother. They soon found a small tropical island with beautiful white beaches and a lush green forest brimming with fruits and vegetables.

"Bestar quickly explored the island and found a black stone mountain in the center. She and her female warriors climbed to the top of the mountain, where they discovered a vast cave. Within two weeks she had converted the cave into a comfortable and fortified hideaway, where they settled in and waited for Mithlass to find them.

"However, the cave was not really empty; it was the home of a Xippon witch, who happened to be on a quest in the south. One week after Bestar had settled in, the Witch, X'larsanna, returned to discover her secluded island now overrun with women.

"At first she was angry but then it occurred to her she could use help on the island, especially after she discovered how commodious and clean her cave now was.

"X'larsanna decided to enslave Bestar and her retainers and turn them to her dark ways.

"To do this, she decided she had to use one of her strongest spells, she had to prick each one with the darkened soul shard of a red dragon."

Stern, who had been listening with a bemused look on his face, suddenly sat up and leaned forward. He asked, "A darkened soul shard? What is that? Is it an instrument of the void?"

Jarllx sighed and answered, "Witches are able to make darkened soul shards from the hearts of red dragons. They kill the dragon and then remove its heart. They roast the heart over extreme heat until it blackens and hardens, like iron. Then they hammer it until it shatters into shards. In all the stories, the witch must find a magicker that is also a blacksmith because only they know how to make the fire hot enough."

Stern sat back and muttered, "thank you." Jarllx cleared his throat, somewhat irritated by the interruption, and returned to his story.

"A month passed before Mithlass found the emerald island he was looking for in the vast Xippon Sea. When his men landed, they were greeted by the most beautiful women they had ever seen. The men were entranced by the witch's magic and easily seduced. Every night the men lay with the beautiful women on the beach. Soon all of the women were pregnant and the men announced to Mithlass that they intended to remain on the island with these insatiable women.

"To this point Mithlass had avoided the women out of loyalty to his sister, Bestar. However, on the night the men declared they intended to stay on the island, the women did not appear. The men searched and searched for them but could not find them.

"Mithlass was relieved. The next morning he tried to persuade his men to leave but they refused. They were filled with grief and demanded more time to find the women. Mithlass bargained with them and promised he would search the forests for them but if the women did not appear in five days then they would depart. The men agreed.

"That night Mithlass began to search the island. Near mid-night he found a clearing near the base of the mountain. Moonlight illuminated the almost perfect circle. He was tired so he decided to sleep for an hour of two in the safety of the clearing, away from the dense darkness of the trees.

"He fell asleep immediately but he soon awoke to the sound of his name. His sister Bestar was calling him, pleading with him to awake. When he saw her, he rushed into her arms and began kissing her cheeks and eyes. His heart was so full of love he thought he would burst. She, however, pushed him away, tears coursing down her face.

"'You must flee, brother. There is a witch here that intends to enslave you and your men.' He fell back and drew his sword. 'You cannot fight her with a sword, my darling. You must flee.'

'But what are you doing here? I can't leave you here.'

"She sighed saying, 'I am a witch, now, just as she is; my life is here. You must flee but before you go, I want you to lie with me. In the morning you and your men must be gone.'

Jarllx grew serious and whispered, "Remember, Mithlass is a god and he knows the truth when he hears it and he knew his sister was telling him the truth. He stayed with her that night and sailed in the morning but he vowed that he and his followers would never slay a witch because the descendants of the powerful witches of the Xippon Sea were his and his men's children."

The men moved away from the fire and began to settle into their bedrolls. It was brutally cold, even the snow had stopped. Stern created a pallet of leaves against a large stone that blocked the northern wind. He wrapped himself in his blanket, covering his head, and settled on his right side, readying himself for sleep. He imagined Mithlass and his sister Bestar and felt a stirring in his loins. He thought first of the Argyll woman but soon he remembered his nights with Gotha. However, before he fell asleep, he imagined he saw a tall woman, wearing a red, silken robe, emerge from a dense dark forest. Her green eyes shone and her long black hair cascaded onto her slight pale shoulders, as a large black wolf with yellow eyes waited at her heels. She reached for him and his heart ached with grief and longing.

Cleave shook him awake. He was cold and stiff.

The sun rose, spreading pink rays through the clear frigid air, and the men stamped their feet to warm themselves. Martz squatted near the fire, blowing on embers to resurrect the dying fire of the previous night, while Jarllx stood on the edge of the camp, urinating onto some dead bushes. They quickly ate and packed up, the men anxious to reach Wyvernne. One of the men called out: "Cleave, do you think that tall red head from the south is waiting for you? You remember the one who broke the water jug over your head."

The men laughed and Jarllx called for the column to gallop. At midday, they left the forest and rode on a rough red clay road that stretched straight ahead of them and traversed a series of small hills. It was obvious to Stern they were now riding up a gradual incline. Soon, they entered a shallow valley. When they emerged they faced a solid wall of rolling hills, which Jarllx ordered them to traverse. At the summit, Jarllx called a halt. Before them, a great mountain range of black mountains loomed.

"The western wall," said Jarllx in a low voice. "It stretches from the northern coast, down the western side, and half way along the southern shores."

He pointed at a white blur on the top of one of the jagged peaks. "There stands Stormcrow, the white citadel. And there to the right, is the beginning of the Wyvernne valley. We are almost there, my brothers, look sharp and be mindful of the King's musketeers." The men laughed and he signaled for them to move forward.

At around four in the afternoon they reached a crossroads. A sign adorned with the word, Stormcrow, pointed to the southwest. Another pointed due west and sported the name Wyvernne. On the side of the road, three men, dressed in black-boiled armor, sat on tall horses. Two carried lances, while the third, obviously the leader, fingered a cavalryman's carbine, balanced on his saddle's horn. The two lancers wore steel helmets, while the leader was bareheaded, his long blond hair tumbling onto his shoulders. His face was gaunt and he sported a week-old reddish beard. He raised his hand slowly, as if he was tired or bored, indicating to Jarllx he was to stop. "Jarllx," he said, "what brings the brothers this way on such a cold day?"

"Viggas, why would a King's lancer venture so far away from a warm fire?"

The man sat up in his saddle and his horse skittered to the left. It was a tall horse, a stallion, a great warhorse but not truly broken.

"Jarllx, have you seen a platoon of the King's musketeers in your travels? News reached us that a daemon attacked Mylla's farm and murdered all of the peons. I await some news."

"We saw your men two days ago. It is true a daemon attacked the farm and killed the farmer and his family, but your men now control the farm and await instructions. I told them I would inform their commander of their valor."

"Well met, then, Jarllx. Now, tell me of this daemon?"

"He fled the field, wounded but still alive."

The answers seemed to make Viggas happy because he smiled thinly. "Shall we ride to the King together, my friend?"

"Alas, Viggas, we must reach our citadel near the docks of Wyvernne by nightfall. Winter is coming and we must board our ship before harbor freeze."

"The King will be disappointed if you do not report the sighting of the daemon."

Jarllx frowned and then smiled. "I will come to the King first thing tomorrow morning, once I have situated my men."

Viggas did not smile now; instead, he squirmed in the saddle and said, "I will inform the King's adviser and we will expect you at eight bells."

"I will be there."

Viggas turned his horse toward Stormcrow and galloped off, the two lancers racing behind him, trying their best to keep up.

The brothers took the road to Wyvernne and Jarllx turned surly and silent.

Chapter Twenty-Two: Wyvernne

STERN HAD NO INTENTION of seeing the King or running into the rogue. He determined to leave the island and find Bedwyr. He had no idea how many days he had passed on Okeanus. He wasn't even sure how many days he had been on the island. When he was in animal form, he had no concept of time. He could have wandered as a wolf for a year and he felt that time was running out for him.

They passed through the great stone gates of Wyvernne at dusk. The streets in the city were narrow and cobble-stoned; hundreds of people moved on the streets, slowing their advance even further. Shops were open on each side of the street; hawkers called out their wares, pointing to shops that sold all sorts of foods and exotic products.

They slowly made their way down the narrow, crowded corridors, turning first right and then left, as the road meandered downward toward the sea. Large white birds with long yellow beaks hovered over the gray stone buildings looking for food. Soon the street opened onto a large plaza and Stern smelled the ocean.

The northern side of the plaza consisted of a huge blue-gray stone edifice, three stories tall. This was the brothers' blockhouse or Keep, explained Jarllx. "This is our headquarters in Wyvernne and the home of our administrative office, our library, and our historical archives. It raises three stories above ground and descends six below. The walls are nine feet thick and the compound houses, when we are fully staffed, three hundred brothers, one hundred horses, ten milk cows, and two hundred chickens."

"How many brothers are here now?" asked Stern.

He sighed and answered, "Eight."

"Eight?"

He shook his head and said, "The King's war decimated us. That is why your quest is so important."

Martz produced a brass hunting horn and blew a long tone into the dusky night. The two great wooden doors of the stockade, framed in iron, opened with a metallic creak. Two brothers dressed in black mail pushed the doors fully open and stood in the breach. One carried a double-headed ax and the other a claymore.

Jarllx, as he spurred his horse toward the opening, called out, "Brothers, you are dressed for war. What is the problem?"

The man with the claymore approached Jarllx and said, "Enter Brother and we will tell you our news. Please hurry."

Jarllx frowned and galloped through the gate, followed by the column down a long covered passageway that emerged into a cobblestone courtyard, where a large stone well dominated its center. Jarllx dismounted near the well and tied his horse to an oaken hitching rail and then took a drink from a running fountain on the side of the well. The two brothers that opened the gate followed them into the bailey. As they approached Jarllx, they removed their black iron helms shaped like the lion's head of Mithlass. The man, carrying the claymore, was tall and thin with wispy white hair. He shook Jarllx hand and then hugged him. Martz whispered to Stern, "His oldest blood brother."

"Brother, tell me why you are dressed for war," repeated Jarllx.

"Two nights ago, a platoon of the King's musketeers tried to enter the citadel. We refused their entrance and they fired several shots at the windows on the second floor. Brother Trek was wounded. We do not know if they were drunk or sent by the King to incite a battle. We have heard nothing since."

"We met some of the King's lancers on our way into the city and they did not try to stop us."

Bekt, Jarllx's brother, shrugged, changed the subject by saying: "Welcome Brother, it is good to see you."

"And you. Renus, escort the men to the barracks. I want to speak with my brother."

Stern, with the others, followed Renus to a wide stone stairway that led to the second floor. Once there they turned to the right and walked down a wide hall with great wooden doors, as Renus explained, "The administrative offices are on this floor. At the end of this hall is the great library. The dormitory for the permanent staff is on the third floor. The barracks are on the first underground floor, because of our small numbers, we have closed the barracks and are using only the dormitory."

They passed the library's double doors and followed the hallway to the right. After a few yards they came upon another stone stairway; one not so wide. They climbed the stairs, turned to the right, and Renus opened the first wooden door they reached. It was a large room with stained glass windows every few feet running along the north wall.

"Pick a bed," he said as they entered.

The men spread out and chose their beds. At the foot of each was a wooden chest, each one different, well-carved and polished. One stained glass window displayed a scene of a knight in black armor fighting a green dragon. It reminded Stern of paintings of Saint Michael and the Dragon he had seen in the cathedrals of La Ciudad. He picked the cot beneath this window. Opening a wooden chest decorated with red runes at the end of the bed, he stored his equipment and weapons.

"Brothers," said Renus, "it is the custom of the Keep to wear our robes when off duty; however, because of our heightened state of alertness, you must don the black mail when away from the sleeping areas. For those new to the Keep, the armory is on the first floor near the gate. We will serve a light dinner at nine bells in the dining hall."

The men began to settle in. Some began to strip off their leather armor. While Cleave poured water into a large bowl, preparing to sponge himself off in lieu of a true bath, Stern approached Martz and whispered into his ear: "I have no robes."

Martz smiled and walked to the far end of the room to a large wooden chest and opened its two pine doors, revealing black woolen robes hanging above three wooden drawers. He opened the top one and pulled out a silk underrobe, moved to the bottom drawer and lifted out a pair of black sandals, and extracted a pair of black woolen socks from the middle one. Taking the garments, Stern smiled saying, "Thanks, Brother." Martz grinned and slapped him on the shoulder.

The men shaved and cleaned themselves and then changed into their black robes. Although it was cold inside the rooms, Stern could find no heating source, the silk underrobes and the heavy woolen robes provided him with ample protection against the cold.

As Martz trimmed Stern's wild hair and his burgeoning beard, he asked, "Tell me, Brother, about your land." Stern cleared his throat and asked, "What do you want to know?"

"Do you worship Mithlass there?"

"No. We worship a God, of course, but Mithlass is not he."

"Who is this god you serve, Brother?"

Stern paused before saying, "I serve him that is both first and last, the one who brought order to chaos."

"What is he called?"

"He has no name, he is simply God."

Martz continued, "Is he a god of war?"

Stern smiled and said, "We were created in his image so what do you think?"

Martz smiled and whispered in Stern's ear, "He must be one mighty warrior then."

Stern nodded in agreement.

At nine bells the brothers marched in a column of two, unarmed to the dining hall on the ground floor. The hall was huge, lined with dark wood and hundreds of exquisitely stone-carved figures of war embedded in the walls, each displaying a magnificent weapon.

Stern asked Martz, "Who are these figures?"

"They are depictions of brave brothers that have fallen in bright battle." He smiled sardonically and then added: "They died bringing order to the chaos of this world."

"Aha, you think that my God is Mithlass?" asked Stern.

"Of course, who else could he be? Why would he have brought you to us at this time and at this place?"

Stern laughed and said, "You may be right, my friend."

"Not friend, but brother."

They all stood when Renus and Jarllx entered the room, followed by a short man, wearing a burgundy robe. Stern looked at Martz, who seemed to read his mind. "He is Felyzz, the Keeper of Wyvernne Keep, master of the Brotherhood's Citadel and ambassador to the King's Court. The man sat and the brothers settled down to eat. The meal consisted of what Stern surmised was roasted venison, boiled potatoes, and ample tankards of ale. Whether it was indeed venison, he did not know but its taste was rich and gamey. Potatoes are potatoes and ale is ale. His mouth watered as he ate the simple food and experienced once again the simple pleasure of eating. When the meal was done, Jarllx, wearing a dark green robe, his long black hair combed to a dark sheen and braided, approached and asked Stern to follow him. Stern pushed his plate back and stood.

They exited the dining hall and crossed the plaza and entered a single wooden door of the eastern wing of the Keep that opened onto a narrow passageway that descended into the Keep's lower levels. At the bottom of the stairs they turned left and followed a hallway for several hundred feet until they reached an iron door, where Jarllx knocked twice before Felyzz opened it. He stepped aside, as they entered a cedar-lined room that contained a large oaken desk and five leather chairs, two walls of bookshelves and a map of the world on the stonewall behind the desk. Oil lamps flickered and illuminated the room that smelled of pipe smoke and leather. Felyzz now in the chair behind the desk reminded Stern of his meeting with the Black Robe priest so many weeks (or perhaps it was months) ago.

"Brother," said Felyzz, "Jarllx has apprised me of the strange circumstances of your involvement with our brotherhood." Stern bowed his head in acknowledgment of his assessment of the situation as strange. "The King grows petulant, violent and, unfortunately, he blames us for his troubles. This is not good for you or us. It is imperative you sail as soon as possible."

"I agree. Not only do I serve you but I have a personal quest that is urgent."

"I am afraid the King is about to make an example of us. We are to be his scapegoat for his military failures and an attack on the Keep is imminent. They will not succeed with their first attack but because we are so weak they will overcome us. Jarllx is to go to the King tomorrow to inform him of the battle with the daemon. Unfortunately, he knows little or nothing. It was you who fought the daemon and when that becomes known, which it will, because of the King's musketeers, the King will want to hear about the battle from you. We have maybe one day at most before he begins to demand your presence and I intend to use it to ship you from the city.

"I have sent Lenark, our quartermaster, to the harbor master to find a ship to Noirrith. This is not an unusual request. Since it is a large outpost of a brother clan we send men back and forth often. I have asked Lenark to find a trustworthy captain with a swift ship and bring him here tonight. After we have negotiated your passage, you are to return to the ship with the captain. Now, it is important you not appear to the ship and its crew as a brother; therefore, Jarllx and I have devised a cunning plan of subterfuge. Jarlzz tells me you are quite the warrior, cognizant of the dagger and the polearm, crossbow, and throwing knife."

Without explaining he was one God's storm troopers, a member of the Black Robes, he simply said, "That is correct."

"It is a shame you are leaving. We could use you in the fight that is coming; nevertheless, we want you to travel under the name of Tatyx, a sellsword from Trint, an island in the south near the southern ice wall.

"If you are challenged on your accent or your deficit language skills, say you are not originally from Trint. As a sellsword, we must give you another tattoo, one from one of the extinct assassins' guilds of Trint. If you are questioned about your brotherhood tattoo, tell them you were once a brother but after the King's initiation of war against the witches, you left the brotherhood because you felt it violated Mithlass' injunction against attacking a witch."

There was a knock on the door and Martz entered with a leather bag in one hand and Stern's polearm in the other.

"Martz will take you to Brother Jankzz for your tattoo. Change into your new clothes there and await the arrival of the Captain. Do you have any other questions?"

Stern was about to volunteer to stay with the brothers but an image of Kylla and her unmerciful death stopped him. Grave sacrifice had already been made a part of his quest. He owed her, among others, to finish what he had started. He accompanied Martz out the door and down the passageway to another iron door and entered a room filled to overflowing with weapons and armor, where a large man, with bronze colored hair and a pockmarked face sat in the corner in front of a small brazier, heating iron needles.

An hour and half later, Stern sat in a straight back chair, dressed in a gray woolen shirt, black leather vest, linen pants, and a pair of boots that stretched to his knees. With long curved daggers, sheathed on each hip, and his polearm on the floor next to a black leather backpack filled with iron rations, Stern sat quietly in a large wooden chair with his left sleeve rolled up to his shoulder, sipping a small glass of green grog to help with the pain of his new sellsword tattoo. It was an image of a long narrow black dagger with a red snake wrapped around its length with two runes inscribed on each side of the hilt. One rune meant order, the other signified dis-order or Chaos. Now a bit drunk from the green grog, he slurred his admiration for the woolen beret that Jankzz wore. "Jankzz, where did you get that beret?"

"What?" the man asked absently.

"The hat," he repeated. "Where did you get it?"

Jankzz laughed. "All brothers who serve the Keep have at least one. We make them in our spare time."

"Could I have one? My head has been wet and cold since I arrived on this island and I lost my stocking cap in the battle against the daemon."

"I will put two in your bag."

Stern smiled, as a tear gathered in his eye. He did not know if it was the pain, the green grog, or leaving the brothers but he was feeling suddenly sad. There was a knock on the door and Jarllx emerged from the shadowed hall. "The captain has arrived. Are you ready?" Stern rubbed his eyes and nodded in the affirmative.

"You go ahead, 'said Jankzz, "I will finish packing your bag and leave it with your polearm at the guard station at the front gate."

Stern followed Jarllx back to Felyzz's office. As they entered a tall thin man, holding a glass of green grog in his right hand, rose from one of the leather chairs. Wisps of delicate white hair framed a gaunt and weathered face. His burgundy eyes were deeply recessed under prominent brows covered with thick curly white hair. His teeth were long and white and his lips thin and flat. He wore a short blue coat familiar to sailors the world over and a flat captain's hat. His hands were wide and red, calloused and strong.

"Tatyx, this is Captain Sollers, the master of the *Whirlwind*, a schooner sailing under the Xipponese flag."

The man bowed at the waist and said, "Well met, Tatyx."

As they found their seats, Jarllx handed Stern a chalice filled with the green grog.

Felyzz explained, as Stern sipped the grog. "We have negotiated your passage to Noirrith and paid your fare. The captain's bargain is to feed you and find a berth. You may work on board if you desire but it is as a volunteer. There will be no pay. Many do it because they are bored. The voyage will take approximately nine weeks. They will only stop to refresh the supply of food and water. The captain estimates no more than three stops. If attacked, you are expected to defend yourself."

"Who would attack us?" asked Stern.

The captain gave him a strange look then said in a flat tone, "Dragons, leviathans, pirates, the King's corsairs, daemons."

The captain cleared his throat and continued. "There will be three other passengers on the schooner: a tradesman, who has hired the entire storage capacity of the ship, a cleric from Lonzst, and a Xipponese diplomat.

"I only have two staterooms. Therefore, you will have to use one of the slots. I am sailing with a crew of fourteen and short-handed. I have two slots available. You will have one and the cleric the other."

Stern looked at Felyzz, who nodded affirmatively. Stern said, "That will be acceptable."

"Now here is something important. You are to stay away from the woman, do you understand?"

"What woman?"

"The Xipponese witch, the diplomat," grunted the Captain.

"What do you mean stay away from her?" asked Stern.

"Do not force yourself on her. Do not try to seduce her. You can stay on the deck and hob-knob with the crew but be respectful of the woman. It goes for you, my men and, by Mithlass's balls, even I must keep my distance. Understand?"

"Yes."

The captain stood and finished his grog. "Are you ready?"

Stern looked at Felyzz, who nodded. "Captain, I need one moment with Tatyx." The Captain bowed and left with Jarllx. Felyzz walked around the desk and handed Tatyx a small leather bag. "This bag contained ten gold coins and ten silver. This is enough money for a man to live a rich life on the Island for many, many lifetimes. One gold coin is equal to a hundred silvers, one silver coin equals one thousand bronzes, one bronze equals one thousand coppers. The yearly earnings of an average man on the Island are five hundred coppers. Do you understand?"

Stern nodded.

"Watch your back and keep this money safe. May Mithlass guide you and watch out for the Cleric. They serve Glanzt, the red god of order."

Martz waited for Stern outside the office and led him first to the central plaza and then to the front gate, where Stern retrieved his leather pack, polearm, and cloak, as Cleave opened it just wide enough for one man at a time to pass. He squeezed through first and checked the street and then whistled. The Captain and Stern followed him through the narrow opening. Pushing the door closed behind him, Cleave set off down the deserted street toward the harbor, with the captain and Stern close behind him. They stayed in the shadows, fearful they might meet a contingent of musketeers.

The cobblestone street wound snakelike down a steep hill. Along the way, the three men passed several taverns that were obviously busy. The temperature had fallen drastically, keeping the men inside drinking grog next to a roaring fire. Several times Stern slipped on patches of ice and he imagined the harbor freezing solid, trapping him in the King's city. Finally, they reached the end of the cobblestone road. A harbor, wide and ample, capable of servicing many ships at once, lay before them. On this frigid night, however, there were only two ships attached to the quay. All other vessels had been either raised or pulled ashore in anticipation of the coming freeze. One ship, a large trireme, flew the King's flag. The other, a two-masted schooner without oars, was the captain's ship. Small and taut, it would be quite fast with a decent wind, thought Stern.

When they reached the ramp leading to the *Whirlwind*'s deck, Cleave said, "I will leave you here, brother. God's speed and I will see you in the spring when you return in the dragon ships with our brothers."

Stern felt an instant pang of guilt. He knew that although the brothers in the keep were in grave danger, he suspected he would never return. He gripped the giant by his forearm and said, "I will not fail you, brother." Cleave smiled and then as he trotted up the hill toward the keep, the captain touched his shoulder and said, "Come, the temperature is dropping and I can see the ice forming." He pointed to the water around the great pylons that supported the wide wooden decks, where bluish green ice formed and spread frozen tendrils out like gnarled fingers and a large white water fowl waddled on a slick patch.

The captain suddenly seemed filled with an urgent need to hoist anchor and sail from the fjord. At the gangplank, he called out to a teen who sat in the shadows of the deck wrapped in a dark-blue cloak: "Roby, wake the boys. We sail immediately."

Once on board, the captain set to work. He had Roby and several other men who arrived on deck lower two long boats. Once in the water, four men descended into each boat. With a command they raised oars and moved toward the prow. Roby, who remained on board with the captain and three others, threw each boat a rope, while two others began unfastening the ship from the pier. The men in the long boat began to count in perfect unison as their labored rowing pulled the schooner from the quay. Soon they were away, heading into the center of the fjord, toward the tide that would pull them inexorably toward the sea.

Stern stood on the stern, facing the city that rose up from the harbor, and watched the few faint lights fade from view. Once again, he was on his way, hopefully he thought toward the end of his journey.

Chapter Twenty-Three: Voyage of the *Whirlwind*

THE SAILORS IN THE LONG BOATS pulled the ship for almost two hours along the length of the fjord before the captain blew a long mournful note on a bone horn. Behind them, the mouth of the fjord appeared as a shadow silhouetted against the eastern sky; the skyline of the island behind them faded into the horizon, as snow fell in wet flakes and a steady southwestern wind blew against the stern of the schooner.

Once the men were back on board and the long boats stored, the captain gave the order to loosen the sails. As the sails dropped into place Stern felt the ship's canvas catch the wind.

The captain stood at the wheel while his men worked in the rigging, turning the schooner due south by southwest. Roby appeared and bowed to Stern. "Sir, the captain instructed me to show you to your slot." Stern yawned, the effects of the adrenalin and the grog over the last few hours were fading and he was growing weary. Roby led him to an opening in the deck and they descended to the first level and followed a narrow passageway to the stern. Roby opened a pine door that glistened from fresh wax; the entrance to a narrow *slot*, a space seven feet long and four feet wide, where a hammock hung from hooks with a built-in wooden box beneath it. Stern sighed realizing this cubbyhole was to be his home for many weeks, yet he knew he had survived far worse.

He pulled the door shut, stored his weapons and leather pack in the cedar box beneath the hammock and changed out of his clothes into a silk undergarment and robe. It was cold, very cold in the room, so he draped his woolen cape over the hammock, fished out his woolen beret and pulled it onto head before climbing into the hammock. He lay on his back and felt the movement of the ship. The captain said the ship could do ten knots per hour but the average was three to four. He calculated the distance, taking into consideration four days of stops to replenish the water kegs and food, to be about five thousand nautical miles. He imagined the miles passing, one after another, as he fell into a deep untroubled sleep.

He awoke when his hammock slammed into the wooden pine paneling of the narrow slip. The plaintive moan of a fierce wind and the creaking song of the ship's timber alerted him that the sea was troubled. He had an urgent need to relieve himself and he was hungry, yet the wild bucking of the ship unnerved him. In the end, the call of nature was strong and could not be ignored. He found his leather slippers and pulled his cloak over his shoulders. Wind or no wind he opened the slip's door and worked his way down the narrow passageway to the ladder that led to the deck.

As soon as he stood on the rough wooden planks of the schooner's deck, the ship plunged downward into a trough of blue-black water. Above the purple sky pelted him with frozen rain and sleet on his face and shoulders, driving him back, causing him to stumble and swear in the *lingua* of La Ciudad. Grabbing a hold on the deck he saw the captain standing at the wheel, his legs spread wide, wearing a black leather slicker; his body tensed against the force of the beleaguered rudder, while two crew members, dressed similarly to the captain, scampered among the rigging, trimming the sail, as the ship dropped and then bucked upwards.

Roby's head appeared at the hatch and Stern watched as his mouth moved but he could not hear over the rush of the wind and splash of the ocean's frantic waves. Finally, Roby, realizing the man could not hear him, left the safety of the passageway and grabbed his arm and dragged him back down into the bowels of the ship, closing and bolting the hatch behind him.

"You cannot go on deck. Do you want to wash overboard and feed the krends?"

"I need to relieve myself," Stern said gruffly.

Roby's eyes widened with understanding and he ran down the passage way towards the stern.

"Now what?" said Stern, leaning against a bulkhead. Soon Roby returned with a large covered tin bucket and handed it to Stern, who carefully walked back to his slip and closed the door. Between the fall and the rise of the ship, he relieved himself in the bucket and fastened the top. Two iron hooks were screwed into the wall and he figured he was supposed to hang the bucket there. Once he mastered this contrivance, he returned to the hammock and fell back into a deep sleep.

Several hours later Stern awoke to the sound of Roby's knocking. The ship no longer rocked and Stern suspected they had outrun the storm. He called for Roby to enter, as he slowly lifted himself out of the hammock's elaborate webbing. The room was frigid with ice formed in the corners of the slip and on the side of the tin bucket hanging from the two iron fasteners attached to the wall.

Roby said, "The captain invites you to dine with him and the other passengers."

"What time is it now?"

"The boatswain just piped six."

Stern scratched his head and straightened the wrinkles in his robe. "Roby," he asked, "Is it possible to get a pan of water to clean myself before dinner."

Roby paused and then answered, "The crew has a head with a mirror, a wash pan, and some towels. You could use that."

"Could we go now?"

"I have to invite the other guests to dinner. I will return for you later."

Stern gathered his razor and a bar of soap from his leather bag stored in the cedar chest underneath his hammock then sat on the chest and waited for Roby to return. He cleared his mind and asked himself a series of questions. How long had he been asleep? How far had they traveled? How long had he been on the watery plane? What was happening in Mittilagart? How was his son? How would he get home? Had he lost his mind and was this journey real or imagined? Just as he was trying to decide if he had lost his mind or not, Roby opened the door.

He followed the boy down the passageway and then onto the deck. The passenger cabins and slots were on the first level at the bow of the boat. The crew's quarters, such as they were, were on the second level at the stern. Stern followed Roby down the length of the deck, past the wheel, to a recessed hatch. The first level housed the galley and the captain's cabin. They continued to the second level, which consisted of a large open space reserved for the crew and a fair amount of storage. Along the sides of the boat were stacked hammocks, enough to sleep twelve. The rest of the area was taken up with wooden barrels, casks, boxes and crates. The space was redolent with the odor of tobacco, which overwhelmed the odor of bilge and unwashed men. Stern surmised the cargo, at least the cargo on this level, was barrels of yellow leaf.

He followed Roby through a narrow *ad hoc* passageway through the barrels until they reached another wooden hatch that led down to yet another level. Here Stern bent forward to avoid hitting his head on the low wooden ceiling. They turned toward the stern and worked themselves through bales of cotton and more barrels until they reached two tiny glass windows at the stern that opened just above water level. Roby opened the windows and frigid air rushed through. A large tin reservoir encrusted in ice hung from a hook against the inside wall of the boat next to a mirror dangling from a leather strap. Roby handed Stern a shallow tin basin and pointed to a copper spigot on the tin reservoir. He filled the basin with cold water and then pulled off his clothes.

"We wash with rain water. It is not potable but it is not filled with brine." Roby stared at Stern's colorful tattoos and assumed a stance, which seemed to illustrate his astonishment. "You are both a brother warrior and a sellsword?"

Ignoring the boy's question, Stern took a deep gulp and then poured the basin of freezing water over his head. As he lathered his body with sweetened rose soap, he said, "I was a brother warrior first and then a sellsword."

"Have you killed a lot of men?"

Stern turned toward the boy and truthfully answered, "Unfortunately, I have."

He asked Roby to pour fresh water over his head as he stood shivering. Roby produced a rough cotton towel from a cedar chest; and, he vigorously dried himself as the soiled water drained off into the sea through two small drainage holes in the stern.

Standing naked at the window, looking out at a pristine sky, sea and horizon, Stern asked Roby if he had a clothing brush. He nodded and disappeared. When he returned he handed Stern a large black brush with stiff bristles and Stern stroked the black robe rigorously. When he finished, he pulled on the robe, realizing he resembled a La Ciudad Black Robe once again.

"I'm ready to return to my slot."

Roby jumped up and like a good hound led Stern back through the labyrinth of barrels and crates to the deck and then to his slot. Once there, Stern retrieved a long leather belt from his leather pack and wrapped it loosely around his waist, then attached one of his curved daggers.

"Is it time yet to join the captain?"

"Not yet, you still have some time."

"Then let's go on deck and watch the fish."

The boy laughed and led the way back onto the deck. As soon as Roby's head appeared, one of the older sailors called out: "You lazy gob, where have you been? The captain's been looking for you. Get to his cabin."

Before running to the captain's cabin, Roby whispered to Stern to come to the Captain as soon as he heard the boatswain ring the bells.

Stern moved to the rail and gazed out at the darkening sea. The sun had set but there was still a bit of diffused light playing on the waters in the west. In the east a harvest moon rose and Stern felt that somehow this moon, the moon of the watery plain, was bigger and greater than in his realm. The air was cold and crisp though it was not as harsh as on the island and each hour that passed the air felt warmer. They sailed south by southwest now, fleeing the ice of the north.

Every time he relaxed, he noticed, his mind returned to the blue-back dragons that ravished Mittilagart, his son, and his quest to this watery world. It was a constant ache, which he had to still in order to focus on the matter at hand, which was simply to survive in an alien world and complete his quest.

Chapter Twenty-Four: The Diplomat

A SIBILANT SOUND shattered his concentration. He turned and caught a glimpse of a slight single figure silently standing in the shadows of the deck. Screwing his eyes into a spare straight squint to see, Stern soon satisfied himself that the shadowed figure was not one of the sailors; it was too small and thin. Unconsciously, his right hand wrapped around the bone handle of his curved dagger and his sudden irrational fear awakened a sense of the bear. His nostrils flared as the spirit of the bare-sark rose into his conscious mind.

The figure, he knew, somehow preternaturally, sensed his presence. The wind changed direction and he detected a faint musky perfume. It was the woman, the Xipponese diplomat, he quickly realized, who walked in the deck's shadows. Remembering the captain's warning, he moved away from her, searching for a darker shadow in which to hide. Unfortunately his attempt to hide was futile because she slowly approached him, granting him a few moments to relax. She stopped a few feet away from him, waiting in a beam of moonlight that was now spreading over the waters.

Although the light was faint he could clearly see her thin figure, her pale white face, and her long black hair pulled back and elaborately braided in a thick cord that hung to her waist. She wore a dark purple robe and flat leather shoes. A silver pendant in the shape of a pentagram dangled around her neck; on her hands were two rings: a large silver one on her left hand and a ruby on her right. She had a prominent nose, thin lips and heavy brows. As she drew closer, her white teeth flashed in the light, strong and straight, her eyes pale blue, like cornflowers, shone in the moonlight that had broken through the storm clouds.

"You have been with Keltoi?" she asked, a slight lisp was evident.

He cleared his throat surprised at the question. "The Keltoi accepted me, trained me for a time."

She took a step forward and reached out her hand to touch his cheek. Her fingers were long and well-shaped. At first he pulled back but when she reached toward him a second time, he let her touch him.

"Where are you from?" she asked.

"I am from Mittilagart and the city, known as La Ciudad."

"Where is this place?"

"The Keltoi call it the Earthern Plane."

"Yes, I have heard stories of this place. She reached out and held his jaw and he suspected she used touch as some sort of lie detector.

She stepped back and he let out a breath.

"How did you come here?"

"Through a portal opened by a witch," he said flatly, as if this were an everyday occurrence.

"A witch?" she asked. "What witch?"

"She was a *lunar bruja*, a moon witch."

"Where does she live?"

"In Mittilagart, like me," he answered. Now it was her turn to breathe a sigh of relief. He suspected she feared a witch from Okeanus, the watery realm, was opening portals.

"Does anyone on board know what you are?"

"No."

"Good. If they did they would throw you overboard. I sensed your presence from the start but you have been asleep and it was difficult to see you. I have a lot of questions but we have little time now. I have agreed to dine with the Captain and I will soon be summoned."

"I have also been invited."

"You must never reveal who or what you are."

He noted for the first time some sympathy in her pale eyes.

"What do they call you, bare-sark?"

"The Captain knows me as the sellsword–Tatyx."

"What is your real name?"

"Stern," he answered.

"I am Sor Michaelsdottir. My friends call me Mikk but now I am a diplomat for the Xipponese and I find I have very few friends. Do you know what that means to be a diplomat?"

"Not really."

"It means power, power in all its forms, and it means magic."

"What were you doing on the Island? I heard the King hates witches."

"The King desires power so he is forced to deal with the Xipponese. But he hates all forms of magic, which makes his intercourse with us particularly distasteful. Nevertheless, we supported him in his war against Brasilika because it was in our interest to do so but now that the war is over, the relations between our two countries are strained. I came to the Island to smooth the King's ruffled feathers."

"Did it work?"

"A little," she murmured. "He lost the war with Brasilika and decimated his mercenary army in the process. He is now weak and needs his allies more than ever. Although it offends him to admit it, he knows he needs us. Imagine, Stern, being afraid of witches, dragons and daemons in our world. It is like being afraid of life itself."

"You are right Sor Michaelsdottir. We do have many things to discuss because dragons are the reason I was sent here."

She cocked her head to the right and Stern knew he had her attention, however, at that moment, the boatswain rang the time and Roby called for them.

Chapter Twenty-Five: The Passengers

THEY FOLLOWED ROBY to the galley, a small room with a low ceiling with a long pine table attached to the floor with two log benches on either side. The captain sat at the end in a rough-hewn pine chair. Stern waited for the woman to sit and then he took a place opposite her. Eight brass lamps burning aromatic leviathan oil provided enough light for him to study her face carefully, just as a short red-faced man, wearing a dirty white robe, rushed into the room. His thin blond hair was cut short and he had a four or five-day growth of ruddy beard. His eyes were a yellowish brown and he smelled of sour sweat. Nervously, he looked about the room, sizing up the dynamics of perceived power, then moved to a place between Stern and the captain. Stern slid down the bench, leaving the man a place opposite Sor Michaelsdottir, who wrinkled her nose in disgust.

Soon another man, with a dark black handlebar mustache waxed to curl upward on each end appeared. He wore a black velvet suit, black silk slippers and sat next to Sor Michaelsdottir. His nostrils flared and a slight ironic smile crossed his face, as he surreptitiously gazed at the diplomat.

The captain greeted his guests. Once they had taken their seats and were comfortable, he lifted a copper bell and rang it twice. A man wearing a white jacket appeared and bowed.

"Please pour the wine, Arndt."

The man bowed and moved to an alcove where a crystal decanter sat on a silver platter with five large cut crystal glasses. The man filled each glass half full then placed a glass in front of each guest. Once they had each received a glass, the captain rose, lifted his glass, and said, "Welcome to my ship."

Sor Michaelsdottor stood and bowed her head. She then lifted her glass and frowned sardonically at the sitting men. At once they realized they should rise and join the captain in his toast. When they were all on their feet, the captain said, "To her and her guests, may we make landfall apace." He then took a sizable swallow of the wine and the others followed.

As they sat, the Captain said, "I usually dine with my passengers on the first night at sea but the weather was so bad that this is the first time we have had smooth enough waters to present a decent meal. We have made good time though because of the strong winds at our back and we should now have a stretch of fine sailing. In five days we make our first stop to off-load goods and take on more."

The man in the black velvet suit interrupted, "This stop, as the Captain says, is due to my commerce and I hope you can bear the delay of a few days. I am exchanging barrels of tobacco and salted fish for more salt and spices. The ship will be redolent with spice when we set sail. I hope you will find the aroma as pleasing as I do." He coughed slightly and looked at the cleric, who was sipping his wine.

The captain continued. "Trong, the major city of the spice islands, has a large natural harbor. We will be able to dock and off-load easily; nevertheless, because we have to await the arrival of the spice, we shall be there for three to five days so if you wish to explore the city you may. Let me warn you though. The Spice Islands do a brisk trade with the rest of Okeanus and the city is a port and, as you may know, port cities have their own inherent dangers. I would advise you to stay on board but you are free to do what you will."

The cleric added, "We have a major mission in Trong so I will be leaving you and staying with my brothers at the canticle house until I can book passage on a ship home."

The cleric looked at each of them to gauge their reactions to his departure.

"I must travel to the spice plantation to alert them of our arrival and make arrangement for the loading of the shipment to Noirrith," said the trader. Stern observed the woman, as she sat quietly, leaving her wine untouched, listening intently to the others.

The captain cleared his throat and said, "I thought we might introduce ourselves while the steward pours us another drink and then serves the meal."

The trader, quick off the mark, said, "My name is Abrahsson. As you surmise I am a trader in commodities, a native of the Island, and a true subject of the King. I specialize in tobacco, wine, and spices and I travel ten months out of the thirteen buying and selling goods. In the winter I am in the south and in the summer I head north."

Stern asked, "What goods do you trade?"

The trader laughed a dry laugh and said, with a wave of his right hand, "Everything and anything. I am driven by the desires of my clients. If the Brothers of Mithlass need weapons, I buy weapons. If the Xipponese need spice, I obtain spice."

The cleric held his empty glass up for the steward to refresh his drink and said, "My name is Tuxk, as you heard, and I am a cleric. I am originally from Lonzst, the capital city of Brasilika, sent to the Island as a missionary. During the war I was imprisoned but with my country's victory, I was released and the King has seen fit to send me home." He paused and with a demure, self-satisfied grin, he said, "Glantz, my god, does not smile on the Islanders and I fear for their souls."

Neither Stern nor the woman spoke and the captain said, "Tatyx, why don't you tell us about yourself."

"I am from a small island in the south, traveling to Noirrith to learn smithing techniques."

He noticed the woman raise one eyebrow.

"Which island?" asked Tuxk. "Do we have a mission there?"

"We call it Trint and no, you do not have a mission there."

Stern gulped. He should have anticipated this and asked a few questions about Trint. He was very vulnerable because he knew nothing about Okeanus except that which he had recently experienced and he knew he could not disclose that.

The woman interrupted, "I know his island well. It is far to the south, near the southern ice wall. It is treeless and barren, is it not?"

"Yes," stuttered Stern. "We cut the trees of the island down hundreds of years ago for our houses and boats and planted no others. It is a rugged land, dependent on fishing and reaving."

"Reaving?" asked the trader with a start.

"Yes, my people are reavers, raiders, pirates and sellswords."

The cleric hissed, "You are a mercenary!"

Glantz either. I serve no god of this world." He smiled at his own little joke.

Stern shrugged his shoulders and said, "Alas, it is true."

"Do you worship that foul god of chaos, Meer?"

Stern thought of the brothers in Wyvernne. "No, but I do not worship

"You are godless?" whispered the shocked cleric.

The captain interrupted, "Enough of this talk of religion. Steward, serve the food before I starve on their measly metaphysics."

Eyeing Stern with suspicion, the cleric raised his empty wine glass to be filled yet again. Stern noticed his fat cheeks were blushing crimson and his tiny eyes seemed to recede into his head. As soon as the steward placed platters of roasted duck, covered in a berry sauce, fried potatoes, and broiled fish down on the rough-hewn table, the captain turned to Sor Michaelsdottir and asked, "You escaped our introductions madam, won't you tell us about yourself?"

She smiled and said in a low voice, "There is not much to tell captain. I am a diplomat, serving at the pleasure of Tangrapra XXIII. She supported the King in his war against the Queen of Brasilika and now our alliance is at an end."

The cleric sputtered and spit up a bit of wine. "What do you mean, the alliance is at an end? Certainly this is excellent news. Has the Emperor made peace with Brasilika?"

"I do not know what is happening. All I know is that I have been expelled and that the king refused me audience three times in a row. The other members of my entourage left on an Imperial galley three weeks ago. I remained to close the embassy and sell off all of our holdings on the Island."

Even though the cleric appeared drunk, Stern suspected he was sober enough to discuss politics and remember the diplomat's responses, as well as his unfortunate confession to being godless.

"Surely, this does not bode well for the King," said the trader. "I mean the brotherhood of Mithlass is broken and the king is taking their property while his Xipponese allies withdraw."

"It would be imprudent for me to comment on the King or his plans; he has alienated his two major allies at a time when his own power is at its lowest. Consequently, I worry for my friends in Wyvernne."

"It is Glantz's will the King should perish. I know this because it has been foretold. Besides, the King's course was set when his great-grandfather cast out all demons, witches, and mages and destroyed the last of the blue-back dragons. Now, he depends upon the power of his muskets and his warrior brotherhood. The Island's greatest strength arose from its ancient alliance with the mage riders of Skaellander and their mounts – the blue-back dragons. Without the alliance of the ancient azure order of the dragon, the Island is nothing."

"I do not know what Glantz's will is but it was foolish for the King to challenge Brasilika," said the captain. "As for mages and dragons, that was a long time ago. Who among us has ever seen a blue-back? Did they ever exist?"

"You are right, of course. Brasilika controls many islands and its galleys sweep the southern seas of any opposition. In order to trade there I have to obtain numerous licenses and letters of passage. Because of the bureaucracy I must charge three and four times more for goods I sell there than the ones I sell in the north."

Stern was interested in Okeanus's politics but he feared to ask any questions, because his basic ignorance of the world and its history would reveal his foreignness. He thought he might find out a few answers by asking oblique questions.

"Brasilika must be the most powerful state in Okeanus?"

The cleric looked at him with a drunken squint and raised a pudgy finger as if to emphasize his point. "It is powerful because of the support of the gods of order but it is not the most powerful. Even I, a loyal subject of Glantz and his majesty, Loovest VI, must admit that the Imperium of Rhiannon in the eastern hemisphere is the most powerful. We of the west are only protected by the vast distance that separates the two hemispheres. Otherwise, we would all be subjects or perhaps slaves of Rhiannon and their demon god, Orobas."

"But if you both serve order, why would they try to dominate you?" asked Stern without thinking.

Wine dribbled from the laughing cleric's slack mouth. "Order demands domination. It is the basic structure of things. The gods of order would see one world with one king."

The trader said, "I have a book that I can lend you, if you are interested, on the rise of the House of Rhiannon."

Stern did not want to admit he could not read the runic language of the Island, so he said, "Yes, I would be very interested."

The woman looked at him knowingly, he suspected she read his thoughts like Kylla. He decided to test his suspicions by calming his mind, as Kylla had taught him, and cast a thought toward her. *"Can you hear my thoughts?"* He waited a moment and decided it was simply his own insecurity that unnerved him and she could not read his thoughts. However, several minutes later, when he had basically forgotten his experiment and was listening to a long involved story about smuggling from the captain, he heard, faintly at first, and then stronger: *"I shall summon the demon Kokabiel to teach you to read. In fact, I have contacted him and he is anxious to meet you. Your appearance on our plane has been foretold."*

Stern, somewhat shaken, asked, "Is he aligned with Focalor?"

"He is no daemon. He is a demon to be called by those he will serve. Do you not know the difference? You are an ignorant man?" He felt her laughing at him.

"How do you summon him?"

"In the same way all magic is performed, through the utterance of a spell taken from a grimoire. In this instance I will use a spell from the Gray Grimoire of Alexa. Tonight, you will come to my cabin after midnight. I will do a body reading and then I will summon Kokabiel, who will teach you to read and write the languages of Okeanus."

"Who is this Kokabiel?"

"He serves the gods of the various planes as a mediator of power, especially between good and evil. It is his role to make sure that neither has a decisive victory over the other. Sometimes he serves as a scribe to the gods. That is why he knows all languages. Legend has it he created language. Sometimes he appears as the black ape, A'an, the god of equilibrium and balance." She paused and then: *"Stern?"*

"Yes?"

"I called upon the gods of order and chaos and asked for a guide to help me with you because I sensed immediately that was what I should do. My feelings were justified because their response was instantaneous. They shouted out Kokabiel's name, the demon of light. It is obvious to me you are fated to have this demon as your guide. If I were not here he would have appeared anyway."

"How can you speak to both gods of order and chaos? This cleric seems to pit them against one another."

"They are always at war with one another but I am not a disciple of either. I have chosen to walk the middle way, like Kokabiel, to hold forces of both in my mind at once."

"There are so many things I desire to know about you and your world."

"We will have many weeks together. We have time to learn about one another."

"Why are you traveling to Noirrith? Isn't it an out-of-the-way island?"

She answered, *"Your lack of information about Okeanus is going to get you in trouble. Yes, Noirrith is small and out of the way but I have an important meeting there."*

He remembered Kylla's prediction and he suspected Kokabiel was the guide she foretold. He sighed audibly and the cleric looked up from his wine. Stern quickly pushed his fears away from his conscious mind; he could not afford to appear weak or confused in front of the cleric or the captain for that matter. Something she had said troubled him. She mentioned Kokabiel mediated between good and evil for both the gods of order and chaos. Who is good and who is evil? The captain interrupted his thoughts with a warning. "In the next few days, we must be vigilant because these waters are rift with pirates looking for ships heading for Trong. They believe any ship here now is either loaded with freight or gold or both to trade for spice. We are fast but in a short run against a pirate trireme we will lose."

The cleric, now quite drunk, slurred his words. "But surely we could fight off an attack?"

"Sadly, probably not, "answered the captain. "We would try, of course, but a pirate trireme could quarter over one hundred and fifty crew members."

"Have you been attacked before?" asked Stern.

"Several times, but each time I was able to outrun them."

"We will be fine," said the trader.

The captain nodded and added, "I, too, believe we will make it to Trong unharmed; however, it is important to be forewarned. If you hear the cry, 'pirates,' arm yourselves and join me on deck. We will need your help."

"I will pray for our safety," muttered the cleric, reaching for the wine carafe.

"Who would like some brandy?" asked the captain, changing the subject.

The cleric sputtered a shower of wine, illustrating his vote in the affirmative. The trader laughed and nodded his head in agreement, as Michaelsdottir rose. "I will take my leave, captain. It was an excellent dinner." She then sent a mental message to Stern. "*Wait thirty minutes and then come to my cabin.*"

The men stood and wished her good night.

Once she was gone, the cleric stuttered, "Thank the gods, the witch is finally gone. Now we can speak freely."

Stern asked, "She is a witch?"

"Are you a fool man?" shouted the cleric. "You don't become a diplomat for the Witch Queen without being a witch. That is probably why the King expelled her from the Island."

"I am a simple man, dear cleric. Could you explain why the King thinks he can conquer a mighty nation? I mean, the Island is a tiny place and from what I have seen of his troops, they are few in number."

The captain handed the cleric a glass of brandy, who took a sip, and said, "Listen, sellsword, it is quite simple. The King is an ambitious man. When he took the throne ten years ago, he proposed to expand his kingdom. His great-grandfather expelled the order of the Skaellander magi and exterminated their blue-back dragons. The King believed in his grandfather's cause, urged on by the clergy, of course, but he was not interested in just ridding his island of magic but in expanding his power. *Islanka* is rather isolated, surrounded by hundreds of deserted islands, and the King reasoned he could begin his expansion by taking control of them; however, custom dictates that in order to claim an island, one must establish a colony.

Establishing colonies necessitates the support of an elaborate social and economic system, which *Islanka* does not have. Nevertheless, the King began his expansion by pressing his unwilling subjects into colonial service, he basically imprisoned them and expelled them from their lands and sent them to the surrounding islands. He concocted a strategy, whereby he would colonize the more distant islands first and then work inward. He thought he could control more area that way. The first island he exiled colonists to, unbeknownst to him, had already been claimed by Brasilika and that, my friend, was what started the dispute that grew into the war."

"What happened to the colonists?" asked Stern.

"It was funny really. *Islanka* colonists, one hundred in number, landed on the northern coast. The year before the Brasilikans had established a base on the southern shore. The two groups were unaware of each other for almost three months, until a Brasilikan hunting party discovered three Islankan women picking berries in the forest. They raped them, beat them and enslaved them.

"The Islankans sent out a search party the next day and tracked the Brasilikan rapists to their base. However, the Islanders were basically farmers, not soldiers, and they did not have the strength or the experience to take on the more organized southern colony, so they returned to their base to think about their situation.

"They had been marooned on the island and they did not expect another ship from *Islanka* for at least another nine months. They estimated the Brasilikan colony numbered two hundred and fifty, too strong for them to attack. Someone suggested they should send an envoy to the Brasilikan base and negotiate a surrender, which they did. The Brasilikans agreed to accept them as indentured slaves. A contract was drafted and signed and the Islankan colonists became slaves to the Brasilikans.

"A year later, when the supply ship arrived from Wyvernne, the colonists' camp was nowhere to be found. The captain sailed around the island, looking for the colonists, and discovered the Brasilikan colony thriving in a natural harbor in the south. When he sent a row boat into the harbor, the Brasilikans fired on it."

Stern asked, "So the war started?"

"Not immediately. The King waited almost a year before hiring the Brotherhood to take the island from the Brasilikans."

"What did they do?"

"They landed one thousand men on the northern coast and attacked the Brasilikans from the forest that skirted the borders of their base. The king ordered them to kill everyone, and they did. Their payment was one half of the island. The Brotherhood took control of the Brasilikan colony and named it Merkheim. They then set about fortifying the town and a year later another two hundred colonists arrived from Wyvernne."

"That started the war?"

"Yes. Now the King had a blood enemy and was tied inextricably to the military strength and prowess of the Brotherhood."

"So why has he turned against the Brotherhood now?"

"Because he never liked them, although he felt they were a necessary evil. When they were defeated by the Brasilikans, the king knew the time was ripe to rid *Islanka* of them."

"Even though they died for him?" asked Stern.

The cleric laughed and shrugged his shoulders.

"The brotherhood doesn't have clean hands. They want to conquer the world for their god Mithlass. It was they who murdered the Skaellander magis in a bloody coup for the King's great-grandfather."

"Enough politics," ordered the captain. "First it was religion and now it is politics. Drink up and have a cigar."

Stern stood and excused himself. "I am sorry but I feel a bit drunk."

The trader said slyly, "For a sellsword, you can't hold your liquor."

The three men laughed and wished him a good night.

Stern quickly left the tight room, gray with smoke, and made his way to the fresh air of the deck. He had drunk very little but he was anxious to see Michaelsdottir.

The sky was cloudless and the winter night's air cold. Steam poured from his mouth, as he took deep breaths to clear his head. He worked himself forward, holding onto the wooden railing, and stopped near the prow. Images of piratical mayhem and demons filled his mind. He shook his head from side to side, trying to organize his thoughts. It seemed to him that every move he made on Okeanus' watery surface took him further away from his goal.

He tried to conjure up a memory of La Ciudad. All he envisioned was his son at the orphan school run by the Black Robes. The last time he saw him he was running with a stick, hitting a small leather ball in a wild game of war. His long legs propelling him down the field with the other boys, chasing him. A heavy splash and a spray of water interrupted his thoughts and he peered out into the darkness. A great leviathan swam alongside the schooner; only a shimmer reflected from the sheen of its oily black skin. Hoping to get a better view of the creature, he listened to the beast threading through the water and the machine-like sound of the ocean spray spewing from its blow hole. Finally, he turned away and worked his way back to the hatch and the gangway; growing excited at the thought of the woman, waiting for him down below.

Chapter Twenty-Six: Kokabiel

AS STERN KNOCKED gently on the witch's door, he felt his stomach knot and gurgle like a school boy's standing outside his first love's dwelling. The door opened and he entered a room with a bed built into the side of the ship and several aromatic candles casting shadows against the polished wooden deck. She stood, waiting for him, wearing a slight, transparent sleeping gown, which startled and pleased him. Ignoring his glance, she directed him to sit in a short wooden chair next to the bed and in a flat voice she began. "The magic I must perform is simple but powerful. During the process you must remain quiet. I want you to pay attention to me because this will be a valuable lesson for you. The first rule is no magic is conducted without consequences. The second rule is that no magic is conducted without the utterances of a word and the spilling of blood. Do you understand me so far?"

He shook his head affirmatively.

"I am now going to explain how I perform this magic. It is imperative you listen to me carefully; otherwise, I could lose you in the airy plane. I will cut a slit in its membrane, which you will step through. I will keep this cut open for one hour. You will take a talisman with you that will, in effect, bind you to me. When you receive the signal from the talisman, you will say the word 'yes' and I will bring you back.

"It is important for you to understand that time is different on each plane. What is an hour here may be a week or a month on another plane. You are not to pay attention to time; instead, you are to return the moment you receive the talisman's message.

"When you return, you may discover you have changed in some way. We will not know at first what traces of the plane remain with you. For instance, when you came to this plane, you discovered you had the power of the bare-sark. When you return from the airy plane, you may discover another power or even a defect.

"I will be sending you directly to Kokabiel. He is a demon and he is untrustworthy. You are there for only one thing – to learn to read and speak all languages. He will try to tempt you with other experiences, other powers. You must turn them down.

"When I say all, I mean all languages of this universe. Our universe contains all languages found on the nine spheres, the four elemental planes and the nine categories of angels. If the spell works and the demon plays his role, you will be a *polyhistor*, at least as long as you remain in this universe. I know this trip is part of your path. Not many make it and those who have gone have had different experiences. Some have returned insane; others cannot bear the responsibility of their power and kill themselves. Only the strong survive."

She sat down on the bed and put her hands on her thighs and leaned toward him. "Are you ready?"

Stern looked deeply into her eyes, trying to read her thoughts or feelings. He could see nothing except flecks of gold in her iris.

"I'm ready," he said with a sigh.

She walked to a small table, where a black leather bag lay open, and removed several pieces of colored chalk, a small cup and a knife. She cleared the center of the room and drew a large circle with white chalk then took the red chalk and drew a straight line from the top to bottom bisecting the circle. With green chalk, she drew a line from left to right, quartering the circle. Once she finished the initial diagram, she marked the four points where the lines met the circle with a rune. Moving in a clockwise direction, she drew a straight line from the first rune to the second, the second to the third, and the third to the fourth, which resulted in the creation of four isosceles triangles. She then retrieved five short red candles from the table and lit one at a time, holding it for a few moments and then allowing wax to drip on the floor to secure the candle over the rune. The last candle, she placed in the center of the circle. The candles were aromatic and their herbal scent was cloying and sweet. After seating all of the candles, she returned to the table, picked up the knife and approached him. He cringed, suspecting the next part of the ritual was not going to be good for him.

"Undress completely," she said, her voice a little hoarse from the smoke.

He looked up shyly.

"Do what I say," she whispered.

He quickly undressed in the cold room, as she, too, pulled off her gown.

When they were both nude, she pointed to the center of the circle. They sat, and she told him to put one foot in the right lower quadrant and the other in the lower left. She then stood facing him and ordered: "Give me your left hand, palm up."

She took his hand in hers then made a cut in the palm of his left hand with the knife. Although the cut was slight, he grimaced, as she dripped his blood into the cup and placed it near the candle burning between them.

"Stand where you are," she commanded, moving back to the table, where she picked up a braided horse-hair necklace. In the center of the necklace, an ornate piece of flat silver, engraved with runes, had been pinned. She brought the necklace to the circle and then pricked her right index finger and smeared her blood on the silver piece and said several words in an unknown language. "This is your talisman. Wear it always while on the airy plane." He pulled the necklace over his head.

She then placed her right palm on his left and his right onto her left and commanded him to stare into her eyes. He felt her breath on his cheek and the warmth of her body near him, resisting the frigid air of the room. She leaned forward, kissed him passionately, then leaned back without moving her hands, chanting in the guttural language. He felt her mind in his and she commanded him to close his eyes. He dozed off and it seemed to him that a long time passed. The freezing room was now warm. He could still feel her hands on him but the pressure now was light, her hands warm and dry. He kept his eyes closed as she had commanded. He felt a warm breeze on his cheek and smelled citrus in the air. The cloying smoke of the candles was gone and the feel of her hands was simply a memory, a vague and diffuse sensation that lingered.

"Open your eyes," he heard her call out from a great distance.

He stood on the top of a tower constructed of ivory-colored stone, perched on the side of a rugged chalk mountain, alone.

He soon figured out that this mountain refuge was situated in a massive range of white chalk pinnacles, stretching as far as he could see. To the right they were higher and more rugged. To the left, they were smaller and seemed to descend to the horizon. He imagined the left was west and right was east. He did not know why he thought this, it was simply an impression he had. He turned and examined his surroundings. The sky was cloudless, a gentle blue ether suffused with light, warm and dry.

A white moth fluttered past his right ear and he noticed a small nest with three colored eggs lodged in a crevice on the side of the lip of the tower's slate roof. He rubbed his eyes. Tired and strained, he searched for a word and then said, out loud, "I feel attenuated."

He sent out a mental message to Michaelsdottir but he heard and felt nothing. He turned toward the imagined east and wrapped his arms around his knees. He shut his eyes and soon fell asleep. Later he awoke to the sound of thunder. The sky, however, was still a cloudless blue. He surveyed the land that surrounded him and saw nothing unusual, except for a white dot in the east, the size of his hand. He faced the dot, staring because it seemed to be growing. He now suspected it was somehow related to the intermittent thunder.

Another white moth buzzed past his head, which he attempted to swat. Rather than flying away, it landed near his foot; its wings beating rhythmically, like a metronome. Soon two moths appeared and joined the first. It thundered and a yellow spear of lightning creased the cloudless blue of the sky. Twenty moths fluttered around his head and then descended onto the white chalky slate of the tower's roof.

The dot in the east grew larger. He was now convinced it was moving toward him and it was not a cloud.

Another mighty thunderclap shook the tower, and a thousand white moths filled the air like snowflakes. All he could hear was the mechanical buzzing of their wings, flapping in unison.

A sizzling stroke of lightening split the sky.

He smelled ozone and he identified the flying dot in the distance as a great white bird.

One more mighty thump of thunder and he could clearly distinguish the bird and its rider. They circled the flat surface of the tower with a million moths trailing in their wake. The rider, with bone-white skin and long, plaited white hair, wearing only a kilt and golden bracelets, circled the tower several times and then the rider pulled back on black leather reins and uttered a high-pitched shriek. The bird responded with a screech that resembled the metallic tinkle of a bell and then spread its great wings and extended its black talons as it landed on the edge of the roof. Swinging a long leg over the great bird's neck, the man jumped to the floor, disrupting the moths that rose like dust around his sandaled feet.

Stern stood to greet him, aware once again he was naked in front of an alien being. He noted the humanoid's strong aquiline features, his thin pale lips; his nose, shaped like a falcon's beak, his eyes, almond-shaped and hazel in color and his pointed ears. When the creature opened its mouth to speak, he displayed straight square teeth, black gums and pointed purple tongue. He bowed his head and addressed Stern by twisting and contorting his lips and tongue into odd shapes to produce strange trills and clucks. Finally, after some difficulty, he managed to say in *lingua*: "Why have you come to visit me, Little Star?" The demon then sat and the white moths lifted from the surface of the tower, clearing a space for him, fluttering about him until they secured places on his legs, lap, and arms to rest. Even after they settled, their wings continued to beat slowly, creating a low modulated hum that Stern found disturbing. He suspected they were not insects but miniature daemons, like the parrots on the first island he landed on, a memory that continued to haunt him.

Kokabiel, the demon, said, somehow sensing the moths disturbed Stern, "They are what they seem to be – simple creatures of this world. Do not worry; they do not yearn for your soul." Stern cleared his throat and attempted to articulate his reason for coming. "Michaelsdottir said you could teach me to read the runes of Okeanus and help me learn its languages."

Slowly, forming his words carefully, the demon gave a slight smile, which revealed his pointed tongue, and answered, "I can help you master languages and I can facilitate an understanding of the runes. But that is only one of my purposes here. To call upon me is to know me and to know me is to serve me. Nothing comes from nothing and nothing is given without a payment. Do you understand?" Stern nodded, although he immediately thought of the gods spewing from nothingness into existence. Kokabiel continued: "If I help you with this, you will be indebted to me. Someday I will call on you for help and you will do as I ask."

"Are you truly a demon?" said Stern, thinking of Focalor and the result of his aid.

The creature laughed and waved his right hand in a flourish and hundreds of moths rose into the air from his movement. "What do your eyes tell you?"

Ignoring the demon's question, Stern asked his own question: "What is your role in this world?"

"Ah, good, you are listening. One of my roles is to develop language but concomitant with that function is translation and mediation between beings, planes, worlds, and universes. Mediation is a subtle art at times but at others it is heavy-handed and blunt. I need help from time to time from creatures of other worlds, especially worlds I cannot visit. I have tried to find a source in your plane but I have been unsuccessful. In fact, I am simply a myth there, unreal to your people. You were so scientific and material before the dragons came that even your religion relied on mathematics. I may need your help from time to time in your realm."

"Help doing what?"

"I am entrusted with building a tower of languages through the axial intersections of the multiple worlds of the universe."

"What do you mean?"

"I am a demon of order and understanding. I oppose chaos and promote communication. I seek uniformity through thought and language."

"I still don't understand."

A vision of imperial wars flashed through his mind. He imagined a polished jackboot crushing down onto a peasant's neck. On an imaginary horizon, black smoke wafted upwards, staining a satin-blue sky, illustrating the fact that Kokabiel was a god of order. He felt chilled.

"Did you produce that image in my mind?"

Kokabiel smiled and rubbed his chin with his right hand.

"I have four gifts for you. They are important and they will become bound to you upon your accepting them. If someone tries to take them from you they will crumble and dissolve into dust. The best thing for you to do is to hold them dear, always. The second best thing for you is to memorize their substance. Memorization is hard, especially such arcane works and your task will be complicated by the fact the works themselves will struggle against you. They will always want to return to their source. They will fight your control over them and they will try to escape. So you must focus your mind and discipline yourself in your study of them. My suggestion is you find a safe place to lock them away, to protect them, and to study them diligently. Do you accept my gifts freely?'

Stern nodded. The demon, however, frowned and asked again. "Do you accept my gifts freely?"

"I do, Kokabiel."

The creature smiled and said, "The gift of interpretation and language is now yours."

Stern felt dizzy and heard a buzzing in his ears that lasted a few seconds.

Kokabiel, then, rose, causing a storm of moths to erupt from the floor, and walked to the giant white bird, which he called a *ziz*. He pulled from black leather saddlebags, decorated with silver studs and buckles, leather-bound books, and a red-woolen cloth. He sat across from Stern and took the first book, which was covered by dark brown leather, and opened it on the floor. The pages were tissue thin with gold edges and tiny runes covered each onion-skin page. Stern estimated there were over a thousand pages in the tome.

"This is the *Book of Beginnings*." He turned the book around so that Stern could see the pages. "You read this book from right to left, quite different from what you are used to." He turned the pages to what Stern would designate the last page. With his beautiful hand he pointed to the first line of the book and commanded in a deep and resonant voice, so different from his speaking voice, "Read that."

Stern saw only finely-formed runes.

In a guttural language, Kokabiel uttered the words and the runes seemed to grow darker and clearer, as if they were magnified gently.

"Now read them."

Stern slowly formed the words: "Now comes that which came not before."

"You can do better that."

He tried again and knew the translation was: "She came forth from nothingness."

"Better, but we expect poetry and philosophy, when reading the *Book of Beginnings*."

"From nothingness she came and spoke the primordial word and created order from her negative being."

Kokabiel clapped his hand and laughed. "You are closer but still not right. However, it takes ages to understand the words. Read the next line."

Stern read: "Her eight legs pinioned the planes of existence and formed a loom for her silk."

"Not bad but it will take you awhile to understand the tropes."

"Does this mean that there are nine spheres of existence?"

Kokabiel frowned and answered, "No, it means there are four elemental planes. Together the four planes make a complete world. Above the world is the one chaotic light and below lies solid darkness. Each plane possesses nine spheres ruled by mathematical laws. The planes lie on top of one another, each wrapped around by the spheres. Only the world tree connects them and commerce of one sort or another exists between them all."

He looked at Stern, giving him a few moments to think about his answer. Realizing Stern was not going to ask another question, he handed him the *Book of Beginnings*. As he touched the book, Stern felt a pain in his arms and his heart accelerated. It lasted only a moment but the sensation was so unpleasant he tasted bile.

When he recovered, Kokabiel placed another book in front of him that was thin and slight and bound in dark black leather with pages lined with silver. Stern estimated it contained no more than a hundred pages.

"You read this book from right to left. It is entitled the *Grimoire of Stone*. The spells are printed only on the right hand page. He opened the book and showed him the finely printed runes in a dark red ink.

"Read the first spell."

This was a different language and Stern could not make out the words.

Once again, Kokabiel read the first sentence.

"Now you read it."

Stern suddenly understood the guttural language and he read the red runes of the grimoire and translated: "I hold the stone against the darkest night."

"Now read the second line."

"To open a passage to a plane, I must hold the stone and say the special words of each."

"Very good but I would translate it thus: 'To open the passage to each world, I must hold my stone and say the sorcerer's spell for each.' This book is a handbook of sorts. It is more important to you than the *Book of Beginnings*, which is history, philosophy, and religion. This book is about power and responsibility. Do you understand?"

"Yes, I believe so."

"Good." He handed the book to Stern, who immediately felt bitter bile rise from his stomach. He quickly turned his head and spewed vomit over the white stones of the tower's flat roof, spraying the white moths, which rose into the air, their wings ringing like wind chimes.

"Magic is not easy on mortals and there is always a price to pay," whispered Kokabiel. "Are you ready to continue?

Stern wiped his mouth with his left hand then examined the book to make sure it was undamaged, as Kokabiel handed him a red woolen cloth, the size of a handkerchief. Extreme heat emanated from the center of the bundle. He unfolded the cloth to find a black stone within, the size of a marble, with golden veins that shone and blinked fragments of light.

"I created this stone of summoning. It is now yours and it connects us. Inside is a soul shard. Because you are not yet strong enough, you must use it to conduct the more complex spells, the ones in the second half of the grimoire. Hold the stone in your left hand."

Stern placed the stone in his left hand. The stone's heat increased and he feared he would soon be forced to drop it back onto the woolen cloth.

"Stand up and extend your left arm in front of you."

Stern followed the instructions.

"Now move your arm slowly from the center of your chest to your left as far as you can."

He conducted the procedure.

"Repeat the movement but say this spell. It is in the grimoire."

Stern repeated the words and an opening appeared to the hill where Kylla died.

"Reverse the movement and say the spell."

He did so and the opening closed.

"Now repeat the movement and say the spell but say Michaelsdottir at the end."

He did so and the plane opened up to the room where Michaelsdottir sat naked in the center of the candles.

"Now close the plane," commanded the demon.

There were tears in Stern's eyes because he knew he now held the way to return home in his hands.

"How do I step through the opening?"

"You must first master the stone and the grimoire." He paused, touched his long middle finger to his lips, and closed his eyes. When he opened his eyes, he said, "Our time is up. Study the books and ready yourself. The last spell in the grimoire summons the demon. Master it and you can open a portal to summon me."

He stood and pulled a black stone from a pocket on his leather kilt. He moved his arm like Stern had done and recited the spell; however, at the end he added another sentence, which included a reference to both Stern and Michaelsdottir, the ship and the captain. The plane opened like a wound and Kokabiel ordered Stern in his deepest voice to step forth through the void and meet fate's loom. Stern stepped forward, lost consciousness and awoke cradled in Michaelsdottir's naked arms. He had a tremendous headache, his throat was sore, and he shivered from a violent chill. He held the two books in his arms and grasped the stone firmly in his left hand.

Chapter Twenty-Seven: Speaking the Spell

"YOU ARE VERY ILL. We must get you to bed."

She dressed quickly and helped him into his clothes. Opening the door to her cabin, she looked both ways before pushing him out into the freezing passageway. She supported him as they worked their way up the passageway onto the deck and then down to his slot. Once there, she helped him stow away the books and the stone. She did not touch anything, knowing the sacred power of the items. She then wrapped him in his cloak and helped him climb into his hammock, where he immediately fell into a feverish sleep, dreaming Kylla came to him in a flat-bottomed punt and together they floated away from their enemies on a calm stream. On the banks of this dreamscape, elf-like creatures sang about the return of the blue-back dragons, while a great white stag bent its majestic head to drink from the shallows.

He slept fitfully throughout the night and the next morning he awoke, shivering; his robe and clothes soaked through. These feverish sweats reminded him of malaria attacks he experienced in the thick jungles south of La Ciudad, where he met the Argyll woman, the mother of his son.

Roby knocked on his door and then peered in to check the slop can, which was empty. Stern croaked out a weak greeting.

"Are you sick?" asked the boy, worry creasing his brow.

"Yes, it's a bit of food poisoning. Was anyone else sick from last night's dinner?"

Roby looked shocked and held back, afraid of approaching the ill man. Too many people fell sick and died within days on the sea.

"No, everyone seems well, except the priest is a bit under the weather." He made the sign of the drunk and Stern smiled faintly.

"Roby, I actually feel a bit better. I had a rough night though. Could you help me up? I must change out of these wet clothes."

"I will get you a clean towel and borrow some clothes from one of the men."

"Wait." It was too late; the boy had fled, fearful that touching Stern would infect him with a deadly disease.

Stern struggled out of the hammock. His hands shook and he felt as if he had lost weight overnight. Finally, he stood on the deck, dizzy and weak. His clothes were damp and it was freezing in the room, causing him to shiver so hard he thought he might break a tooth. Once he had shed all of his clothes, he toweled down with one of his woolen shirts, hung his cloak on a peg to dry, and spread the other clothes of the floor, hoping they would dry rather than freeze.

He pulled on his only other clothes, some woolen leggings and the shirt he had used to dry his body. Roby returned with a blanket, a towel and a woolen sweater.

"Thanks, Roby, this will help, especially the blanket."

He toweled off, slipped into the sweater, wrapped himself in the blanket, and crawled back into the hammock. He fell asleep before Roby closed the door.

Stern did not eat for the next four days. During that time he slept almost constantly. When he was awake he thought about Kokabiel and the books hidden in the chest, although he did not have the energy or strength to climb out of his hammock and study them. His illness, he knew, was payment for dealing with demons and their magic.

On the fifth day, the brilliant brass bray of a trumpet and the crew running over the roof of his slot awakened him. As he lay still, trying to collect his thoughts, he heard someone shout, 'Land ho.' He pulled himself up and stood unsteadily on the planks of the slot. He smelled his sour body and frowned. Roby opened his door and smiled, relieved the man was up at last.

"We will be docking within the hour."

Stern noticed someone had cleaned his clothes and folded them on top of the wooden chest.

"Roby, do I have time to wash?"

The boy frowned, "I have so much to do. Can you find your way to the stern?"

He nodded. The towel he had used several days before was gone. A clean one, folded next to his clothes, had replaced it. He took the towel and worked his way feebly to the rear of the boat to the crew's makeshift bath.

An hour later, clean, with his beard trimmed, wearing fresh clothes, he worked his way slowly onto the deck. Flakes of wet snow fell from a gray sky onto the purple water, obscuring the outline of a city on the edge of a wide horse-shoe shaped bay. It was filled with hundreds of vessels: junks, barges, biremes, triremes, dragon ships, schooners, galleys, corsairs, and one large warship, sporting two rows of twelve-pound guns, flying *Islanka*'s flag. They had all outrun winter, he thought, and many of the ships were anchored away from the shore, their crews in the city, waiting for spring or a load of cargo going south. Michaelsdottir stood on deck, wearing a hooded, scarlet cloak and he walked toward her, stopping a few feet away.

"You are up, finally," she said with a smile.

"Yes, I feel better."

"I look forward to hearing your tale."

He grunted and changed the subject. "That ship, the warship, is it from *Islanka*?"

"Yes, it passed us in the night two days ago. I would suggest you stay on board and keep out of their way."

"Have you sensed anything from it?"

"No, I feel nothing emanating from the ship; however, it is a warship, as you pointed out, and it probably houses a company of musketeers."

"Why would it be in these waters?"

"I have no idea but we should know something soon," she said, pointing at two long boats being rowed toward the schooner. From the nearest one, a man dressed all in black linen called out to the boat, asking if the Captain wanted a tug to the pier. The captain, at the stern, negotiated a price and two of the crew threw thick, heavy ropes to crewmen on the long boats, who tied them off and began tugging the schooner to a loading dock on the eastern side of the harbor. The cleric and the tradesman appeared on deck, carrying their bags, ready to disembark as soon as the ship reached the pier.

Stern breathed deeply, filling his lungs with the cold clear air. This was the first time in almost five days he did not feel like retching. An image of the great white *ziz* appeared in his mind and he felt a slight vertigo. It was as if the demon was with him now; a part of him, conscious of his actions. He had a lot to tell the woman and many questions. He hoped they would have some quiet time alone on the boat. He did not intend leaving it.

After almost an hour, they reached the pier, and once they tied the boat to the wooden dock, the crew sprang into a frenzy of activity, setting the gang plank, tying down the sails, opening the hatches. The tradesman was the first one off the ship, quickly working his way through the gang of workers waiting on the pier. He waved his hand and shouted out to the captain that he would be back in a day or two with a manifest for the new cargo.

Stern drew closer to the woman and whispered: "We have a lot to discuss about my adventure."

She turned to him, her eyes sparkling with energy, anxious to hear him tell everything that happened to him in Elysium, the aery plane.

The captain approached them and said, "You may leave the ship if you want but don't go far without an escort. This is a dangerous town full of pirates and thieves."

"I don't intend disembarking, captain," said Stern.

The captain examined him and asked, "Are you still sick?"

"I'm better but a bit weak."

"When was the last time you ate?"

"Days," he said.

"We will have fresh vegetables and meat for dinner tonight." He clapped him on the shoulder and said: "We will soon have you shipshape."

"Captain, did you notice the warship in the harbor?"

He cleared his throat and answered, "I saw them when they passed us on the sea. They scared me. I thought they were after us. They came on so fast."

Michaelsdottir asked, "Isn't it unusual for them to be out at this time of year?"

"You are correct. The King usually pulls his ships in for the winter. They will not be able to return to *Islanka* until the spring."

Roby was on deck talking to a man, dressed in black velvet, with a great silver chain hanging heavily around his fat neck. He displayed no weapon but two men dressed in black leather stood on each side of him, each sporting a rapier on one hip and a long curved dagger on the other.

Michaelsdottir said, "The harbormaster has arrived for his sack of coppers."

Stern shivered and noted the snowflakes falling now were fatter and wetter than those in the morning.

"Will the harbor freeze?" he asked.

"It's possible but it won't last long. Winter takes longer to arrive here than in the North. We should be all right."

"I think I will go back to my slot."

"We should meet tonight in my room after dinner to discuss what happened," she whispered.

When Stern reached his slot, he locked the door and opened the wooden chest. He removed the books from his leather knapsack. The first thing, he thought, he should do was to ask Roby for a waterproof bag. He had seen the men making some from the skin of the narllxx, a seal-like creature. For the time being, he tore his extra shirt in two and wrapped the *Book of Beginnings* carefully in one half of it and stuck it deeply into the knapsack, hiding it under his extra clothing. He then examined the *Grimoire of Stone* slowly, rubbing his hands slowly over its leather cover. He immediately felt an unpleasant sensation of heat and electricity in the palm of his hands.

Slowly, he opened the book and turned the first few onion-skin pages until he reached the title page, marked with the silver embossed runes for *g* and *s*. He turned this page slowly and carefully and noted that page two was titled, which he translated roughly as *evocation of the north wind*. Without translating the complete second page, he turned to the third page, which was titled: *evocation of the south wind*. Growing excited he skipped to the sixth page, which was entitled: *evocation of the wind elemental*. He sat down on the wooden floor beneath his hammock, using the wooden chest as a desk and thumbed through the book quickly, deciding that the first twenty pages concerned weather spells and the summoning of elements. The last ten pages involved the summoning of demons and the opening of portals.

He set the book aside and began to think about the strategy necessary to approach this arcane knowledge. He felt completely out of his depth and wondered yet again whether he had lost his mind. After an hour, he determined to approach the book slowly and methodically. There would be no skipping around. He would read and interpret the first page and learn it completely before he turned to the next.

Turning to the first page of text, he read its title out loud, pronouncing the strange words in Kokabiel's language. He read through the approximately five hundred words once and intuited that the page contained a spell to evoke the north wind. He read it again and the meaning of the words became clearer. He read and re-read the page for almost eight hours; the time passed without his awareness until he could read it as easily as he read his mother tongue.

Roby knocked at the door and Stern answered flawlessly in the complex language of Elysium. The startled boy knocked again. Stern rose and opened the door. Roby calmed down when he surmised Stern had simply been reading a book out loud.

"Dinner will be ready in an hour, sir."

"Thank you, Roby."

Once the boy had pulled the door shut, Stern wrapped the book in the other half of his woolen shirt and hid it beneath the *Book of Beginnings,* then locked the knapsack in the wooden chest. He washed his face and hands before going on deck. It was dark and the night air frigid. Fragile flakes fell and froze as they landed on the wet wooden planks of the deck. One crewman, who stood near the gangplank, held an iron pike in his hand, his head nodding as if he were about to fall asleep; a sign the captain was concerned about the thieves that populated the port. Stern worked his way to the back of the boat, which now faced the north, and raised his hands to the sky as the grimoire instructed and repeated the spell softly and slowly. He waited several minutes but nothing happened. He chided himself for believing in this claptrap. As he turned away from the stern on his way back to his slot, he felt a cold breeze from the north swirl past his cheeks. His heavy cloak billowed out gently as it filled with air. Encouraged, he spoke the words of the spell louder and faster and the wind in eager response blew quicker and harder, creating small whitecaps on the water, forcing the schooner up, as the waves passed under its hull. He chanted the spell louder and faster and the wind responded by almost knocking him from his feet. And as the waves deepened and quickened, the ship rose, waking the guard from his slumber.

Chapter Twenty-Eight: Arrested and Chained

STERN PANICKED, afraid the wind and the waves would inundate them, sinking all the ships, junks and barges in the harbor. However, after a minute or two, the wind resided. He sighed in relief but quickly realized he felt strained and weakened by just this momentary foray into incantation.

The guard, fully awake now, called out to him, asking who was there and he responded with his name. The man waved, recognizing him, and then returned to his post, now alert and nervous. Stern moved to the hatch and headed to the ship's galley, where he found Michaelsdottir seated and laughing at some story the captain was relating. The captain stood and shook his hand warmly: "You scared us, man. We thought you were done for. Many a man has fallen ill to some unknown contagion on the sea. These old ships seem to be full of poison for some."

"Sorry, Captain. I served the brotherhood in the jungles of the south and contracted some malady that comes and goes. I have so far been able to cast it off."

"You must relate some of your tales."

"Someday, sir, but tonight I would like to hear of your exploits and, if she would be so kind, something of Michaelsdottir's life."

The captain called for the steward to fill their wine glasses and he toasted his guest's renewed health. The wine was better than before and Stern suspected the captain kept the best vintage for special occasions.

They were beginning their third course, when they heard the sound of rushing boots across the decks and the discharge of a musket. The captain jumped up and pulled a pistol from his coat's voluminous side pocket and rushed out of the galley and toward the stairs that led to the deck. Stern looked at Michaelsdottir, whose face had paled. "They have come for you. I sense it. Go to your slot and prepare yourself."

"Me? Who would know I was here?"

"That was a musket and I fear it is the King's musketeers from that man-of-war we saw in the harbor."

Although he was not sure he trusted her powers completely, he feared for his books. He quickly made up his mind and fished out the large brass key that opened the chest in his room from a pocket on the inside of his robe. As he pulled out the key, his hand brushed the stone Kokabiel had given him on Elysium. It was warm to the touch. "Take my things to Bedwyr on Noirrith."

She took the key from his hand. "I swear I will do this thing you ask."

"I have another favor." He heard boots on the steps from the deck.

"Name it."

"I want to put a message in your mind to be delivered to the brotherhood on Noirrith."

A frown crossed her brow and he realized he was putting her in an awkward and dangerous situation but he had promised the brothers who had saved his life.

"I am ready."

Silently he spoke the message.

"Shall I repeat it?"

"No, I have it."

The door to the galley sprung open and a man dressed as a King's musketeer entered with a cocked flintlock pistol in each hand.

"On deck, the both of you!" he spat in the guttural patois of *Islanka*.

Michaelsdottir went first and Stern followed her down the passageway and up the worn wooden steps to the deck, where the few remaining crew were sitting, watched over by ten musketeers. Standing near the railing was a man dressed in black leather armor with a great black cloak draped across his shoulders. Stern noticed his boots first. He had seen those boots before, he thought, and he shuttered as his eyes met those of the King's assassin, Flymtt.

The musketeer with the pistols pushed Stern toward Flymtt, while another moved quickly to Michaelsdottir's side and guided her with a firm grip on her forearm to the sitting crew members.

"Stern, I am very surprised to find you here."

"Why? I thought you were hunting me. Or did you think I died on the rocks with Kylla."

"No, I seek the brother who fought Focalor to a standstill several days ago. But since you mentioned it, how did you escape the kroaxx?"

"I didn't escape. They mauled me badly."

"But you live my friend. Very few men have survived one kroaxx, let alone three."

"Kylla didn't survive but her courage saved me."

"Somehow I think you are being modest." Flymtt rubbed his chin, darkened by several days' growth of beard. "You have changed. Just weeks ago you did not speak my language and now you talk like one raised in the gutters of Wyvernne."

Stern changed his voice and imitated Flymtt's accent.

The rogue looked surprised and said, "Now you are speaking the Northern dialect, my dialect, by the way."

Flymtt rested his right hand on the steel hilt of the rapier he wore on his right hip and Stern felt the stirring of the bear; he tasted bile and he heard Kylla's screams echoing through the hills. His vision blurred and he saw everything as a variation of red. Fearful of the musketeers' response, he forced the blood of the bare-sark down; he could not afford to reveal himself now. He needed a plan. An attack too soon might jeopardize the lives of the others and forestall his reaching Bedwyr. He must think rather than react, although his desire to kill Flymtt was growing second by second and he feared he did not have sufficient control over his murderous impulse.

"So your innocence and confusion when we first met was an act to deceive me?"

"No, everything I told you was true. Your world and the daemon Focalor changed me. He unloosed things in me that I did not know existed." Stern paused and said, "You cannot truck with daemons and dragons and remain unscathed. They poison you, and I imagine, will ultimately kill you."

"You met Focalor?" asked the rogue.

"Can't you guess? Focalor sent the kroaxx. He has been chasing me since I arrived on the island. He is still chasing me."

"So it was you that fought him?"

"Of course, did you think you would find a great warrior on this schooner?"

"My orders were to apprehend the sellsword Tatyx."

"It is I, my friend," said Stern bowing like a character in a historical romance sold for a copper on the streets of La Ciudad.

Flymtt's eyes widened. "Pratt, take this man into custody. We have found our sellsword."

"May I gather my things from my slot?"

"No. I have everything you will need aboard our ship. We sail at dawn."

Pratt tied his hands behind his back with thin strips of hide and then placed a rough hempen rope around his neck and led him from the deck and down the gangplank. Flymtt walked next to him and the remaining musketeers fell into single file behind him.

"Where do we sail?" Stern asked.

"Back to the island, my friend. The King wishes to speak to the man who fought Focalor and lived."

"How is that possible? I thought the harbor was frozen and inaccessible."

Wyvernne is frozen in but Cathair, a small fishing village on the southeastern coast, is not. It is seventy-five kilometers further south than Wyvernne and it is protected on the north by the Ebon Mountains, the highest mountains on *Islanka*. We will land there and then take sleds to the King's winter palace near Milieu."

"How did you know I was on the *Whirlwind*?"

"We caught the man that escorted you to the ship. After a few days in the dungeons of Stormcrow he gave us your name and the name of the boat you escaped on."

"What happened to the brother?"

"Don't worry. He awaits you in his cell in Stormcrow Keep. However, I don't know what shape he is in, there is no heat and as you know the winters are brutal on the island."

As the musketeers and their prisoner wound their way through the narrow stone streets of the town, Stern could hear people singing and laughing in the bars and hostels. Streetwalkers hooted at him as he passed, relieved that someone else was suffering. Kids threw clumps of mud at him and sailors laughed and called him names. Finally, about two kilometers north of the *Whirlwind*'s berth they reached a wide stone pier that jutted deeply into the harbor. Two long boats awaited to ferry them to the *Gemmell*, anchored in the deeper waters of the harbor.

Once they had wrestled the bound Stern onto the deck of the ship, Flymtt cut his leather binding with a short, sharp dirk. Stern rubbed his hands and quickly scanned the deck, looking for a way to escape. He noted a full score of musketeers and as many sailors on the deck. Snow fell and ice formed blue patches.

"Take him down to his cell, Terzis."

Stern felt a pike point in the small of his back and Terzis, a small dark musketeer, wearing a tin helmet, sneered and growled, "Let's go."

They descended several flights of stairs and Stern realized the warship had three decks and many cannons. The second deck was open and housed the cannons and the sailors. Hundreds of hammocks hung from the ceilings, their makeshift home. The musketeers were quartered on the third deck, near the stern, where Terzis untied him and forced him into a small closet and barred the door, which only opened outward. Stern sat in the corner and noticed mouse droppings spilled over the rugged wooden decking. He studied the door and noted it was ill-shaped and poorly constructed. The cell was obviously an add-on, an afterthought created by an amateur carpenter, probably one of the musketeers. He pushed on the door with his boot and it gave a bit; the green wood warped and thin.

The cell was damp. Water seeped through the wall of the ship and ice formed in the corners and floor, as Stern hugged himself to foster some warmth. A few weeks in this hole, he thought, and he would die of pneumonia. He heard the musketeers talking and storing their gear, the captain barking instructions, and then the grating rumble of the iron anchor being raised. The Islanders were not going to wait for dawn. They were in a hurry to return to *Islanka* and the King.

He felt the movement of the ship as the Captain turned it toward the north and shivered from the cold, as he unconsciously fingered the small hot stone in his pocket. Once again his quest was being detoured and he bristled at the thought he was being taken back the way he came. He folded his arms around his knees and lowered his head and Gotha entered his mind and he imagined her pregnant, riding her zebra. It all seemed too fantastic, he thought: his present reality consisted of the King's warship and the hatred he felt for Flymtt.

He fell asleep. When he awoke he was stiff and sore, cold and wet. He called out that he needed to relieve himself. A musketeer angrily shouted for him to close his mouth and urinate on the floor. He heard laughter from the other side of the wall, as a gray mouse crawled through a small rough hole in the side of the makeshift cell. He remembered the well and the Freedmen and the taste of rat.

He needed a plan to escape. He had no idea how long they had been sailing but he suspected from the sounds on the other side of the door that the men were asleep and it was still night. He did not want to go north and any escape must be accomplished before they got too far away from land. He sat and thought, running scenarios and plans through his mind, rejecting most immediately. He thought of Kylla's prediction that he would arrive at Noirrith in the guise of a great sea turtle and he wondered if he could transform into yet another animal. He concentrated on the sea turtle as he remembered it, as it existed on his plane. He imagined swimming beneath the surface of the sea, his large flipper-like legs moving silently, the sun rippling and distorting through green waters. He soon gave up because he felt nothing; no possibility of imminent transformation. Perhaps, he could only change into a wolf and bear or bird with assistance or as a result of emotional trauma. He thought about the stone and a portal but he had not yet mastered the spell and his books were with Mikk.

He fell asleep for a second time and awoke to the sound of someone raising the bar on the door. Terzis pulled the door open and stood above him. "Get up! The Captain has ordered you to eat and then walk on the deck. He doesn't want you dying on us."

"What time is it?"

"Dawn."

Terzis pushed him up the stairs onto the deck. The sun rose and frigid wind blew from the north. Frozen flakes of snow filled the air and gray clouds of breath billowed from his mouth, as he walked. In the distance he could see land, obviously the island they just left. For some reason the captain was hugging the shore as long as possible. The sight of the island gave him hope and he smiled realizing he still had time to implement his plan.

"Is that Trong?"

Terzis turned and looked at the island. "No, that is one of the smaller islands of the Trongian archipelago. There are probably a hundred of them."

"How far are we from Trong?"

"Maybe sixty nautical miles to the southwest," he spat back.

"When do we turn to the open sea?"

"In the evening," he sputtered. "The Captain is hugging the shore as much as possible. Winter is coming and he is afraid of blizzards and whirlwinds."

As Flymtt approached them with a swagger, Stern felt the pulsating anger of the bear, rising to the boundaries of his consciousness. He swallowed and rubbed his eyes and concentrated on his plan to escape. If the bare-sark appeared now, he reasoned, it would ruin his chances.

Flymtt rubbed his hands together vigorously. "We are making good time but winter is coming in fast. Soon the whole northern sea will be frozen and even Trong's harbor may close this year."

"What happens when so much of the sea freezes?"

"We take sleds across the ice to the connecting islands. It is more convenient in some ways."

A green wyvern flew off the starboard side and one of the sailors called out a warning.

"You better go back to your closet. We don't want you ending up as dragon food. Terzis, escort him back and lock him in."

Before disappearing into the bowels of the ship, Stern watched the small dragon circle in the distance.

Chapter Twenty-Nine: Shipwrecked Again

AS SOON AS HE HEARD the wooden lock fall into place and the faint sound of Terzis walking away, Stern sat on the floor and began to recite the summoning spell for the north wind, one of the few spells he had mastered. He repeated it over and over again until he felt the ship rock and dip on an ever-widening trough of waves, deepening now, pushed forward by a rushing storm.

The rocking, falling ship, creaked and cracked, against the onslaught, as Stern struggled to maintain his stomach and voice. He stood and pressed his hands against the sides of the cell and spread his feet wide apart for stability. He shouted out the spell now; the howling wind drowning out the sound of his voice, as the temperature dropped and the moisture on the walls of the cell froze into a blue sheen of ice. He felt the boat turning in the wind and he noticed fissures and fractures forming in the ship's gunwale. Up above, on the deck, he heard screams and the fall of debris. A loud crash signaled the demise of one of the three masts and then the ship turned onto its side and water rushed over the deck and down into the lower decks. Frigid water rose around his feet before he fell forward with the overturning of the ship. And, as the ship sank, he continued to shout the spell, hoping the wind and waves would scuttle them onto a beach. He feared he might drown himself but he drove onwards, pushing through his fear and panic, calling the spell and forcing the ship to its limit of endurance. Finally, with a solid whack, the ship broke in two against the rocks of an island and he fell against the floor, smashing his head, and passing out.

He woke in silence and ice. His clothes, soaked, were now frozen rigid and he was shivering so hard his teeth knocked together. The ship lay at an angle, the gunwale crushed against the rocks and the door to his cell facing up toward the sky. He pushed against it but the lock held. He knew if he didn't free himself soon, he would freeze to death. A sudden fear took control of him and he imagined his death in this cell on the beach of a deserted island in the frozen ocean of a strange world. He turned and lay on his back, his feet pressing against the door. He pulled his legs to his body and then struck out, both feet hammering into the door. Nothing happened. He repeated the action ten times. His legs now ached and vibrated. At the very least, he thought, the noise should have brought someone but no one came; he heard nothing. He wondered if the storm had killed everyone. He continued attacking the door on and off during the day but he failed to budge it. When night arrived the temperature dropped further and he climbed up as high out of the water as possible and huddled in his wet clothes. He fell asleep sometime in the night. At dawn, he awoke to the sound of voices, speaking a new and unknown language. He pressed his eyes with the palm of his hands and concentrated on the words of the strangers, trying to learn the language as quickly as possible. When the voices grew nearer, he began to pound on the door again with his feet and call out for help. Soon, he heard several people gathered around the door of the cell. They seemed to be heatedly discussing whether they should open the door and free whoever was trapped there. Their language was unknown to him but he could sense they were puzzled and afraid. The more they talked, however, the more he deciphered. Soon he began to call out for help in their language and their arguing abruptly stopped. One of them said in a hushed voice that the room contained a daemon that could mimic their language. Another offered the explanation that the captive must be one of their people taken in a raid. Finally, one suggested seeking the war master and asking his advice.

Stern relaxed and stopped screaming and listened as carefully as he could to the men whispering on the other side of the door attempting to learn as much of their language as he could before the war master arrived. Just the title scared him and he prepared himself for the worst. After some time, he heard the sound of many iron-shod boots working their way through the capsized boat to his door and a unified grunt from the waiting men, recognizing the power and authority of newly-arrived war master. Then a baritone voice asked, "Who are you?"

Stern thought for a moment. "I am prisoner of the King of *Islanka*."

There was mumbling on the other side. Several suggestions were made to the war master: questions the other men wanted answered before they smashed the door open.

"What is your name?" asked the same baritone voice.

"Stern," he answered quickly.

"From where do you come?"

"I come from an island in the far north. I am on my way to see the magus—Bedwyr."

Only silence existed now. In fact, it was so quiet Stern could hear the waves beating against the sides of the battered ship.

"Stand away from the door, Stern!" the war master called out.

Stern moved back and pressed himself against the hull's remnant. There was a loud smashing sound and the head of a huge war hammer penetrated and split the wood of the door. He covered his eyes to protect himself from hundreds of splinters thrown off from the stout whack of the war hammer that in just a few hits destroyed the door completely. Once he realized the attack was finished, Stern opened his eyes to stare into the pale clean-shaven face of a creature wearing a metal helm. He guessed he was facing a man but the creature's features were so delicate and fine that Stern thought at first that it was a woman. Long reddish blond hair hung loosely around the creature's shoulders, adding to the confusion of gender. He was approximately six feet tall, slim, slight in build; chain mail that glittered like red and green fish scales draped his body and extended past his knees. Greaves similar in color to the chain mail protected his legs, while a pair of sturdy black leather hob-nailed boots covered his feet. Besides the war hammer, which he held in his hands, protected by reddish green mail gauntlets, a long curved dagger dangled from a wide leather belt tied tightly at his waist. The blade of the dagger shimmered red and green like the mail and reflected an eerie glow into the shadows of the capsized boat.

Before Stern could speak, the warrior backed out of the space to allow another, taller man to approach. Older but similar in build, he wore a helm with black metal wings sprouting from each side. Blond hair hung down his back in two long braids and he sported a thick mustache. He too wore shimmering red and green mail but instead of a giant hammer, he carried a two-headed ax in his right hand, while two short red swords shimmered on each hip. He smiled and said, "Well met, Stern. I am Axel, the war master of Svenqvist's dragon ships."

Wet and tired, Stern felt embarrassed in the presence of these glittering warriors. He straightened up as best he could in the leaning wreck and said as clearly as possible in Axel's language, "Well met, war master. I thank you for freeing me from my cell."

"Come Stern, let us leave this ship."

Stern, stiff and sore, followed the war master out of the wreckage. He did not have to climb up any stairs because the ship was severed neatly in half and he was able simply to step out of the cracked hull onto the beach. It was cold and gray but he could see clearly in the wintry sun. Debris and bodies covered the white sand. A hundred or so of the war master's warriors wandered about the wreckage checking the bodies and the debris for loot. If a sailor or musketeer was found alive, the war master's soldiers dispatched him. Stern surveyed the field to find Flymtt's body. He did not see it. He could have been washed over board or he could have escaped into the woods of the island.

The war master set off down the beach with his men and Stern following him. Shortly, they came upon five brightly painted beached boats; each sporting an avatar on the prow. Stern named each avatar out loud and in the language of the reavers: stag, wolf, bull, lion, and dragon.

As they marched down the beach, the warriors fell in behind the war master, their arms full of loot, weapons and glittering swag. Stern wondered why he had not been killed with the rest, as he marched along the beach with the war party, and he suspected his ability to speak their language plus his captivity had saved him. The sun rode low on the horizon and it would soon be dark. He shivered from the cold wind and his wet clothes, as he realized the dragon ships had no cover and he would spend a cold night in the elements in wet garments. He would be lucky to survive the night under these conditions.

When they reached the boat with the dragon's head carved in the prowl, the war master ordered him to climb aboard and take a seat on a rowing bench near the till. A young warrior with dark hair and piercing blue eyes sat down next to him and growled: "When the command comes we row. Do you understand?" Stern shook his head in the affirmative but the man glared at him, not understanding the significance of his nodding up and down. "I understand," said Stern.

Approximately forty men took their places at the ten oars on each side; two men to an oar. The war master stood in the front, while a tall man with flaming red hair and beard took his place in the rear, grasping a giant wooden till firmly with both hands. Several warriors on the beach pushed the dragon ship into the sea and then the war master gave the command to row in a loud voice. A man in the center of the boat began to bark commands to the rowers. Slowly by following his instructions the men turned the boat toward the sea. A young man took his place near the till and began to beat out a cadence on a large drum, while two men unfurled a great red triangular sail with the head of a black ram embroidered in the middle. The war master called for the ram's horn and one of the men in the prow stood and blew a long, loud note. Four other horns answered the call as the five ships lined up in a "v" formation, like geese, and sailed north. Snow fell and a cold wind blew over the ship. The men rowed silently and steadily. From time to time the war master called for the horn and Stern guessed he used the instrument as a device to keep the boats together in the dark.

Chapter Thirty: Heorot

STERN'S ARMS ACHED and blisters formed on his hands. Dismissing the pain, he suspected this was just the beginning of his agony. They continued to row several hours after the sun set. Sometime in the evening, a command was given to add sail to take advantage of a fresh breeze from the south. The men pulled their oars in and up and then lay across them, resting from their hours of unceasing work. Like the others Stern leaned across his oar and fell into a deep sleep. He awoke to the sound of a ram's horn and the men once again lowered their oars into the water. Stern had no idea how long he had slept. The southern wind had died and the men now strained against the oars, driving the ships against a hostile and frigid north wind and a wet snow. None talked, as they mechanically pulled on the wooden oars.

Several hours later, morning light seeped across the surface of the sea. Snow continued to fall and Stern could make out pieces of ice floating on the rough surface of the water. Horns sounded and the man sitting next to Stern said, "Thank the gods, we are approaching Heorot. My ass is frozen to this damn bench." Several of the men around them laughed and then they all began to sing a song about Heorot and the women waiting for them with ale and a warm fire. As the song progressed through several verses, the lyrics became more and more obscene. Stern found himself laughing along with the reavers, although he had no idea what would be waiting for him when they arrived at Heorot. He did not even know why he was still alive.

The lead boat turned toward the mouth of a river flowing into the sea. Whitecaps danced where the rapid river water met the ocean's waves and Stern felt the boat lift as it crossed the whitecaps. A call to pull and the reavers strained against the wooden oars, fighting the strong, savage current.

They rowed for almost an hour upriver. Along the banks, a thick growth of tall evergreen trees and dense vegetation seemed to cover the island. Finally, a break in the foliage revealed a clearing that housed a village comprised of fifteen or twenty long, log buildings. Ten wooden piers extended into the water, where the reavers docked their boats, as horns shrieked and people poured from the long houses and ran to the docks to greet their returning warriors.

The people, mostly women and children, dressed in green and red robes, were as tall and pale and as handsome as the reavers. One man, wearing a multicolored cloak of parrot feathers, carrying a black staff covered in several runes, walked at the head of twenty or thirty others.

The people stopped at the edge of the beach and made way for the tall man to walk through them and step upon the wooden dock. The metal base of his staff banged against the wooden planks of the pier. As the man approached the boats, the war master climbed onto the pier and bowed. The old man placed his hand on the war master's head and sang a benediction to the gods of the sea, while the people on the beach and in the boats knelt and bowed their heads. Stern imitated the reavers and as soon as the man finished the war master called for Stern, who made his way awkwardly through the length of the boat and climbed onto the pier. His arms and back ached, his hands were a bloody mess, and he was still wet, as he approached the man, who said, "Stand, Stern. I am Olivar, the *hejtman* of this kraal. I welcome you on behalf of Svenquist, our king."

Stern replied, "Thank you Olivar for rescuing me from the Islanders."

The man grunted and turned toward the village. As he walked away, he said, "Follow me and we will tend to your wounds."

Stern fell in behind the *hejtman*. As he walked he surveyed the primitive camp, noticing there was no wall and the people carried no weapons.

The *hejtman* set a steady and rapid pace toward a long, narrow log house perched on the top of a hill overlooking the rest of the village, as blond-haired and blue-eyed children ran next to them, laughing and touching Stern. Compared to them, he thought, he must appear quite bizarre with his bedraggled robes, black hair, brown skin, and massive black beard. Several children called out to others to come and see and touch the black bear.

206

They entered a long, log building at its south end. The north end solid to protect its inhabitants from the frigid wind. A large stone fireplace dominated the center of the building, where gray, acrid smoke wafted upwards through a circular opening in the roof. Dogs lay in packs around the hall and between and under several sleep platforms that extended from the walls. The *hejtman* led him to one such platform, where furs lay strewn over its rough wooden surface, and pulled a massive black bear's fur to the center of the platform before signaling for Stern to sit near him. A woman with a lit clay pipe with a long stem in one hand and a tankard of ale in the other approached the *hetjman*, who took the pipe with a half-bow, puffed, and then drank a deep draught of the ale. "The woman will be back to serve you," he said with a laugh.

Stern replied as graciously as possible: "Thank you, Olivar."

"Tell me your story Stern," he said, taking another puff on his pipe.

Stern related the story of his journey from the north, leaving out most of the pertinent details and simply concentrating on Flymtt's cowardice in the face of the kroaxx and his subsequent trip to the city. He wanted Olivar to believe he was a simple traveler, betrayed by the King's men.

As he was finishing his story, two women dressed in multi-colored shifts and dark red cloaks appeared and bowed before Olivar, who turned to Stern and said, "Go with these women and they will tend to your wounds, provide you with clothing and feed you."

Stern followed the women from the long house. Outside, they set off down the hill, through the village and onto a beaten trail that led into a forest of beech and ash. The women who from time to time turned toward Stern, sniffed and then laughed. Stern interpreted this as being their way of telling him he stank. Finally, they reached a bath house on the bank of a rushing stream. Smoke rose from its stone chimney.

Inside the bath house they tried to strip off his clothes and he asked: "What are you doing?"

"We are going to bathe you and give you clean clothes."

Stern pushed them back and then dug into a small pocket inside his cloak and retrieved the demon's stone.

"I have a relic that is sacred to me," he muttered, grasping the stone.

One of the women walked to a chest and opened a drawer. After some rummaging, she drew out a brown leather pouch that hung from a braided black leather strap. "This pouch and strap are made from the skin of a minotaur warrior. Use it for your relic."

Stern took the pouch and opened its small mouth and inserted the stone inside and then pulled the leather strap over his head. It was a tight fit but it worked. The demon's stone now hung around his neck, radiating heat.

"Are you ready?" The younger woman laughed and took his hand, leading him to an adjoining room where she also undressed. The older woman examined his wounds and his scars. His tattoos interested her, she said in a whisper, as she turned him around to see them better.

"What are you?" she asked quickly, looking at him directly. Her blond-white hair, now damp from the heat and wetness of the room, rested loosely on her shoulders.

He shrugged at the complexity of the question, as the younger woman signaled for him to sit on a wooden three-legged stool, where she poured a large bucket of hot water over him and rigorously soaped his back and arms, while the older one doused his head and began to massage his head and beard. When he was lathered from head to foot, they poured several buckets of hot water over him, rinsing him clean. The older woman then took his hand and led him to another room where there was a large pool of scalding hot water, lowered herself in and then signaled him to follow. Swimming to the corner of the pool, he lay back, resting against a smooth wall of stones, as the two women floated to the opposite corner and gossiped. He closed his eyes and felt extreme exhaustion taking control of him. He could barely hold his eyes open and soon fell asleep.

He awoke with a start, as the young girl with the pale blue eyes pulled on his hand. Climbing from the hot water, they moved through yet another door and stood on a deck, open on three sides, with a smooth pine floor and a round wooden tub in the center. Snow fell and a brisk northern wind blew across the rushing stream that ran from the mountain past the bathhouse. He shivered as the older woman dropped into the tank with a scream and the younger one pushed Stern in before her. Stern felt his breath escape in a whoosh from his body, as they bobbed up and down for several minutes and then climbed out laughing. The women rushed through the next door, a room lined with yellow pine, where they had piled rough towels on wooden planks. They dried off and the blonde asked Stern to sit next to her. She took his hands and rubbed a thick cream over his bloody calluses and applied a poultice to his cuts and bruises. The other woman quickly dressed and left the room. She soon re-appeared with dark red woolen pants, a white linen gray shirt, thick woolen socks, and a multicolored vest, some leather high-top moccasins and a thick woolen red cloak with a hood.

Now dressed, in his new clothes, they led him outside where a young boy, holding the reins of two gray and black ponies, waited. When the boy saw him, he moved forward and handed him the reins of one of the ponies and said, "She awaits us." He then mounted his pony and started off down a narrow trail through the trees. Stern followed on his pony, his legs dangling from each side.

Pulling the hood up onto his damp head to protect him from the falling snow and the frigid air he followed the boy up the trail toward the river before turning back toward the hills. The ponies climbed slowly, breathing with great gasps in the cold air, as they strained against the steep incline and Stern's weight.

They rode for at least an hour, climbing higher and higher into the hills. Stern's stomach growled and he felt faint; it had been days since he had any substantial food.

As they climbed above the timber line, Stern looked over his shoulder to see the village, the harbor and the dragon boats. Before him, he could make out a small stone cottage, a wisp of smoke curling above its chimney.

The boy halted his pony in front of the stone house and Stern rode up next to him and sat astride his horse, waiting for instructions. The boy leaned forward and took the reins of the pony and said in a worried voice: "She waits inside. Please hurry."

Stern dismounted and walked stiffly to a wooden door, festooned with all sorts of relics and designs, wild flowers, animal skins, and wooden totems, pulled the handle and pushed the door open. The smell of incense and cooking food made his mouth water.

Chapter Thirty-One: Hochangsttraumerin

HE OBEYED A STRONG feminine voice that ordered him to close the door. Inside he stood quietly, as his eyes adjusted to the shadows of the room. To the left of the fireplace a woman sat in a dark wooden chair, her long leather-clad legs extending toward the center of the room, her head and torso hidden in shadows. Her feet covered in high-top leather boots were crossed at the ankles, indicating she was comfortable and relaxed. He looked around for another chair and spied a three-legged stool in the corner opposite her. He moved toward it slowly, allowing her to stop him if she wished. She watched him closely and then placed her hands akimbo and sighed.

"You should not fear me. I found you and sent the dragon ships to save you from the King's musketeers."

Stern sat down facing her. The stool was short, causing him to look up at her.

"Who are you?"

"I am called, in our language, Hochangsttraumerin. There is no translation in the Island's language."

Stern, because of the demon's power, immediately had a sense of the word's meaning but he asked her to explain.

"I dream the fears of the tribe and work out a way to overcome them."

"I don't understand."

"Right now the tribe fears the onset of winter. Already, we have had colder days and nights than in recent memory. There are legends of great winters but no one living has experienced them. Suddenly, their dreams are full of their fears. The oceans freeze. Snow falls in massive amounts and great beasts from the north migrate south over ice bridges. The leviathans flee the northern waters and the dragons hibernate in ice caves."

"So what do you do?"

"I do the dreaming spell and I figure out what we should do?"

"How did I enter your dreams?"

She laughed. "The words you used mean, how did I come to sleep in your dreams. In our language your expression has a sexual connotation."

"Sorry. I guess what I am asking is, how did you find me?"

She straightened up and by moving, she exposed her face to the reddish glow of the fireplace. She had the delicate features of her tribe, pale white skin, long raven black hair and pale blue eyes. Two silver earrings hung from each ear lobe and six to seven silver chains hung around her neck. From each chain dangled one or two silver trinkets and tokens, while numerous silver bracelets glinted and glimmered in the fire's light.

Before she answered his question, she smiled revealing her straight, strong teeth and pale, full lips. "Olivar dreamed that an *Íslensk* battle boat entered our harbor and fired on our kraal. During the dream he boarded the ship, fighting his way to the lower decks. Along the way, he discovered all types of creatures and humanoids enslaved in chains. In one cell, however, he discovered a dragon. It was not one of the common dragons we know but an extinct blue-back dragon, a battle dragon, the type of dragon the ancients rode.

"When he told me his dream, I immediately felt its numinous quality. Here was a special dream, a big dream that demanded elucidation. Therefore that night I ordered Olivar to sleep with me here in front of this fire. I gave him a draught of an elixir that facilitates a sacred dream state.

"As we slept, I entered his dream. Once again the *Íslensk* battle boat entered our harbor and sailed up the river toward our kraal. Once again, Olivar boarded the ship and fought his way to the lower deck. When we reached the cell I could smell the dragon and feel the heat of its breath. He was correct it was a blue-back, a war dragon of the ancients. Olivar wanted to awaken it but I forced him to stay asleep and face it. I cajoled and screamed at him. I threatened and insulted him. I was relentless in my attack. I was determined to see the dragon.

"He relented and broke the lock on the cell. Inside was a pregnant blue-back. I approached and spoke the ancient commands of the dragon masters and she responded. It was then I noticed you in the corner of the cell, sleeping. I approached you and put my arm around your shoulders. You were feverish and muttering in your sleep but you responded and snuggled into me, like a baby.

"At that point something miraculous happened. I entered your dream. I had never been in a dream within a dream. I saw you struggling against all odds to reach the magus, Bedwyr, and I decided to help you if I could. Once I told you I would help, a demon appeared riding on the back of a great white bird. He wore silver armor and he was very beautiful. He told me I was now part of the quest to return the blue-back dragon to Okeanus.

He warned me there were others and he showed me the fate of those who had already fallen. The most vivid vision contained Kylla's death. He also showed me the future. I watched from a mountain peak the mobilization of the Brotherhood and the creeping ice of the north. I heard the King of the Island rant and rave before his lords and I saw Dra'ghan ships set sail from the south, seeking the place of the dragon's return. I witnessed a great battle on a frozen ocean and several naval ones. But most importantly, I was present at the return of the blue-backs to the island of Grun and the end of your quest.

"When the visions ceased, I awoke and the demon handed me a stone and instructed me to hold it in my left hand as he recited a rune poem. He sang the words that told me your name and the location of your ship. I also saw all active players in the quest tangled in the skein of fate. There were hundreds on Okeanus but thousands on the other planes. Never before had I felt so much power and hope connected to one thread of fate.

"The last thing he showed me was you, chanting the spell of the north wind.

"Afraid, I awoke from both your dream and Olivar's and roused him. I explained to him that to stop the attack of the battle boats, he must kill the crew of the King's ship and rescue the man known as Stern from a cell on one of the ship's lower decks. He set sail immediately."

Stern did not know how to respond. Everything she had seen was true but he was no nearer Bedwyr than before so he asked, "Now that I am here, what will happen to me?"

"We wait for the dragon ships. They are expected in ten days. During that time you need to dream so that I may guide you."

"You mean sleep?"

"Yes, each night you will drink a tea and we will dream together. I will learn about you and the quest. Through the process I will help soothe your fears and help direct you. For instance, I know you fear what you are. The black bear lives inside you and you are afraid it will escape and hurt someone. I can help you accept your chaotic nature. You have the blood of the bare-sark. It was dormant in your plane but here it is very strong. You also question your role in the dragon quest. You fear the power and the control of the demon but you are attracted to and tempted to take his power. You feel guilty about Kylla's death and you plan to seek vengeance on the man known as Flymtt and the daemon Focalor."

"Your analysis is precise and a bit unnerving."

She smiled and bowed her head. "I also sense you fear your own power. You have acted passively several times, when you should have attacked. You are also confused by the politics of Okeanus. You sense the world is huge and you have only seen a small portion of it."

"You are correct. I don't understand the King's power. His is a tiny island with a small population. Why does the world concern itself with him?"

"He is an ambitious man, who seeks to extend his power and his brand of order throughout Okeanus. By destroying the dragons on his island and killing its witches and wizards, he is attempting to destroy magic and assert a political realism, which he calls order. He has sent men like Flymtt throughout the world to spy for him, gather allies, and foment revolution. He has also spent millions to develop weapons that are superior to most of those of the rest of the world. There are rumors he has devised a machine that turns water into steam and can move his ships at great speed."

"What is the name of your people and what relationship do you have with the King?"

"We are the Carnelians and we have no relationship with the King, except to raid his coast and sink his ships. Our homelands are far to the north, spread through an archipelago. Heorot is only one of several winter bases for us. From here we raid into the south. Soon the ice will be nibbling at our toes and we will move even further south. We know of the King because we are known in every seaport in this hemisphere."

"What is your relationship to the blue-back dragons?"

"The dragons of this plane are sacred to us. The blue-back is probably the most loved because it was the only domesticated dragon. We were never dragon riders like some but we still hold the dragon sacred as a symbol of our world."

Stern had hundreds of questions about Okeanus. Except for Kylla he had asked few questions of anyone because he understood his questions revealed his ignorance of Okeanus.

"What am I?"

She leaned forward and looked directly into his eyes. "You share some characteristics with the Keltoi but you are something else. Kylla was right in naming you a bare-sark but that does not make you a Keltoi." She sat back and then sighed. "There was a race of men here once that were bare-sarks, shape changers and wizards. They were the masters of the blue-backs, the keepers, if you will, or the riders of the domesticated dragons. They disappeared with the dragon."

"Who were they? I mean what did you call them?"

"They were the Skaellanders, the northern sea people, and they lived in vast cities carved into the sides of the island mountain of the northern seas. They were sometimes known as the men from Thule, the shadowed island."

Stern thought of the abandoned city where he met Focalor for the first time. He guessed it was a city of the Skaellanders.

Stern changed the subject. "Do you know Bedwyr?"

"Everyone knows about the magus. I have never met him though."

"What type of power does he possess?"

"I have heard stories but all I know is that our magic is more primitive. We tend to trust in our shaman, our ships and our swords rather than the type of magic Bedyr makes."

Stern tried to remember everything she had said about her dream. "You said you saw the return of the dragon?

She nodded. "I saw them return to the island of Grun."

"Where is that?"

"It is far to the south in the western hemisphere."

"Was I in the dream?"

She smiled and waved her hand. "A portal opened and three dragons flew through: two males and a pregnant female."

"Dragons?" he felt immediate panic. "There was more than one? There were three."

"Most definitely," she said with a frown. "But you did not see me?"

She felt his anxiety and watched as chaotic colors surrounded him in an aura of panic. "I will help you with your fear," she said, as she moved to his side. She was thin and as tall as he. She placed a dry warm hand on the back of his neck and began to sing. He felt his immediate panic recede and warmth filled his mind. He had a momentary feeling of well-being before a long plaintive note on a horn interrupted her song and she moved away from him. "Is that better?"

"I feel much better. Thank you."

The horn calls us to the hall for the evening meal. "The red reavers are gathering to meet the bare-sark."

"They know what I am?"

"Of course they do. I told the war master and from him the word spread like wild fire through Heorot. Few secrets exist in such a tiny place." She laughed, as she pulled a multicolored cloak of parrot feathers over her shoulders and picked up a black staff, capped with silver and engraved with hundreds of tiny runes.

He followed her down the hill. Fat flakes fell steadily and several inches of snow covered the ground. She stopped half-way down the hill and sniffed the air. "Heavy snow is coming. It is too soon for us. I must consult with the shaman. Something is changing the weather."

"Isn't a shaman a magician?"

She stopped and turned towards him. "A shaman does not make magic. He controls nature in all its form. He heals the sick, he makes it rain, he calls the sacred animals, he tracks the game, he blesses the ships, he sings the runes. A magician deals with power and death. More often than not he engenders and uses chaos. He uses fire to destroy the ordered substance of things to transform and mangle. He is the master of technology, alchemy, and herbalism. He is a trickster and a voyager. I trust a shaman but I run from magicians."

"But what about Bedwyr?" he stuttered. "Is he a trickster? Should I see him?"

"He is integral to your quest. You must see him one way or another. "

They reached the door of the crowded long house, where cauldrons of soup bubbled over fires and women moved through the group handing tankards of mead to the men. The crowd made way for the Hochangsttraumerin as she worked her way through the dense group to a platform elevated a few inches above the ground to Olivar, who sat surrounded by his warriors.

To the chagrin of the men sitting around him, Olivar signaled Stern to join him on the platform, then attracted the attention of a young woman carrying steins of mead and pointed at Stern. As she pressed her way through the crowd of men toward Stern, receiving pinches and pats along the way, she expertly slapped their hands away from her hips and legs and laughed at the awkward displays. She handed Stern an overly-full tankard. Mead splashed on his tunic and the reavers guffawed and hooted at his ineptitude. He smiled, understanding quickly it was important to be considered one of them as soon as possible. As he laughed, he remembered the red reavers cutting off the heads of the king's men. These men were neither frivolous nor gentle. If he wanted to keep his head, he first must keep his wits and pay attention to his surroundings.

Like the maid, Hochangsttraumerin also worked her way through the crowd of men. They made way for her. She received no pats or hoots rather he saw both fear and respect in their faces as she passed. As she took a tankard of mead from the maid, she whispered in his ear: "The reavers celebrate their victory tonight. It would not be wise to try to meet them drink for drink. As soon as we have eaten and toasted the war master, we will leave."

The crowd was manic and Stern saw the wisdom of her suggestion immediately. People continued to enter the hall until every space was filled. Maids moved throughout the group serving mead and platters of roasted meats, as the group laughed and sang. From time to time fights broke out, in other locations men and women began to couple on the dirt floor. When one of the men drunkenly leaned forward and challenged Stern to wrestle, she stood and said, "Thank you Axel for the food and drink but I have much work to do with Stern this night."

Axel waved his right hand drunkenly, as she took Stern's arm and led him off the platform and through the crowd. A frigid wind howled and he braced himself as he passed through the door.

Chapter Thirty-Two: The Reavers Sail South

A GELID RAIN FELL and patches of ice covered the ground. Dogs huddled beneath the empty houses and the wind raged around the ragged rocks of the fjord's cliffs. Limbs broke from trees and the temperature dropped.

Hochangsttraumerin pulled her cloak tight around her neck as she trekked up the hill to the stone house with Stern, his head bowed, protecting himself from ice shards, following her. Wet and sober by the time she pushed open the cabin door, he hesitated: he had to relieve himself. He walked a few feet away from the house and stood on the stony precipice above the river they called the Eisveldt. As he urinated with the wind, he watched her rekindle the fire.

Later after they were warmed from the fire, she draped a great water buffalo robe over the wooden bed and undressed quickly before the fire before crawling beneath the robe. "Undress and join me," she said. He quickly shed his clothes and ran to the bed, shivering. Beneath the heavy robe, with only their heads uncovered, she said, "Tonight we shall dream of the past. I want to know all about you." She reached down at the side of the bed and retrieved a small glass bottle with a crystal stopper, unplugged it and handed it to him to drink. The bottle contained a few swallows of a green liquid, which he drank quickly. He handed her the empty bottle and she returned it to the side of the bed. "Lie on your right side and I shall lie next to you." He followed her instructions and turned over. He felt the elixir working its way through his body and he quickly became drowsy and warm. As he fell asleep, he felt her snuggle against him.

Throughout the night, Stern dreamed his life. In many episodes she asked him questions. In others she requested he repeat memories and situations in the dreams. When they reached the battle with Focalor, she commanded him several times to relive the experience and when Kokabiel arrived she moaned as if in pain and begged him to hurry though the dream. Finally, she ordered him to stop his dreaming and sleep like the bear sleeps in winter and he remembered no more until he awoke to the sound of her stoking the fire.

Frost covered the glass windows, casting a silver sheen over the room. "Winter has truly arrived," she said. "There will be no more false starts. Part of the Eisveldt is frozen and Olivar will soon sail further south."

"Is this a problem?"

"Why do you ask?"

"Because you seem very nervous," he answered from below the warm covers.

She sat on the edge of the bed. She had dressed and braided her hair. "I know now that we must get you to Bedwyr as quickly as possible. You have done well in this world alone. Frankly, I am surprised you are still alive but time is passing quickly on your plane and the dragons are growing in number. Do you realize you are much younger now than when you arrived; our plane runs counter-clockwise to yours." She laughed. "I had no idea how different the planes were until I dreamed your world."

Her explanation of the passage of time stunned him but he didn't really believe it. He felt stronger but he thought that was because of the exercise he had been getting. "I thought we were waiting for the traders."

"We are. Olivar will not take you to Bedwyr. He must move the tribe further south, if they are to survive the winter. But if the sea freezes the Dra'ghan will not arrive. They will turn back so if Olivar starts the migration today we may have to go with him."

"Where to?" he asked, supporting his head on his hand and looking at her.

"They will sail to the south to another archipelago."

"How far is it? Will it take me out of my way?"

"Bedwyr's island is southwest of here. By dragon boat, it would take ten weeks or more. Olivar will sail southeast, in the opposite direction."

Stern felt both frustration and anger welling up in his chest. The image of the bear flashed into his conscious mind and rose on its hind legs. It seemed to him that every step he took toward Bedwyr was frustrated or deflected. He remembered Kylla's vision of his swimming as a great sea turtle toward Bedwyr's island. Maybe he should have tried to transform himself into a turtle and swim alone to Bedwyr.

"How do you know the Dra'ghan are coming?"

"I dreamed their presence. They are caught in the web of the dragon's fate. They are important to your quest and they somehow know this. They are coming to this island as fast as their ships will bear them."

"Dress and let's see what Olivar plans to do. This icy weather is strange and precipitous."

Stern dressed and pulled his cloak over his shoulders. Once he stepped outside, he pulled the hood over his head as far as it would go to protect him from the frigid wind and the chill rising up from the ice-covered ground. They slid down the steep hill and located Olivar on one of the wooden docks directing the loading of a boat. As they approached, Hochangsttraumerin asked, "When do you sail?"

"The first wave leaves today. I'm sending twenty dragon boats with supplies and warriors to open the new camp. Twenty more boats will leave tomorrow with women and children."

"When will the last boats leave?"

"We have to wait until the forty boats return. I'm estimating twenty days."

Stern interrupted, "What if the sea is frozen?"

"Then we march across the ice to the boats, which will wait at its edge."

"What do you think about the weather? Will it continue to be this cold?"

"I have never seen it this cold this early in the year. Winter surprised me."

They left Olivar on the docks and walked to the long house, looking for breakfast.

Later, Stern sat on the wooden platform, eating a bowl of warm oats, spiced with dried apples and cinnamon. He washed it down with a half tankard of mead.

"We will wait for the last boat but then we must go," she said.

"I will not go. I must use my time here wisely."

"What does that mean?"

"I don't know. All I know is that I will no longer diverge from the path. I must reach Bedwyr. You said my plane's time is outpacing us. If I don't get back and retrieve the dragons, our worlds may be changed irrevocably for ages."

Once he finished eating he climbed the slippery hill to the stone house. She stayed in the village to pack and load the boats. As he trudged upwards, Stern noted everyone in the village was working frantically to pack their few belongings for the voyage south.

At the house he carted more fire wood inside and built a large roaring fire. He rubbed his hands in front of the flames and began to think. He had, through others' help, transformed himself into a sea bird, a wolf, and a bear. Kylla told him he would someday swim in the ocean as a great sea turtle. He knew he possessed the ability to transform himself into an animal but he had never shifted into a new form alone; someone always showed him how the first time. He did not believe he could fly the distance to the island as a bird. As a giant turtle he might have a chance. He began to meditate on the turtle, imagining himself transforming into the great sea creature. After a long while he stopped.

Since nothing was happening, he began to meditate on the wolf, just as Kylla had shown him, and after a few minutes of meditation, he felt the change coming, the black wolf rushing from his inner self. He stopped the onslaught of the transformation; he did not want to make the change now. Instead, he fingered the leather pouch around his neck and contemplated calling on Kokabiel, the demon from the airy plane. However, he remembered the illness he felt from their last meeting and he could not afford to be incapacitated for days. The last time he had the healing presence of a witch to help him. Here he would be all alone. He realized he was trapped; his fate was dictating yet another detour...another delay.

That night the hall was half full. Twenty ships had debarked and twenty more waited for dawn. Stern drank mead and listened as the reavers sang songs about the brutal winter and their ever valiant battle against it. They were a handsome people and he enjoyed their moving about in their colorful clothes. As he watched, he absently scratched his ever-burgeoning beard and rubbed the stubble on the top of his head; he suspected the reavers were laughing at the clown from the earthen plane.

When they left the hall, the icy rain had stopped. Thousands of stars dotted the sky and a large full moon rose. At the cabin, as Hochangsttraumerin prepared the bed for dreaming, Stern admitted to himself although she was a beautiful woman, he did not desire her. It was as if she were simply a part of him.

When he lay down next to her, he thought of all the women he met on this journey and the way he felt about each. At one point, the idea of a daughter flitted through his mind, which reminded him of his son, abandoned in the priest's orphanage, he felt both sadness and anxiety. At the moment of anxiety, however, he felt her behind him and her thoughts soothed away his fears. At this point, he was in that state between sleeping and waking and she was already waiting for him.

He dreamed four black ships with two black masts each entered Heorot's harbor. It was snowing and ice floes dotted the water. A large white polar bear slid down their hill on its belly into the water, as sailors on the black ships cheered, raising trident-shaped spears into the air. They hauled the bear aboard the largest ship and it stood on its hind legs next to the captain at the wheel. The captain was a tall, black lizard, standing upright, with yellow eyes, and well-defined muscles, wearing a yellow leather vest, red leather pants, and a steel helmet, and sporting two curved swords on his hip.

The ships turned in the harbor and set sail toward the west where on the horizon a large red dragon flew languidly toward the south. Ice floes floated past the boats and sailors called out warnings to the captain, as a school of gray leviathans churned the water into a white froth.

Stern felt Hochangsttraumerin turn in her sleep and moan. The dream morphed and he stood on the dock, waving farewell to her, as the sun caught on the silver head of her staff, illuminating runes he discerned easily. He translated the words but he could not understand the meaning, as her figure darkened and disappeared along with the reavers' boats as they passed the horizon.

When they woke the next morning, she was somber and quiet.

"What's wrong?" he asked.

"I realized last night that I will soon pass out of the quest. I will leave with Olivar and you will travel alone."

Suddenly, he was sad. "I dreamed of reptiles," he said, to change the subject.

"You saw the Dra'ghan."

"Who are they really, these traders?"

"They are another form of dragonkin. We call them the dragon's children and they are a ruthless nation. They breed prodigiously and their numbers are legion. They stay away from the north for the most part because of the cold; they cannot bear it. Moderate cold makes them lethargic. Brutal cold kills them. The reavers have an uneasy alliance with them. We build their ships and they send us food from the south. Those ships you saw in your dream were loaded with fruits and vegetables."

"Why are we to be separated?"

"I don't know bare-sark."

"I realized something last night, something that had not occurred to me before arriving here."

"What is it?"

"I am on three quests really. To you and the Dra'ghan I am the bringer of the dragon. You look to me to succeed in opening a portal and ushering the dragon back into the world. To the King and the Brotherhood, I am a force to fight and kill the daemon Focalor, and to the witches of my world, I am a hunter, searching for a way to destroy or remove the dragons."

"What is important about this insight?"

"Last night, I dreamed the positive aspect of this quest. Suddenly, I felt I had a purpose greater than that of a hunter. I felt myself bound up in the threads of all of your fates."

"How did it make you feel?"

"At first, I felt important, prideful really then I became frightened and overwhelmed with my quest. I asked myself, what could I do? I am just a blacksmith. What am I doing here?"

"How do you feel now?"

"Better. I have decided to continue as before, simply trying to accomplish the first step of the mission, reaching Bedwyr."

"You are not without power but you are green, green as the newest sprout in the garden. You need time to develop and learn to control your powers."

"That is what Kylla said before she died."

"She was right." She frowned and then continued, "I will help you as much as I can before we separate."

"You are sure the dream was correct?"

"In some form or fashion we will separate. Yes, I am sure of it."

They dressed and joined the reavers down below and helped with the packing.

Each night they explored his dreams and during the day they packed and stored supplies. After twenty days, Olivar showed signs of strain. The weather grew worst each day and the boats were overdue. Several times, he cursed the weather and asked Hochangsttraumerin whether she sensed any magic. Each time she sniffed the air and shrugged her shoulders. "If it is magic," she said, "it is coming from a long ways away."

On the thirtieth day, the boats worked their way up a narrow ice-bound channel of the Eisveldt. Both sides of the river were frozen. Olivar slapped his hands together in relief and ordered the remaining reavers to immediately load the boats. That night they feasted in the long house and Olivar asked Stern, "Do you still intend to stay and wait for the Dra'ghan?"

Stern nodded his head in the affirmative. "They do not like the cold. If they were coming they would have already arrived. Come with us and I will take you to Bedwyr in the spring on our return home."

"No, I must find my way. No more delays or detours. I must finish the quest."

That night he dreamed he flew a blue-back dragon over the ramparts of a gray castle. He wore black mail and carried a silver spear. Large armies marched toward the castle in the wide verdant plains below it.

When he awoke, she was dressed with her parrot feather cloak draped over her shoulders. She held her staff in her right hand and a leather pack was slung over her left shoulder. "Goodbye Stern. Before I leave I must warn you that the dream world is calling you. Do not believe the images of power that flow from its dark depths. The powers there seduce men with images of power; without learning, meditation and patience you could go mad or become vainglorious. Tread the middle way, the way of the shaman. Your dream last night frightened me. You are not prepared for the power you wielded in the dream. Maybe someday you will be ready but not any time soon. Learn the power of the stone, study the grimoire, listen to Bedwyr and prepare yourself before you plunge head forward into your quest. If you come with me now, we could spend the winter dreaming. You could learn the ways of the reavers and fight alongside the war master."

Stern wanted to go with her. The reavers would protect him and he could safely wait in the south until spring. It was tempting and he knew Kylla would have advised him to go. Hochangsttraumerin contained his anxiety and soothed his spirit. She mediated between him and the representatives of the dreams. Without her, he knew he would fear to sleep. She had opened many doors and took him deeper into his psyche than he had ever been before in his life.

However, in the end, he chose to stay behind and wait for the dragon men. "If the Dra'ghan do not come," he said, "I will find a way. If the sea freezes I will walk to Bedwyr's island."

She kissed him on each cheek and left. The frigid wind blew through the open door into the stone house.

He dressed quickly and ran to the docks. As the last ship squeezed through the narrow channel between the banks of ice, he waved and entered the war master's long house to discover she had left him a bag of grain and a basket of shriveled apples.

Chapter Thirty-Three: The Dra'ghan

THE DAY AFTER THEY SAILED it snowed for twenty-four hours. He found it difficult to leave the cabin so he made a raging fire and dozed beneath the bear skins. He dreamed several times of the polar bear and reptiles in black ships. Three days later he heard water running. He went to the door of the cabin and pushed against the snow, forcing it open. The sun was shining brightly and the snow on the roof of the cabin was melting: long icicles hung from the eaves. Summer-like weather had descended onto the island. He dressed and worked his way down the hill. The melting snow formed rivulets of icy water flowing toward the Eisveldt. From the wooden dock he noted the ice on the river also melting. Maybe, he thought, if this weather continued, the Eisveldt would open.

The warm weather continued for a week, nearly all the snow and ice disappeared. From what the reavers had told him, the current temperature was within the normal range. Fifteen days later, he was fishing off the deck. It was warm enough to wear only his shirt and a woolen sweater. Suddenly, he heard a horn in the distance, looked up, and saw a black mast enter the mouth of the Eisveldt. He felt fear and wondered if he should run and hide. Maybe it wasn't the Dra'ghan. It could be pirates or another clan of Carnelians. He waited weaponless to see if his dreams were true.

The dream predicted four ships so he waited, believing in the Hochangsttraumerin's power to manage a dream. He counted the ships and there were four. He waited as they laid anchor in the protected harbor at the mouth of the Eisveldt. The crew dropped a long boat into the water and eight figures, humanoid, climbed down ropes hanging from the side and rowed a longboat toward the dock. The black ships were larger than the dragon boats of the reavers. One figure stood in the lead longboat and called out to Stern in a sibilant version of the reavers' language, "Ho, on the dock."

Stern waved and shouted back, "Ho, to the longboat."

They ran the boat up the side of the dock and one of the rowers jumped out and tied it off. Climbing up the wooden ladder eight reptiles, Dra'ghan, soon stood before him. The one who had called out wore a yellow leather vest and red leather pants and no shoes. His webbed feet possessed three toes with ebony nails that glistened in the sunlight and his hands consisted of an opposable thumb and three webbed fingers and dark black nails. His skin was a tight web of dark blue scales; his eyes almond-shaped and yellow and his teeth long and sharp, like a fish.

The Dra'ghan stood quietly, waiting, watching him, as he studied them. One spoke in the sibilant language to the captain and Stern immediately began to decipher the complex syntax, recognizing it contained colorful metaphoric images. He discerned quickly that the captain's name was Grek'kan, *kan* being a designation of power or leadership. The deckhand had asked Grek'kan whether they should reconnoiter and determine if the human was alone. With a flick of his ebony nail and a slithering wash of s's and z's Grek'kan ordered four of the Dra'ghan to investigate the camp. The captain then asked Stern in Carnelian: "Where are the reavers?"

"They sailed to their southern bases."

"It is odd they would leave so early in the year."

"There was an ice storm several weeks ago and the Eisveldt froze."

The captain shivered and said, "We were delayed because of strong winds and extreme temperatures. Our shaman suspected magical resistance to our arrival here."

"Who knew you were coming?"

Grek'kan shrugged his shoulders. "We come every year to trade with the reavers."

"So you did not come for me?"

The captain's yellow eyes watched Stern, waiting for some sort of explanation. When Stern did not explain, he asked: "Why would we come for you, little brother?"

Stern decided to say nothing about his dream. Instead, he asked: "Do you know Bedwyr?"

"Some call him the blacksmith?"

"That's the one."

"Of course, we know of him and his talents."

"Do you know where his island is located?"

He waved his left hand, which Stern quickly perceived meant the same thing as a human nodding his head.

"Could you take me there?"

Stern was unable to read the Dra'ghan's face, which seemed rigid and fixed; however, he picked up something through the subtle change in his expression but he could not determine the meaning behind the movement.

"It is far to the southwest. We must go south and find the reavers. Our hulls are full of fruits and vegetables. They will spoil soon if we don't get to the reavers."

"You do not know of my quest then?"

He waved his right hand in the negative.

Stern swallowed nervously. Suddenly he doubted everything the Hochangsttraumerin had told him.

Another long boat glided up to the dock with a tall Dra'ghan standing in its center, wearing a dark green robe and carrying a white staff covered with green runes from its top to its base. Tak'seth, his name, climbed onto the dock; his scaled skin darker than Grek'kan's. Moving to the end of the pier, he raised his arms, stretching them away from his body. He held up his staff and the stone hanging around Stern's neck warmed and he began to chant. He faced the east first, then the north, the west, and the south.

After chanting for several minutes, Tak'seth pounded the staff three times on the boards of the dock and turned toward Stern, pointing a finger at him and shouting in his strange sibilant language. "He brings the blue-back dragon."

Grek'kan, startled, stepped back, pulled a curved black-bladed dagger from the sheath on his right hip and ordered his followers to surround Stern.

Stern nervously backed up a few steps and felt the power of the bear, lurking on the edge of his conscious mind, and the stone, dangling around his neck, growing warmer. Taking a deep breath, he addressed the shaman in his language. "It is true my quest is to return the blue-back dragon to Okeanus but to accomplish this task Grek'kan must deliver me to Bedwyr, the magus." Grek'kan sputtered, obviously disturbed by the statement.

The shaman moved toward Stern who braced himself, preparing to be hit by the white staff. Instead of striking him, the Dra'ghan bent forward and whispered into his ear: "We must speak in private."

Stern backed away, the creature's size intimidating him. "We can speak in the long house."

The shaman started off in a determined stride and Stern ran to keep up with him.

In the hall, the shaman pulled a long yellow feather from a green leather bag, hanging on his left side and began to chant and strike every object in the room, including Stern, with it. When he struck Stern a white spark danced off his head and extreme heat emanated from the stone hanging in the pouch around his neck. The shaman seemed aware of the stone and reached toward it. He did not touch the pouch, rather, he waved his palm over it and whispered the word for demon in his language. He pulled a small glass vial from his bag and sprinkled oil about the room. Finished, he sat on the floor and made a gesture, indicating he wanted Stern to join him.

"You speak my language?" he asked.

"Imperfectly, I am sure."

"How have you learned it?"

"You are teaching me."

The lizard man's eyes seem to swell and Stern interpreted this to mean he was surprised.

"Where are the blue-backs?"

"They remain in my world, on the earthen plane."

"You have a way to retrieve the dragons for this world?"

"I must complete my quest and then I will bring the blue-back dragons to Okeanus."

"Where will you deliver them?"

"It has been foretold that I will bring them to the island of Grun."

"Grun?" The shaman scratched his chin with a curved black nail. "That is good. Very good. How may I help you?"

"I must reach Bedwyr and be trained."

"Tell me your quest tale."

Stern was not quite sure what he meant so he told him his story instead. When he finished, the shaman said, "You have left something out."

Stern had not told the shaman he was a bare-sark or that he was being hunted by the King's men. He used the gesture that was similar to his shrugging his shoulders and the shaman leaned toward him: "You are a shape-shifter. Why have you failed to disclose that? And you are being hunted by a daemon. Important facts, don't you agree?"

Stern cleared his throat and told him about Focalor and the series of changes that he had undergone. When he had finished describing each one of his transformations, the shaman leaned back, closed his eyes and began to chant in a low voice. The room filled with steam and the temperature rose. He felt drowsy and he had difficulty keeping his eyes open. A vision of the Hochangsttraumerin emerged from the fog and sat on his right. The shaman continued to chant and Kylla appeared and sat on his left. Neither she nor the Hochangsttraumerin spoke. The shaman continued to chant and Mikk entered wearing a red robe and sat next to Kylla. Then, the lunar *bruja* materialized on the Hochangsttraumerin's right. With the five seated, the shaman changed his chant. Gotha entered, accompanied by two children, twin girls, and joined what was now beginning to be a circle.

The shaman's tone deepened still and his dead Argyll woman, Mara, with their son joined the group. The circle was almost complete. Two men, who Stern could not identify, appeared and took places in the circle, and then Grek'kan took his place. Two seats remained. A tall gaunt man with long white hair, wearing black armor filled the penultimate spot. Only one place left and the shaman called out for the final player to enter. Stern guessed the place belonged to Bedwyr, it had to be. The shaman called out again and a tall figure appeared draped in a white robe, its head hidden beneath a large hood. Stern could not make out if the figure was a man or woman. The shaman, however, seemed satisfied. He mumbled deeply now, almost incoherently, calling out for the spirits of the four planes to look through the eyes of the quest members and reveal the blue-back dragons. A light appeared above the circle, illuminating the center. In the light Stern saw blue-back dragons circling high mountains like pigeons circling a church spire on a sunny summer's day. The shaman gasped and collapsed and the fog and circle disappeared.

The shaman lay in a heap on the floor unconscious. Unsure of what he should do, Stern rose and sought Grek'kan. When he found him he told him the shaman had collapsed. The Dra'ghan said, "He passes into a deep sleep after his séances. Do not worry." Stern turned and looked at the house on the hill, wondering if he should go back and watch over the shaman.

Grek'kan interrupted his thoughts. "You should gather your things, if you want to sail with us. I intend to leave with the tide."

"Will you take me to Bedwyr?"

"It is up to the shaman. However, winter is coming. This warmer weather is simply a respite. I don't intend be trapped here when it arrives."

Stern walked back to the stone house on the hill, deciding he would not leave with the Dra'ghan if they would not take him to Bedwyr's island. A voyage to the south would delay his journey for weeks, maybe months. He would have to succeed in transforming himself into a turtle or a bird and reach Bedwyr's island on his own. Kylla was right, he decided. He needed training to complete his quest. He was ill-prepared for this journey.

The shaman was still sleeping when he returned. The creature looked more at ease and relaxed than when he left. Before, he looked like a lizard that collapsed. Now, he simply appeared to be a sleeping man.

In the late afternoon, Stern heard Dra'ghan horns trumpeting. The shaman turned over, coughed and awoke.

He looked at Stern and said, "Gather your things. Grek'kan will take you to Bedwyr." Stern laughed as he gathered a few pieces of clothing and stuffed them into a leather bag.

Chapter Thirty-Four: The Voyage to Noirrith

THE SUN SET and the tide turned. Stern stood on the deck of a Grek'kan ship, with Dra'ghan sailors and soldiers tightly packed on the deck. Twice the number of Dra'ghan populated the boat than a similarly sized human one and at night the Dra'ghan slept tightly compressed in every available space. Stern moved about the vessel stepping over bodies until he found a free space to lie down. As he slept the mass of Dra'ghan bodies edged toward him, seeking his high body temperature.

The four ships sailed due west and Grek'kan informed him it would take many weeks to reach Bedwyr's island and that the estimated time was contingent upon the weather holding. Stern spent the time huddled on the deck with the shaman, who questioned him about his world and his meeting with Focalor and Kokabiel. Stern told the shaman he had trouble shape shifting. He could transform into a wolf or a bear when stressed because Kylla had trained him but he could not access other forms he suspected he could become. The shaman thought for a few moments and said, "You have had no real training. A shaman trains for years to learn the technique and then he usually only has access to one or two spirit animals. You obviously have a great talent but you are like a child." He paused and

230

rubbed his large hands up and down the shaft of his staff. "I can help you with the technique but you must remember this is but a beginning. To become a magus or shaman takes a lifetime."

The shaman began Stern's training the next day in a secluded spot in the lower level of the boat. The smell of overripe fruit almost overwhelmed Stern at first but through meditation he soon overcame the smell. The shaman ordered him to undress and sit on the floor of the lower deck. "Close your eyes and relax your body. Now, open your mind to images. Tell me the first animal spirit that appears to you, he will be your guide into the subtle world."

Stern sat quietly, letting his thoughts arise freely. Initially, he thought of La Ciudad and the dragons, then Kylla and Gotha. Eventually, these surface thoughts passed and newer, darker images began to surface. Soon two yellow eyes peered at him from the darkness, preventing all other images or thoughts from entering his conscious mind.

The shaman asked him what was happening and Stern explained that since the two yellow eyes had appeared no other thoughts or images followed. All he could see were the eyes of the wolf.

"Good, the guide has appeared. Invite him in. Welcome him with a smile and a wave."

Stern whispered, somewhat shyly, embarrassed by the playacting: "You are welcome. Please come forward."

He waited and the shaman said, "Keep talking. Coax him forward."

Stern repeated the invitation so many times it became a mantra. Finally, the eyes moved forward and Stern could see a gray snout, white teeth, and a black tongue. The wolf seemed shy and distrustful and Stern described the wolf's behavior to the shaman, who said, "He has not arrived yet. Invite him again. Talk to him and make him feel at home."

Eventually, a wolf, fully formed, appeared in his mind and Stern felt the urge to shift but the shaman stopped him before the transformation. "We must make the spirit guide feel comfortable. We must train him to come when we want him, not just when you are emotionally needy or frightened. You shifted shape before when you were afraid and in need of an escape. Now we must train the guide to be available whenever you call, not to help you escape but to guide you. I want you to learn how to hold onto your true self in this process."

They spent several days calling and dismissing the spirit guide. On the fourth day, Stern called the wolf and the shaman ordered him to shift. He transformed in a matter of minutes and then calmly changed back. They practiced the transformation over and over again until he felt in total control of the operation. The shaman said at the end of a particularly long day of training, "Tomorrow we will ask the wolf to send your authentic guide."

"What do you mean? Isn't the bear my true shape?"

"Maybe, but I sense a guide hidden in the recesses of your psyche. The bear and wolf come too quickly. The true guide is not so easily found. It usually hides and manipulates the spirits."

Stern thought about the shaman's words as he settled down on the deck amidst a pile of Dra'ghan bodies. He was becoming accustomed to the communal nature of the reptiles and even beginning to discern the different features and characters of the creatures.

The next day was clear and warm. Grek'kan had turned toward the southwest and they were sailing away from winter. The reptiles had discarded what little clothing they wore and were relishing the heat of the sun. At mid-day, Stern noticed the Dra'ghan were excited and somewhat agitated. They ran toward the front of the boat, causing it to dip downward. Officers yelled for them to move back and to distribute their weigh equally. However, they refused and continued to press forward. Stern, curious, joined them and saw on the port side, three large green dragons, five times the size of a blue-back, flying just a few feet above the water. The beasts were indifferent to the four ships running full sail parallel to them.

The shaman called Stern from the rail and they descended into the bowels of the boat, seeking a private space. Once there Stern undressed and sat upon the rough planks. Once again, he closed his eyes and summoned the wolf, who quickly appeared. The shaman whispered into Stern's ear, "Tell him you know he is but an emissary for the true guide and you demand to meet him."

Stern complied and conveyed the message to the wolf, who responded by lowering his head, baring his teeth and growling. Stern felt an unreasonable fear. It was as if the wolf were real and not simply a part of him. He repeated the command and the wolf jumped at him and he fell back, hitting his head on the rough planks.

The shaman ordered him to repeat the command a third time. This time the wolf backed up, growling, saliva dripping from its fangs and disappeared into the shadows. "It's gone." The shaman relaxed and said, "Now we wait. Continue to meditate on the guide."

Several hours passed and his legs were numb and his back throbbed. The rough planks ground into his buttocks and he was sleepy and bored. The shaman was asleep, snoring lightly and Stern was about to give up when he saw two shining yellow eyes in the darkness. They were not the wolf's eyes; they were different: brighter, keener, more intense. He was no longer sleepy. He focused his attention on those eyes and imagined they were filled with savagery and cruelty. He asked himself, 'Does this thing live within me?' Using the techniques the shaman taught him, he invited the spirit guide to come forth out of the shadows of his mind. The yellow eyes blinked and Stern sensed its curiosity. He invited it again and he saw the beginnings of a beautiful black feline face emerge from the darkness. He imagined a panther raw and primitive, more primal than the wolf. He heard its low purr like a savage growl vibrating in his own throat.

The shaman awoke with a jerk and the panther disappeared back into the darkness. Stern felt it running deep down into the caverns of his psyche and called for it to return. He desired to see its beautiful face again.

"What was it? I felt its presence."

Stern answered, "It was a panther."

The shaman smiled. "You have made some progress today Stern. But you will never become a shaman or a magus if you have not met your true spirit self."

They spent another ten days coaxing the panther from the darkness. During that time, Stern felt his conscious mind expand and change. He ended each session with the shaman with a splitting headache, which only several hours of sleep would ameliorate.

On the eleventh day following the appearance of the panther, the shaman asked Stern to shift into a turtle. Stern hesitated. He had tried before to shift into the great sea turtle but had had no luck yet he had come to trust the shaman so he crossed his legs on the planks of the deck and imagined a turtle swimming in the sea. He shifted and felt the great weight of the multicolored shell, pushing down on the deck of the ship. He sniffed the odors of the sea and felt the urge to work his way up the ladders to the deck and plunge into the waters of Okeanus.

From a great distance, he heard the shaman calling him and he shifted again.

The shaman smiled. "The turtle is a very ancient creature. To access it takes a great deal of skill and power. You have done it. We will soon reach Bedwyr's island. You will have to continue your study with him but be aware. A magus is not a shaman. They are dispensers of magic, which is just another word for power. The shaman is a greater calling. We battle the chaos of the world and attempt to maintain balance. The magus seeks ever greater power. They desire control over the material. I have seen your soul and your shadow. You will be tempted by the power but your true calling is to create balance. Your fate is tied to the blue dragon.

"Do you remember the spirit circle?"

Stern nodded his head.

"It is significant to know who appeared in the quest circle but it is more important to know who wasn't there."

Stern asked, "Was the cloaked figure Bedwyr?"

"No, the cloaked figure is hidden from you because its role has not yet been fixed. It is as if the figure is the trump card in a child's game. Its presence could signal success or failure."

"I did not recognize everyone."

"They will be revealed."

Stern ended another day at the prow of the boat, watching the horizon for a glimpse of Bedwyr's island, when Grek'kan approached him and leaned against the railing.

"How do you feel, Krassnith?"

Stern smiled at his name in the Dra'ghan's language. It literally translated as 'little star.' Of all the names he had acquired on his journey, he liked Krassnith the best.

"I feel stronger. The shaman has taught me how to control my gift."

"He says you will make a great shaman."

"I am not seeking a new occupation, Grek'kan. I simply want to get home."

"At dawn you will see the ebony crags of Bedwyr's island, Noirrith, the black rock."

Stern repeated the name and asked, "What is it like, Noirrith?"

"The island was once simply three volcanoes that grew together over time. The volcanoes form the boundaries of the island. Between the high peaks lies a flat plain of rich volcanic soil. This is where the two cities are and the fortress home of the warrior monks. Bedwyr lives on the western mountain in a tiny village near the top.

"We will land on the eastern side in the harbor of Simic, the larger of the two towns. You will then need to journey to the west to Bedwyr's mountain, which the locals call Crucix. That will take two days of hard walking."

"The brotherhood's base lies in the center?"

He lifted his hand. "We are not welcome in Noirrith. The Brotherhood hates us because we sided with Brasilika in the last war. We will enter the harbor but we will not dock. I will fly the flag of truce and then we will leave you."

"I thank you for your help and for that of the shaman."

"The shaman tells me we will see you again and I believe him; therefore, I will save my goodbyes."

Later, Stern curled up with his usual crowd of Dra'ghan and fell into a deep sleep.

Chapter Thirty-Five: Noirrith

AT DAWN, THE BOAT exploded into a whirlwind of activity as their ship, flying a large pale blue flag, a symbol of truce, entered the deep harbor of Simic. A sloop sailed from the harbor toward them and Stern saw several men armed and wearing armor leaning against its railing. He had no weapon and he experienced a moment of panic, as Grek'kan yelled out a command and the Dra'ghan formed defensive ranks, preparing to repel any boarders.

As the sloop neared the boat, a man called out for the commander of the Dra'ghan to identify himself and Grek'kan boldly climbed some rigging to reveal himself.

The sloop slowed, as the man shouted: "I am Brother Castor, a cohort commander, of the Brotherhood."

"I am Grek'kan, war master of the Tarkan clan, and I bring an envoy to the Brotherhood. He flees the King's musketeers and seeks asylum."

"Under what name does he travel?"

Grek'kan looked at Stern.

"Tatyx," called out Stern to Grek'kan.

"Tatyx," repeated Grek'kan.

The sailors on the sloop trimmed its sails and laid anchor. The cohort commander called out: "Send Tatyx to us. We have been expecting him and rejoice at his appearance."

Grek'kan turned to Stern and asked in his language, "Shall we trust these black-hearted crows?"

Stern nodded and said, "I have no choice. I must follow the quest."

Grek'kan turned toward the sloop and shouted: "He comes now."

Stern found the shaman standing on the quarter deck. "Thank you for your guidance and wisdom." The shaman placed his hand on Stern's shoulder and said, "Remember, silence is more powerful than any word. Good luck and bring me the dragons."

After he thanked Grek'kan, the Dra'ghan lowered a long boat and ferried him the short distance to the sloop. He climbed a rope ladder up the side of the boat until two brothers grabbed his arms and lifted him onto the deck. The captain gave the command and as they weighed anchor and began to turn the boat, the cohort commander approached him and took his hand. "I am Castor, commander of the Twelfth Cohort of the Noirrith Brothers."

"I am Tatyx, messenger of Blut, commander of the *íslensk* Brotherhood."

Stern watched the Dra'ghan ships turn and sail toward the south.

The sloop soon reached the Noirrith docks, where many warships, flying the Brotherhood's flag, anchored.

Castor noted Stern's interest in the ships. "We are preparing for war with the King. Michaelsdottir arrived several weeks ago and delivered your message."

"Is she still here?"

"No, she left on a Brasilikan ship three days ago but she left your things."

This news saddened Stern. Another quest member had exited the stage.

"I come also to see Bedwyr."

"First, we must report to the Magister and then you and he will decide what to do next."

Turning back to the war ships, Stern asked, "Do you expect an attack?"

"Not really. The north is freezing and we do not expect anything until the spring but the fact that you were taken by one of the King's ships indicates he sent his corsairs out before the freeze. We anticipate there may be some attacks on our ships and maybe even a raid on some of our outposts."

The cohort commander led Stern to a carriage, drawn by four roan horses, waiting patiently on the dock. "We have a five hour trip ahead of us," he said climbing into the carriage.

The men working on the docks stopped their tasks to watch the oddly dressed Stern walk to the carriage. He was lean and muscled, much stronger and even taller, than he had been in Mittilagart. He was dressed as a reaver, wearing a parrot feather cloak over a yellow leather vest, bright red leather pants, and black boots that reached his knees. He had pulled a red woolen stocking cap over his head. His thick, burgeoning black beard bounced on his chest as he walked and his green eyes sparkled with new psychic energy.

He was weaponless and yet the men stepped aside to let him pass. Stern was aware of their staring. He was also painfully cognizant that the demon's stone, hanging around his neck, was suddenly generating a blistering heat. He did not know what it meant and he determined to puzzle it out as soon as he obtained a free moment alone. He had learned from the shaman that silence produces answers to most questions.

As they rode in the open carriage he studied the black mountains in the distance. The bright black road, recently graded, wound through lush verdant fields. Crushed remains of grain stalks covered the ground and Stern guessed the last harvest had only been a few days ago.

Once they left the small harbor town, which consisted of mostly warehouses and offices, he saw few people. An hour away from town he spied a dragon lion, the first one he had seen since his adventures with Gotha in the north.

"A dragon lion," he said pointing to the northeast.

"Bedwyr protects all creatures on this island, although some, like the dragon lion, can be a great nuisance. That thing can grab a full-grown sheep before you can snap your fingers."

"You know Bedwyr?"

"It was his island before we came."

"Why would he allow the brotherhood to establish a base here?"

"I have no idea. The lease was granted many years ago."

"Does Bedwyr follow Mithlass?"

The cohort commander shrugged his shoulders. "He only interacts with us, when we buy his weapons, which, in my opinion, are the best in the world. We buy every halberd he makes."

Two hours into the journey they stopped at a small village to eat. Among the eight or nine brick houses, there was a two-story wooden tavern with an attached stable. The commander ordered the driver to feed and water the horses. When they entered the tavern, the four or five patrons stopped eating to gawk at the reaver now in their midst.

Stern pulled off his stocking cap and rubbed his head, his hair now grown long and coarse. A woman, wearing a soiled apron, approached them and the commander ordered two mugs of beer and lunch. The woman looked at Stern and asked him in a language new to him, if he was a pirate. Stern slowly puzzled out the meaning of the question and answered her haltingly in her own language.

"No, I am from the north. I was captured by the Carnelians."

She gasped and asked, "How did you survive the ravishing of the reavers?"

"They respected me because we were both enemies of the King of the Island."

"Aye," she said, nodding her head.

One of the men at a nearby table stood up and walked toward their table. He carried a beer mug in one of his ham-sized fists. "You escaped the Carnelians, did ye?"

"In a matter of speaking," he answered.

"What do ye mean, 'in a manner of speaking'?"

"They left me on an island to face the winter alone, without food or drink."

His eyes widened. "How did ye survive?"

"I was rescued by a Dra'ghan battle boat that brought me here."

The man stepped back, his face turning a bright red, and spat out, "Ye are a damn liar. No human man survives the Dra'ghan."

The commander interjected, "Calm down brother. I received him from the Dra'ghan battle boat myself."

"It canna be true," he whispered. He turned back to the other people in the room as they huddled next to the fire to discuss Stern.

The commander laughed and took a deep draught of the beer. "You will soon be famous."

The girl put plates of steaming food in front of them and Stern puzzled out that it was mashed vegetables of some sort and a chop.

The commander asked with his mouth full, "How do you know their language?"

Stern shrugged and answered, "I'm a quick study."

Once they had finished their meal and the commander had a second beer, they climbed back into the coach and continued on their way. Two hours later they crested a hill. A fortified encampment spread out along the shore of a large lake at the bottom of it. "Welcome to the home of the Brotherhood. This is base camp Alpha, the largest camp of the Brotherhood on Noirrith and headquarters of the Magister Militum, Brother Blatt."

The brotherhood had laid the camp out in a grid and Stern could see from the hill that a large wooden blockhouse dominated the center. A wooden and stone stockade surrounded the camp. Twenty yards beyond the wall the brothers had dug a wide deep trench. Wooden observation towers marked every fifty yards of the wall and there were four gates, corresponding to north, east, south, and west. The commander and Stern entered the east gate.

The camp was clean and organized and seemed to vibrate with activity. The driver drove the carriage to the center of the encampment and halted in front of the stone blockhouse, where two brothers, armed with black halberds, stood guard in front of a double iron door. The commander saluted and announced that Tatyx had arrived and sought an audience with the Magister. The guard on the right turned and pounded twice on the iron door.

A brother wearing black robes opened the right side of the door and received the message, nodded his head, and then pushed the door closed once more.

"Why is there so much security?" asked Stern.

"The King has sent assassins against the Magister twice this year. Luckily we were able to foist both attacks but the Magister is always guarded now."

The door opened and the man in the black robes invited them into the blockhouse.

The bottom floor was open. Ten armed men sat around the large room on black wooden benches playing cards, their halberds stacked in the center of the room. The man led Stern and the commander up a wooden stairwell to the second story. On the second level, twenty or thirty clerks worked at long wooden tables in the center of the room. They wound their way through a maze of desks to a third flight of wooden stairs. The brotherhood had divided the third floor into offices. The door to the Magister's office on the west side was open and Stern noted a tall, gray-haired man, wearing black robes, like a priest of La Ciudad, rise and approach them with his hand extended.

Stern shook the Magister's hand. "Please sit down Tatyx. We feared for your life. Michaelsdottir told us you were captured by the King's musketeers."

"She told the truth," said Stern sitting down in the offered chair.

"Please forgive me, Stern, but I must check your identity."

"You think I am an assassin?"

The Magister smiled and shrugged his shoulders. "It is a mere precaution."

"How do you intend verifying my identity?"

"I would like to see your tattoo."

Stern stood and shrugged off the parrot-feather cloak, unbuttoned his leather vest, and removed his linen shirt. He showed Magister Blatt the tattoo he received in Wyvernne. The Magister retrieved a magnifying glass from his desk and examined the tattoo. "There's Blut's special mark, designating you as one of his messengers." Blatt returned to his seat on the other side of the desk. "One other test, please."

Pulling on his shirt, Stern said: "Continue."

"What items did Michaelsdottir leave in our custody?"

As he buttoned the leather vest, he recited the list of things he left in Mikk's care. "I left her everything in my slot when I was taken: my clothes, my weapons, and two books."

"Can you describe the books?"

"I would tell you the titles but they are in an archaic language and I would be surprised if you could verify whether I was telling you the truth."

"Excellent. Thank you for cooperating with me, Stern."

He leaned forward, placing his elbows on the desk: "Please recite Blut's message."

Stern sat up straight at the edge of his chair and recited the message verbatim.

After the recitation, Stern asked: "Will you go to their aid?"

The Magister grimaced and replied, "We cannot go until the spring. You saw the ships in the harbor?" Stern nodded in the affirmative. "The *Hawkmoon* arrived yesterday from the north. They fled the freezing ice all the way. Winter has come early and the captain told me the island is completely closed off."

"Flymtt, the King's assassin, told me there was one place on the southeast corner of the island that was accessible."

"I know the place. Our troops would be massacred. There is a narrow harbor and no beach to speak of. I must land ten thousand men to take the island. The only place for such a landing is in the north. The rest of the island is impenetrable, high mountains mark the coastline. But enough of this subject, I am told you have business with Bedwyr."

"It is urgent I see him."

"Tomorrow, I will provide a mount and an escort to Crucix in the west."

"Commander, show Tatyx to his tent and to his things."

Stern shook the Magister's hand and then followed the commander out of the blockhouse. As he walked he imagined the island encased in ice and he wondered if Focalor was still there.

That night, he bathed, changed into fresh clothes provided by the Brotherhood, and retrieved his books wrapped in one of Mikk's silk scarves in his leather pack. He carefully opened it and removed the grimoire, reviewed the pages he had memorized weeks before and then moved on to spells concerning the summoning of wind elementals and the beginning pages concerning fire. He slowly translated the runes and repeated them. Once he finished the section on wind and moved into the section on fire, he found one spell particularly fascinating. After an hour or so of practice, he was able to produce a small fire ball in the palm of his hand. After some patient practice he threw the ball through the half-opened flap of the tent. A passing soldier yelled out a warning and quickly stamped out the tiny blaze. Soon a crowd of angry and frightened brothers gathered outside his tent. He heard strident shouts of witch, witchcraft, and black magic and he realized he had been foolish and naïve.

Over the din of the frightened men, he heard a commander calling his name, ordering him to come outside. The brothers were obviously afraid to enter the tent and remove him. He wrapped the grimoire in Mikk's silk scarf and pushed it deep within his leather pack, took a deep breath, and opened the flap of the tent.

Forty or fifty brothers had gathered outside, along with a commander, who asked in a soft voice, "Did you produce a fireball, Stern?"

"No, of course not, I was reading a message from Michaelsdottir and I touched the candle in my tent. It went up in flames and frightened me. I threw the paper through the flap."

The commander called out for the man who had stamped out the fire ball and a young brother pushed his way through the crowd. "Brother Sestus, was the fire you saw a magic fireball cast by a wizard or a burning parchment cast from the tent?"

Brother Sestus cleared his throat and said, "It was not a fireball. The flame was small and dwindling."

"Like a burning piece of parchment?"

"It could have been, commander. I am not sure."

The commander turned toward Stern and said, "I appreciate your service to the Brotherhood, brother, but please be careful. You could have started a riot and gotten yourself hanged before we could get to the bottom of things. The Brotherhood shares the king's hatred of magickers. It goes against our beliefs."

He turned to the crowd and lifted his voice in a command: "Get to your tents. Night's trumpet will sound in thirty minutes."

After the trumpet's woeful lament, Stern lay on his cot staring at the canvas ceiling. Tomorrow, he would find Bedwyr and hopefully the key to freeing the earthen plane of the blue-back dragons. He tried to count how many days and weeks he had been on Okeanus but he was unable to reconstruct all of his days. Sometimes he had traveled as a bird or a wolf and he had no sense of the time he spent in animal form.

Chapter Thirty-Six: On the Road with Sestus

HE WOKE AT REVEILLE and quickly dressed. The air was cold. Even this far south winter was coming. He lined up with the brothers for breakfast and received a mug of hot tea and a bowl of boiled oats and honey. He ate at a long wooden table outside with a large contingency of monks, enjoying their banter and community. As he was scraping the bottom of his tin plate, the Cohort commander approached him, accompanied by a young soldier.

"Stern, you remember Brother Sestus from last night?" Stern nodded. "He is going to guide you to Bedwyr's village. Can you be ready to leave in an hour?"

"I am packed and ready."

"Good. Retrieve your gear and meet Brother Sestus at the paddock in thirty minutes."

Stern returned to his tent and checked his bag. The two books, wrapped in Mikk's scarves, lay at the bottom. He wrapped the soft deer-skin boots, the pants, and vest given to him by the reavers in a weathered cloth and placed them on top of the books. He then slung the pack over his left shoulder and set off for the paddock, which a young brother told him was near the western gate.

When he arrived, Brother Sestus was mounted on a large black gelding and holding the reins of a pure white mule with a plain, worn cavalry saddle, on its back. Stern adjusted the pack firmly on his shoulders before climbing onto the mule. Brother Sestus leaned forward and handed him a large canteen, with a wide leather strap. He pulled the strap of the canteen over his head and then took the reins of the mule.

"Ready?"

"Ride on, Brother."

The horse set off at a gallop. Stern gently pressed his knees into the mule's flanks and it reluctantly followed the Brother's gelding. He nudged him harder to pick up speed, as he followed Brother Sestus down a black dirt road. After an hour they passed another camp to the north, nestled against a high wall of black volcanic mountains. Past the second encampment, at an intersection, the mule wanted to turn toward the right but brother Sestus continued west. Stern had to kick the mule firmly three times before he would follow the gelding, as Brother Sestus explained, "That's his home base. He has a twin and he probably thinks he is there."

"Why did you pick a mule for me?"

"Horses on the island are a premium. This gelding belongs to the cohort commander."

Soon Stern saw the faint outline of yet another camp to the south. They reached a second crossroad but this time the mule followed the gelding through without a hesitation. Brother Sestus pointed to a copse of trees to the north and turned off the road. Thick grass scraped Stern's knees and they disturbed a covey of large speckled brown birds that exploded in a flurry of feathers. As they ascended into the clear sky, Stern sighted several giant rodents burrowing into the grass.

A small stream meandered through the thick veldt and formed a pool in the center of the copse, where they dismounted and let the animals drink. Brother Sestus pulled a brown sack from his saddlebags and moved up the hill and stretched out beneath a large hard wood and stretched out on green velvety moss. Extracting a hunk of hard cheese and four stale rolls from the sack, he pulled his dagger and cut several slices, which he laid out carefully on the bag. While the animals grazed, they ate the cheese and bread and washed it down with water from their canteens.

"How much further is it to Bedwyr's village?" asked Stern, with his mouth full.

"It will take us another two hours to reach the road that leads up the mountain. From there, we will climb for several hours."

"Have you met Bedwyr?"

"No, but I have seen him at the docks."

"What does he look like?"

"He is tall and stout with huge arms. He usually wears just a leather vest and a woolen kilt. He has long curly black hair and a beard like yours but a bit longer. In the winter he wears a black woolen cloak with a wolf skin collar. The only weapon I have seen him carry is a tall black staff with a silver tip and base, both engraved with tiny runes."

"How old is he?"

"I have no idea but I would guess in his forties, although people say he has been around for many decades."

As they talked, Stern heard the flat thump of leather wings above their head and looked up to see a mottled brown dragon about the size of a large dray horse fly a few feet above the tops of the tree.

"Don't worry; it's only a swamp dragon. There are about twenty of them holed up in the bog in the northwest corner of the valley. They steal a lamb or two but mostly feed on the veldt rats. You probably noticed them moving through the grass as we rode."

Stern took another piece of cheese and slowly chewed as he cocked one eye toward the tops of the trees.

Two hours later they stopped at the end of the dirt road and the beginning of a black cobblestoned way that headed at a steep angle up the side of the tallest volcanic mountain on the island.

"The road runs almost straight up, so lean forward on the mule. Keep it to the right side and stay as close to the rocks as you can. There is no rail and the drop is straight into the sea."

The cohort commander's gelding was skittish on the cobblestone pathway but the mule seemed to calm down and move forward naturally.

An hour later they turned a sharp corner high above the valley. The sun was setting and Stern was struck with the beauty of the view over his left shoulder. When he turned back to the road, he realized they were about to enter a tunnel that led them directly into the black mountain.

For almost thirty minutes they rode through the dark, the sound of the animals' shoes on the cobblestone the only sound. Then they saw light and emerged onto a narrow plateau overlooking the western sea. At the northern end of the plateau was a village, consisting of forty or so buildings built out of the black volcanic stone. Perched on the rocks above the village on the highest peak in view was a black tower.

They crossed a black stone bridge stretched across a crevice. On the other side several gardens and animal pens bordered each side of the road.

Four or five young boys ran from a barn and called out to them. Startled, Brother Sestus' gelding backed up as the boys approached.

"Let's dismount. I don't want this horse stepping on one of these kids or throwing me because it is skittish."

They led their horses to a large two-story building on the edge of the village that displayed a sign–*The Wizard's Whistle*. By the size of it, Stern guessed it was a tavern and inn. They tied their animals to a hitching post in front and climbed a steep stone stairway up to a large covered porch. A stout man with a head of unruly red hair and a full beard, wearing a flannel shirt, corduroy pants, and worn brown boots, greeted them, smiling broadly, his green eyes twinkling, as he reached out a paw-sized hand to Brother Sestus.

"Welcome to *The Wizard's Whistle*. I am Cratus."

Brother Sestus shook his hand. "Good day to you, sir. I am Brother Sestus and this is Tatyx. We would like a room, some food, a stable and feed for our animals."

"Well gentle sirs," he said with a wink, "we have exactly what you need."

He called out and a tall teenage boy with wild red hair and a wisp of a beard emerged from the inn. "Take care of their animals, Rufus." He then turned to Brother Sestus and said, "Follow me and I will show you the rooms. Dinner will be ready at dusk so you have time to clean up."

The ground floor was open. Ten or so long tables occupied most of the space and a long bar ran along the far wall. They followed him up some wooden stairs to the second floor, which was divided into twelve rooms of various sizes. He showed them two small rooms at the end of the hall.

"How much is room and board?"

"A small copper penny per day," said the man. Brother Sestus gulped at the price and Stern said, "That's fine." He rummaged in his bag and pulled out the pouch of coins that Magister Blut had given him and paid the inn keeper.

"Thank you, Tatyx. You know we swear a vow of poverty."

"I did know that and you are welcome."

Once in his room, Stern took off the black cloak of the Brotherhood, washed his face and hands with water from a porcelain bowl on a mahogany washstand and examined himself in a small mirror hanging on the wall. His face was deeply tanned but fuller, younger looking. After his travails he thought he would look the worst for wear but somehow this journey seemed to agree with him. He hid the coin purse beneath the mattress and slid his pack under the bed. There was no lock on the door.

Brother Sestus was sitting at the bar drinking a pint of the local ale; its rich foam stained his blond mustache. Cratus stood behind the bar and Stern asked him for a pint. It was growing dark and three other men, obviously craftsmen, were sitting at the far end of the bar, sipping the local brew and throwing glances at the two strangers. A young stout woman with long red hair set two places on one of the long tables and called out that dinner was ready to be served. Stern and Brother Sestus moved to the table and she served them two large bowls of stew and fresh baked bread. Within thirty minutes, the tavern was full of people, laughing and talking, drinking pints of the fresh beer. A young man with blue eyes and a thick head of black hair sat next to Stern and said, "Hello, brother." Stern finished his mouthful of stew and said, "Hello, friend."

"Are you here to buy arms?" asked the young man.

"We came to see Bedwyr."

The boy frowned and asked, "Does he know you are coming?"

"I don't think so. Will that be a problem?"

"Wilmot, the foreman, handles all business. Bedwyr stays in his tower inventing things. He doesn't meet strangers."

After they ate, Brother Sestus suggested they check on the animals and then take a walk. The night air was cold but pleasant. Unexpectedly, the young man stopped and asked, "Who are you, really, Tatyx?"

Stern didn't know what to tell the young man. He decided to relate the same story he told Magister Blut, plus his adventures with the reavers and Dra'ghan. He also told him his real name. When they returned to the tavern, twenty or so men sat in the corner drinking. Brother Sestus wanted another pint so Stern excused himself and went to his room. As soon as he entered, he checked to see if his money and books were safe. He breathed a sigh of relief when he felt the pouch. He removed the grimoire from his pack and laid it open on the covers of the bed, undressed completely, and climbed beneath the comforter. Reading, he rubbed the demon's stone between his thumb and forefinger. It was cold now and he wondered if Bedwyr's power dampened magic in the village.

The next section of the grimoire involved the summoning of a wind elemental. He settled back into the bed and began to translate the spell. At some point, however, he fell asleep and dreamed he was hiking alone across a great sheet of green ice. He awoke to singing coming from Brother Sestus' room; he obviously had more than one more pint of ale downstairs with the locals. The candle next to his bed, melted down to its metal holder, flickered once and then extinguished itself in the liquid wax.

He climbed out of bed and opened the window. The night air was cold and clear; a full moon filled the southwestern sky. Restless, he dressed and went down stairs. All lights were out and the front door of the tavern was barred. He walked to the back of the dining room and found the door to the kitchen. The kitchen was dark but he soon found an unlocked door that opened onto a yard behind the tavern. He passed through the yard and followed a stone pathway that made a gradual decline toward the cliffs, past a building that was obviously the stables and then continued on it as it turned gradually to the right toward the mountain and the black tower.

A red light burned at a window near the top of the tower. Suddenly, yellow sparks flew out the window, illuminating the structure. Engrossed in the light show, Stern did not notice a creature approaching him at a rapid pace. He jumped, startled by a sudden pain in his right thigh. Turning quickly to confront his attacker, he was surprised to see a large bird with a splendid tail that, at that moment, screeched a loud warning to him that it intended to strike again. He backed up, watching the peacock display its plumage. In the shadows, he perceived three more of the creatures coming to the aid of his attacker. He did not want to harm the birds so he quickly moved away from them, running down the stony trail that led him away from the tower. As he turned the corner, he heard the birds' chilling shrieks. Later, in his room, he examined the wound. The skin was torn and blood stained his robe. He found another candle in the drawer of the chest near the bed, climbed back in bed and resumed his reading. It was nearly dawn when he finally fell asleep.

He had only slept for an hour or two when Brother Sestus woke him. "I must leave after breakfast."

Stern rubbed his eyes and pulled on his clothes. "Wait downstairs. I will be there in a few minutes."

Twenty or thirty people were eating in the tavern. The innkeeper had opened the doors and windows and a fresh breeze blew in from the sea. The server girl placed a large mug of hot tea in front of him, a bowl of hot cereal, and a shriveled apple. Midway through his meal, a large man, wearing a leather vest, linen shirt and a kilt, with a full head of curly black hair that fell freely onto his shoulders and a thick long beard that parted naturally in the middle, entered the room. Stern knew it was Bedwyr.

Chapter Thirty-Seven: The Magus

THE PATRONS GREETED BEDWYR warmly as he walked toward
Stern, who sat quietly, studying the man, he had spent the last few months
struggling to reach.

Bedwyr stopped a few feet away from Stern and asked, "Was that you
my peacocks attacked last night?"

There was slight grin on his face and Stern did not perceive any anger
in the question.

"I was distracted by the lights and your birds snuck up on me."

"Did they draw blood?"

"They tore a hole in my robe and scratched the skin."

He slapped his large meaty hands together and laughed.

"I'm Bedwyr, the blacksmith."

"I am Stern and I have come a long way to ask for your help."

Every eye in the room was on the two men. "Sit with us, Bedwyr. This
is my escort and guide, Brother Sestus."

Bedwyr nodded at the brother, whose mouth was open.

The girl with the red hair placed a large mug of the tea in front of
Bedwyr. "Thank you, Suze." She bowed and backed away, as he sat down.
"I have been expecting you for a long time, Stern."

"How did you know I was coming?"

He simply sipped his tea and smiled without answering.

"Michaelsdottir was here?" asked Stern.

"She spent three nights with us."

"She helped me a great deal."

"Maybe she did and maybe she didn't." He sipped his tea and turned to Brother Sestus. "Do you stay with us?"

He cleared his throat. "No, I leave after breakfast."

"Since you will soon be alone, Stern, I would like for you to visit me in the tower. We have much to discuss."

After they finished their breakfast, Bedwyr and Stern accompanied Brother Sestus to the stable. The stable boy had saddled both the gelding and the mule and Stern held the mule's reins as Brother Sestus mounted the horse.

"Take care Stern."

"And you."

They watched him ride down the cobblestone path until he reached the mouth of the tunnel.

"Let's walk to the forge. I want you to see my facility, my shop."

Stern followed Bedwyr to the center of the village, where the magus turned right, passed between two large stone houses and then climbed up a series of steps leading to the narrow entrance of a crevice in the mountain's wall. The passageway was approximately two hundred meters long and opened onto a flattened, circular space, surrounded by the black walls of the volcanic mountain. An open air forge dominated the center of the space. Two large wooden storage facilities stood on the southeast corner of the space, where ten or so men and boys worked at the forge, making swords, halberds, and horse shoes.

Stern picked up one of the halberds. He judged its weigh and balance first, then he sensed or imagined a silver aura. He moved to a sword and lifted it. It too seemed both balanced and solid. This time the aura seemed to be platinum in color.

"Bedwyr, this sword seems to be a better quality than the halberd. And I seem to feel an aura."

Bedwyr smiled. "Check the mark on the sword. There is an imprint somewhere on the blade."

Stern held the sword close to his eyes, trying to locate an imprint or marking. "Here it is. Looks like two dragons fighting."

"That is Wayward's mark, the older man there at the forge. He made the sword and his aura is brighter than most of the others."

"Talmidge," called Bedwyr, "bring us what you are working on."

A slim young man approached them, carrying a *zweihandler*. As he approached, Stern noted a thick dark gray aura around the sword. Talmidge handed the sword to Stern, who took it reluctantly.

"See, every maker has a personality that imbues the sword. The spells cast in this forge produce the aura you are seeing. It is a way to understand the personality, as well as the quality of the weapon."

As soon as Talmidge moved away, Stern asked about the sword's dark aura.

"Talmidge was a sellsword that fled the King's island. He has killed many men and his soul is not pure. His weapon is deadly and needs to be wielded by a man that can handle the ambiguities of life. Wayward was born here in this village and learned the craft at an early age. He is a simple man with a wife and children and he puts every ounce of his being into his craftsmanship."

"Are his weapons better than Talmidge?"

"Better? That is not the issue. Both have exquisite quality, they are just different. A sellsword, looking for a weapon, might prefer the feel of Talmidge's sword. Most people cannot see the auras but they can sense the sword's being."

"Let's go to the tower. It is time we began our work."

They followed the trail back through the crevice into the village square and then turned toward the tower. Its iron doors were open. The ground floor was deserted and sunlight illuminated the tessellated floor. Dark red tiles formed a six-point star in the center. A stone stairwell angled upward to the upper stories and an opening in the floor on the opposite side of the chamber revealed a stone stairwell that descended into the mountain.

"There are seven stories above us and seven stories below us," said Bedwyr.

Stern studied the room, noting a gray-black aura emanating from the stones. When he studied the stairs leading down into the mountain the aura darkened, extinguishing the light. Bedwyr, seeming to read his thoughts, said: "You cannot use your simple human qualifications on these auras. Black does not mean evil, nor white good. Here, the blackness of the aura arises from the stones burned by the lava of the volcano. It might be easier to say the stones have been purified by the fires but not destroyed."

He moved to the stairs leading up to the upper levels and began climbing. Stern, thinking about his pronouncement on the color and meaning of auras, shook his head and followed the magus.

The stairs wound like a snake through the upper levels. No level after the ground floor was open. Most were divided into rooms with black iron doors. Open windows let in light and air. After the first level the floors were polished wood. They were clean and shining and Stern imagined an army of servants waxing them each day, although he saw no one nor did he hear any sounds, except for birds on the ledge of the windows.

The top level was open, like the ground floor with seven windows, a black polished wood floor, covered with multicolored rugs, four chairs in front of a large fireplace, and a stack of wood organized in the grate, ready to be lit.

Standing in the open space, Stern felt chilled from the wind off the sea.

"Winter comes early this year," said Bedwyr.

"You think it has something to do with Focalor?"

"Not Focalor but his master, Typhon. When he created the storm to deter you, he started a cycle that will not stop for quite a while." He sat in one of the chairs near the fire place.

"Sit down. We need to talk."

Stern sat across from him, stretched his legs out across the elaborate rugs and waited for him to begin.

"The Xippon witches told me of your coming but they were not clear when and where you would arrive. I used the scrying bowl and I saw the ancient home city of the Skaellanders. I meditated on the image and I used the scrying bowl until I was sure you were coming soon and you would land in Thule, the dead city perched on the island mountain.

"That unnerved me because Thule is inhabited by lesser air daemons, brought to this world many years ago by a demon to destroy the power of the Skaellanders. I was also worried by the amount of biological contamination that might still reside in the stone." He paused for a few seconds, blinked and then cleared his throat. "Did you notice the ocean has a red tint near Thule?"

Stern leaned forward and nodded.

"Tiny creatures from the fiery plane turn the water red in summer. They die back in the winter but ever since the great war of the north they have been there. They eat everything in the waters of the north that would feed the fish; consequently, the fish population has been decimated. The Skaellanders were great fishermen but the demon made sure he contaminated the food supply.

"Once I figured out when and where you would arrive, I contracted with the Tandraxx Amazons to send out warriors to find you. They reported they found you but then lost you in Typhon's storm."

"They found me, but not at Thule. And it is true that the young Amazon and I were separated in the storm that washed me onto the shores of *Islanka*."

"You must tell me everything. I want to know about your life on Mittilagart and then I need to know everything that happened after you arrived on Okeanus."

Stern began talking. At first he didn't know where to begin but he soon warmed to the telling and continued non-stop for several hours. At midday, Bedwyr raised his hand and said, "Enough for now. Let's go to the tavern and eat.

The tavern was full as Bedwyr and Stern pushed their way onto one of the long benches. Several of the guests were workers at Bedwyr's forge and they nodded to him as they entered. Lunch consisted of lamb chops, potatoes and a leafy vegetable, which Stern washed down with a pint of the ale. As soon as they finished, Bedwyr said, "I have to check the forge. I will meet you at the tower in three hours and we can continue our discussion. Tonight we will start."

Stern returned to his room and promptly fell into a deep sleep, dreaming of the daemon parrots and the red sea of Thule. He woke at dusk, his mouth dry and his head aching. A cold breeze blew through the window and gray clouds amassed in the north.

Chapter Thirty-Eight: Wizard Talk

HE DRESSED and walked to the tower. The large iron doors were open and a black cat sat in the entrance cleaning its paws. Stern found a heavy knocker on the right door and banged it twice. The cat jumped, annoyed at the sound, and scurried down the cobblestoned path to the village.

Stern waited in the frame of the portal. After a while he grew bored and began practicing the spells he memorized from the grimoire. He whispered the fire spell, his favorite so far, and small red flames appeared on the fingertips of his right hand. He flicked his index finger and a tiny ball of flame shot forth across the cobblestone and struck a weed growing between the cracks. The flame consumed the weed in one withering blow, which frightened him. He stamped out the fire.

The sunset and shadows lengthened around the black stone buildings of the village. Drops of rain began to splatter down onto the stones and Stern moved inside the tower. He sat in the shadow of the door, as the rain fell harder and the wind stiffened, rushing out of the north. He began to imagine he saw figures hiding in the shadows of the buildings and he wondered where Bedwyr was.

An hour later, the rain stopped and he heard someone coming up the path from the center of the town. It was Bedwyr walking slowly, talking to himself. Stern emerged from the shadows, calling out to Bedwyr, alerting him to his presence.

"Stern, why didn't you go up to the study? Surely, a fire is roaring there by now."

"I knocked but no one answered."

"There is only Kathe but she is almost deaf. Let's go up."

The man that Stern followed up the stairs seemed older than the man he shared breakfast with that morning. When they reached the chamber at the top, Bedwyr dropped his cloak on the floor and fell into one of the chairs in front of the fire.

"I had to help strengthen some of the siege weapons ordered by the Brotherhood. I used magic to unite the joints and springs. It is a tiring business—magic."

Kathe, with salt and pepper hair that fell loosely onto her narrow shoulders, entered the room, carrying two tankards of dark ale.

"Shall I serve dinner here or in the dining room?"

"We will come down after I warm up," mumbled Bedwyr.

He took a large gulp of the ale and then wiped the foam from his mustache with a wide swipe of his right hand.

"I have been thinking about your quest and I believe I know what is happening." He paused, watching Stern's face. "The worlds are out of balance and the appearance of the blue-back dragons in your world is a result of their extermination in this world. The dragons have thrived in Mittilagart because they have no natural predators and the humans were unprepared for them. They had no weapons to fight them."

He stretched his legs toward the fire, warming his feet.

"You were sent to bring the worlds back into balance: to return the dragons to the natural habitat and rid your world of an unnatural predator."

Stern laughed. He found the notion he was here to re-balance the planes too ludicrous for words, laughter seemed to be the only sane response. "Why would I be chosen to fulfill this most serious quest?"

"In a way you chose yourself. Why did you allow the witches to throw you through the portal? Why did you accept the Black Robes' assignment to travel north?"

Stern shrugged his shoulders. He had been so busy running since arriving on Okeanus he had not had time to ask such questions.

"You told me the Dra'ghan shaman helped you find your animal spirit, which was a panther, although you had shifted several times before into the shapes of other animals?"

"Yes, but I had help each time."

"Focalor awakened your powers?"

"That is correct. I had never shifted before."

"Focalor is here for a reason greater than obfuscation. You and Kylla thought his purpose is to stop the return of the blue-back dragon but I'm not sure."

"Why do you think he is involved?"

"I haven't figured it out yet. All I know is that the shape-shifting is integral to the quest and that Focalor initiated your powers. With his help, either on purpose or inadvertently, you have started on the path to becoming either a mage or a shaman. From what I have seen you seem to possess the talents of both. My goal would be to help you along that trail as best I can. In order to accomplish this you need to finish the books given you by Kokabiel and to further train your abilities to shift shape. When you are ready, you will return to the earthern plane and lead the dragons through the portal and back to Okeanus."

He paused to measure Stern's response to his thoughts.

"I'm not sure yet but I think we will need some help from your friends, the Dra'ghan. You told me the reaver witch saw the blue-backs returning to Okeanus through a portal on the island of Grun."

"Yes."

"Grun is a tropical island far to the south in the western hemisphere. It is a long journey by ship but from everything you have said I think it is essential for your mission to travel there and open a portal to Mittilagart as soon as you are ready."

"How do I get ready?"

"First we will eat and then I will determine if you do indeed possess the blood of a Skaellander."

"How will you know?"

"The Skaellander through the aid of a powerful drug made from the dragon shard of the blue-back could shift into a dragon. I will dose you with a diluted tincture of a drug, known as *dragonskin*; and, if you succeed in shifting, then we will know that you are a descendent of the ancient race. It will take us weeks to train but if I'm right, we'll know the reason the witches chose you and will have a way in which to accomplish your quest. It seems to me you are a pawn of the witches of both Mittilagart and Okeanus and in some unknown way they have been working in tandem."

They descended to the level below and entered a large dining room with a great wooden table. Kathe served them beef stew in large silver bowls and fresh bread. They washed the food down with cold dark ale that was superior to that served in the inn. When they finished, Stern followed Bedwyr to the stairs descending into the mountain. They passed six levels and entered an open room, illuminated by torches. The floor was a solid black slate, polished to such a degree that Stern could see his hirsute self in its surface.

Chapter Thirty-Nine: The Dragon Appears

BEDWYR LIT KINDLING with a torch and then crossed to a work table in the far corner of the room. "You had better undress," he said, pulling a vial from a cabinet behind his desk.

Stern draped his clothes over the arm of a wooden chair, as the man transferred some of the elixir to a glass. "I will give you a diluted tincture of the dragonskin, which will make you drowsy at first. Remain as still as possible and concentrate on the blue dragon you saw on the earthern plane. I'm not expecting much but you may experience hallucinations and nausea."

Bedwyr approached the naked Stern with the blood-red liquid and said, as he extended his hand toward him, "This is your chance to back out."

With his arms crossing his chest, trying to maintain some body heat, Stern asked: "If I shift, how do I come back?"

Bedwyr explained, as Stern took the glass: "The process is the same as you have experienced with the bear. The difference, of course, is the use of dragonskin to facilitate the change. You might say this experiment is against your nature."

Stern closed his eyes and began to meditate, calling forth his spirit animal. The moment he felt the stirrings of the shift, he swallowed the dragonskin. Containing a touch of mercury, its metallic bitterness made him gag. However, he swallowed it all. The liquid burned his throat and slammed hard into his stomach.

As the potion acted on him, the bear bounded from his conscious mind, retreating into darkness, into his unconscious. Stern coughed and felt a stirring in his groin. A blue tail, angled and shaped like the head of an arrow, flicked across his mind's eye, and a wave of dizziness assaulted him. He pressed the palms of his hands against the shining slate floor to steady himself, as his mind whirled and images and visions pummeled his consciousness.

A burst of liquid flame flew past his inner eye and he smelt rotten eggs and brimstone. A cry of pain echoed against the far wall, as an apparition of the Argyll woman, the mother of his son, ran naked through the room, followed by Kylla, bloody and torn, naked and crying. Mikk followed her, flying through the arched rafters of the room on a broomstick, and calling his name, while Gotha waddled into the room pregnant. As the images poured relentlessly into his mind, Focalor, brandishing a pitchfork, threatened Gotha and a blue-back dragon, the size of a dray horse, reared up; its black leathery wings spread across the width of the room. Resting on its haunches, it stared into Stern's eyes, and then opened its long maul, disclosing rows of sharp yellow teeth.

Stern tried to control his mad thoughts by concentrating on the dragon, imagining himself, rather than the beast, flying above the Sun Mountains, seeking currents to hold him up. Suddenly, he was hungry, hungrier than he had ever been before, and his yellow eyes searched the pastures beneath him for food. A flock of black sheep grazed on a hill. He prepared to sweep the hill with his liquid fire, when he heard someone screaming his name, pleading with him to stop, throwing his timing off and interfering with the physics of his turn.

The human Stern stirred and demanded to be returned, fighting with this thing within him. The beast was hungry, refusing to relent. The wind felt good to it and food was near.

Stern opened his eyes to see Bedwyr near the fire, holding his black staff; his eyes burning with fear and anger. Stern coughed and asked for water and Bedwyr handed him a silver cup.

"How do you feel?" the man asked.

"I am thirsty and tired."

"You shifted. Were you aware of it?"

"No, I thought I was dreaming."

"I thought you were about to attack me. The dragonskin was too strong. I need to dilute it further."

"I was flying above the Sun Mountains."

Bedwyr shrugged, not understanding the significance of his statement.

"I was either within the creature or I was seeing the future."

"You must get some sleep. There are some sleeping rooms on the floor above us. I want you to stay here so I can watch you through the night."

Bedwyr helped him up the stairs and Stern lay on a narrow cot in a small cell and immediately fell asleep. He woke once during the night, covered in sweat, even though the cell was cold. Naked and shivering, he pulled a blanket off the bed and wrapped it around him before falling back onto the bed.

He dreamed of the Argyll woman again. She begged him to call upon the Black Robes to help him, to free him from the clutches of the demon. He bowed before an altar and called out and then the man in the hooded cape from his vision entered and spoke to her. She bowed her head and listened intently and he heard her say, "Yes, I promise. Yes."

Bedwyr shook him awake and he coughed several times, his throat sore and aching.

"Come with me and we will break fast. It is midday."

As they descended the stairs, Stern felt a bitter cold seeping through the stone walls. "It's colder, much colder than before."

"A storm came in last night and dumped several inches of snow on us. The kids are dancing up and down in the stuff."

As he ate a bowl of hot vegetable soup and drank a tankard of the dark ale, Bedwyr said, "We should skip tonight. Return to the inn, sleep and study. We will try again tomorrow night."

An hour later, Stern, wrapped in a heavy black cloak, its hood pulled forward, covering his head and face, waded through the snow to the inn. The innkeeper looked at him strangely, as if he suspected that he and Bedwyr were performing magic in the tower. Once he reached his room, he fell into a deep sleep, fully clothed, with the cloak pulled over his head. In the middle of the night, he stirred from a troubling dream; a strong wind rattled the shutters and he could see his breath by the light of a candle burning on the table next to his bed. Someone had checked on him, lit the candle, and left bread, cheese and dried fruit, which he ate like a ravenous dog. Finished, he lay back on the bed and pulled the grimoire from its hiding place under the bed and read for three hours before he blew out the almost extinguished candle.

He woke at the first bell. Ice glistened on the inside of the window pane and he smashed the patina of ice on the porcelain wash bowl and washed his hands and face.

He felt good, very good in fact. As he walked down the stairs to the dining room, he took two and three steps at a time. His legs felt like steel coils and his arms seemed bigger, more muscled, and stronger. He devoured his breakfast with relish and he drank two tankards of pale ale.

He asked the innkeeper for some more candles before returning to his room to study the grimoire. Finishing the spells on water, air, fire, and earth, he moved on to the invisibility spells. His energy was boundless.

Chapter Forty: A Second Night with the Dragon

AT DUSK, he trudged through new snow to the tower and knocked several times before Kathe pulled the door open enough for him to enter.

"He's downstairs, waiting for you," she said.

Stern found Bedwyr at his worktable, diluting the dragonskin with a clear viscous liquid that smelt like almonds. When the magus finally turned his attention to Stern, he said, "You have gained a lot of muscle in the last two days."

"Have you seen this side effect before?" asked Stern.

"Not really. But I have never used this potion before." Stern's face reflected his dismay and Bedwyr laughed, as he handed him a tiny vial of the red liquid, and said, "This time try to maintain consciousness."

Like the night before, he sat on the cold floor and meditated. However, the bear refused to appear and he feared he would not return. The first thing he saw were the yellow eyes of the dragon, then its black leather nostrils puffing out a small red flame sporadically. He heard Gotha call his name and then twins with long curly blonde hair tottered across the tiles.

The scene changed and he flew along the banks of the Rio Concho. Horns blared as ornithopters appeared on the horizon. He plunged head first into the rushing waters and swam downward toward the entrance of an underwater grotto, far removed from the noise, to a cave. "So this is where you are hiding?" he thought. The entrance was tight and almost too small for him as he struggled down the tunnel.

He turned his inner mind backwards and he was in the tower, where the man dressed in a kilt and leather vest stood, waiting for him. He fought for his consciousness. He tried to remember the man's name. He knew he could say it. The man was calling him. He held a black staff with a silver cap covered in elaborate runes.

Stern remembered the man's name and willed himself back into the room with Bedwyr and fell face first onto the cold slate floor.

"How do you feel?" asked the magus.

"I am not as sick as before but I lost consciousness."

"That was better but you cannot give yourself completely to the dragon. You must be able to maintain and control a portion of your conscious mind in the beast's body."

He wrapped him in the heavy cloak. "Let's eat and then you need to sleep."

He stayed in the tower in one of the smaller cells above the magus' work room and dreamed of a night in La Ciudad. An Argyll woman with raven-black hair approached him. It was hot and humid and he wiped away beads of sweat forming on his brow. In her heavily-accented voice she asked if she could sit with him.

"I don't have money to spend on a bottle."

"Black Robes always have." Her eyes were dark black and her teeth very white.

"If you sit, I can buy you a beer but that is all."

"She sat next to him and put her hand on the inside of his thigh."

In the dream, her hand felt warm and moist. However, he heard a phrase in his mind: her hand was like fire acting as water. He awoke in a room so dark he could not see his hand. He was cold and he felt around for a blanket. His cloak was folded at the end of the bed and he pulled it over him, as he fell into a deep, untroubled sleep.

The next morning he emerged from the tower to find it had snowed again during the night. Bedwyr placed his hand on his shoulder. "I have never seen it snow this much this far south. The planes are tilting out of balance. Your world must be really suffering from the heat now."

"How long have I been away?"

"It is hard to tell. Okeanus and Mittilagart move in opposite directions. It could be one year or fifty."

Chapter Forty-One: The Return of Brother Sestus

WHEN HE REACHED THE INN, he was surprised to see Brother Sestus sitting at one of the long wooden tables. He asked, as he sat down opposite him: "Brother, what brings you back?"

The man wiped his mouth on his sleeve and answered with his mouth full. "Magister Blut wants to talk to you."

"What does he want with me?"

"He did not share his thoughts with me. He simply asked me to bring you back to the camp."

"I'm working on some important things with Bedwyr. If I came with you, when could I return?"

"He told me we can have you back here within two days."

"I will have to discuss it with Bedwyr."

Brother Sestus nodded and then returned to his food.

Stern set out for the forge. A light snow fell onto the black stones of the village, as crows, ravens, and jackdaws gathered on the roofs and cawed plaintively in the frigid gray air. He found Bedwyr at the largest forge, working with a gray powder. "Mercury for the potion," he said. "You need to stand back."

From across the room, Stern shouted. "Brother Sestus is here and has asked me to return to the Brothers' camp to meet with Magister Blut."

Bedwyr, naked to the waist, pulled his thick black hair back from his forehead with his thick fingers and answered: "You have to go. This is my island but since they came they have continued to amass power. I could stand against them but it would be disastrous for my people to resist them."

Stern was shocked. He had come to think Bedwyr was all powerful.

"You almost sound like the Brotherhood's presence here is insidious."

"The Brotherhood has good impulses; however, their fanaticism coupled with their bellicose nature can be harmful. I have never understood their real purpose, other than serving their god through war. Leave your things with me in the tower. I would hate for them to fall into the hands of the Brotherhood."

"Who do you favor—the King or the Brotherhood?" asked Stern, worried by this turn of events.

Bedwyr removed the substance from the flames and wiped his hands on a large black towel. "Neither force appeals to me. They and all the petty kings and despots like them are responsible for destroying the balance of this plane. As you develop, you will discover our role is simply to maintain balance between chaos and order. The Brotherhood and the King work from a different impulse; theirs is a totalitarian wish to exert control over their natural environment." He signaled for Stern that he could come closer. "I imagine the Brotherhood wants to enlist you in their war against the King. Humor them and return here as soon as possible."

Stern shivered as he left the heat of the forge. The howling northern wind beat against the walls of the village and surged through the alleys and streets. He gathered his things and left them with Kathe at the entrance to the tower. Brother Sestus had followed him on a black mule with brown markings on its face and leading the white mule for Stern. They rode slowly through the deepening snow, heading toward the valley and the Brotherhood's main camp.

Because of the weather, the trip took two days. They spent the night in an abandoned shed on the side of the road, huddled under their cloaks. That night Stern dreamed he shifted into the bear and slept in a warm cave on the edge of a red sea. The next morning the snow had stopped and the sky was clear. It was late afternoon when they reached the block house, where Stern warmed his hands in front of the Magister's fire.

"Brother Stern, I appreciate your coming in such weather."

Stern nodded, waiting to hear the Magister's request.

"We are sending a ship north to *Islanka* and we would like you to accompany Brother Sestus and a small party."

Stern turned to the Magister, his eyes wide with shock. "Why do you want me to go, Magister? You know the King is looking for me."

"You fought Focalor and won. We have news he is harassing the Brotherhood on the island."

Somewhat panicked, Stern said: "Magister Blut, I thought *Islanka* is iced in."

"It is. We plan to drop you off on the ice. You will travel across the ice fields on skis to Wyvernne and then proceed to the Brotherhood's encampment. We will land in the spring with an army and resolve this struggle with the King once and for all."

"My mission takes me to the southwest. I cannot go back to the Island."

The Magister's eyes narrowed and Stern could feel his anger. "What is this mission you speak of and what are you doing with Bedwyr in that cursed tower of his?"

Stern realized he had said too much. "When do you send this expedition?"

"The ship is ready now. The winter has fallen upon us and we must go before the Port of Noirrith freezes completely."

"You do intend for me to return to Bedwyr and pick up my things?"

"No, you will equip yourself from our stores and leave with Brother Sestus and his men at dawn." With that pronouncement the Magister rose and extended his hand. "I wish you a good and safe voyage, Tatyx."

Brother Sestus escorted him to the armory, a large stone building near the northern edge of the camp, where he walked up and down the stacked arms, running his hands over the weapons and sensing the blackness emanating from a six-foot-long polearm. Another whose aura was bright silver attracted him and he suspected Bedwyr had a hand in making it. He chose it and a dagger he knew Talmidge had crafted. Next he selected fur-lined boots and gloves that fit and a red stocking cap and a close-fitting quilted jacket he intended to wear over his leathers and under his cloak.

Fully equipped, Brother Sestus escorted him to his tent to store his weapons and then accompanied him to evening mess. The fact that Sestus refused to leave his side alerted him to the fact they suspected he might bolt for Bedwyr's village.

A frigid wind blew across the lake when he finally lay down on his cot in the tent. He wrapped himself in his cloak and pulled the blanket over his head. As he closed his eyes, he saw the blue-black maul of the dragon and he felt its strength running through his veins. He quickly cleared his mind and shooed the dragon image away.

They left at dawn, heading for the port. It had snowed during the night and snow covered the road. Stern, on the white mule, followed behind

Brother Sestus and a squad of six brothers, hand picked for this expedition. For the first time in weeks, he felt the heat of the stone around his neck. Kokabiel was telling him he was going the wrong way and that his fate lay far to the south on a tropical island the Dra'ghan and Bedwyr called Grun. It was time to go home, he thought. He felt resistance and anger rise as they moved inexorably toward the east. It entered his mind that he could just turn around and head toward Bedwyr's tower. He asked himself what action would Brother Sestus take to stop him; and, if they tried to stop him, was he prepared to kill seven brothers and leave their bodies in the snow.

Chapter Forty-Two: The Magicker Awakes

AS HE RODE, he began to work out a plan to escape the brothers without killing them. He knew he could escape and probably make it to Bedwyr but how would he get off the island. The weather and his need to travel south worried him.

Because of the ice and snow, the animals had trouble with a slight hill that overlooked the harbor. When they reached the top, Stern counted six large galleys and one sleek corsair. Sheets of ice floated in the harbor.

He made up his mind and began to chant the spell of the north wind. At first, he whispered the spell until he felt the frigid air against his face. He spoke louder and the wind picked up the loose snow on the ground. He pulled back on the mules' reins to slow her and repeated the words louder still. One of the brother's horses went down, slipping on some ice, buffeted by the wind. Stern yelled out the spell again and the wind pushed against the coast like an electrical shock. Boats in the harbor lifted and fell, as thunderous waves pushed as the wind slammed against the volcanic rocks of the coast.

He could barely see the brothers now. He turned the mule away from the wind and headed south. As he rode he sang the spell at the top of his lungs and he heard above his head the wind's shrieking roar, the cracking masts of the ships, and the torn rigging falling to the deck.

He kicked the mule into a wild gallop on the ice and stood in the stirrups and howled the spell until his voice broke and he could no longer speak. His mind filled with the power of the wind and he felt the dragon thrill in his unconscious mind.

He rode mindlessly before the wind for hours before heading back to Bedwyr's village.

He passed the southern camp, which was a shambles of overturned tents and broken walls. Fires burned throughout the camp and men screamed for help in the debris of the storm. He called out the fire spell and watched his right hand form a ball of flame, which he hurled toward one of the guard towers. He whispered the spell of speed and the flaming ball smashed against the logs and ignited. He kicked the mule into a run, as he ignited three more towers, confusing the brothers even more with this unexpected onslaught.

Later, he slept in a cave a half day's ride from the entrance to the road to Bedwyr's village. His head ached and he was exhausted, worn from the magic and the journey.

The next day was clear. A slight wind blew from the north, a residue from yesterday's storm. Several hours later, he found the trail up the mountain. The snow was deep and the trip arduous. It was dusk before he tied the mule to the post in front of the inn. He left the mule there and climbed the hill to the tower, where he pounded on the iron doors, calling Bedwyr's name, as Kathe opened the door enough for him to slip through.

"You have disturbed the heavens." Kathe said.

Stern studied her face. She was angry.

"Is he here?" he asked pushing past the woman who was distraught.

"He is in the observation room at the very top."

Stern left his weapons at the bottom of the stairs and climbed the stairs. He had never entered the observation room, above the top floor. He found Bedwyr hunched over a scrying bowl. Without looking up, he whispered, "You have destroyed two galleys and damaged the rest. Countless brothers are injured. Ten are dead. The weather is shifting drastically and there are heavy snows falling even in Brasilika."

"I did not want to return to *Islanka*."

"I see that."

"I have a plan."

"I hope so, because I don't have any idea how to help you. Your training has only just begun. You need a lot of work and now you have offended and enraged the Brothers."

"I need to study your maps. I must find an island that I can fly to."

"You intend to shift into a bird and fly to an island? In this weather you will freeze to death."

"If the island is close enough, I can fly away in the morning and then return at night. If it is safe, you will fly a white flag. If it is not, you will hoist a red one. I will spend the nights here training and reading the grimoire. After a while the brothers will stop looking for me."

Bedwyr scratched his beard. "I have an alternative plan based on your ideas. We will proceed along your course but I will attempt to contact the Dra'ghan. There is an island sixty kilometers to the south. It is a small volcanic rock with six or seven large caves. There is nothing there but sea birds and an occasional dragon or dragonkin. If you survive, I will send the Dra'ghan there to pick you up.

He cleared his throat and then asked: "How did you get here?"

"I rode the mule."

"We must send the mule back down the mountain. While you eat, I will have Cratus take care of it. One of the boys can ride it to the valley and turn him loose.

"I will show you the map tonight and you can sleep here in one of the cells. I have already retrieved all your possessions from the Inn but it is imperative you leave at dawn."

Before cock crow Bedwyr shook Stern awake. "You must go now. The boy left last night and has just returned. He saw campfires on the plain. They will be here soon."

Stern stripped off all his underclothes and stood before Bedwyr with only the leather pouch hanging around his neck. Kathe gathered up his clothes, folded them and then packed them away in a large canvas bag that she hoisted onto her shoulder and carried from the cell. Bedwyr and Stern climbed the stairs to the very top of the tower.

"Wait a few days before coming back."

Stern shook his hand and then sat on the cold tiles and began to meditate on the osprey. Soon he imagined himself flying over the tower, circling on the brisk morning air, squawking into the now rising sun. He shifted and flew in a circle around the tower. He climbed higher on an air wave and he could see the road leading to the valley, where now twenty mounted Brothers rode toward the village. He flew east first toward the plains where the Brothers' camp lay in geometrical neatness. He found a cornfield covered with snow, landed and began to scavenge for food. A murder of crows joined him and began to assert their territorial imperative over the cornfield so he pushed on. He circled the field and turned south. The brothers had arrived and he saw them moving toward the mountain.

Stern felt a pang of guilt as he flew out over the water.

He reached the tiny island at dusk. Several dragonkin hovered over a beach on its south end. Without drawing too close to them he found a leviathan beached on the sand, where thousands of sea birds fed on its bloated carcass. His hunger was immense so he dipped down, skirting the dragonkin, and joined the white sea birds, feeding on the blubber of the sea beast. He fed until he could hold no more, and then flew away toward the northern end of the island, where several volcanic mountains protruded into the air, found a shallow cave, and landed on a pumice ledge.

Stern took shelter in the deep recesses of the cave but it was cold and he feared he might freeze. He began to contemplate the form of the bear and soon shifted into a great black bear, shaggy in its winter coat of fur. He settled into the back of the cave and fell asleep. A cold wind blew from the north and sometime in the night snow began to fall.

He remained in bear form for four days, during which he killed several birds and even fought a dragonkin. He was constantly hungry on the barren island. On the fifth day, he shifted into bird form and flew back to Noirrith. The farther north he flew, the colder it became. The village lay under a deep covering of snow and a white flag flew from Bedwyr's tower.

He landed on an icy ledge and then hopped down on the frigid tile floor. He cawed several times until Bedwyr appeared, wearing a heavy fur coat over his shoulders and carrying another one in his arms.

\

Chapter Forty-Three: Calling the Dra'ghan

STERN MEDITATED on his human form. When he shifted, he fell onto the tiles shivering and Bedwyr wrapped him in the furs and helped him to the stairs.

"You have lost weight," said the magus, as he supported him up the stairs.

"You would not believe what I have been eating."

"Kathe has made a thick stew. Let's get you cleaned up. You smell like a bear." He wrinkled his nose and Stern laughed. "I have been a bear for a week. The ice has even reached the island in the south."

"I have never seen snow like this before. The world is out of order."

"When did the Brothers leave?"

"Three days ago when the snow began to fall they searched every house at least three times and questioned every resident, even the children. You have made a serious enemy."

Stern shrugged. "Could I have been wrong? Is the King right and the Brotherhood wrong?"

They reached the baths on the ground floor; steam poured from the open door.

"No, they are equally bad, if that is the word you want to use. I think they are just power hungry. Okeanus is a huge world with thousands of islands and peoples. For these small fry to decide they want to conquer the world is the height of hubris."

Stern lowered himself in a large stone bath and Bedwyr sat on a bench near the edge.

"Who is the most powerful?" asked Stern, reclining in the hot water.

"In the west, Brasilika controls about nine percent of the land mass. They are probably the strongest western nation but the Bouc are the most numerous of the humanoid."

"What about the Dra'ghan?"

"It is hard to say. They are great traders but they care not for the acquisition of land. The sea and the jungle are their homes."

Stern soaped himself thoroughly and then slid under the hot water. "When he emerged, Bedwyr said, "As long as the snow blocks the pass, I don't anticipate the Brothers coming back."

"Good, I need rest and food. Is the grimoire safe?"

He nodded in the affirmative.

After his bath, Stern joined Bedwyr in the dining room, where he ate several bowls of Kathe's stew and drank three tankards of the Noirrith ale. When he finished he went to his room and slept for four hours.

Late in the afternoon, the now-rested Stern joined Bedwyr in his study at the top of the tower.

"What are your plans?" the magus asked.

"I will continue my studies of the grimoire and work with you on the transformations."

"Do you realize the dragonskin potion has changed you?"

"What do you mean change?"

"You are probably two to three inches taller. You have put on muscle and your hair is returning thicker and darker than before."

He rubbed his hands over the top of his head to feel thick hair growing there.

"Your beard is considerably thicker now as well."

"Even though I was starving, I felt stronger."

Bedwyr changed the subject.

"I have tried to contact the Dra'ghan without any luck. Do you remember any of their names?"

"The shaman's name was Tak'seth."

Bedwyr stood up and motioned for him to join him at a five foot tall iron table, supporting a clay bowl, filled with water, centered on its black surface.

"Let's see if your connection with Tak'seth will produce a better result."

Stern gazed into the shallow water, which turned darker as he gazed into it. Soon a dragon ship appeared, emerging from a raging squall; the Dra'ghan huddled at their oars. Tak'seth stood, his left hand griping a rope tied to the mast, chanting at the top of his lungs, his right hand lifting his staff high into the air.

"Are they in that storm now?"

"It could be now or tomorrow or a week ago. It is hard to say. Call out to him."

"Tak'seth. It is Stern. I need your help."

The storm raged around the ship and Tak'seth struggled to stand on his feet. He pulled a blue amulet, hanging around his neck on a silver chain, from beneath his robes. He grasped the stone in his right hand and began to chant, calling on the sea gods to calm the waters around the Dra'ghan craft and to preserve the lives of all on board.

As Stern watched the scene, the waters calmed and the ship ran before the storm. Reading the shaman's lips, Stern watched as Tak'seth raised his head and thanked Okeanus, then turned to the captain and announced that they must change course.

Bedwyr described the island several times, hoping the shaman understood.

"Do we know where they are?" asked Stern.

"I have no idea; and, unfortunately, this is as good as the communication will be."

"He can't hear us?"

"It is a feeling. Suddenly, you think of a person and you understand they are asking for help. Most people would ignore it but someone like Tak'seth will know we are calling him."

"If they are heading to the island, should I return and wait?"

"We should continue to work on your transformation skills and every other day, you should fly to the island and check and see if they have arrived."

They continued to work throughout the night on the transformation. During the day, Stern slept and studied the grimoire. Every other day for two months, he flew to the island in the form of an osprey. Snow continued to fall, assuring the village the path up the mountain was closed to the Brotherhood.

The unnatural weather and the impassable trail prevented all food supplies from reaching the village, as the goods manufactured by the villagers stacked up in the warehouses, waiting delivery to the traders, merchants, and the Brotherhood. The villagers began discussing opening a path wide enough for a pack of mules and horses to make it to the harbor and Bedwyr warned Stern: "We must open the road. Once we do the Brotherhood will be back here looking for you."

"Only you and Kathe know I am here. I'm sure it will be safe to open the way." Bedwyr shook his head in such away that indicated that he disagreed. "There are no secrets in this village. You must leave as soon as the road is cleared. I have made a leather saddle with bags for the dragon. You should take all of your clothes, books, and weapons to the island and await the arrival of the Dra'ghan."

"What about the dragonskin?"

"You no longer need it. I have been feeding you a placebo for a week. Your transformation is flawless."

Stern ran his right hand through his dark black hair that now fell to his shoulders, laughed and asked: "Will I keep the hair?"

"I believe so. Every time you change into the dragon, you become the dragon. Its residue remains in your blood."

The villagers dug for three weeks until they finally broke through to the plains below the mountain. A train of forty horses and mules set off to deliver weapons and various other craft items to the harbor. A week later, a brotherhood patrol of thirty men accompanied the traders back to the village. The night before the patrol arrived Stern in the form of a male blue-back dragon flew from Bedwyr's tower with all his worldly goods strapped to his scaly back.

Stern had studied Bedwyr's charts and he believed if he flew along the coasts of the intervening islands he could make it to Grun in half a year.

Both he and Bedwyr agreed he would only wait one more month for the Dra'ghan and then he would set out. Once he reached Grun, he would open a portal and step though to the earthen plane.

Chapter Forty-Four: Stern Flies South

WHEN HE REACHED the volcanic island, he changed into his human form and carried his clothes, food and books to a cave on the southern end of the island near a beach. From its ledge he had a panoramic view of the southern sea, where he passed the time studying the sky and the weather.

Several weeks passed and he resolved to leave the island in two days.

He was chewing some hard tack at dusk, when he saw the black sail of a dragon ship appear on the horizon and realized Tak'seth was coming for him. The Dra'ghan ran a small boat up on the black sand of the southern beach of the tiny island, while Stern waited for them on a hillock above the beach, his saddle bags packed and the dragon saddle next to him. Grek'kan jumped from the prow and landed squarely on both feet, a cutlass of black steel in his right hand. Looking about, he sniffed the air and shouted: "Hello, Krassnith. We meet again."

Stern waved. "It is good to see the valiant Grek'kan."

"Tek'seth awaits you in the south."

"He is not with you?"

"No, he set sail for Grun to prepare the way for the dragons."

Three Dra'ghan joined Grek'kan on the sand and he ordered them to carry Stern's belongings to the boat.

"Come, let's leave this cursed rock. We have a long way to go."

Stern smiled. He felt his journey was nearing its end.

They pushed the boat off the sand and out into the sea. On board, the Grek'kan gave orders to hoist anchor. As the mast filled, the reptiles began to sing and whitecaps danced around the prow of the ship. Stern stood on the elevated deck with Grek'kan and white birds fluttered around the sail and dolphin-like creatures swam escort. Two firedrakes the size of a great Dane crossed the bow.

At night, he slept on the deck amidst the Dra'ghan, as he felt the dragon ship carving the sea. Three days later, he woke before dawn and stood at the rail, studying the outline of a dense rain forest on a large island to the west. Grek'kan drove the Dra'ghan ruthlessly and Stern wondered at their urgency. Over a lunch of bananas, coconut milk and boiled eggs, Stern asked Grek'kan if there was trouble. He turned his yellow eyes to Stern and watched him closely. "Tek'seth intends landing on Grun and establishing a base. The Bouc will oppose us. The shaman feels confident we will succeed but I feel anxious, knowing my battle brothers are in harm's way."

"So Grun is populated?"

"Grun is a large tropical island south of the equator. It is covered with thick, almost impenetrable jungle. Beside the Bouc, there are dragonkin of every size and nature. The place is a dragon paradise."

He sipped some coconut milk. "Every Dra'ghan warrior is dropped off on Grun for three nights as soon as he reaches his twelfth year. Only one in five survive. Can you imagine how dangerous the island is?"

"So you survived the test?"

"I would not be sitting here if I didn't. In that three day period I killed three Bouc and a firedrake."

"At this pace, how long will it take us to reach the island?" asked Stern.

"We cannot keep this pace up, of course, but I anticipate we will reach Grun in six to eight weeks."

"Will we stop on the way?"

"We must. We have supplies for only a few weeks at sea. You will see a large part of our world, little brother."

"Did you find the reavers?"

"No, they were not at any of their usual places. They must be hiding from the King's musketeers."

Every few weeks, the Dra'ghan found a place to beach their boats and hunt for food and water. Stern stayed close to Grek'kan, learning as much as he could of their language and culture. He discovered they were fearless warriors with a deep sense of honor among the members of the clan; however, they were merciless with their enemies. Several times they encountered other peoples on the islands and the Dra'ghan cut them down, burned their villages, and sank their ships and boats.

After nine weeks at sea and numerous battles and adventures, a lookout shouted that Grun lay ahead. Stern ran to the prow of the ship to get a better view of the island that was now, for him, imbued with honor and valor, after his hearing the stories of initiatory battles from many of the Dra'ghan warriors that he now knew well by sight, sound, and smell.

Chapter Forty-Five: Grun

THE ISLAND was green and black. A prodigious forest began at the edge of the black sand with five volcanic mountains, rising from the forest, dominating its center. Above the trees ten green dragons flew in formation to the north, while several firedrakes, the size of kroaxx, buzzed the ship.

As the boat drew near the shore, mosquitoes, the size of humming birds, circled their heads. The thick leathery skin of the Dra'ghan was impervious to their bites but Stern's was not. Grek'kan produced an ill-smelling paste, which Stern rubbed onto his skin, to ward off the bugs.

"The fat of the wattle bug will protect you," he said.

"It smells like the sour earth of a pigsty."

They worked themselves around the island, seeking Tek'seth's boat. It was a large island that might take weeks to explore.

At dusk they laid anchor on the southeast coast and the sounds from the jungle terrified Stern. Besides the metallic hum of millions of insects, there were roars, growls, calls, and screams of birds, animals and dragons.

Grek'kan set twice the number of guards around the ship than usual and then threw himself on the deck amongst his battle brothers and slept. Stern curled up under the edge of the polished railing, as far away from the coast as possible, and listened to the cacophony of the island's inhabitants.

Although winter had arrived in the north, it was warm on Grun and Stern did not need his cloak; nevertheless, he wrapped himself completely within it as feeble protection against the island's insects.

They set sail at dawn and moved inexorably around the edge of the island. By mid-afternoon they reached the southernmost tip of the coast. As soon as they turned toward the west, they found four dragon boats anchored in a sheltered lagoon. A thin wisp of white smoke rose from the jungle and Grek'kan ordered the boatswain to have the pilot bring the boat up to the anchored vessels. They lowered two long boats and twenty Dra'ghan and Stern approached the shore. There was little or no beach so the lagoon formed a perfect refuge for the boats.

They ran long boats up on the miniscule beach and Grek'kan sent off scouts in every direction, looking for an entry into the forest. Hopefully, they would find one recently hacked out by Tek'seth's warriors. In a few minutes, Stern heard the muted horn of Tang'gath, the scout sent to the west. As they hurried to Tang'gath's side, he pointed to a freshly hewed trail leading into the dense undergrowth, which they followed for almost three hours until they discovered a clearing and, in its center, a round stockade. Smoke rose from a longhouse and two Dra'ghan warriors stood guard at the gate. Tang'gath blew his horn, announcing their arrival and one of the guards beat his short sword against his brass shield and a horn answered from within the stockade.

Signs of battle marked the ground. Broken arrows lay scattered in front of the gate and large blood stains soured the spot where either a Bouc or a Dra'ghan fell.

There was no sign of the dead, however. The Dra'ghan had either policed the area or burned or buried the bodies.

Tek'seth emerged from a long log cabin near the center of the compound and raised his staff in recognition of Stern. "You have grown strong and tall, little brother. I see the dragon breathes in you."

"It looks as if you have been busy," answered Stern.

"The Bouc are good fighters but rather primitive. They know only brute force. I thought this camp would be a good base for the return of the blue dragon and their master, the Skaellander."

"What do you mean—the return of the Skaellander?"

"We will discuss it tonight. We have much to talk about."

In the distance, Stern heard the faint sound of a drum and Grek'kan bared his razor-sharp teeth, which Stern interpreted as a smile.

"What is it?"

"I thought Tek'seth had killed all the Bouc but now I hear their war drums and I know there will be plenty for Grek'kan to slay."

"They have attacked every night since we took their village," said Tek'seth.

Grek'kan called for Tang'gath. "Take ten warriors and go to the ship. Bring half the warriors back. Tell the others to guard all the boats and be alert."

"I set a strong watch over the boats," explained Tek'seth. "They were safe but we need to be careful. We can't be here without an escape route."

Stern followed him to the log house; his nose wrinkling at the foul odors of the camp.

"The Bouc live in their filth. We have spent weeks cleaning and still it reeks."

Inside, Tek'seth led Stern to an elevated platform near the back and said, "Put your things here next to mine."

He sat on the platform and waited for Stern to store his pack next to the shaman's leather bag, then said, "Tell me everything that has happened to you since we dropped you on Noirrith. Stern took a deep breath and began to relate in minute detail his adventures over the past months. From time to time Tek'seth would interrupt him and ask questions. He was particularly interested in Stern's transformations into the blue dragon. When he finished, Tek'seth sat quietly. Then he said in a low voice, "It is true. The legend is unfolding. The Dragon Lord is coming and with him, the dragon's son will bring the world into balance. "

"Tell me the legend."

"When the dragons disappeared, the weather began to change, growing increasingly colder each winter. The harsh northern winters and the King's musketeers took their toll on the Skaellanders and then Focalor opened a portal for a daemon to finish them with a contagion.

"Mordant, the last Skaellander shaman, escaped on a reaver ship and lived among them for many years. One winter's night he had a vision of a great blue-back bull arising from the south, from Grun. Riding him was the dragon's son, a Skaellander. Together they led an army of dragon riders.

"Mordant predicted the dragon's son would bring balance to Okeanus and that the Dra'ghan would be his ally."

"So that is why you are helping me?"

"Of course, I spent two years with Mordant and learned a great deal about the vision. I am convinced I am part of it."

Horns blasted through the cacophony of night sounds.

"The Bouc are attacking again. We need to join the men at the wall." Tek'seth stood and moved toward the door, where he stopped and scratched his snout with a long, sharp nail. "Can you shift into the bear? I think it might stop the Bouc's incessant attacks."

Stern paused, feeling nervous and afraid. The time had come for him to reveal the dragon and let it fly freely into battle. He picked up his polearm and followed Tek'seth to the east side of the stockade. Approximately two hundred Dra'ghan spread out around the perimeter of the camp, while thousands more of the centaur-like creatures emerged from the shadows of the forest.

The Bouc possessed the head, arms and chest of a man and the body of a goat. The largest of the beasts had black fur and dark red skin, while the smaller ones possessed fur of brown and white. Stern thought the word 'small' was a relative term in discussing a Bouc because the smallest one stood over six feet, while the large dark ones were close to eight. They carried axes and spears. Some of them employed round wooden shields, which they beat with their ax, adding to the noise of their attack.

The twelve foot tall stockade enclosed five acres. An elevated mound of dirt running around the inside of the wall provided a firestep for the Dra'ghan to see and fire over the fence. Twenty of Grek'kan's men carried crossbows, while the rest held axes and spears similar to the weapons used by the Bouc.

When Stern and Tek'seth reached Grek'kan, who stood near the gate, the shaman murmured, "We are outnumbered at least fifty to one."

"I have never seen them so well organized," said Tek'seth. "There must be a new leader somewhere in this mob."

"Why don't they charge us?" asked Grek'kan.

Tek'seth signaled he did not know with his left hand.

Suddenly, the tumult died down and the wall of Bouc warriors separated. Focalor, the daemon from the fiery realm, walked through the crowd, his black leathery wings spread in a display of power. When he reached the clearing, he walked a few feet toward the gate and signaled for a black Bouc to blow a great hunting horn, delivering nine mournful notes.

As the demon paraded in front of the Bouc, his naked muscles pulsing in his shoulders and neck, Stern studied his body, searching vainly for any sign of the wounds he inflicted on the daemon at their last meeting. A vision of Kylla being torn apart by the Kroaxx entered his mind and he staggered, dizzy from the scene and felt the dragon emerging from his unconscious mind. He could not control it. It was coming with or without his consent. He turned from the dirt rampart and walked to the center of the stockade and began to undress. He called for a young Dra'ghan to take his clothes and weapons to the long house, as Grek'kan called out, "Get back up here. Have you lost your mind?"

Stern sat naked in the dirt of the stockade and began his meditation on the dragon. In the distance, he heard the Bouc beating their weapons against their shields and the low mournful moan of their great horn. His training over the last few months worked and he was able to ignore the sounds of battle as he guided the dragon from his unconscious mind. He shifted and a blue-back dragon bull stood in the center of the stockade.

Its yellow eyes scanned the walls and the stockade, as it blew a spray of fire toward the gate. The flames spread across the ground and stopped a few feet from the ramparts. The Dra'ghan fell back away from the beast, as it spread its wings and lifted slowly off the ground, rising above the walls so that the Bouc could see it. The horns ceased and the Bouc cringed. Murmurs ran through their lines. Some turned and ran in fear back into the jungle but Focalor rallied them on, popping a long leather whip, calling for them to attack.

A giant black Bouc handed Focalor a long spear with an iron head and he reared back and threw the spear toward the dragon. The dragon waited and then rose another two feet and the spear plunged downward into the soft sand of the stockade's center.

Focalor called for another spear and the dragon flew higher and then turned in a left-handed tumble toward the earth. Twenty feet above the ground, the dragon leveled out and sprayed the Bouc with liquid flames. Many fell, their hide singed and their skin peeling away from their bodies.

The dragon rose up at the end of the run and climbed even higher. The Bouc, realizing it was going to attack again and there was little or nothing they could do to stop it, broke ranks and fled into the jungle. Focalor stood his ground and threw another spear at the approaching dragon. The spear creased the leathery skin of its left shoulder, drawing black blood.

Though the pain was immense, Stern ignored it and cleared his mind by thinking of Kylla. Hatred and revenge flowed into his mind, strengthening his resolve and bolstering his dragon shape. He rose and circled for another attack. The black Bouc handed Focalor yet another spear. The daemon rose a few feet off the ground, steadying himself with his black wings. He flicked his forked tail, readying himself for the dragon's attack. As it neared Focalor, the dragon turned like a corkscrew and the daemon's spear passed across its chest. It spewed liquid fire striking the black Bouc assistant full on, melting his features, as stray flames splattered Focalor's right wing, causing the daemon to fall to earth and roll in the sand to extinguish the fire.

Stern rose above the trees and flew toward the black volcanic mountains, turning his dragon head from side to side, watching the Bouc spreading out through the forests below, each seeking their own hiding place. The dragon's blood lust was high and its body shuttered with hunger. As the dragon's body demanded food, Stern struggled for control, knowing that Focalor was not dead, only wounded. Reluctantly, Stern, now barely in control of the dragon body, lowered his right wing and turned back toward the south and the stockade. Focusing his yellow eyes on the edge of the forest, he searched for Focalor, making three passes over the stockade without catching a glimpse of the daemon.

Each time he flew over the encampment, he felt Tek'seth calling him in, like a falconer calling his bird of prey. The dragon body, however, resisted the call, hungry for more blood, as Stern wrestled control and hovered over the center of the Bouc kraal.

He landed and through a concerted effort of sheer will shifted shape and collapsed in a heap on the sand. Tek'seth was soon by his side ordering water and food. He knelt down and touched Stern's naked shoulder and said, "You did not tell me you had mastered the dragon."

Stern coughed and spit onto the sand, "I wasn't sure I had. At first, it was the dragon fighting alone. Only near the end did I take over."

"The myth is alive. The first step in the return of the blue dragons has now occurred."

"I don't know about the myth but I'm now ready to open the portal and return to the earthern plane."

Black clouds formed over the island and a heavy rain began to fall. Two Dra'ghan helped Stern stand and walk to the longhouse, as three quarters of the warriors gathered in the house, while the rest waited on guard on the walls.

Stern lay on the wooden deck near the rear, eating a bright yellow melon and drinking water from a leather bag. His strength was returning slowly. He had a tremendous hunger and thirst, which he knew fruits and vegetables would not satisfy.

Across from him Tek'seth sat with his legs crossed, smoking a clay pipe, filled with herbs and hemp. The rain ran off the thatched roof and thunder rumbled in the distance.

"What will you do now?" he asked.

"Once I have gained my strength, I will open a portal to the earthern realm. I'm concerned, however, about the time I have been away. I was told that time here runs in the opposite direction from my world and I'm growing younger. I have been here for a long time. Maybe years have passed on my plane since I left. I just don't know. And I don't know where this portal will open. I could open it in the middle of the sea or on a mountain."

That night he slept on the platform, waking twice from nightmares of Focalor. In the first dream Focalor led an army against the King at Stormcrow. In the second Gotha, defending two children, twins with blonde hair and pale blue eyes, fought the daemon on the gray cliffs of a mountain next to the sea.

Chapter Forty-Six: Back Again

IT WAS STILL RAINING when he awoke. He ate strange red and green fruit and drank as much water as he could stomach. He felt his arms and he shook his head, suspecting he had grown stronger and younger in the night. He pulled his long black hair back and braided it in a queue that now hung half way down his back. At midday the rain stopped and he stood on the deck of the longhouse with Tek'seth and watched the sun emerge from the dark clouds. Black insects, the size of his hand, crawled in and out of the logs of the dwelling and giant parrots squawked loudly in the forest.

"I will open the portal here in the center of the stockade. If I am successful, I will return with the dragons."

The shaman said: "As you know time is fickled. You could be back in an hour or a year. I will leave fifty men and voyage to my island. I will then return with a larger party and several shamen. While you are gone, we will make this a Dra'ghan outpost."

He then handed Stern a small pouch.

"What's this?" he asked, opening the mouth of the leather pouch. Jewels, diamonds, and gold coins glittered in the light.

"You might need to pay for something in your world," he said.

He nodded his thanks and patted the shaman on the shoulder, then hoisted his backpack on, and walked to the center of the stockade, while checking the two curved Dra'ghan blades sheathed on his hips and Michaelsdottir's trinket bag beneath his leather vest. He opened and removed the demon's black stone of summoning from the pouch and unwrapped the red cloth that surrounded it and held it between his thumb and forefinger. As he moved it from right to left, he said, in the ancient language of the demon, Kokabiel, the sentence: "Open a portal on the earthern plane, where Grun intersects the lines of Mittilagart."

A shimmering portal opened and Stern saw blue water with whitecaps beating against a white, pristine sandy beach. Seagulls fluttered in the hundreds above the water and a bark with three masts moved parallel to the horizon. This must be his world, he thought, the earthly plane, but the landscape was unfamiliar and he remembered for the first time in months the witch's warning, to return to Mittilagart from the same spot he entered Okeanus. But it was too late. Too many things had occurred and he had no way to return. The north was frozen solid and he was a hunted man. He felt extreme heat pulsing through the opening; and, as he stepped across the diaphanous pink membrane of the portal, it closed, and he stood on a wide beach of white, sugary sand with a clear, translucent blue-green tide lapping against the shore. He could see no trees, no house or road or any other evidence of civilized life other than the boat disappearing into the haze of the horizon.

He marked the spot of the portal's entrance with an "x" with the heel of his boot. He, then, marched across the flat beach to the dunes, looking for stones to build a *herm*. Once he had found some sizable stones, he stripped off his leathers, as he worked. This beach, he guessed, was somewhere south of the equator. He stopped several times because of the heat. When he finished, he gathered his clothes and pack and set off toward the west, away from the beach. He would dress when he saw signs of civilization. He slept that night in the shadow of a dune. Crabs scuttled across the sand throughout the night and he awoke at dawn, his lips swollen from the sun and thirst. If he didn't find water soon he would be in dire straits and he had no idea where he was. Relentless sun beat down during the day and the mosquitoes, scorpions and fleas tormented him throughout the night.

He walked west away from the beach; at dusk he discovered a road, just two ruts really, running straight north and south. Heat rose off stones in waffle waves and, even though it was hot, he dressed in the leathers to protect his skin, as he turned north. Hours later, drenched in sweat, he took cover from the heat under a withered tree, where he slept, making gurgling sounds, his tongue swollen and his skin blistered. Tomorrow, he dreamed, he would shift into the osprey and fly to civilization.

He slept a long time, from setting sun to dawn. He squatted naked in the shade of the tree and gazed at a flat prairie with tall grass undulating in a soft wind. In the distance black specks moved south parallel to the road. Cattle, he thought, grazing. And if there were cattle, there would be water. So he pulled on the hot, impractical leathers and set off west toward the herd.

Soon he could make out large black cows with long silver horns, slight humps on their backs and white faces. He counted several hundred, grazing on the yellow grass. As he approached, he saw a bull moving on the edge of the herd, guarding it from predators or other bulls and he angled his approach to get down wind of this bull that seemed strange and atavistic to him. These cows, he soon surmised, were longhorns, wild cattle, not the domesticated creatures like those of La Ciudad.

He followed in the wake of the grazing cattle throughout the day and at dusk he smelled water. Just as the animals did, because they began to low and turn southwest toward the dampness he detected.

As the sun set, the cattle reached a shallow but wide river. On its far bank a wall, several feet high, followed the course of the river in both directions. His lips were cracked and bloody and his tongue swollen but rather than rush to the water he gaped at the structure in front of him and knew there were people somewhere near.

Later, after the cattle moved on, searching for grass, he hiked up stream, stripped off his clothes, and waded naked into the river, where he drank his fill. As night fell, bats fluttered in the twilight, devouring mosquitoes breeding in the shoals and predators including, wolves, coyotes, and large cats, emerged from their dens to stalk their prey along the banks of the river. Stern found a tall cotton tree, whose roots reached into the river from an eroded bank and climbed as high as he could to find a place to sleep.

The next morning he followed the river northwest, away from the coast. If there were people in this brave new world, he thought, they would be on the river and away from the sea. He also knew he could find food near the river: frogs, fish, bird's eggs, berries, and nuts. He would not starve.

He traveled for four days before he saw any evidence of human life. A strange craft, which resembled the witch's ornithopter, an insect-shaped vehicle with transparent wings, sped across the northern horizon, traveling east to west. A day later he spied a winged-serpent, an elongated reptile, covered in multicolored feathers and wide wings, heading south toward the river and the wall. He accepted this wasn't his land, it was something else and he toyed with the idea of opening a portal and returning to Okeanus.

A week later, he came upon a stone house with a wooden door with a sign posted in *lingua*: "Stay Out." The sign was good news. Maybe he was in Mittilagart after all. He touched the demon's stone but it was cold and lifeless. Magic seemed not to work within this plane. That night he slept in a copse of conifers near the building and at one point he tried to shift into the wolf but failed. He extracted the stone from its case and spoke the words of the portal spell but to no avail. Although the stone seemed to emit a small amount of heat, which at first encouraged him, this plane seemed to have no exit. He curled into a ball like the wolf and fell asleep and dreamed of his home.

At dawn he heard a mechanical rumbling and the earth vibrated in unison. Two thousand feet above him, a giant machine, heading southwest toward the wall, cast a massive shadow, as it passed over him. People moved about its expansive cupola and he could have sworn he heard piano music.

At mid-day, he followed a gulley to the river to drink. After undressing, he waded into the water and cupped his hands to rinse his grimy body and soak his wild thatch of hair and beard. Later he lay in thick grasses growing on a natural shelf above the river and dozed. A cottontail unaware of him drew near, nibbling green sprigs of grass. He grabbed it with a sudden strike and wrenched its neck. As he skinned it, he felt a slight heat emanating from the stone ensconced in the pouch hanging from his neck. With sudden insight, he removed it and smeared it with the rabbit's blood; a spark flew from its surface and its mineral veins pulsated. Suddenly he felt hopeful.

Perhaps, with enough blood, he could open a portal back to Okeanus or, at least, contact Kokabiel. But he remembered the witch's warning this time to return to the exact spot of the portal's opening. So, after feeding on the rabbit and gnawing its bones clean and sucking the marrow, he started his trek back to the beach to the exact spot of the portal. Along the way, he killed things, small animals usually, sometimes reptiles, snakes and turtles, and fed the stone its ration of blood. At times, this act bothered him but more often than not it didn't. Instead, he found himself thinking of the demon on the *ziz*, flying languidly through the sky.

Several days later, he crawled into a shallow cave to sleep. An hour or so after he fell asleep he awoke to a sound outside the cave. A foot fell onto some dried leaves, then a twig cracked, and finally a hushed voice. At least two men, maybe more, outside of the cave stalked him.

Stern meditated on the bear but, although he was able to conjure its image, it fled from him, running deeper into his unconscious, unavailable or unwilling to aid him. He grasped the stone and felt heat radiating from it and he heard faintly, from far away, the strange voice of the demon, saying,

"Invite me into your world. I can help you but not from here. It is too far away." He recalled Mikk's warning to fear the demon and ignored its siren call. He pulled the blades from the sheaths and moved slowly to the opening of the cave and peered into the gloom. A mist rose off the ground, there was no moon to illuminate the night, only the feeble light of the stars. No movement outside and no more sound. Had the men ceased waiting for him to leave the cave?

They knew, he thought, they had awakened him with their awkwardness alerting the creatures of the night. He sensed them holding their breath, expecting him to turn over and go back to sleep. But their ploy did not work; he could smell them now. Their sour sweat, covered with the smell of smoke and cinnamon, was close. His mind whirled with questions. Should he dash from the cave and hope his movement would startle them into disclosing their location? Should he remain as he was, still, ready and wait for them to enter the cave, one at time, so that he could drive his curved knives into their spines.

As he waited, the demon spoke, its voice excited, expectant, "Their blood will be the sacrifice the stone needs to become attuned to the earthern plane. Kill them and sacrifice their blood to the stone." He shrugged his shoulders and shivered, waiting for the men to make their attack. An owl hooted in the distance and he heard a snap of a branch breaking and the cicadas rubbing their wings, the men had moved on. They feared the unknown of the cave and passed. The demon sighed, disappointed and the heat in the stone waned.

Dawn was still several hours away but he dare not fall back asleep. He sat near the entrance of the cave with his knives drawn, waiting for the first light.

A low-lying mist covered the ground and wafted beneath the trees as the first rays of sun light filtered through the leaves. Stern had fallen asleep, sitting up, with the knives crossed in his lap. He had to relieve himself, so he crawled slowly out of the cave and sniffed the air like the black bear. Birds greeted the morning with songs and flew under the low-lying limbs of the hardwood trees, as he worked his way away from the cave and into the rocks above, where he found a secluded crevice overlooking the forest and the cave. Finished, he climbed higher in the rocks to find a spot high enough to survey the forest. From the pinnacle, he surveyed the horizon and spied a thin thread of white smoke about a mile to the northwest. The hunters' camp, he thought.

From the height of the rocks he scanned the hills and valleys below him. Suddenly he realized he was lost. This was not the way he had come before; somehow in the last few days he had made a wrong turn. He could not see the wall, the river or the sea; instead, rolling hills with outcroppings of stone and narrow valleys spread all around him. He checked the location of the sun and marked the directions. The sea had to be to the east and the wall and the river to the south. Had he somehow turned north, thinking it was east? He slapped his forehead and cursed himself. Should he head south until he found the wall or should he just go east until he found the sea? And who were those men sitting around their fire? Would they try to kill him or help him? The demon whispered: "kill them and sacrifice their blood to the stone and all will be revealed." He pushed the thought away, as his stomach rumbled from hunger. The men had food and water and he knew where they were. They were men like him; surely they would help him. He brushed these thoughts away. Mittilagart was a world besieged by dragons and desperate men. If he approached them, he would have to do it on his own terms and safely. Approaching them seemed not to be the viable solution at this point. The stone was almost dormant; its powers being stifled by a demon, who wanted access to his world. His magical powers, learned on Okeanus, seemed not to work on Mittilagart. He still possessed them because he could feel them as a vague ache in the back of his mind. Here, in this world, he was on his own with no super powers for him to fall back on, no god in a machine to save him from wolves or dragons. Here he would have to work out his own problems in his own way.

At mid-day, he climbed down from his roost and set off to find the men; not to approach them directly but simply to follow them and study them. By dusk he reached the remnants of their fire. From the tracks in the gray dust around the campsite he counted tracks for four men, wearing moccasins. Bones and skin in the dead ash indicated they had killed a picador, a wild pig, the size of a dog. Their trail headed south so he used the last few moments of dying light to determine their exact route before choosing somewhere safe to sleep. At dawn, he followed a cold trail as quickly as he could. The men were careless, unaware they were being dogged. He had made good time.

They marched due south. At noon, the sun shone directly above him, when he discovered their camp from the previous night. They had dined on grouse on the edge of vast grasslands, the bones and feathers of several birds stacked near the dying fire. He tightened his belt and checked his knives, rubbed his tongue over the rough film of his teeth and then spat on the thick green-blue grass that undulated in the wind. Once he stepped onto the prairie he would be visible for miles. He ran his hands through his hair and adjusted the queue, raised his shoulders and huffed, then set off at a comfortable jog, a pace that he could maintain throughout the day. He would catch the men at dusk and then he would decide what to do.

As the sun settled on the horizon, causing pink and blue hues to spread across the grasslands, he paused and sat on his haunches to listen. Something had been nagging him for an hour or so. He bent down and pressed his ear against the earth and heard the dull thud of approaching horses. He rose slowly and scanned the horizon. Two men on galloping horses rode toward him from the north. "The hunter is also the hunted," he heard the demon whisper. He knew he could not outrun the horsemen; his only alternative was to stand and fight, so he loosened the blades and spread his legs, readying himself for the assault.

Chapter Forty-Seven: Cooper and Jerah

TWO MEN ON HORSEBACK, leading two mounts with empty saddles, approached, slowed, and then stopped several feet away from Stern, who stood with his hands on the hilts of the long curved knives of the Dra'ghan. The stone in the leather pouch hanging around his neck pulsated with heat as he waited for the men to speak. Both men, tall and thin, wore dark-gray hooded cloaks that covered their buckskin clothing and shadowed their faces. Stern's first thought was that it was too hot to be wearing the cloaks. His second was to question if the riders were even men. His third concerned the riderless horses.

The taller of the two men leaned forward and rested his arm on his saddlehorn, then pushed back his hood, revealing a gaunt face, weathered and wrinkled by the elements. Speaking an archaic form of *lingua*, he asked his companion, an Argyll half-breed: "Jerah, what do you think we have here?" The other man removed his hood with a laugh, revealing his almond-shaped eyes, pale blue skin, and pointed ears, and said, "He ain't no Argaunt; that's for sure." The other man addressed Stern: "So what are you? My Argyll friend here says you ain't an Argaunt."

Stern cleared his throat and answered: "I'm a blacksmith from La Ciudad."

One of the horses skittered and the Argyll pulled on the reins and made soothing sounds, while the taller man rubbed the whiskers on his cleft chin. "You are a very long way from home."

"I was shipwrecked several weeks ago and washed up on a beach. I have no idea where I am."

"Shipwrecked, was it? How did you get here on the pampas, deep in Argaunt territory," asked the man, now fingering the hammer on the strange musket laid across his saddle.

"I was looking for civilization and got lost," answered Stern, eyeing the rifle. He had never seen one like it and he would have relished a good examination of it. From its length, he figured it had a tremendous range.

"Where you headed now?"

"A couple nights ago, four men came upon my camp and tried to take me. I hid in a cave until they got tired of looking for me. When they left, I decided to follow them and see if they would lead me to a town or city."

"You're following four Argaunt dog soldiers, members of the Moon clan. They ain't going to lead you anywhere except your funeral," answered the man and the Argyll laughed.

Stern looked at the two riderless horses and said: "Maybe you've met these warriors before?"

The man sat up in the saddle and looked off into the distance, over Stern's shoulder, and said, "The last time we met there were four of us and ten of them. When we meet again, there will just be us."

"You don't suppose I could ride along with you?" asked Stern.

The man leaned across the saddle horn again and looked Stern in the eye. "Now why would we trust a stranger to ride along with us?"

Stern shrugged his shoulders. Finally, he said: "I can't think of a reason. If I were you, I'd ride on. But if you think you can take on these dog soldiers, as you call them, alone, then God's speed. Just point me in the right direction. However, if you think you might need some help, I'm willing to sign on for a fight against these savages for a ride to the nearest town."

"That's assuming we're still alive afterward, right?" asked the Argyll with a wink.

The man laughed and said, "Take the mare. She's right gentle and a good sturdy mount. She belonged to my cousin Bertram."

The Argyll pulled the reins and drew the horses toward him, then separated those of the roan mare and handed them to Stern, who took them into his left hand, stepped into the stirrup, while grabbing the leather horn with his left, and pulled himself up. The horse whinnied and he patted her broad neck and spoke softly into her ear. As he settled comfortably into the saddle, he felt a carbine in a leather boot and he pulled it clear and held it in his hands.

"You know how to use one of those?" asked the tall, gaunt man.

"I earn my living making weapons like these. Yes, I know how to use it."

The man nodded and pointed: "There's ammunition in the saddle bags and probably some jerky if you're hungry." Stern nodded, as he returned the carbine to its boot.

"My name's Cooper, by the way. What's yours?"

"Stern," he answered, as he turned in the saddle and dug out a square of dried meat."

"All right Stern, lead the way. Get out aways ahead of us and show us what kind of tracker you are."

Stern cut off a chaw of the meat and stuffed it in his mouth before returning the rest to the bag. "Don't trust me yet?" he said with his mouth full.

"Why should we? Just ride up ahead and find those dog soldiers."

The man called Cooper was correct, when he said the roan mare was a gentle mount. Responsive to his touch, she moved to the right or left by just a simple flick of his wrist. He trotted out ahead of the two men and leaned forward in the saddle, watching the trail for signs of the dog soldiers. He had been following them for awhile and he knew their individual marks and prints. He soon found one and pointed toward the ground, alerting the men behind them they were on the right course, as he urged the mare into a gallop. An hour later, he found where they had rested and relieved themselves. They were very close now. So he waited for his companions to catch up, allowing the mare to graze quietly on the long grass of the pampas. As he waited he removed the saddle bags and the carbine. He found cleaning materials in the bags and sat upon a rock and cleaned the weapon. Bertram was not a tidy man, he concluded. The weapon was dirty. He quickly rectified that, scrubbing off grease and patina from the barrel.

Almost thirty minutes later the two men approached Stern at an easy gait, preserving their horses. These were patient men, thought Stern, as he stood and inserted the now loaded and clean carbine into its boot.

Cooper addressed him before he pulled up on the reins, slowing the tall, black gelding. "What is it? Why have you stopped?"

Stern walked over to the signs and said: "They rested here maybe three hours ago."

Cooper bent down and examined the excrement. "You're correct; we're almost on top of them."

"So, how do you want to handle it?" asked Stern.

"Handle it?" the man said, rising up and looking off in the distance. "I'm going to kill them."

"But how are you going to do it? That's what I mean?" said Stern. "Are you going to ride them down and have a pitch battle or you going to use your wits?"

"My wits?" asked the man, as he scratched his head. "I suppose you have a plan?"

Stern looked up at the sun and explained. "We probably have six hours of light left. If we gallop the horses, we probably could catch them before dark."

Cooper placed his hand on Stern's shoulder and said, "We're not going to run up on them. We're going to ride until dusk and camp; then, tomorrow we'll swing around and ambush them. With this long carbine of mine I can kill two of them before they even hear the shot." He smiled and then continued, "I'll leave the other two to you and the Argyll."

As they rode, the stone warmed and vibrated in its pouch. Suddenly, Stern felt the bear lingering on the edge of his conscious mind and he heard the demon whispering, "I can help you. Please, let me help you." Something Mikk said nagged at him but for some reason he was having difficulty remembering as the demon murmured and whispered, warning him that something ahead of them was amiss.

They continued due south until it was too dark to ride safely across the undulating emptiness of the pampas. As the last light faded on the horizon, the Argyll found an outcropping of white stone to shelter them for the night. They stripped the saddles from the horses and rubbed them down with grass before staking them out to graze and then huddled next to the rugged and jagged stones, chewed the tough jerky until their jaws ached, and sipped water from their canteens to wash the tough and stringy mash down. A slight wind rose up from the south bringing with it the smell of woodsmoke and they knew the moment they sniffed the acrid aroma the dog soldiers were very near.

The Argyll was the first to notice the smell and without saying a word, he picked up his long-barreled carbine and climbed to the top of the outcropping, while Cooper crawled to the eastern side and hunkered down, listening to the sloughing wind and the whispering grass swaying in the southern breeze. Without being told, Stern knew his job was to cover the western side with the short carbine. As he took his place, the demon whispered, "There are more than four and they know you're here. Beware. Invite me into your world and I will bring magic with me."

Stern ignored the demon's wheedling cry and concentrated on the darkness, the wind, the carnal smell, wafting on the wind, and the nervousness of the horses that were pulling on the stakes that hobbled them and snorting in fear. Forgetting the horses for a moment, he concentrated on the sour odor, intermixed with the woodsmoke, and discerned something feral and bitter, like the lair of a cougar soaked in urine and musk. Before he could say anything, he heard the metallic click of the Argyll pulling back the hammer on the long carbine and he knew the man had also sensed the presence of something wild and untamed near them. He loosened the Dra'ghan knives and prepared for the onslaught, as Cooper opened the front of his cloak, revealing two revolvers, one on each hip.

The first beast, a man-sized, dog-like creature, roared toward him on all fours out of the right, charging so fast that Stern barely had time to swivel and fire the carbine point-blank into its maul before a second one rose out of the grass to his left and jumped, hitting him in the shoulder and rolling him backwards. All through the attack, the demon, Kokabiel, screamed in his ear, begging him to open the way for him to enter Mittilagart to help him; to save him from the shape-shifting dog soldiers of the Argaunt by bringing with him the magic of Elysium. Oddly, it was as the creature, the dog soldier, in its canine form, barred its fangs and bite down into his shoulder that he remembered Mikk's warning to never allow the demon into their world. And, as he grabbed the canine's ears and pulled its sharp teeth away from his throat, he cursed the demon and with the curse, he felt the stone burn into his flesh. He could not access the power of the bear but he had the heightened strength of the dragon still coursing through his veins and he was able to slowly lift the snarling beast off his chest and twist its neck so viciously he heard the bones crack as its spine broke. Taking a deep breath, he pushed the dying creature to the side and pulled the curved knives and waited for the next attack.

Above him, he heard the Argyll cursing in his language, as he struggled with one of the creatures that had him pinned to the ground. Stern quickly climbed the jagged stone wall of the outcropping and plunged both knives into the back of the dog soldier and lifted it off the slight frame of the Argyll. Three down, at least, he thought, when he heard the report of Cooper's revolvers and turned to see two snarling creatures approaching the man, whose back was pressed against the rock's wall. Three beasts lay dead at Cooper's feet. The demon's advice was correct, thought Stern, there were more than four. He pulled the knives from the beast and jumped from the rock onto the ground next to Cooper and began to snarl like the beasts and wave the curved knives. Cooper holstered his empty revolvers and pulled a knife from his belt. "It's tooth and nail time," he said with a gruff laugh. As they started forward, one of the dogs rose up on its hind legs, readying itself to spring. But the Argyll, from his vantage point atop the outcropping, shot him through the heart and whooped, leaving just one dog soldier facing them, who seeing its companions lying dead around him and three foes facing it, turned and fled into the darkness of the pampas.

All three men had suffered wounds. As soon as the dog soldier disappeared, Cooper ordered the Argyll to build a fire. "We must treat these wounds quickly, their fangs and nails are poisonous."

While Jareh searched in the dark for something to burn, Stern went to the beast he had shot and dipped the demon's stone in its blood. The veins in the stone flared up bright and clear, as the stone's extreme heat stung his fingers. He felt the bear awakening in his mind, as he whispered the spell of fire and watched tiny tendrils of yellow flame awake on the tips of his fingers. He put the stone back into the blood and rubbed his eyes in disbelief, as the stone lapped up the blood, absorbing it into its pulsating veins. Minutes passed as the stone absorbed the blood. Finally, Cooper called him and Stern awoke from his trance, suddenly aware he had been in a momentary dream of blood.

"Come here and let me look at your wounds," ordered the man, who was haunched over a small fire that the Argyll had made from dried longhorn chips.

Returning the stone to the leather pouch around his neck, Stern painfully removed his leather corselet to reveal the wounds suffered from the beast's bite. "Not as bad as I thought," said Cooper. "That leather saved your life."

As Cooper examined his wounds, Stern asked, "These creatures, they are the dog soldiers? They shifted shape somehow?"

Cooper grunted as he set a tin bowl filled with water into the fire. "That's right. The Argaunt are shape-shifters. Cursed, they are by the gods."

"But they're not really shape-shifters are they? I mean, although they are dog-like, they are not dogs. A shape-shifter becomes a wolf. It's as if these dog soldiers are a different species. They aren't really human, are they?"

"What do you know about shape-shifters?" asked Cooper as he removed herbs from a leather pouch and sprinkled them in the boiling water.

"I met one once in the mountains. He shifted into a wolf, a real wolf. He was not one of these monsters."

"He was probably one of those *indio* shamans. They supposedly can shift into birds and animals," he said, as he cleaned Stern's wounds with the water mixed with herbs. "But you are correct, the dog soldiers of the Argaunt are different from men. An Argyll and a man can mate. An Argaunt and a man cannot. Oh, they can rape a human woman but no child will be produced.

"The Argylls are human," said Stern with a slight snarl, thinking of his son.

Cooper looked him in the eye and said: "You will get no argument from me. That one," he said pointing at Jareh, "is like my son."

Stern nodded and grimaced as Cooper slathered on the herbal broth. "Now the question I have for you, Stern, is: what are you?"

"What do you mean?" asked Stern, looking down and hiding his eyes from Cooper.

"Well, first of all, you say you are from the North, from La Ciudad. If you sail from the port in Buenos in a fast ship you might reach the port city of Leone in six weeks and then spend a week marching to La Ciudad. It's possible that you sailed from Leone but you would be the first man that did so in years and ended up with us in the pampas. We haven't seen a man from the north in ages. So why have you arrived now, alone, here on the pampas, away from Buenos? What brings you so far south?"

Stern sighed and decided to tell a portion of the truth. "It was an accident. I never intended to land here. I was on my way back north and I got terribly lost."

"On your way back, you say? Where were you coming from?"

Stern rubbed his face with his dirty, blood-soaked hand. "I was returning from a voyage to the east, on my way to La Ciudad. But somehow I ended up here."

The man handed him a wet rag and told him to clean his face.

"To do what? What were you going to do in La Ciudad?" asked Cooper as he signaled for Jareh to come closer so he could wash the cuts and scratches he received from the dog soldiers.

Stern cleared his throat and said: "I was heading north to hunt the blue-back dragons."

Both the Argyll and Cooper looked at him to determine if he were joking.

"Are you serious?" asked Jareh.

"Yes, I'm telling the truth. I have been ordered to hunt the blue-back."

Cooper quickly asked, "Who ordered you to do such an insane thing?"

"This part, you are not going to believe."

"Try me," said the man.

"The Black Robes of La Ciudad ordered me north to find the dragons."

Cooper's eyes narrowed as he considered Stern's latest pronouncement and Stern closed his mind for a moment and remembered the witch.

"And your assignment was to hunt the blue-back?" asked Stern.

"Among other things," he responded.

"Ah, it's those other things that are probably the most interesting."

"Suffice it to say, Cooper, that I have undertaken a long journey and learned many things."

"I can imagine," he said, now washing his own minor wounds. "But before we hear that story, you and Jareh ought to round up the horses. Dawn is approaching and I want to be on my way as soon as first light. I fear the hunters are now the hunted."

An hour after first light the men galloped north away from the scene of the attack. Stern suspected the four they followed were members of a splinter group, broken off from a larger raid, and that they had followed them to their meeting place. As they were saddling the horses earlier in the day, Cooper had said, "Argaunt won't track us for long; they become bored if the prey takes too long to catch. We just have to outrun them until they lose interest."

They rode for two days across the pampas, not even stopping during the night, just slowing, usually dismounting and walking the horses; afraid they might stumble and fall in some rabbit hole. On the third day, they camped at dusk along the banks of a shallow stream underneath some cotton trees, whose gnarled and twisted roots extended into the water. Stern had not heard the demon's voice since the stone drank the blood of the dog soldier so, as a way to test the stone, while he searched for dried chips to burn, he recited the spell of fire. Yellow flames appeared on his finger tips, he laughed and recited the spell again. Once again the flames crackled and flickered up from his hand. As he calmed his mind, extinguishing the nascent flames, he imagined the stone was becoming attuned to the magical currents of Mittilagart through the ingredients of the blood. Suddenly, he feared the damage he might be creating by introducing Elysium magic into this world. Was he contributing to the imbalance of the worlds just as the Skallaenders and the dragons had when they came through the portal from Okeanus?

Later as Stern sat near the fire, eating porridge from a wooden bowl that the Argyll handed him, Cooper announced between mouthfuls of mush, "We'll reach Chambre tomorrow afternoon."

"Chambre?" asked Stern.

"It's a cattle town on the edge of the pampas. You'll be able to get some decent clothes there and buy a ticket for the stage to Buenos." He ate another mouthful of porridge and asked: "You got any money?"

Stern lifted his eyes. "I'll get by," he said, thinking of the shaman's jewels in his pack.

Several minutes passed in silence as Stern thought about Buenos and civilization. He argued with himself, fearing he was losing the thread of his quest. Suddenly, returning to Okeanus with the dragons no longer seemed important to him. Why, he asked himself, was he torturing himself for some world that was not his own. And then he thought of Kylla and Gotha and the Dra'ghan and he asked, "Are there any blue-back in the area?"

The Argyll sputtered and Cooper gave him a long look before responding to his question.

"Some nest in the Arkadies, on the spine of the pampas. How many do you need?" he asked with a laugh.

"At least a breeding pair," responded Stern seriously. The Dra'ghan had never been clear about how many he had to return to Okeanus. The creatures had bred for decades on Mittilagart and there was no way he could return them all to Okeanus. But a breeding pair that should be possible, he thought. And the witches, the witches had only instructed him to find out the secret of the dragons from Bedwyr, they said nothing about returning them to Okeanus. That quest came later.

"You're pulling my leg, aren't you?"

"No, I'm not, so how do I find the Arkadies?" asked Stern.

The man pursed his lips and shook his head before answering in a dry flat tone. "We're traveling northeast toward Chambre. The Arkadies are due west; they run from the tip of the world near the ice wall, north to the jungles of Colonia. It would take a man on horseback six months to reach them from Chambre. But chances of his making it alone are nil. He would need supplies, lots of supplies, and enough firepower to dissuade the natives from gutting him and eating his innards."

"Natives?" he asked.

"Argaunts, Scalas, Myrtoi and a legion of other clans and tribes of indigenous peoples stand between you and those mountains."

Stern remembered an Argyll map of the southern continent and a thought occurred to him. "You call the southernmost point of land on the southern continent the Horn of Agahast, don't you?"

Cooper nodded. "Could I catch a boat to sail around the horn and land on the west coast?"

"It's possible but it would take you just as long."

"But it would be safer?" he asked and the man nodded.

"What about one of the airships?" asked Jareh.

"Airship?" said Stern and then he remembered the monstrosity that flew above his head on the beach.

"It would cost a fortune but it is fast. Flying from Buenos to Pima on the west coast takes about a week."

Stern scratched his head, pulling a louse from the wild thatch of hair. "So how long will it take me to get to Buenos.

Cooper smiled as he watched the man smash the louse between the nail on his thumb and forefinger of his right hand. "You might have to wait a month for the coach, then a week or two to Buenos."

"Nothing is ever easy in this world," sighed Stern.

"That's the truth," agreed Cooper, as he measured coffee into a tin pot.

Two days later they came upon a herd of cattle being driven toward Chambre by a cadre of Argyll cowboys. The trail boss, with two young men, rode out to meet them. As they approached at a gallop on their small painted ponies, Cooper advised Stern to keep his mouth shut and let him do the talking. The boss pulled back on his reins just a few feet from the men, causing his horse to stop abruptly and almost rear. Stern suspected the boss was displaying his finesse as a horseman.

The three men, mounted on black and white spotted ponies, dressed alike: flat hats with short round brims, red checkered cotton shirts, with long colorful scarves—some red, others yellow—wrapped around their necks, leather vests over the shirts, leather chaps over leather pants, worn boots with high heels and long silver spurs strapped to the boots. A long knife sheathed and a pistol holstered on their hips accompanied long leather whips held confidently in their right hands. Their blue skin darkened by the sun was clean except for the boss' handlebar mustache, which was waxed stiff and curled at the ends; an effect, which Stern guessed, along with the clothes, marked his status as the boss.

Cooper waited patiently for the boss to calm his horse and address him first. Finally, the man raised his left hand, holding the reins tightly in his right, and pronounced his Argyll name and the *rancho* he represented in a patois that Stern had never heard. The power of the demon's spell worked, however, and within minutes, he began to understand the language, as Cooper introduced himself and his men. With the niceties of the introductions over, Cooper told the Argyll boss they had encountered a hunting party of Argaunt dog soldiers five days before and they were now on their way to Chambre. The dark-blue face of the boss darkened further when he heard about the raiding party but Cooper quickly explained he had not seen any evidence of the dog soldiers in days and he believed they had dropped their pursuit. The Argyll was not persuaded and he ordered one of the young men to take a small party and scout south of the herd in the direction from which Cooper and his group had come. He then turned to Cooper and apologized because he could not welcome them into their camp. If the Argaunt were tracking them, he said, he did not want to be associated with the white hunter. To emphasize his position, he gave Jerah a shrug and a sad look, as he turned his horse and rode back to the herd.

"Just as well," said Cooper. "We can travel much faster on our own but I was hoping we could have camped with them tonight: the safety of numbers would have been a relief. I'm tired of sleeping with one eye open."

Days later, they rode into Chambre, a small cow town on the edge of the pampas. It appeared to be populated by butchers, tanners, leather workers, candlestick makers, bone grinders, broken down cowboys, brothel owners, whores, saloon keepers, cattle agents, tax-agents, auction-barn owners, haulers, ostlers, blacksmiths, bankers, gunsmiths, speculators, thieves and scoundrels.

They checked into the only hotel without a saloon. The first thing they did, after Stern sold one of the Dra'ghan diamonds, was to pay for a bath and barber. Stern took the bath but he refused to cut his hair; instead, he paid an Argyll woman to wash and even-up his hair, oil and braid it. For an extra copper, she trimmed his beard and eyebrows and his ragged nails. At the urging of Cooper he allowed the Argyll woman to burn his leathers and sell him a pair of linen riding pants with the seat reinforced with leather, a white cotton shirt, an embroidered vest, a linen coat with large pockets on each side, a pair of black leather riding boots that reached his knees and one of the Argyll's flat gaucho hats.

Dressed in his new garb, Stern strapped on his belt with the sheathed knives and pulled his worn bag's strap over his shoulder as they left the bathhouse and headed to a cafe owned by a friend of Cooper which was located on the edge of town, near the only church and cemetery.

Argyll and human cowboys crowded the streets. Several herds had arrived, After their long journey, the men were hungry and thirsty with a modicum of coin in their pockets. As they walked, Cooper warned Stern and Jerah to avoid any confrontation with the men, who if not yet drunk, would soon be.

The cafe was crowded but the owner forced a couple of drunken cowboys to vacate their table for the three men. Lucille, the owner's daughter, served them and Stern immediately recognized the attraction of the cafe.

Lucerne, the owner, joined them at the table for dessert and Cooper asked, "When's the next coach to Buenos?"

The man sipped his coffee and looked up at the greasy ceiling of the cafe and said, "The last one left three days ago, so I would say we will see the stage from Buenos in a week or three, maybe."

Cooper scratched the skin under his right eye and said, "The herds seem to be arriving early this year."

Lucerne leaned forward. "There've been several raids in the south; two or three *ranchos* have been burned and the owners are nervous. In fact, if you intend getting a seat on the stage you had better buy your ticket tomorrow, first thing. Owners are sending their families to Buenos. Most have their own coaches but you never know if there will be room or not."

Sporadic gunfire punctuated the night as they walked back to their hotel and several drunken Argyll cowboys called out threats to Jerah in their patois, challenging him to a knife fight. The young man refused to respond but continued to walk straight ahead.

Stern asked Cooper, "Why are they singling him out for their challenges?"

"Can't you guess," he responded with a huff. "He's not pure Argyll, he's only half-human."

Stern swallowed and blushed, thinking of his own son in the Black Robe School in La Ciudad. "My son's half Argyll," he said and Jerah stopped and looked him directly in the eye.

"You married an Argyll woman?" he asked.

"I met her in the south during the Mayan wars."

"Where is she now?" the young man asked.

"She's buried in Maya-tan City."

"And your, son where is he?"

"The Black Robes are holding him in a Black Robe School in La Ciudad."

Cooper asked, "Is that why you went looking for the dragons on your own?"

He did not want to explain or tell them everything he had experienced since he left La Ciudad so he just nodded.

The next morning he left the hotel with two things to accomplish. The first buy a ticket on the coach to Buenos and the second to find a gunsmith. Before falling asleep he had drawn a diagram for a shoulder holster. He wanted someone to make it for him and he wanted the right gun to fit it.

A few hours after dawn, the city was quiet. No drunken cowboys filled the streets; no gunfire interrupted its quiet. A few shop keepers swept the wooden sidewalks, citizens were preparing for their workday. The cowboys were on the pampas with their herds, sleeping off their hangovers, resting for round two tonight.

Stern found the stage office and purchased the last seat to Buenos from an old man with gray whiskers and a bald pate, who informed him the next coach should arrive in four days. The old man also directed him to Taras' gunshop just a couple of blocks away.

Taras was stooped and very old. The Argyll lived longer than humans so Stern had no idea how old he was.

His shop was small but very clean with hundreds of guns displayed in glass cases. He had models and styles Stern had never seen before. He showed the man the pattern for the holster, then wandered around, while the smith studied his drawing.

Finally, the old man said in perfect *lingua*, "I've got a woman, an Argaunt that can make this holster in two or three days."

"I'll need it before the stage arrives from Buenos."

"She can do it but it will cost you one silver piece."

Stern smiled and nodded.

"In advance," the man said with a slight giggle in his voice.

"Half up front and the rest upon completion," answered Stern, examining a four-barreled derringer. Picking up the weapon, he held it loosely in his hand and he knew he had to have it. It would make a perfect back-up weapon but he would also need a revolver to fill the holster. "Do you have a revolver that would fit the holster?" he asked and the Argyll shuffled from behind his counter to a case near the door leading into his shop and produced a five-shot revolver with a shortened barrel. Stern examined it, noting it was the same caliber as the derringer, which pleased him, but to be sure, he quickly dismantled it and checked the parts. 'I could make it better,' he thought, 'if I had the time.' But he didn't have the time, so he purchased both weapons and told the Argyll he would pick the revolver up with the holster, as he pocketed the derringer and a box of cartridges.

That night they ate at Lucerne's again and returned to the hotel late. Cowboys crowded the street and twice men challenged Jerah to a duel. One man even spat on him to provoke a fight but Cooper held the young Argyll back, as the drunken Argyll cowboys cat-called and simpered in the background.

"Maybe we should eat at the hotel in the future," suggested Stern.

"A good idea," said Cooper. "As soon as you leave I think we will be on our way. This town during herd gathering is more dangerous than the pampas."

As they moved away from the men, Stern heard a grunt and then Jerah fell face-forward onto the wooden sidewalk. He turned to see the drunken men leering at them, waiting for them to react. Cooper knelt next to his friend and pulled a knife from the young man's back. "I got to get him to a doctor fast."

"You go now and I will delay these thugs," whispered Stern.

Cooper looked up at him and began to argue, but Stern quickly cut him off. "Don't worry about me. Just get the kid some help."

Cooper hoisted his friend up and staggered off down the sidewalk, while Stern stood between the five cowboys and his retreating friends. In their patois, he asked, "Which one of you threw the knife?"

The tallest one stepped forward and flashed a crooked grin at Stern. He had very white teeth, thought Stern, as the Argyll loosened his whip and allowed it to unravel at his feet.

"I'll give you a choice," said Stern. "I'll fight you hand-to-hand with a knife but if you use that whip I will strike you dead." As he talked, he felt the stone hanging around his neck heat up and the voice of the demon whispering, 'burn him.'

The man spat on the ground and Stern smiled, as the Argyll raised his whip hand to lash out at him. As his hand came up, pulling the whip back, Stern yanked the derringer from the pocket of his coat and fired one round that struck the man between the eyes. The back of the man's head exploded. The four other Argyll stood shocked as the dead man's body fell backwards into them.

Before they could react, Stern fired a second round into the chest of the man that had spat on Jerah and then stepped forward aiming the gun. It was at that point that the remaining three turned and ran.

Stern walked to the dead man and removed the stone and allowed it to lap up his blood, while the second man held his chest and whimpered.

"Help me," he gasped.

Stern turned to him and stared into his eyes. "Don't worry; you're suffering will soon be over."

"Dom Carlos will come for you," he said.

"I'm sure he will," said Stern, pushing the satiated stone back into its pouch and pushing it under his shirt. He then slid one of the curved Dra'ghan knives from its sheath and slit the man's throat.

Standing over the bodies he loaded the derringer and then followed the fleeing men. One thing the last few months had taught him was that very little justice existed in this world or any other and that among men the need for vengeance seemed to be insatiable. He would deal with Dom Carlos and his men now; he would not flee them like he did Flymtt.

He pushed through the swinging doors of the crowded tavern and soon spied the three men standing in front of a table near the back, gesticulating frantically in front of a well-heeled man sitting with two women, who listened calmly.

Stern remained in the doorway with the derringer in his hand until one of the three survivors turned and saw him. With a shudder, the Argyl pointed at him and pulled his knife. Dom Carlos stood and ordered the women away, while the rest of the patrons backed away from the door, waiting.

"So you're the one who killed my men?"

"That's right. They stabbed my friend in the back."

Dom Carlos frowned and turned on the nearest cowboy. "Is that right?" The man looked sheepish and moved away from the trail boss. Turning back to Stern, he asked: "Is your friend dead?"

"I don't know. I didn't wait around to find out."

"What do you intend doing now?" asked the man, unbuttoning the middle button of his coat.

"Well, we can stop it now and call it even or you and your men can seek revenge."

"You must understand that it is a matter of honor; you killed two of my men outside the confines of a duel."

"I offered your men a duel with knives but they chose not to fight me one-on-one."

"Will you fight me now with knives? If you win, I promise on my word that will be the end of it."

The demon whispered, "Kill him. He is lying; he will cheat."

Stern looked around the room and saw a slight movement from the gauchos and he felt emotional pressure building near his temples, as his senses compared the charged emotions around him to the rattler that slithered out the driving sheets of rain several months ago in the Sun Mountains. Just as Coyote came to his rescue then, the demon entered his mind now and reminded him of the spell of binding. He whispered it and the people in the tavern fell silent and still. Running his tongue over his teeth, he sighed and asked the demon, "Why are you so present now in my world and so silent in Okeanus?" The demon did not answer but he suspected the demon sought an entry into his world, and he feared for a moment that he was giving him one.

He walked over to Dom Carlos, whose eyes had widened in fear. He could not move his body but Stern could tell from his eyes that he was alert to his present danger.

"Dom Carlos, unfortunately, you and your men are stupid and dangerous. Your sense of bravery and honor are corrupting and dishonest so I cannot trust you to stop harassing me and my friends; consequently, I will have to crush you.

He bent down and wrapped his arms around Dom Carlos' waist and lifted him, allowing the gaucho to fall across his left shoulder. He then walked from the saloon. At the swinging door he turned and recited the spell of long sleep, which he cast on the patrons and gauchos before stepping into the street.

Stern carried Dom Carlos to the stable where he saddled his horse. He then threw the recumbent body over the saddle and led the horse from the stable toward the pampas.

Stern rode south throughout the night. Thunderstorms gathered in the west and jagged bolts of lightning illuminated the landscape. Toward dawn, he stopped on the banks of a narrow stream and pulled the body from the back of the horse at the base of a gnarled cotton tree. The gelding drank from the stream as he tied the gaucho's body to the trunk of the tree and recited the spell of awakening from the *Grimoire of Stone*. Dom Carlos' first words were a vile curse, his next were pleads of mercy.

Stern held Dom Carlos' knife in his hand, as he listened to his pleas. When he finished, tears rolling across his cheeks and urine running down his legs, Stern said softly, "I have learned over the last few years that men are savage beasts. Only through strength of society is humanity able to carve out any semblance of order. Here in the south, on the pampas, the gauchos rule and men like you control them. If I were to let you go, you would attempt to kill me and my friends; consequently, my recourse is simple." In a sudden motion, faster than the rattler, he thrust the blade of the knife deeply under the man's ribcage into his heart. Blood gushed over his hand as he held the blade steady against the man's body spontaneously exploded into vicious movement to escape its inevitable death.

Moments later Stern released the blade and extracted the demon's stone and watched as it absorbed the gaucho's blood. As its veins bulged and turned red with savage heat, he heard the demon Kokabiel singing in satisfaction and he felt the dragon's rage thrilling throughout his body, just as it it had done on the island of Grun.

Later, he washed his hands in the stream and then mounted the gelding and turned it toward the town. Fifty feet from the tree, he turned in the saddle and whispered the spell of fire and cast a firebolt toward the dead body tied to the tree. It ignited in yellow and scarlet flame that quickly spread along the bark and the leaves above. As he galloped away, the fire extinguished the last remnants of the night as the sun rose.

At noon, Stern rode into town and tied his horse off in front of the stagecoach office. The stage was delayed a day and he breathed a sigh of relief. He walked his horse to the hotel where he found Cooper sitting in a straight-back wooden chair of the covered veranda.

"How's is Jerah?" he asked, tying the horse's reins to a hitching post and knocking the dust of the pampas off his stained clothes.

"The doctor says he will live but he will be laid up for a few weeks."

'Good," said Stern taking the chair next to Cooper.

"Where have you been, if I might be so bold to ask?" asked Cooper.

Stern fished his pipe from his coat pocket and stuck it in his mouth. As he removed his tobacco pouch, he noticed dried blood on the sleeve of his coat but he just ignored it, as he said, "I took a little ride to clear up a few matters."

"Should I be looking over my shoulder?" asked Cooper.

Stern lit his pipe and sucked smoke into his mouth, holding it for a few seconds before exhaling. "Nope," he said.

"The constable showed up here this morning asking question about a couple of dead gauchos," said Cooper. "I told him the truth, I had no idea who killed them. I suggested it might have been the same man that attacked us."

"Did he ask about me?" asked Stern.

"It's an odd thing. No one asked about you?"

"Odd indeed," said Stern, as he settled back into the chair and puffed on his pipe, listening to the low internal happy humming of the demon, Kokabiel.

Chapter Forty-Eight: Bueno

AFTER WEEKS on the coach with five strangers, the first thing Stern did when he arrived in Buenos was hire a rickshaw to a hotel near the harbor and rent a room with a view of the sea, where he ordered a bath, followed by a steak dinner and a bottle of the blood-red wine favored by the gauchos. Dressed in a silk robe, provided by the hotel, he handed his wrinkled and soiled clothes to a porter and asked for them to be cleaned. Later, he soaked in a tin tube in the center of his room and gazed out through open glass doors at the natural harbor of Buenos filed with ships, mostly sailing ships from the Eastern continents, purchasing beef from the pampas, but also junks from the west, bringing spices, silks, indentured workers, steam ships, large paddle boats from the north and even further, trading iron or wheat for beef.

Open and spacious Buenos was different from La Ciudad, which was a walled city, built on a plateau in the middle of the country, far from the sea. At sea-level, Buenos consisted of low apartment buildings constructed around a horseshoe-shaped natural harbor. As a seaport, it was filled with strangers, exotic peoples from all over Mittilagart and it was rich. Being rich, Buenos sent its ships, filled with its products, around the world to trade. Gauchos might dominate its vast prairies but its navy and its merchant ships scoured the seas.

The next day Stern rose early and walked through a light rain to the ticket office of Cosmonautic Airship International Corporation. A trader from Bretagne had told him over breakfast that Cosmonautic owned ten zeppelins, rigid airships that flew between the five major cities of the southern continent, and their hangar, located just outside the city. He also explained that the Teuton businessman and engineer, Lothar Raben, controlled fifty-one percent of the stock of the corporation, that traded briskly on the local *bourse*.

The small office constructed of white stone was a part of the aero-base, which consisted of an iron derrick that rose above the city and functioned as the dock for the zeppelins, a spacious hangar, where engineers serviced the crafts, the dormitory where the pilots and crews rested while on duty between flights and an office that served as both a ticket booth and accounting center. Today, the docks and dormitory were empty because all ships were underway. As Stern pushed the mahogany door of the office open, a slight bell rang and a man in a black rumpled suit rose from a wooden rocker in the corner and moved behind the counter. "May I help you?" he asked.

Stern approached the man and nodded, as he reached into the inner pocket of his linen jacket to extract a very fat wallet; he had sold another Dra'ghan jewel and exchanged it for paper money. "I want to purchase a one-way ticket on your next airship to Pima."

The man bent down and pulled a large leather ledger book from beneath the counter and said, "You may be in luck; we just had a cancellation on our next flight." As he flipped through the pages, he added: "Most seats are purchased months in advance."

Stern counted out the fee and the man handed him a ticket and warned him to be at the derrick's entrance no later than seven o'clock the next morning. It was necessary, he explained, to get everyone on board at least two hours before departure. He then asked: "How much luggage are you carrying?"

Stern pushed his wallet into his pocket and answered, "A leather knapsack and a small valise." The man nodded and recorded it in his book.

"How many passengers will be on the flight?" asked Stern.

"Twenty, of course," the man looked up; his eyes wide. "Is this your first trip on one of our ships?"

Stern nodded and the man smiled, as he explained, "Most of the hold is filled with goods. We make little or no money off passengers. You might say they are an afterthought, although the trip is quite enjoyable for them. Afterall, only the wealthy and important are able to afford our service. So for forty hours you will travel with our best citizens. I think you will find it quite stimulating."

Stern smiled and stifled a laugh, as he walked from the ticket office and walked toward a rickshaw stand, where he hired a driver to return him to his hotel. Bruise-black clouds formed in the west, signaling a storm forming over the pampas. Stern leaned back against the rough leather seat of the rickshaw and thought about his friends, as the driver padded through the labyrinthine streets of Bueno.

Tomorrow, he would cross the pampas; heading toward what he hoped would be the penultimate leg of his journey. All he had to do was find a matched pair of dragons, a male and a female and get them to the spot in which he entered Mittilagart, a beach somewhere south of Bueno and open a portal to Okeanus. He laughed at the absurdity of it all and suddenly felt the stone hanging around his neck heat up precipitously, as the voice of Kokabiel whispered in his ear, saying, 'Invite me into your world and the full power of the stone shall be yours.'

He remembered the power he felt on Grun when he shifted into the blue-back dragon and he was tempted to give in, to invite the demon to help him. Because without the demon's help, he had no idea how he would accomplish his quest and satisfy his promise to the *bruja*. And as he thought of her, he remembered her promise to be with him at the end. But when would he come to the end? And what was the end? Was it the final opening of the portal or now when he was close to finishing the quest but without any real hope he could accomplish what he had set out to do so long ago? He could use her help now. And he could use the power of the stone and the aid of Kokabiel.

He stepped out of the rickshaw in front of the hotel just as the rain clouds opened and a heavy rain fell on the city. He ran up the stone steps and stood on the veranda, watching the heavy traffic on the narrow cobblestone streets quickly disappear. Across the street, a woman opened the double glass doors of a dance hall, the Prada, and walked out and stood under a canvas awning, watching the rain fall. With the doors open he could hear the sound of an accordion and a pair of violins playing the strident music of the roundelay, the savage dance music of the pampas that was currently the latest craze of Bueno. The woman, dressed in a low-cut, tight fitting floor-length dress, crossed her arms, as if she were cold. With a strike of lightning, she shivered and held herself tighter. Stern pulled his pipe from his pocket and walked over to one of the several wooden rockers on the veranda, sat and lit his pipe. Soon, a haze of blue smoke surrounded him. He suddenly felt very happy and he knew it was the combination of rain, smoke, music and a beautiful woman that filled him with the sudden conviction that he would accomplish his mission. He would just have to take each step as it came. "Baby steps," he said out loud, "will win the day."

That night he ate a steak in the hotel's restaurant, drank a half-bottle of the gaucho red and then crossed the wet cobblestone street and entered the dance hall, where he sat at the bar, smoking his pipe and watching couples dancing the roundelay.

An hour before dawn, the hotel's carriage rattled over the cobblestone streets to the aeroport and delivered him. He was several hours early but he could not sleep. As the driver pulled the pair of horses to a stop in front of the gates of the port, the sun was just rising. The first sunbeams of morning bounced off the metal struts of the framework and illuminated the name painted on the black and gold gondola—*The Arabesque*.

Stern smiled. The rain had stopped sometime after mid-night, leaving a clean fresh smell in the air. He paid the driver and then walked to the gate and dumped his bag onto the ground, pulled his pipe and tobacco pouch from his coat pocket, and slowly filled the bowl. Once again the thought flitted through his mind: 'Why the hell didn't he just go back to the hotel and climb back into bed. Did he really want to step through the portal into the chaotic world of Okeanus once again?' Suddenly, he felt a taste of blood on his tongue and the raspy, roughness of a fur ball in his throat and he shuddered.

A man in a black uniform and white shirt exited the ticket kiosk and walked toward the gate, rattling a set of keys. "Morning," he called, as he splashed in a puddle of water, "beautiful morning for a flight."

Stern stuck his pipe into his mouth and picked up his bag as he marched through the gate, determined to see the quest through to its end.

Chapter Forty-Nine: The Arkadies

"THE ARKADIES RUN THE FULL LENGTH of the southern continent of the western hemisphere, forming a backbone of stone," explained Captain Marks, over dinner with his passengers, most of whom were new to the Argantine. "They are the highest mountains in the west and Pima the highest city. West of the Arkadies is a ragged coastline and east of the mountain range are pampas in the south and jungles in the north. The eastern face of the Arkadies is sheer and rugged, making access to Pima only possible from the west. Therefore, travelers either take a ship and land on the coast or one of our zeppelins."

He took a sip of champagne, licked his full lower lip and continued. "Pima's population numbers less than ten thousand, mostly soldiers, engineers, and bankers. The reason is that Pima has only one product: minerals and only one industry-mining. The soldiers are there to protect the mines from bandits and pirates. So, everyone in Pima, except for the *indios,* are there for the money."

Stern interrupted the Captain's disquisition and asked, "But there are dragons, aren't there?"

The Captain smiled and twisted one side of his thick blond mustache. "The dragons are high above Pima. You need not worry about them. Some days, when the haze burns off, usually in the summer, you can see the giant condors or fire serpents flying above the peaks."

"But what about the blue-backs?" urged Stern.

The Captain put his crystal glass down and rubbed his hands. "The blue-backs, migrating from the north, nest in the highest peaks. I bet you cannot find a citizen of Pima that has actually seen one up close."

A mining engineer from Bretagne asked in his bird-like accent, "I have heard that some of the mines at higher elevations have been attacked by dragons."

The Captain rubbed his red bulbous nose and laughed sourly. "That's a myth, made up by people, who have never seen the Arkadies. Dragons are a fact these days, just as caribou or polar bears are a fact. But I have never seen either."

"But you have seen a dragon," said Stern.

The Captain frowned and answered, "Of course, I fly over the Arkadies twice a week in the summer. We usually spy them flying between the higher peaks, but they do not fly as high as we do, and they have never bothered us."

No one asked a follow-up question; it seemed as if they were all imagining the dragons flying above the peaks of the mountains.

The Captain then finished his champagne in one swallow and stood. "Tomorrow, at dawn, we cross the mountains and land at Pima at noon. I recommend you rise early and watch the sun rise. It is a spectacular sight. And, just maybe, if we are lucky, we will see one of those dragons." He excused himself and left the passengers to finish their meal.

The next morning Stern stood on the observation deck with four or five of his fellow passengers. The sun had not yet appeared but light was seeping over the horizon. Below gray clouds covered the mountain tops and one of the men pointed out it was snowing.

Just at dawn, the Captain joined them and said, "Summer snow is falling on the Arkadies, gentlemen. We may have a rather rough landing."

"But it is the middle of summer," exclaimed a just-graduated mining engineer from Bueno.

"It's normal at this altitude," responded the Captain.

As Stern watched the clouds moving across the surface of the mountains' peaks, he imagined the sheer cold at that height and saw, in his mind's eye, the dragons huddled in caves, sleeping; their leather wings folded on their backs. And he envisioned himself, once he found the dragons, climbing ice-covered rocks, full of fear, on the way to their lair. Suddenly, he knew he was not up to the task and with that intimation firmly in his mind, Kokabiel entered his conscious mind and said, "I will help you. You are not alone." Stern shook his head, trying to clear away the demon's voice, and remembered the witch's promise to be with him in the end. Where was she?

As the engines slowed, the zeppelin turned slowly and the Captain announced, "We are beginning our descent toward Pima. You will need to return to your seats in the next half-hour." He straightened his jacket and then said, almost as an aside to no-one in particular, "I must return to the bridge."

Instead of returning to their seats the small group huddled around the cold glass on the observation deck and peered at the mountains, the clouds and the falling snow. Most were excited at the prospect of landing in the snow but Stern felt anxious and frightened. After all he had been through over the last year, he wondered why he was undergoing a crisis of faith now, so close to the end. He had been naked and alone for a long time and survived the most horrendous adventures. Perhaps, it was the demon working on his mind, undermining his confidence. He separated himself from the group and headed toward the door and the steps that led to the passenger seats.

Kylla had died and so, too, Coyote in the pursuit of the quest. He could not give up now. If he had to have the demon's help to complete it, then he would ask for it. As he came to this conclusion, the shadows receded and he felt himself again. He suspected the demon was somehow manipulating his thoughts and affecting his emotions. But the ends must in some cases justify the means. If he could not accomplish the goal alone, then he would call on Kokabiel.

As he sat in the passenger seat, the stone vibrated within the leather bag hanging from the rawhide strip around his neck. Heat radiated through the leather and warmed his skin. And when he closed his eyes he saw the eyes of the dragon peering out the darkness of his unconscious mind and he suspected, if he called upon the dragon now, or the bear or wolf, he would shift, just as he had on Okeanus. Somehow, through his doubts and fear, he had opened Mittilagart up to the demon's magic and he wondered what evil machinations he had beget as a result of his weakness and fear.

Two hours later the zeppelin docked at the iron derrick in the center of the small walled city of Pima. Snow fell steadily as Stern exited the gondola onto the iron platform. A crew member warned him to watch his step, ice had formed on the platform and the stairs.

Frigid air and a strong wind pushed against Stern's body. He wore only a light linen suit and he was totally unprepared for the temperature. When he grasped the railing of the stairs, he felt the jolt of the frozen metal on his hands and he remembered his days and nights on Bedwyr's island, huddled before a fire with the magus, as cold, brittle winds blew from the North Sea.

The passengers marched down the stairs and huddled around the base of the derrick. No one seemed prepared for the weather. Even the crewmen shivered. Unlike Bueno, there was no ticket booth beneath the iron framework of the derrick, no rickshaws queued up outside the gates and no carriages. Snow fell steadily onto the narrow, unlit cobblestone streets.

"Is there a hotel or inn nearby?" asked Stern, rubbing his hands together vigorously.

One of the crewmen, tying off the zeppelin, pointed down a narrow, dark street to the left, and said, "The *Red Fox Inn* is about two hundred meters up that street. That's where we spend the night."

Stern nodded and set off; his head bowed and his shoulders hunched against the wind and cold, as several of his fellow passengers grunted and fell in behind him. The city seemed to be of a piece, each dwelling shared a wall with its neighbor on both sides and the cobblestone streets and alleys were the same gray stone of the houses. The only other colors in a very gray world were the stained dark brown doors and shutters, and the red tile of the roofs.

Stern broke trail through the mounting snow and grumbled under his breath, as the other passengers followed behind him like ducklings. Finally, he reached the first three-story edifice he had seen since arriving in Pima, the *Red Fox Inn*. He pushed open the right side of a two door entrance and entered a short passageway that led to an atrium. The true entrance of the hotel was there on the north side of the small courtyard.

A tall, thin Argyll hovered near the tavern's entrance, smoking a cheroot. He wore the livery of a hotel page. When he saw Stern and the others, he pressed the cheroot against one of the posts supporting the roof of a narrow porch, extinguishing it, and then inserted it into a pocket of his waistcoat, rubbed both hands through his thick black hair, and then ran to open the door of the hotel.

"Welcome, gentlemen," he called out in a sweet tenor, as he bowed to Stern.

Stern stamped his feet on the wooden porch to clear the wet snow from his boots.

The entrance opened onto a large room with blond wooden floors and a large stone fireplace roaring against the north wall. To the right, behind a small mahogany secretary's table, a man in a black suit and white shirt sat, scribbling in a thick book of accounts. He wore a pince-nez on his narrow nose.

The man looked up from his figures as Stern entered the room but seemed reticent to leave them. He blinked his black eyes like an owl and then slowly focused on the number of guests arriving. He pushed back his chair and stood, pulling the glasses from his nose and inserting them into a pocket of his coat.

"Welcome, guests," he said with a wide smile that waned quickly. "I take it the zeppelin has arrived from Bueno."

Stern nodded to the man and then walked over to the fireplace, where he dropped his bag and dug his pipe from his coat pocket and slowly filled it with tobacco. *First things first*, he thought, as the other passengers lined up to register for rooms.

From his vantage point near the fire, Stern could survey the entire room; as well as look into the dining room, where several guests occupied tables, eating lunch.

He lit the pipe and puffed contentedly. There was a sense of harmony about the room, which comforted him, relieving the anxiety he felt when the zeppelin descended through the clouds into a blizzard. Maybe things would be all right after all.

He sat in a large leather chair near the fire to wait his turn to check into the inn. As he sat and smoked, he began to plan his next move. His first step was to find maps of the region and a guide. Not only was the demon pestering him, he too was anxious to be on his way. He clearly could not lounge in this tavern for weeks, waiting for a thaw. The demon would devour him, if he did not feed the stone.

By the time it was his turn before the officious little man, once again wearing the *pince-nez*, there was only a small room available on the third floor; a maid's room really. But it was either that or share a room and he did not relish being under the watch of one of the engineers or miners. He had enough of their questions about his business on the trip over from Bueno.

After storing his gear, he descended the stairs and took a table in the dining room. Over a cup of coffee, he smoked his pipe and scribbled a few notes in a small leather-bound notebook. Most of the guests had finished eating and only a single woman, occupying a table near the kitchen entrance remained. She wore all black clothing and a veil, as if she were in mourning, and the wait staff treated her with the utmost respect, whispering their questions to her. Rather than answer, she simply lifted her hand or nodded.

Later, Stern approached the clerk in the lobby and asked for a moment of his time. Once again, the man seemed to be in a trance, mesmerized by his accounts, as he slowly focused his eyes on Stern. "Yes, how may I help you?"

Stern cleared his throat and stammered his question. Now that he was articulating what he wanted, he found he was unsure of himself, "I want to talk with someone who is familiar with the mountains." He paused and scratched his nose absently before continuing: "A man who could function as a guide."

The man turned his head slightly, like one of the parrots in the empty city, "Are you seeking someone to help you pan for gold?"

Stern bowed his head slightly, avoiding the man's eyes, as he said, "I'm a hunter. I hope to find the lair of the blue-back dragons."

The man sputtered.

"An unusual request but an interesting one," he said with a slight smile. "You are serious, I take it?"

"Most serious," answered Stern, placing one gold angel on the man's desk. "I will pay you two more if you find me a satisfactory candidate." The man's eyes widened and a smile stretched across his greedy face, as he pocketed the angel.

"I will have one for your review by tomorrow, if that is satisfactory."

Stern nodded and walked toward the stairs. In his tiny room, he opened the one small window and watched snow fall onto an alley running behind the inn. Three cats rummaged in a midden and a cook entered one of the many outhouses along the far wall of the alley. In the distance, above the roofs of the city, the Arkadies, barely visible because of the storm, beckoned. He was almost to the end, he thought. And then a faint knock at the door awakened him from his reverie and he opened the door.

The woman in the mourning weeds stood at the door, her black veil hiding her face from the nonplussed Stern.

"May I come in?" she asked softly; her voice a bit hoarse and deeper than he would have imagined. He stepped aside to allow her to pass but she hung fire at the lintel.

"You don't understand," she said. "You must invite me to enter the room."

He blinked and cleared his throat, "Would you please come in?" he asked.

She reached down under her veil and pulled it up and off of her head, as she stepped across the threshold and into the bedroom.

Stern stepped back to make room, as she threw the veil onto his bed and undid her black hair, freeing it from the tight bun. "Please close the door,' she said, as she ran her hands through her hair and loosened the buttons at the neck of the black dress to reveal pale white skin.

When she turned toward him, he knew she was a *bruja*, but not his witch.

She appeared young but he knew she could be old. Her face was heart-shaped and her eyes a pale blue. And when she sat on the wooden strait-back chair and looked up at him, her eyes seemed to twinkle.

"You've been difficult to track down," she said.

"I opened a portal in the south seas on an island called Grun."

She rubbed her chin and said: "We know that. You didn't pay attention did you? Not only did you open a portal in the wrong place, you brought a demon along for the ride."

Stern rubbed his tongue over his teeth and then sat on his bed. Cold wind filled the room and he hopped up to close the window.

He examined her face and could discern no anger. She was simply listing his mistakes.

"Everything I did seemed necessary at the time."

"It was expedient to enlist the help of a demon from Elysium?"

He felt the stone move within the pouch. "In my opinion I would have never made it to Bedwyr without the powers I obtained from the stone and the grimoire. Or escaped from the Brotherhood or survived Focalor's attacks."

"Maybe," she said.

He leaned toward her and explained: "I'm near the end. I can feel it. I will succeed."

She tapped her full lower lip with her index finger and opened her mouth slightly. She was a beautiful woman, he thought. And, with the window closed, he could smell cinnamon and musk, smells he found alluring and seductive.

"We know you're almost finished. That is why I'm here. She told you that she would be with you at the end. And, as you have said, the end is nigh. But we have a problem: you carry a demon spirit with you. Kokabiel cannot be allowed to remain on Mittilagart. You must return him to Elysium."

"But how?" he sputtered.

"If you think about it, you will know what to do. But first you must finish the quest. You must return the blue-back dragon to Okeanus and prepare the way for the return of the Skallaenders. But if you remain here with the demon, we will intervene."

He felt his temper rise, as well as the stone begin to throb around his neck. Something was happening that he had no real knowledge of; some type of inter-dimensional struggle between Kokabiel of Elysium and the lunar *bruja* of Mittilagart. And was it fair, he asked himself, to expect him to understand any of it. Suddenly, he felt betrayed and abused. First they cast him into a foreign world without any help or instruction and now they were criticizing how he had moved between two worlds and survived.

Kokabiel whispered in his mind, 'Kill her.' He blinked, angry at her but also at the demon, who had helped him with his quest, but who had done so out of some nefarious plan to inhabit not one but three worlds. *"Shut the hell up, demon"* he thought, as he took several deep breaths to calm himself. *"I thought you were a mediator, not a murderer?"*

As calm as he could be under the circumstances, he asked the witch: "How are you going to help me?"

She smiled and said: "I just did. I gave you your instructions."

"That's it," he asked with a sardonic laugh.

She stood and walked toward him, taking his hand and pulling him up from the bed. She then leaned into him and kissed him, while flicking her hand and reciting a spell in a guttural language that Stern did not at first understand, but when he repeated it silently, allowing Kokabiel's language spell to interpret for him, he soon knew it was a simple extinguishment spell that doused the candle and plunged the room into darkness. As she nibbled on his lower lip and then moved to his ear lobe, he absorbed the language completely and wrapped his arms around her narrow waist and pulled her close to him.

He awoke with a start. Naked, he pushed back the bedclothes and swung out of bed. The woman was gone and someone was knocking on his door. Light shone through the tiny window and he could see icicles, hanging from the tile roof, melting.

"Who is it?" he called.

"The manager asked me to tell you he has found you a guide and he will be here at noon, sir."

"What's your name?" Stern asked, running his hands through his long hair, pushing it back.

"Jaspers, sir," answered the man.

"I need a bath, Jaspers. Can you arrange it?"

"In the basement, sir," he said. "Our baths are in the basement."

At noon, with his clothes cleaned, his hair braided and his beard trimmed, Stern waited in the main room next to the fire, smoking his pipe. Although he bathed, he could still smell the musk of the witch and feel the incipient rage of the demon.

A quarter past the hour an Argyll with long hair and a beard entered the hotel, nodded to the hotelier at his desk and walked toward Stern.

"I'm Hagen," he said, taking the seat next to Stern. "I hear you are looking for a guide into the mountains to hunt dragons."

Stern observed his face to discern if there was smile there.

"That's right," he said around the pipe's stem.

"What type of dragon are you hunting?" the man said calmly, crossing his leg and pulling a cheroot from the pocket of his long leather coat.

"The blue-back," answered Stern, lighting the man's cigar.

"There's a cave in the Manner, a mountain not far from here, where two are nesting. Young ones but mature enough to breed. Does that interest you?"

Stern pulled the pipe from his mouth and spoke to the Argyll in his own language. "That's exactly what I am looking for," he said excitedly.

The Argyll's eyes opened wide at the use of his language but he soon covered his surprise and asked: "Why would a man want to kill a breeding pair of dragons?"

Stern pointed the mouthpiece at the Argyll for effect. "I don't want to kill them. I want to save them."

"Save them from what?" asked the Argyll.

"Not 'from what,'" corrected Stern. "I want to save them for breeding."

The man used the Argyll word for crazy and Stern laughed.

"What do we need?" asked Stern.

The man rubbed his chin with his weathered right hand and said, "Tents, blankets, sleeping bags, climbing equipment, warm clothing, food, lots of food, rope, and a couple of llamas to carry it all."

Stern pulled a ruby from his pocket and handed it to the Argyll. "Will that cover it?"

The man turned the stone in his hands and said, "Several times over."

"Get what you need and keep the rest." The man's mouth fell partially open but he quickly recovered.

"When can we leave?" asked Stern

"Day after tomorrow," answered the man, as he pushed the ruby into a pocket of his leather waistcoat. "I will be here at first light. Be ready to go. And buy some warm clothes and decent boots, if you don't have any."

Stern nodded and re-lit his pipe.

Chapter Fifty: The White Apes

THREE WEEKS HAD PASSED and Manner's peak still seemed far in the distance. Hagen had not spoken a word all day; he simply marched ahead, pulling on the rope, leading the two malodorous llamas along the mountain trail, carved out of the stone by one of the Argantine mining companies years ago.

Finally, near dusk, Hagen raised his left hand, and stopped. To his right was a wedge of rock, fairly flat. Stern recognized it immediately as the type of place the Argyll liked to make camp.

Since their first meeting at the *Red Fox Inn*, the two men had spoken to each other only in the Argyll language. And even though they knew each other fairly well by now, they hardly talked about anything other than the weather and the mountain.

Later, sitting on camp chairs in front of the tent, both smoking, Hagen said, "In a day or two, we will have to leave the llamas behind."

Stern guessed the answer but he asked the question anyway. "Does the trail end so soon?"

The Argyll nodded. "There is an abandoned mining camp ahead and then the mountain goes straight up. We will climb after that."

"How long, after we leave the trail, until we reach the dragons?" Stern asked.

"Maybe a week," he answered. 'If we are lucky, that is."

"What could happen?" asked Stern. "We haven't seen a soul in days."

"You could fall," said the man with a laugh. "Bandits could attack us. Dragons could eat us. A pack of snow apes could rip us apart and beat us with our arms."

"Snow apes," said Stern. "Is there such a thing?"

"Of course there is. Why do you think they closed the mine? Snow apes attacked the camp and killed everybody."

"You're making this up, aren't you?" asked Stern with a laugh.

"Speak of the wolf," said the Argyll and pointed his cheroot toward the edge of the mountain several meters from the trail.

A snow ape sat on a large gray rock, tearing the meat from a dead bird's chest. "Speak the name of the wolf and he appears," said the Argyll, who began to recite a warding spell.

"I'll be damned," said Stern standing up to better see the huge white ape.

"Sit back down!" whispered the guide. "They are very territorial, these apes."

Stern heard the demon say, "Kill it, I'm hungry."

The next day, the Argyll stopped mid-afternoon and began setting up camp. The wind picked up and snow flakes flittered through the air. Stern pulled the hood of his green woolen cloak over his head and grumbled: "Why are we stopping?"

"I don't want to reach the mining camp at dusk. There are too many ghosts there."

Leaning on his stave, Stern looked over his shoulder. Last night, the white ape disappeared down the mountain as soon as it finished eating. Stern, however, since waking, had felt a prickly feeling between his shoulder blades and wondered if the creature had followed them. Shrugging the feeling away, he helped Hagen pitch the tent and then went looking for something to burn. They were way above the tree line now and he found little or nothing. They spent the afternoon sitting in front of the tent, puffing away on pipes and cheroots, as the wind howled through the rocks. At dusk they chewed iron rations and drank water from canteens, as flakes of snow whirled about in the wind. The temperature was dropping and Stern pulled his cloak tightly around him.

"Should we take turns sleeping?" Stern asked, as he painfully swallowed the last bit of the dry iron ration.

The Argyll removed the cheroot from his mouth and scratched his nose with the long ragged nail of his thumb. "Do you feel something?"

Stern nodded and said, "Ever since yesterday, I've felt something watching us."

"Me, too," responded the Argyll.

"Do you think it's the ape?" asked Stern.

The man shook his head. "If it was the ape, the llama would be nervous."

"So what is it?" asked Stern.

"My guess is that it's a man or men."

"Bandits?" said Stern.

"We spent a lot of money in Pima. Maybe someone saw you flashing the money around and decided you might be an easy mark."

Stern reached inside his cloak and touched the revolver in his shoulder holster. "So, do you think they will attack us tonight?"

The Argyll placed his rough hands on his knees and looked down the trail. "They have come closer to us today than ever before. I suspect they are beginning to feel impatient. Most people fear the old mines, so they probably want to hit us before we pass them."

Stern felt anger well up in his chest. "Why the hell did you stop here? We should have pushed on to the mines, if they scare people."

The Argyll cut his eyes quickly to Stern, who felt his anger. "People fear the mines for a reason. I didn't relish fighting a ghoul or a ghost, while a bandit was trying to stab me in the back."

They sat silent for a few moments, letting their tempers cool in the frigid air. Finally, Stern pulled his pipe from his mouth with his left hand and nervously stroked his beard with his right. "Let's talk about this," he said in a soft voice and the Argyll nodded. "If we think they intend jumping us tonight, let's do some planning." He stood and surveyed the ground. They had pitched the tent on a level piece of solid rock a few feet from the ragged and rugged trail, a remnant of the days when the mine was in operation. Several meters to the north of them, a pile of rocks rested on the edge of a jagged cliff. To the south, the face of the mountain posed an obstacle. The attack would come from the west, they would creep along the edge of the trail in the dark and jump them. The east would be the only avenue of escape and the rocks to the north the only defensible point.

Stern spat out a curse in *lingua* and then turned to the Argyll. "This position will be impossible to defend."

The Argyll shrugged. "I will not go into the mines at night."

"What's there, at the mines?" asked Stern, trying to think.

The Argyll, his face almost unreadable, said in a flat voice, as if he had already accepted his fate, "About twenty shacks, a foundry, a few barns, a two-story office building, a clinic, four or five barracks and several storage buildings and, of course, the mine itself."

"In other words, plenty of places to hide and defend ourselves," he said bitterly. He wanted to lash out at the man for being so obtuse and manipulative.

He looked up at the gray clouds and tried to find the sun. "How many hours until dusk?" he asked the man.

"Maybe three but I refuse to enter the mining camp. There are worst things than death."

"Like what?" asked Stern genuinely interested.

"Being possessed by a devil or a demon," answered the man.

Stern walked down the hill, away from the tent, heading west toward the attackers, if they existed, and opened his hand, palm upward, and whispered the words of the first fire spell. A tiny flame erupted in his hand and he smiled, as he called the demon. "Kokabiel, I will feed you, if you help me?"

The demon laughed and said: "Have I ever failed you?" Stern closed his hand, extinguishing the flame. He stood peering down the road. He could see no-one but he felt them.

Walking up the trail toward the tent, away from the hidden enemy, he made up his mind. "Hagen, strike the tent. We're going east through the mining camp. We must find a defensive position."

The man's eyes widened and he said gruffly. "Did you not hear me? I will not go into the mining camp."

"You do not have to. I want you to take the llamas and our supplies and go past the camp. I will stay behind and fight whomever follows us. I will join you later."

"What if they kill you?" the man asked, as he pulled up a peg.

"Then you are on your own."

Thirty minutes later they were on their way. Two hours after that they reached the mining camp and Stern took his knapsack, a canteen, and his walking stave and entered a two-story building on the side of the trail, as Hagen continued east, following the trail. Stern could hear him reciting warding spells as he walked.

As the sun set and night fell onto the camp, snow fell steadily on the mountain, covering the trail and any tracks of the Argyll and the llamas. Stern sat and stared out of a window on the second floor of a building near the trail, focusing intently on the west and listening carefully for any sounds of the men following them. He feared he might not hear them pass and they would fall on the Agryll.

Hours after midnight, Stern heard a man curse and the sound of boots slogging through the wet snow but he could see nothing. The sound came from down the hill; the bandits were on the move, trudging toward the camp.

Stern pulled off his heavy cloak and folded it, placing it in the corner away from the window. He then undressed completely. Shivering, he sat on the rough wooden boards of the floor and meditated, just as Kylla had instructed him many months ago on Okeanus. Kokabiel, good to his word, did not obstruct his metamorphosis, as he had when Stern had first returned to Mittilagart.

The wolf, its black fur, thick and warm, shivered not from cold but from transformation. Its yellow eyes burned bright in the dark and its teeth shone white in the shadows of the room. The scent of the bandits, heavy on the air, caused the wolf's nostrils to flare and widen, these men smelled of sweat, tobacco, cinnamon, and blood. Stern counted five men and one Argyll, climbing the trail in two columns. He also detected something else nearby: the rank foul odor of the apes. Maybe twenty in all, they were spread around the mining camp, moving now toward the trail.

Stern, as wolf, padded down the narrow stairs and out the back door and into the snow, where he almost collided with two white apes moving quickly to flank the men. He paused, letting the apes, which ignored him, pass. Should he let the apes attack the men or should he help his kind? The demon answered the unspoken question: *Draw blood and hurry the process. These men are no friends of yours.*

Stern quickly discerned a pattern in the apes' action, many of the males took up positions on the men's flanks, while several of the larger ones moved to the center of the trail ahead of the approaching men and a fairly sizeable group of young females moved down the trail, cutting off the avenue of retreat. Once in their positions, the apes advanced toward the column of bandits, who seemed oblivious of the danger they now faced. Stern fell in behind the bandits and quickened his pace. Consistent with the demon's wish, he intended hamstringing the last man in the column, bringing him down and filling the air with the scent of fresh blood. If Kokabiel were right, his attack would trigger the apes and a melee would ensue.

The last man was taller and heavier than the rest. He carried a musket in his right hand and he was breathing heavily, tiring from the quick march up the slight pitch of the trail. Stern charged his left leg and tore into the ragged and worn boot, sinking his teeth deeply into his flesh. The man let out a scream, as he raised the musket and slammed its butt into the shoulder muscles of the wolf. Stern yelped and broke off his attack; his mouth filled with blood and flesh. And, as he backed away from the man, who was now falling, his left leg no longer able to support him, Stern heard the grunt of the apes and the hollow thumping of a slab of wood, being struck repeatedly against a stone; a primitive signal to attack the column.

At least two men were able to get off shots from their muskets before the apes tore into them, crushing them under their weight. Screams and curses filled the air, along with the stench of released bowels and blood, as Stern slunk away, avoiding the apes that now moved in for the kill, the fight almost over.

Seconds later the bandits were dead.

Stern in wolf form ran toward the building where he had left his clothes, pack and weapons. He hurried because he knew it would not be long before the apes hunted him. As he ran the demon's stone dangled from its leather strap around his neck and he toyed with the idea of simply running, leaving everything else behind. But he remembered the dragons and his quest and so he climbed the stairs to the second floor.

The snow ceased suddenly and dawn arrived shortly thereafter. Light rays illuminated the room, where Stern lay curled, listening to the terrible sound of apes feeding on the bodies of the bandits. He returned to his human form and as he quickly dressed, he looked out the window onto the trail, where blood and viscera stained the snow. Twenty or thirty apes picked at the bones and flesh, while others, now satiated, wandered away from the sight of the mayhem.

With the sun, the shadows of the mountains receded and Stern could see the gaping entrance of the abandoned mine. As he watched, a horned head of a dragon emerged and sniffed the air. Stern rubbed his eyes, not really believing what he was seeing. The blue-back waddled from the cave's mouth on its hind legs and raised its head to expel a breath of flame, as it spread its wings. The apes stopped, wherever they were, and began to chatter and pant, warning each other of the dragon's appearance.

The blue-back was a young bull, the size of a large dray horse. As he flapped his wings, a female, a bit smaller and lighter in color, pregnant and heavy, emerged from the cave, stretched and sprayed fire into the air. Stumbling as she walked into the sunlight, unbalanced by the size of her stomach, she fell against the male. Startled, he snapped at her and screeched, causing her to recoil and spit a burst of flame at him.

Stern had found what he was looking for: a matched pair and one of them pregnant. He quickly undressed and once naked he snuffed his clothes into the knapsack along with the two grimoires he had received from the demon. Everything else—guns, clothes, tools, tobacco and pipe— he left behind.

As he walked from the building, he watched as the male dragon pounced on a female ape, took her head into his maul and bit down; the body fell away gushing blood onto the snow.

Stern sat naked in the snow and meditated on the dragon. At first, he could feel Kokabiel blocking him, slowing the transformation process. He warned him away and cursed him but the demon simply laughed. "Promise me," he said, "That you will honor the pledge you made on Elysium." Agitated and fearing the female dragon would attack him, she was already watching from one black eye, he agreed and Kokabiel stepped aside and even aided the transformation. Stern, once again in the guise of the blue-back, rose up on his hind legs and screeched a warning to the pair of young dragons, causing the male to leave off tearing out the stomach of a white ape and focusing his attention on the male dragon.

Stern spread his leather wings and rose slowly into the air, spewing flames from his mouth, as the female, with one eye cocked, fed on the innards of an ape and her mate, the blue-back bull, challenged and threatened by Stern's sudden appearance, followed him. At first, they circled high above the mining camp, speeding through the snow-covered peaks of the Arkadies, sizing each other up by testing the others' abilities and speed. As Stern flew, he struggled against the division of his conscious mind into the primitive brain of the dragon, ruled by instinct and rage, hunger and power, and his own, rational mind that was trying desperately to figure out a strategy to lure the two dragons back to the beach on the coast of the Argantine, the place where he had entered Mittilagart several weeks before. His initial plan was simple: lead the dragons to the beach, open a portal over Grun, and send them to their ancestral home. However, the male was not cooperating; instead, Stern's very existence threatened him and he was intent on demonstrating his dominance by fighting him. And, even though Stern was in dragon form, which brought a certain amount of innate instinct with it, his divided thoughts slowed him down and placed him at a distinct disadvantage to the young bull that acted solely on instinct. As Stern planned, the dragon acted. Consequently, Stern ran and the bull chased. It soon became obvious to him that the young male was gaining on him, spraying liquid fire that ultimately scorched his spiked tail, unbalancing him, causing him to slow. The pain of the burns frightened him and for the first time Stern began to consider killing the male. The female was pregnant, he thought. If he could get her and her offspring to Grun, his task would be complete, he would have returned the blue-back to Okeanus and fulfilled the demands of the witches. His *ad hoc* plan now was to fight and cow the bull dragon, but if that didn't work he would kill it.

Stern realized the first step was to reverse the current situation; he had to take the initiative away from the dragon. Spying a narrow crevice between two peaks, he turned toward it and beat his wings as quickly as possible. His sharp turn toward the narrow pass and his increase in speed took the bull unaware, allowing Stern to widen the gap between them.

He sped through the narrow opening, clipping the tip of his wing against jagged stones. Once through, he turned sharply and landed on the sheer face of the rock and waited for the bull to follow him through and pass. He heard the growl of the dragon and then a scream as it, too, scraped its wings against the walls. Stern prepared himself. As soon as the bull exited the crevasse, he launched himself from the rock face and dived toward the back of the younger dragon. With his talons bared in front, he dropped on its back and drove his razor sharp claws into its rugged skin, attaching easily, allowing his momentum and his weight to push the dragon downward toward the rocks below.

As the bull struggled and turned, its wings folding and twisting as it fell through the air, plummeting downward, Stern let loose a blast of fire that engulfed the young dragon's head and shoulders. Then, he released the dragon, freeing his talons from its back and beat his wings, flying upward. The bull singed and bleeding struggled until its wings opened and filled with air, stopping its free fall.

Circling above the wounded young bull, Stern roared and sputtered out fire. He stayed close to the dragon but did not attack. Instead, he followed the blue-back to the mining camp. He had won the skirmish; his conscious mind had out-witted the instinctual mind of the bull. Now he had to convince or coerce them to follow him through the mountains and across the pampas to the site of the portal. The zeppelin flight from Bueno lasted forty hours; he figured the dragons could make the trip in half the time. Twenty-four hours from now, his quest could be finished.

The bull landed near where the female fed on the carcasses of men and apes. Cowed, it approached a dead ape, looked over its shoulder at Stern, as if asking for permission to eat, and then, seeing that Stern made no move to stop it, tore into the body.

Stern flew to the top of the administrative building. From its third floor he surveyed the area, as several surviving white apes scampered away into the rocks. Stern turned slowly toward the female and wondered how much time he had to get her to the portal. It would be a disaster, he thought, if she laid the dragon eggs before they departed Mittilagart.

He allowed the dragons to feed and then he roared. The two looked up; their mauls covered with viscera and blood. He flew up and called for them. At first they hesitated and growled back, spitting little flames of fire. He dived toward the male and landed near him and sprayed fire across the ground. The male turned its body, exposing its underbelly. Stern grunted and strutted in front of the two, spreading his leather wings wide. He remembered Phobus and Deimos, his dogs, and named the dragons the same.

He flew up again, circling and calling, until they rose up to join him.

The three turned toward the east.

Chapter Fifty-One: The Portal

THEY STOPPED TO FEED on the abundant life of the pampas twice in the next twenty-four hours. Each time, Stern refused to release them until his own stomach ached with hunger and he felt as if he could not fly another mile. When they were freed to hunt, Stern sensed their pleasure in the amount of food available on the pampas: herds of wild oryx roamed freely in the south, while thousands of the long-horned cattle of the gauchos grazed in the more populated north. After they fed, the dragons slept on the ground for an hour or two; their wings folded tightly against their bodies. They would have slept longer but Stern drove them on; anxious to finish the quest and return to La Ciudad and his son.

As they flew high above the pampas, heading northeast toward the sea, Stern heard the demon, Kokabiel, mumbling in his ear, and he wondered what devilment the demon was up to now. On the second day, they reached the white-sand coast and Stern turned north, looking for the rocks that marked the site of the portal. At sea-level it was still summer. Warm rain fell on them as they flew.

At sunset, Stern found the stones. He flew up above the spot and released the dragons to feed. He wanted them full and groggy when he morphed into his human form to open the portal. He realized he was in a very precarious situation. To open the portal, he needed to be in his human form. But if he faced the dragons as a human, there was a high likelihood that the two would devour him. As this thought passed through his mind, the demon whispered into his ear. "Summon me and I will open the portal and the three of you can pass through as dragons."

He shook his head as the demon's voice buzzed and vibrated in his ear. "The witch warned me it would be folly to allow you to enter Mittilagart." The demon hummed and then said, his voice now as smooth as honey: "Remember my role. I'm mediator to the world. It is my task to build the tower of language. Without access to Mittilagart my purpose is frustrated. Invite me to enter and I will open the portal and you can complete your quest." Stern flew higher; he had lost sight of the dragons in the rain and the fading light of dusk. Finally, he said, "I must change into my human form to complete the spell of invocation."

The demon let out a laugh and said, "Do so and I will keep the dragons away long enough for you to complete the spell."

Stern landed on the beach near the stones. The sun had set completely and the gray dusk was quickly absorbing the last remnants of light. He meditated on his human form and then he changed. Naked, filthy, smelling of blood, offal, brimstone and ash, he shivered in the summer rain. With the demon's instructions firmly in his mind, Stern found a stick–some dried drift wood–in the sand and drew a pentagram within a circle. Then he wrote Kokabiel's name in runes within the circle. Finished he sat in the center, facing east, pricked his palm with a clam shell and dripped blood on the runes, as he spoke the spell, holding the black stone in his right hand, summoning the demon to him. A portal opened and Kokabiel stepped through into Mittilagart and laughed. His long white hair billowed in the wind and his red eyes flashed in the night. "You have done well," he said, walking across the white sand toward Stern.

As Stern started to rise, the demon pushed him back down onto the sand. His left hand, encased in a leather gauntlet, gripped Stern's right shoulder and squeezed until he yelped in pain. With his right hand, he demon ripped the black stone from Stern's hand. "You will not need this any longer, my friend," said the demon.

Stern felt the bear emerge from his unconscious mind; full of rage and anger at being betrayed.

Kokabiel spat out a spell of binding and Stern's body froze into implacable rigidity.

"Listen, my friend, I'm going to call the dragons in from their hunt. If you wish to live, I suggest you shift shape into the bull dragon and prepare yourself to lead them through the portal to Okeanus." Stern moaned but he could not move. "I promised Michaelsdottir that I would not harm you and I do not intend betraying my word to that witch." Stern's eyes widened at this revelation. "I'm going to release your mouth so that you can promise me that you will do what I say."

Kokabiel spoke a few words in his guttural language and Stern felt his mouth move. "You bastard," he spat, "You tricked me."

"Tricked you?" the demon laughed. "Everyone you met warned you about me and yet you took every step necessary to achieve your goal with me by your side."

"What do you intend doing here?" asked Stern. His mind was buzzing with questions but he asked this one first.

"I will continue to mediate between the forces just as I have always done. Those witches of yours have frustrated me long enough." He paused and looked out on the night sea. "In the long run, you have done a good thing, Stern. You just don't know it yet. But because you have betrayed the lunar *brujas,* you have burned your bridges here, or should I say closed your portal. They will never let you back in and I don't need you here either."

"What about my son?" he asked.

"He is fine with the Black Robes. Don't worry about him. Besides he hardly remembers you, now."

"What am I to do in Mittilagart?" he asked softly.

"Ah," said the demon. "You will continue to learn. Seek out Bedwyr and continue your apprenticeship. The only difference will be that you do not have me at your side and you can no longer open portals between the worlds."

He ran his hand through his long white hair. "If I were you, I would go back north and suss out your true heritage. Learn the ways of the Skaellanders. I mean that's what the Black Robes are seeking anyway. And frankly, my friend, once a Black Robe, it is very difficult to be anything else. You still have most of the powers you had before. Use them to increase your knowledge. You just can't summon me or open portals between the worlds. Leave that to demons and witches."

The demon opened his right hand and let the wind blow away the black dust in his palm, the only remnant of the stone, disappearing into the night.

The demon bent down and knelled next to Stern's head. "Will you now do as I say, transform into the dragon and lead the dragons to Mittilagart?"

Tears rolled from Stern's eyes, as he said, "I will on one condition."

The demon stood and placed the heel of his black leather boot on Stern's neck. "What is it?"

"Protect my son," he said firmly.

The demon rubbed his chin and smiled: "I will protect your son."

"And I will do as you say," promised Stern.

The demon lifted his left hand, said one word in his language, which Stern now understood, and the binding disappeared. "Change into the dragon!" Kokabiel ordered. "Your charges return."

Sitting naked on the wet sand, Stern meditated on the form of the dragon. Without the demon's interference, he effortlessly shifted shape, stretched his wings to their full length and rose up on his hind legs, towering over the demon with the white hair and red eyes.

Kokabiel laughed, knowing Stern wanted to crush him, as he recited the spell of opening. A portal appeared and, through it the island of Grun glistened; its jungles wet and steaming.

Stern called to the two young dragons, returning from the hunt and then plunged through the portal. Phobos and Deimos hesitated, circling the demon and sputtering fire.

Flying up above the humid jungle in the south seas of Okeanus, Stern called the dragons who reluctantly left the demon standing on the white sand of the Argantine.

As the two dragons entered the portal, the demon raised his hand in a flippant wave and spoke the words of closing.

The portal disappeared, terminating Stern's life in Mittilagart.

Proof

27909976R00200

Made in the USA
Charleston, SC
23 March 2014